KINGS, QUEENS
THE WARDSTC

M... ....

ISBN: 978-1-946187-12-3

2016 Modernized Format Edition
Created in the United States of America
Worldwide Rights

If you enjoy this read, please tell a friend or write a review.
Enjoy, M.R. Mathias

This is for my mother and father.

Jack Hoyle is responsible for these amazing 2016 Modernized Edition covers
Find him at www.t-rexstudios.com

Thank you JT, for the formatting help. It was timely.

To hear about new releases, sales and giveaways, follow M. R. Mathias here:
www.mrmathias.com or @DahgMahn on Facebook, Twitter, and Instagram

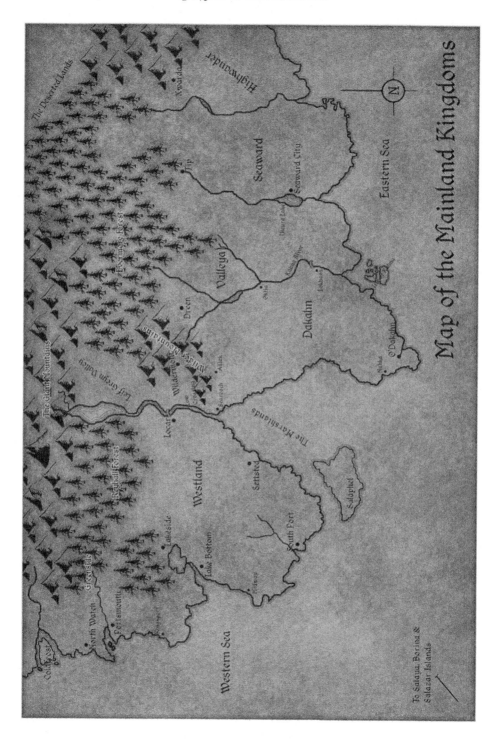

Kings, Queens, Heroes, & Fools

Chapter One

Lord Alvin Gregory opened his eyes sometime in early winter. They'd been closed since summer began. The unfamiliar room was dark, but warm and earthy, tinged with the smell of fire smoke and roasted lamb. He tried to rise, but his body would not allow it. With the pain came the memory of the wounds he'd taken. *From what?* He shouldn't be alive, he knew, but he could tell by the intensity of the pain he was in, that he was. He lay there for a long while before the hazy memory of a woman, elegant and beautiful, carried him back into sleep.

The next time he opened his eyes he found a woman sitting next to him. She wasn't the woman he had been dreaming of, but she was no less beautiful. It seemed that his waking had startled her, but a warm smile crept across her face soon enough and she went back to cleansing his skin with the damp cloth in her hand.

She had long, straight jet black hair, and dark motherly eyes. The edges of which were just starting to show the lines of age. She was no noblewoman, her clothes were made from doeskin and plainly cut. He wasn't back in his Westland stronghold at Lakebottom, he knew. He couldn't sort through the fog in his brain to say where exactly he was though. It was a safe place, he sensed, but it was a long way from home.

"How do you feel?" she asked.

He tried to reply to the question, but his throat was thick with mucus and would not work for him.

"It's all right, Lion Lord," she said. "I'll fetch some broth and my mate."

Lord Gregory suffered the pain of turning his head so that he could watch her go and felt the chill of the icy-cold air that blew in when she opened and closed the door behind her.

Lion Lord, she had called him. It stirred memories from the mix of his mind, but nothing complete enough to comprehend. He closed his eyes again and drifted.

"He can remember nothing," the woman said sometime later.

Lord Gregory opened his eyes to find her and two men standing in the room.

"Ah, he's waking again," the older of the two men said. He was seventy years old if he was a day. His long hair was streaked with silver and gray and the skin on his clean-shaven face was sun-darkened and wrinkled. The old man shrugged off a thickly furred cloak that had been made from several different animal skins. Grayish brown, black, and snow-white long-haired goat skins had been hemhawed together. It looked warm though. Lord Gregory grew curious when the old man winced his way down to take a seat at the edge of the bed.

"Lord Gregory," the old man said. "Lion of the West. Lion Lord. Do these names mean anything to you?"

"I know who I am," Lord Gregory croaked. His own voice sounded unfamiliar to his ears. It was weak and hoarse and it reminded him of his injuries.

"Good, good," the old man said with a pat on Lord Gregory's arm. "Do you know where you are?"

Lord Gregory racked his cloudy brain and found the knowledge, but the name of the place escaped him. Then he wondered if it even had a name. He managed to get out two words: "Clan village," but even though he knew that was correct, he knew it was incomplete.

"Yes, yes, this is the village of the Skyler Clan. I am Halden Skyler, the Eldest, and this is my second son Harrap and his mate Karna. They have kept you while you were resting. Their son, my grandson, Hyden was amongst your group when the dark creature attacked. Do you remember?"

Some of it came back to him. A fleeting feeling of hope bloomed. "Mikahl?" he croaked.

"Aye," Harrap joined the conversation. He was standing at the foot of the bed. "And an elf." The word 'elf' was spoken with more than a little contempt.

"A tattooed Seawardsman was with you as well," the old man added from beside him. "You killed a Seawardsman at the festival. Do you remember that?"

Summer's Day, a great fight with another brawler; gamblers, wagering, thousands of people cheering them on, blood and knuckles and pain—these were the images that came to his mind.

"I lost, I think." Lord Gregory tried to grin.

"Aye," the old man looked to his son at the foot of the bed. His grin was full of satisfaction. "This lion will roar again. He just needs a little more time to lick his wounds."

"He's not heard of the Dragon Queen and the fall of Westland yet. And..."

A raised hand from the Eldest cut Harrap short. Harrap shook his head in frustration.

"Lord Gregory's mind's not ready for all that yet, son. He's been unconscious for more than a season. Filling his head with too much at once might hinder his recovery." The Eldest turned to his son's mate. "You've done well, Karna. Could you ask Tylen to come for a while each day to help our Westlander get his body used to moving around again."

She nodded that she would and hurried out the door. The old man's gaze settled back on Lord Gregory. Their eyes met, and the old man's look was serious, yet reassuring. "It will be no small task to get you walking again. We will see if you truly have the heart of a lion beating in that chest of yours."

"That his heart still beats at all, after being dropped from the sky by that evil beast, shows that he has a lion's heart," Harrap said.

It didn't escape Lord Gregory's notice that Harrap had spoken of him, but not to him. Maybe his eyes had been closed, or maybe he'd been lying there so long that he didn't seem like a person anymore to Harrap. Before he could think much more about it he slipped back into a deep and heavy slumber.

The young man named Tylen came later that day. He and Lord Gregory spoke for a while of the legendary brawl from a few years earlier, when Lord Gregory beat a fighter called the Valleyan Stallion. He won his place on the Summer's Day Spire that year. The great needle-like projection of polished black stone rose up out of the sacred Leif Greyn Valley and the names of each year's winners were carved into its base. No one knew who built the Spire or why, but for as long as any man could remember, on the first day of summer each year, men from all across the realm gathered there to trade and compete in the spirit of fellowship and peace. The winners of events such as archery, brawling, hammer throw and various foot and horse races won a bit of immortality and heavy prize-purses of gold and silver, but it wasn't the honor of having his name engraved into the Spire twice that drove the Lion Lord to battle again last year. He'd been there for far more important reasons.

King Balton, the king of Westland, had been poisoned just before the festival. From his death bed he had ordered Lord Gregory to attend. The Lion Lord had done so, and was poisoned himself, beaten half to death, and left to watch helplessly while most of his men were killed by the Blacksword soldiers of Highwander. The whole festival had turned into a battlefield. It was all too much to think about.

Tylen eventually took the covers off of the Lion Lord's legs and manually worked his ankles and knee joints as his grandfather had instructed him to do. It was agonizing for the Westlander but, with clenched teeth and many curses, they got through it. When the young man was done he fetched the Lion Lord a strong drink of some horrible tasting liquid and helped him get it down.

That night, Lord Gregory dreamed of the regal lady again. When he woke, her identity and the vision of her most beautiful face were fresh in his mind's eye. She was his wife, the Lady Trella. She was his best friend, his lover, and he found that he missed her dearly.

Later in the day, just before Tylen started his exercises, Lord Gregory asked for the Eldest. He was ready to hear what the old man was keeping from him. Somehow he knew it involved his wife. In his dream she had been fleeing something and he couldn't come to her aid. As he waited for Halden Skyler, he prayed to the gods that his wife was safe. He swore to get his legs working again so that he might find a way home to her.

"There's much to tell," the old man said, as he took a padded stool and sat on it near the hearth. "Are you sure you're ready to hear it all?"

"Sooner or later I'll hear it, sir," Lord Gregory said. "I'd prefer to hear all of it now."

"Well then, as you know, us clansman are not kingdom men. We only ventured down from the mountains a few times a year. Two of my sons, Harrap and Condlin, made one such journey in the fall. They went to the city of High Crossing to purchase animals and other provisions like they do every year before winter sets in. Only this year the town was nearly empty."

This grabbed Lord Gregory's attention.

"Harrap and Condlin continued south to the city of Castlemont. I guess I should say where the city of Castlemont used to be." The old man leaned forward on his stool, took up a poker and began prodding the fire back to life.

"Used to be?" Lord Gregory asked.

"What few folk they came across told them that the city was sacked by your new king and then was destroyed by his wizard. The ones that didn't hide well enough were rounded up and herded to that slaver city by the sea."

"O'Dakahn," Lord Gregory said. "But…but that's impossible."

"Oh there's much more to tell," the Eldest said. "While your Westland king was herding the people of Wildermont to the south, and his army was making passage through the Wilder Mountains to attack the Red City, a dragon rider led an army out of the swamps and took Westland for herself."

"But—"

The Eldest cut Lord Gregory's protest off with a wave of his hand and a healthy harrumph. "Walking lizards from the marshes, the zard, Harrap called them. Huge man-like beasts that aren't true giants, but wild half-breeds from beyond the Giant Mountains hold Westland under the Dragon Queen's rule. They destroyed the bridge at Castlemont. That alone amazes me. I've seen that bridge with my own eyes and it would take powerful forces to tear it down. I wouldn't believe these things had my own two sons not told me of them. They are good fathers, and good men. They have no reason to lie."

Lord Gregory had crossed the magnificent bridge that led from Wildermont over the Leif Greyn River into Westland at least half a hundred times in his day. A spectacle of archways wide enough for five, maybe six, wagons to cross abreast, it was the only land passage from the eastern kingdoms into Westland. If this Dragon Queen really existed, then she wasn't planning on giving Westland up anytime soon. The fact that she had destroyed the only land access into Westland showed that she meant to isolate and defend the territory. He could only hope that his lady wife was alive and well. Surely his friend Lord Ellrich, or another of his peers, had seen to her safety.

"What of your kinsman Hyden, and my countryman Mikahl?" Lord Gregory asked. Inside him the desire to get his legs working again so that he could go see if these things were true, was growing from a spark into a fire.

Mikahl was the true king of Westland, though the boy didn't know it yet. *I may have told him,* Lord Gregory said to himself, but he wasn't sure. Mikahl had been raised a bastard, but King Balton brought him up well. Mikahl was Lord Gregory's squire in his adolescent years, and the king's squire up until King Balton was murdered. Mikahl was smart, well trained, and capable. Lord Gregory hoped he was still alive, and still had possession of his father's sword, Ironspike.

"Borg, the Southern Guardian, a true and noble giant, came out of the deep mountains in the early fall," the eldest said. The reverence he held for the giant was clear. "He brought with him three horses and a tale as wild as the news of the Dragon Queen. Hyden, Mikahl, and the elf, met with King Aldar. What transpired at the meeting, I do not know." Halden stirred the fire again and adjusted his old body on the stool. "The Seawardsman who was with them was killed in the Giant Mountains by the same beast that got you. Borg spoke of Mikahl's bravery in the battle, and for Borg to make such compliments is no light matter. King Aldar sent them through the Evermore Forest to the kingdom of Highwander. Borg was very vague about why, but my grandson Hyden and his hawkling, and that... that *elf* went with him. They rode on the backs of King Aldar's great wolves no less. Can you imagine crossing through the Evermore Forest on the back of a great wolf?"

Lord Gregory couldn't even imagine Mikahl fighting the hellcat, much less anything else. He knew that King Balton had sent Mikahl to the Giant King. It was the only place he knew that Prince Glendar and his wizard Pael might not hunt them down. It was why Lord Gregory had been with them in the mountains in the first place. He'd sworn to help Mikahl get to the Giant King. He was relieved to know that he would not live on as an oath-breaker; almost as much as he was relieved to know that Mikahl was probably alive. He wondered why King Aldar had sent them to Highwander. The Witch Queen's Blacksword warriors were the ones who started the bloodshed at the Summer's Day Festival. At least that's the way Lord Gregory remembered it.

He also remembered thinking that he was dead after sending his page Wyndall to take a message to Lady Trella. If Wyndall made it, Lady Trella would have been warned of the coming trouble. Hopefully big Lord Ellrich or Wyndall or someone else had helped her to survive. In a rush of angry passion, Lord Gregory tried to rise up from the bed only to end up howling as his soft, un-worked muscles gave fiery protest.

At once, the old clansman was at the door yelling for young Tylen. The boy came and went, then returned with another cup of the horrible concoction they had been feeding him. The Eldest helped him drink it down and waited patiently until Lord Gregory slipped back into his deep dreaming slumber.

Lord Gregory dreamt a memory of the big half-breed beasts he'd fought in Coldfrost. He, King Balton, and Lord Brach had led the men bravely against the huge brutal creatures. Then King Balton used the power of his sword, Ironspike, to create a magical boundary that the creatures couldn't pass. Borg had spoken for King Aldar there in that frigid bloody place. The true giants wanted no part of the breed beasts, and in fact were pleased with the way King Balton had imprisoned them on the glacial island.

In his dream, the true giant, Borg, fought alongside him, young Glendar, and King Balton against the creatures. They battled to free the Lady Trella from a prison of ice where huge hairy half-men were trying to tear apart her body.

Lord Gregory woke in a cold sweat. His legs ached from the movements Tylen had put them through, but he wanted more of it. From that day forward his whole existence was about getting his legs back under him. It took half a month for him to be able to sit up on his own. He had Karna and Tylen place his food across the room. He crawled, slithered, crumpled and cried, but he didn't give up, even though he went hungry many a mealtime. In the evenings, he worked his legs while lying in the bed, bringing his knees up as close to his chin as he could, one after the other, over and over again. He used a rock the size of his fist for a weight to exercise his arms, but gradually worked up to a head-sized chunk of granite. His arms regained muscle much faster than his legs, but he didn't get discouraged.

He talked to Harrap and Condlin about their journey into the ruined cities of Wildermont for many hours. He questioned them in great detail and learned that the half-breed giants had been released from Coldfrost and had helped tear down the great bridge between Westland and Wildermont before taking over rule of the Westland trade city called Locar. They were building great wooden watchtowers all along the Westland bank of the Leif Greyn River when the two clansmen had been in Castlemont. Some said King Jarrek had fled his kingdom. Others said that he had died by the hand of the wizard Pael.

As hard as he tried, Lord Gregory couldn't learn much more than that from the two men. They weren't kingdom men. They'd been born and raised and lived here in the mountains their whole life. Kingdom men seldom dared to venture here, and the things a kingdom man might notice about a place were lost to them.

Harrap helped his nephew Tylen support Lord Gregory the first few times he tried to stand and walk. It was hard and painful and even comical at times, but finally, near midwinter, Lord Gregory took some steps on his own.

"This lion might not yet be able to roar," he told them. "But at least I can still growl."

He began using a cane that the Elder had carved for him out of a witch-wood bough. The handle was the head of a snarling lion and the base a wide lion's paw. It was crude work, but heartfelt. Lord Gregory cherished it dearly.

By the time spring was upon them, Lord Gregory was hobbling along fairly well. When he left his room the first time, he found that he had been living underground all winter. The clan folk all lived in stone rooms built right into the sloping walls of their little valley. Narrow passages that reminded Lord Gregory of mine tunnels led from the open valley into the homes. Giants and dwarves, Halden told him, had supposedly built the burrows long centuries ago.

The clansmen didn't own or ride horses, but on several occasions Lord Gregory rode on the dead Seawardsman's mount. It wasn't long after that he was feeling well enough to leave the Skyler Clan and their hospitality behind him. The desire to find his wife was gnawing at him like a starving dog at a bone.

He would have rather taken Mikahl's proud and well trained horse, Windfoot, but he left the steed because Borg had promised Mikahl that it would be there when he came for it.

He waited until it was warm enough to get out of the mountains without freezing, and then, after a long respectful goodbye, he left the Skyler Clan behind. He pointed the horse south toward Wildermont, and with all the hope in the world, he set off to find his wife.

Chapter Two

Mikahl reared back with his blade as he slipped to the side of the sword the dark haired man before him had just thrust out. To the onlookers, Mikahl looked like a young lion with his intense expression and his thick golden mane flying about. The man he was fighting, Brady Culvert, growled in frustration through gnashed teeth because he had to spin to get clear of Mikahl's gleaming, arcing swing. He managed it, but barely. He lost his balance in the process and almost fell. Mikahl rode the momentum of his slash all the way around, but this time, instead of resuming his guard, he feigned a chest-high slice. As soon as the other man committed to his unbalanced defensive guard, Mikahl deftly lowered his blade to thigh level, and struck with force.

Mikahl's dulled steel thumped wickedly into Brady Culvert's leather thigh pad. The small group of swordsmen gathered in the training yard grimaced with sympathy then called out praises and jests alike. Brady couldn't hear them over his own cursing. Mikahl had horse-knotted his leg and it hurt like hell. Brady wasn't angry though. He had just won a small fortune in wagers by lasting over five minutes sparring against High King Mikahl. It was a record. No one in all of Highwander had managed to make it even three minutes against the treacherous young king of the realm.

"If he'd been using Ironspike, Brady, you'd be legless," King Jarrek, the displaced king of Wildermont, commented as a squire began unbuckling Brady's leather armor from the back. Another squire took the dulled sword from the combatant's hand.

"If he had Ironspike in his hands, I would have been fighting with him, not against him, Highness." Brady smiled back at King Jarrek. After settling their debts, the men broke up and went back to their practice drills. The victor smiled at his congratulations, then went over to a small table where an old retired warrior was keeping time with minute glasses.

King Mikahl hadn't been wearing armor at all—only a pair of calfskin britches, and a green silk shirt trimmed in gold. Those were the colors of his dead father's Westland banner, and after several long minutes of dodging and deflecting Brady Culvert's blade, he hadn't even darkened them with sweat. His hair had gone wild though, and he made a futile attempt to smooth it back into some sense of order before making his announcment.

"Seven full minutes and almost half a glass more," King Mikahl called out with a nod of respect. "The cream of the crop, without a doubt."

Brady Culvert was twenty-two years old, three years older than High King Mikahl. Brady had been one of King Jarrek's feared and revered Redwolf guards and had worn his crimson enameled plate mail proudly. Their kingdom had been decimated last summer by the Westland wizard Pael. Brady, acting on orders from his King, rode all the way across the continent warning the other kingdoms of the approaching doom. He'd been in the Red City of Dreen warning the Valleyans when that battle started. He escaped the evil wizard's hordes only to be captured later by a group of Queen Rachel's Seaward soldiers. Somehow he'd won free of them and made it all the way to Xwarda, where Pael and his undead army were already attacking.

Most of the people of Wildermont, including Brady's family, had been sold into slavery, and all winter long, King Jarrek had been here in Xwarda training a group of handpicked men to go into Dakahn to free them. High King Mikahl, being a great swordsman, trained with them rigorously. In fact, he trained easily twice as hard as any man in the group. He had a temper, and in order to keep it under control, he intentionally exhausted himself at least once a day.

"…not good enough to stay alive if we faced each other in actual combat," Brady was saying in response to Mikahl's comment.

"Aye," the High King grinned proudly, but without cockiness. "In actual combat, Sir Culvert, you'd have never had the chance to draw your sword."

For the most part formalities and titles were forbidden on the Royal Training Yard. Unlike the yards where Queen Willa's Blacksword soldiers trained, where sergeants and captains put regiments of men through long brutal repetitions, often accompanied by much yelling and screaming, here, men were just men. Crowns and thrones and holdings meant nothing. It was one of the few places a man might jest with his king without fear of reproach. The use of the word 'Sir' by King Mikahl when speaking to Brady displayed volumes of respect and Brady Culvert beamed for it. So much so that he'd missed the humor in the High King's ridiculous boast. King Jarrek didn't miss the jab though, and he laughed heartily.

"That one will do," Mikahl said after Brady had gone. "I want him to go with Hyden Hawk, if you'd spare him. My friend needs a sword he can trust on this wild expedition he is planning."

"I thought you'd keep him for yourself Mik," King Jarrek said a little disappointedly.

"I would if there were someone as capable with the blade going along with Hyden," replied Mikahl. "Why is it that you refuse to take him with your group? He's your countryman, and you've known him his whole life, or so he says."

"It's true. I was drinking with his father when he was being born, but his father was killed right before his eyes, by Westlanders, and his mother, sisters, and cousins may be the very slaves we come across in O'Dakahn. Just like another great swordsman I know, his emotions are too highly strung. Besides that, if one of the slaves recognizes him, then it could jeopardize the others. The men I hand-picked are all from Highwander. They have no emotional involvement in what we're going to do. I think it's better that way."

It pained Mikahl deeply to hear of the horrible deeds that his Westland countrymen had done under the leadership of his stepbrother King Glendar and Pael. Mikahl sometimes wondered how Jarrek kept from hating him for being a true Westlander.

"It makes good sense then, to send him with Hyden Hawk, but what if one of the slaves recognizes you?" Mikahl asked.

"I had no beard when I sat my throne at Castlemont, and no one in all the lands, save for a few here in Xwarda, have ever seen me dressed as anything less than a king. It will be easy for me to go unnoticed, I assure you."

"Not if you keep speaking like a king. Commoners don't use words like you do. Maybe you should spend some time out in the markets, or at the Squalor, where they speak with less pomp and formality." Mikahl laughed at the idea of it. King Jarrek was naturally as regal as a man could be.

"I may just do that," said Jarrek as they started toward the bath-house. His expression showed that he was seriously contemplating Mikahl's suggestion and it made Mikahl laugh even harder. When the mirth died away, Mikahl changed the subject.

"Can you believe that Queen Willa actually wants me to propose to this Princess Rosa?" The High King's voice was incredulous. "I don't even know her."

"It might be necessary to secure Queen Rachel's full support," explained Jarrek. "The Princess is as pretty a girl as there ever was. Have you seen her?"

"No, but it's not fair!" He felt like a little boy whose mother was calling him to come inside early instead of letting him stay out in the cobbles to play with his friends. "Her mother tried to attack Xwarda after sacking two Highwander cities. I don't understand how Queen Willa could even think of us making such an alliance."

It was Jarrek's turn to laugh. After a moment he grew serious and stopped Mikahl to look into his eyes . "Seaward has fighting men, Mikahl. The few thousand men Queen Rachel sent to help King Broderick attack here was a token offer at best. You have to remember that Glendar, or Pael, or whoever was behind the attack at Summer's Day, set all of this into motion. They flew Willa's Blacksword banner when they did it. Rachel had to do something, and thankfully she did as little as possible." He put his arm around Mikahl's shoulder in a fatherly manner. "Remember, it's a proposal, not a marriage. Later, after Queen Rachel has bowed to you publicly, then you can politely change your mind, but I doubt you'll do that. You'll not find a more beautiful and polite girl in all the realm."

"If and when I marry, I want it to be for love," Mikahl said naively. "Anything less just doesn't seem to be, what's the word? Honorable?"

"Being a good king isn't a very honorable business sometimes," said King Jarrek. "Every single time we do something good for somebody, someone else is upset about it. That is why honorable men don't usually want to be king."

"Aye," Mikahl agreed with a huff of frustration. "I should've gone a few more rounds out in the yards," he mumbled to himself as King Jarrek was pulled away by a question from one of his men.

Queen Willa was having a welcome feast for Princess Rosa later in the day. It hadn't even started yet, but already Mikahl was getting aggravated by the mess. The bath was hot and relaxing and went far toward easing his tension. It was peaceful in these particular bathhouses, which were for the use of those training in the Royal Weapons Yard. If Mikahl tried to bathe anywhere else he'd be swamped with bowing servants, over eager attendants, and all the other amenities of his position that made his blood boil. What he'd give to be able to eat anonymously with the squires and pages this night. The only formalities he'd find there were belching contests, dice, and the laces on a willing servant girl's girdle.

A sharp repetitive thumping sound caught his attention and he turned in the wooden tub to see what it was. A wide wingspan of dark brown feathers swirled the steam and the tiny, yet widening yellow ring of a hawkling's focusing eye found him. The bird gave a weak apologetic caw then proceeded to flap its way out of the room, dragging Mikahl's robe with it.

"Talon, no!" Mikahl screamed as he looked around and saw that there was nothing at all to cover himself with. "Blasted Hyden!" he swore. As angry as he was becoming, he couldn't hold back the smile that stretched across his face. He and Hyden took great pride in the pranks they pulled on each other, and this was a good one. Princess Rosa was here at the castle, and by the time the feast gathered this evening, the gossipers and rumor mongers would have a lot to talk about. Mikahl wasn't about to be meek about it. He would strut across the practice yard naked if he had to. His fierce pride wouldn't allow any less.

"You just wait Hyden. I'll get—" Mikahl was yelling as he burst out of the door that opened into the corner of the training yard. His voice died quickly away. His heart leapt into his throat when he saw the girl who was waiting there with Hyden. She was suddenly wide-eyed and having to stifle her giggles. Talon leapt from Hyden's wrist and flew to perch on a piece of training equipment a fair distance away and began preening himself innocently.

The well-bloomed young girl with Hyden was beautiful beyond reason, with sparkling blue eyes, full pouty lips, and long wavy brown hair that flowed down over her shoulders. Her day dress was colored the very same shade of green as the

Westland banner, and it hugged her curvaceous figure well. Her skin was golden, but mottled roses had suddenly appeared on her cheeks.

"Oh, sorry, Mik," Hyden shrugged with an ear-to-ear grin on his face. His long black hair was pulled into a tight ponytail, and gave his face a hawkish look that eerily resembled Talon's. "They told me you were taking a hot bath, not a cold one."

Princess Rosa's mouth had formed a perfect 'O '. She whirled and whacked Hyden across the chest. Hyden could barely contain himself. He was about to explode with laughter.

"Yew seed that he was feeding some earphaned beer cubs!" she shrieked in a heavily accented voice as she stalked off. A pair of equally flustered and giggling attendants, and a slightly older woman who was still openly eyeing Mikahl's naked body, appeared from the background to receive the girl and usher her off.

Hyden lost all control of his mirth and was laughing so hard that he actually fell to a knee and held his stomach. As the training yard door slammed shut behind the Princess of Seaward and her entourage, applause erupted from some of the braver men; there were whistles and jeers as well.

Chapter Three

Hyden Skyler spent the winter up in Dahg Mahn's tower learning to read and write. It was Hyden's tower now, even though everyone still referred to it as Dahg Mahn's. The great wizard had disappeared ages ago, but had left a trial, a series of tests that one must pass to win entry into his sacred Xwardian abode. Hundreds of magi had tried to enter, but only Hyden Hawk Skyler had done so.

Targon, the old High Wizard of Xwarda, had died with the elf Vaegon in a mighty battle against a Choska demon on the outer wall, as Pael's undead hordes swarmed into the city. Queen Willa had named two of his underlings to take his place. The new High Wizards assigned apprentices to help Hyden in his endeavors. Hyden's desire to overcome his ignorance drove him, and now he was reading well, if a little haltingly at times. His writing skills were still lacking, however. He could scratch and scribble enough to get by, but nothing more. His favorite apprentice, a skinny blond-headed orphan boy of fourteen summers named Phenilous, had given him the most help. He and Phen had become fast friends. Hyden was nearing twenty summers himself, but was still a boy at heart. He had a natural gift for magic and he could communicate with animals through his familial link with his hawkling, Talon. Phen's grammatical skills were superb, but his magical skills were lacking in the sense that they were stiff and studied, and came not from the heart, but from repetition and memory. Hyden Hawk's magic was pure—not learned, but felt. Over the winter, the two of them garnered a great deal from each other and had serious fun in the process.

Hyden was planning a grand quest. Since it was Phen who had done the bulk of research into the great blue dragon, Cobalt, and the treasure he had stolen from the pirate Barnacle Bones, Phen was trying to get Hyden, and the two High Wizards to let him go on the adventure. Hyden didn't mind at all. In fact he liked the idea of Phen going, but there would be danger, and the boy was only an apprentice. Hyden wouldn't dare disrespect Queen Willa's wizards by assuming anything. Only if they agreed, would he add Phen to his growing roster of campaigners.

"What did they say?" Hyden asked the boy as he was getting dressed for the evening's feast. Phen was a lowly apprentice and hadn't been invited to the event, but it didn't bother him. He didn't really want to have to use manners and act serious all evening long.

Phen smirked in approval as he entered the room. Hyden had sensed him there before he had seen him. It was a simple awareness spell they had been working on, and Hyden had used it perfectly.

"Master Amill seems to think I could learn a lot on such an excursion," Phen said. "Master Sholt, on the other hand, thinks that it will be too dangerous, and that I'll just be underfoot."

"When I was your age, my father had me harvesting hawkling eggs on cliffs higher than this tower," Hyden said, a little miffed at the reasoning. "I'll try and talk some sense into them this evening, Phen. Master Sholt is coming to the feast, is he not?"

"I believe so." Phen seemed pleased that Hyden was going to speak for him. He had been worried that Hyden had only been pacifying him with his talk of taking him along on the quest for Barnacle Bones's stolen booty. "We don't need treasure, though, Hyden. Queen Willa's got all the gold in Highwander already."

Hyden laughed. "You can do better than that, Phen."

"Why won't you tell me what it is that we're really after?" the boy asked with an ear to ear grin.

"I'll tell you only this…" Hyden turned from the reflecting glass and looked seriously at the boy. Phen stifled a laugh. Hyden's robe was bunched all wrong on one side.

"What is it?" Hyden turned back to the reflecting glass.

"Here," Phen came over and straightened the fancy silver trimmed white robe. "Now what were you going to tell me?"

Hyden loved drawing stuff out with the boy. Phen's impatience was entertaining, but he was in a hurry, so he told him what he wanted to know—at least part of it. "When the dragon, Claret, and I finished sealing the demon back into the Nethers, she told me…"

"I know, I know this part," said Phen as if the balance of the world's fate hung in what came next. "She told you about Cobalt the blue drake, and the pirate ship, but what is it we are really after? What's in that booty that you want so badly, Hyden?"

Hyden laughed aloud at that. Phen was as sharp as a whip's crack. It was one of the reasons he liked the boy so much. "Claret told me that among the treasures the dragon stole was a silver skull with eyes of jade, but if you tell a soul that that's what we're after, I'll skin you and hang you from a banner pole."

"The Silver Skull of Zorellin, but…"

"But nothing! You keep your mouth shut about it or I'll have Talon pluck your eyes out."

Just then Talon flew from his perch near the open window and landed on Phen's outstretched arm. The hawkling was as tall as Phen's arm was long, and he had taken a liking to the boy.

"Traitor," Hyden said to his *familiar*. "I guess I have no choice but to convince your masters to let you come with me now that I've spilled the stew."

"Spilled the stew?" Phen giggled. "You really are a bumpkin, Hyden. King Mikahl was right. I can't believe you grew up in a place where people don't ride horses and live inside dirt hills."

"In the Giant Mountains, even in the spring and fall, you'd be glad to be inside a hill. And besides, the walls are made of stone, not dirt." Hyden frowned into the mirror, not liking what he saw at all. "Blast this! It just doesn't suit me." He pulled the fancy wizard's robe over his head, and then began stripping off the awful itchy woolen leggings that went with it. "Grab my kid-skin pants from the closet—the new black ones—and my old horsehide boots for me, would you Phen?"

"Sure." Phen went into the other room and found the items. As he returned with them he asked, "Is it true, what they say you did to the High King and the Seaward Princess this afternoon?"

"I suppose that depends on what they say I did," Hyden chuckled from behind the changing screen. "But if they say I lied to the pretty girl with promises of bear cubs, but showed her the High King's sword instead, then yes, it's true."

Phen laughed deeply at that. "They'll have you hanged for insolence or treason," the boy managed between giggles.

"Nah, nah! High King Mikahl was my friend back when he was just Mik the Squire." Hyden stepped from behind the blind in a pressed white shirt with ballooned sleeves that was tucked neatly into his leather pants. Unlike what the current fashion trends dictated, he wore the legs of his snug fitting pants over his boots instead of inside them. "Besides," he continued. "I'm not from the kingdoms of men. I'm a human from the kingdom of giants. I am a free man here, and if I did have a king it would have to be King Aldar."

"The cloak," Phen offered his fashion advice. "Wear the black one with the silver flames along its edges."

"That was Dahg Mahn's cloak," said Hyden. The idea of wearing it stopped him completely. For a long moment he just stood there contemplating. He rarely messed with the long missing wizard's personal things. It just didn't seem right. Yet to wear that cloak to this feast seemed to be the perfect thing to do. "All right then," he nodded.

Phen was already up and bringing him the ancient garment. Hyden put the cloak over his shoulders, pinned it with a silver broach shaped like a diving hawk, then checked himself in the glass again.

He had mussed up his long black hair when he'd pulled the robes off. He started to brush it, but changed his mind and instead tied it back behind his head with a silver wire. He gave the mirror another look and decided that there was only one thing missing. He reached into his shirt and pulled forth the silver medallion that he always wore around his neck. The brilliant tear-shaped jewel mounted in it sparkled at his collar. Finally, Hyden decided, he was ready.

Talon cawed out his approval of the look.

Phen nodded as well. "Not so bad, for a bumpkin, I mean."

"Keep an eye on that boy, Talon," Hyden said to his hawkling with a grin. "He's as sharp as a iron orb."

As soon as the door closed behind Hyden, Phen sat Talon back on his stand and started rummaging through the piles of books at the study table. He would know everything he could about the Silver Skull of Zorellin by the end of the night. Little did he know, that was exactly what Hyden Hawk intended.

Later, at the gathering, Hyden gawked openly at the size of the arms on Princess Rosa's two guardsmen. They were huge. Each bicep was as big as Hyden's head. Both men wore spiked and studded boiled leather armor vests that weren't just for show. Each of them carried long, well used swords at their hips too. Studded gauntlets and knee-high hard leather boots finished the uniform, save for their long blue cloaks with the orange setting sun of Seaward emblazoned on the back. As were most of the men of Seaward, these two were baldheaded, and covered with tattoos—one giant tattoo actually.

One of the guards had what looked like a bird's beak that started between his eyes and bent backwards over his head. Hyden had seen the same style on a lot of Seawardsmen. Feathers started where his hairline should have been, and strange yellow eyes were inked in over his ears. The other had a simpler design of lightning streaks jagging back from his temples and forehead. The man reminded Hyden of Loudin the hunter. Loudin's tattoos had been of tiger stripes, and he had been as fierce as any wildcat there ever was.

The Princess was beautiful. Her dress was a rosy color, with crimson and sea-blue trim. It set off her eyes and the jewels on her dainty wire crown. The dress was less shapely than the one she'd worn earlier in the day, but it revealed more of her ample cleavage. A thumb-size sapphire had been cleverly hung around her neck. It rested perfectly at the top of the deep line her breasts made. At her side was an older woman. Hyden thought he heard someone say she was an aunt.

Queen Willa looked regal and beautiful in a powdery blue gown. Her little blue-skinned pixie friend Starkle fluttered around her head like a butterfly, giving her an unearthly, surreal appearance. To further the look, at either side of her was a dwarf. Dugak was on her right, and his wife Andra was on the queen's left. They were dressed in a darker shade of blue that was trimmed in lavender. Though her expression didn't show it, Hyden knew that Queen Willa would have rather been wearing her studded leather girdle over her chain mail. And Dugak would surely have rather been drinking in the cellars, for if you wanted to find him for anything, most of the time that was where you would go. Queen Willa smiled brightly at Hyden when she saw him. He smiled back and made a cringing funny face. She was forced to feign a cough to hide her laugh.

King Jarrek wore the deep black shades of mourning, trimmed in blood red. He was making a statement for the Princess to carry home to her mother. "My kingdom was destroyed," the look said. "My people are now slaves. Will you just sit there and do nothing?" Jarrek's expression was stern behind his dark bangs and beard, and the fierce determination in his eyes added a perfect exclamation point to his attire.

Then came the High King. Hyden had to shake his head in wonder as the court announcer called out his lengthy title. "I give you High King Mikahl Collum, the Uniter come again, the King of Kings, the wielder of Ironspike, and Defender of the Realm..." and so on for a full two minutes. Mikahl looked the part too. Layers of emerald and forest green, all trimmed in gold, were draped over him, and a fur scarf made from what might have actually been a lion's mane gave him the appearance of a young, golden crowned lion's cub. The emerald-eyed lion's head medallion that King Aldar had hand carved out of dragon bone hung proudly around his neck. He looked the part of a mighty king, in all his splendor, but the look on his face was pinched. Mikahl despised this sort of pomp and ceremony.

Hyden knew without a doubt that with only a few words he could create a scene here for the ages to remember, but he held his tongue for the sake of Queen Willa and King Jarrek. To begin rebuilding in earnest, they needed Seaward's aid badly. Hyden was sure that was the only reason his friend Mikahl was suffering through this farce as well.

When King Mikahl's eyes landed on Princess Rosa, it was hard to say which one of them blushed a brighter shade of crimson. After a moment, both sets of eyes found Hyden. All Hyden could do was shrug and grin. High Wizard Sholt saved him from their glares by handing him a goblet of Valleyan honey wine and engaging him in conversation.

"The only two things Valleyans can do well are raise horses and make wine," the middle-aged man said. He was wearing the high collared, black-trimmed, white robes of his station. The master wizard kept his beard in a neat goatee, but his wild graying hair always seemed to be in disarray. "In fact, it's the only two things they do at all," he continued. "It amazes me that King Broderick is pleading for exoneration for his great mistake, but is too afraid to ask to be forgiven in person."

"Would you want to face King Mikahl and that sword of his?" Hyden asked. He hated politics, but liked Master Sholt. "Or what about Willa the Witch? Would you like to have to face her after sacking two of her cities?"

"Nay, sir, I would not, on either count," agreed Sholt with a forced chuckle.

"You will allow Phenilous to continue tutoring me while I'm on expedition, I hope," suggested Hyden. His words hadn't been framed as a question, more like a subtle order.

"I've been meaning to talk to you about that," Sholt started. "I wasn't sure if he was truly needed on such a dangerous venture. I thought that it might have just been kindness on your part that was indulging his fancy. He tends to be a little highly strung, if you haven't noticed. Confined on a ship, on a long sea voyage, he will become a nuisance, I assure you."

"No," Hyden looked the master wizard directly in the eye as his father had taught him to do. "It is more than indulgence, Master Sholt, I assure you. And no one will be more antsy on that ship than I. I trust Phen, and he helps me with Talon. He is fluent in several languages, including Salazarkian, for which I may need him as a translator when we reach the islands. But most importantly, he is my friend, and he really wants to go."

"I see." Sholt swirled his nearly empty goblet a few times then downed the last of the wine. "What do you plan to do with the items you find on this expedition? I suppose that is the pertinent question. As scholars and educators in the arcane, we would want to study anything of importance. And I'm sure you know that we don't want any dangerous items ending up in the wrong places."

Hyden was certain the high wizard was fishing for information just like Phen had been doing earlier, only with a little more tact. Phen couldn't have told them yet, and wouldn't have told them about the Silver Skull. "I assure you that anything of interest to you, Master Sholt, and your colleague, Master Amill, will be handed over once I've returned," Hyden said directly into the man's eyes. "My interest is only in the adventure of finding the old pirate ship." *And using the Skull of Zorellin to go into the Nethers and get that blasted ring away from the thing that my brother has become. Once I've accomplished that you can have the Silver Skull too, for all I care.*

"Any scrolls, or texts would find their way to me or Master Amill before any other eyes delved into them, I pray," the high wizard said seriously. "Neither you nor Phenilous are skilled enough in the arcane to do more than cause harm with something you don't understand. When it comes to spells, potions, and artifacts, extreme caution and careful study is always the best route to take."

"Of course, Master," Hyden said from behind a forced, but convincing smile.

"Then I will inform Phenilous of his good fortune later this evening." Master Sholt's smile wasn't forced at all. The prospect of acquiring new spells and artifacts excited him and set his mind to wandering.

The "tink! tink! tink!" of silver rapping on crystal grabbed everyone's attention. The feast, it seemed, was about to begin. Oddly, Queen Willa's place at the head of the table had been given to High King Mikahl. Queen Willa sat at the other end of the table with the round and balding, but extremely capable head of her Blacksword soldiers, General Spyra, on her right and King Jarrek on her immediate left.

Hyden was seated at High King Mikahl's right hand, next to a large fleshy man who he thought might have been the mayor of Xwarda. Across from him, and to the King's left, sat Princess Rosa. The aunt, who sat beside the Princess and almost directly across from Hyden, was staring at him with a dark, angry look in her eyes. The white of her knuckles as they squeezed around the handle of her meat knife wasn't lost on him. Nor was Princess Rosa's subtle amusement at the discomfort that her aunt was causing him.

He gave her a mock apologetic shrug and sighed. It was going to be a long meal, followed by an even longer, and less interesting series of negotiations masked as polite conversation. Hopefully Phenilous had taken the bait and was researching the Silver Skull of Zorellin. If he was, Hyden mused, at least something was getting done this night.

Chapter Four

"...thes weel intereast yew, Kang Jareek," Princess Rosa was saying in her heavily accented, girlish voice.

The dinner dishes had just been removed and everyone was anticipating the desserts that were yet to come. Hyden was just glad that there were no more knives left at the table. The daggers in the eyes of Princess Rosa's Aunt were as sharp as razor blades.

"A men neemed Dreeg, and hes company, are claiming up the iron mines around yer ruined Castlemont, and all threw the rest of Wildermont as weell," the Princess continued. "It seems that he's taking your people back to their homeland as slaves to do the werk—the digging and the smething, I thenk mother called it." She touched a finger to her pouty lips and squeezed her huge dark eyes shut in concentration. "No, smeelting not smething, was whet she said," she finished with a smile.

The room fell silent for a few long heartbeats. The subject was a tender one for both King Jarrek and High King Mikahl. Her information was welcome, though, and the fact that her mother had obviously told her to tactfully relay the news showed that Queen Rachel might be serious about helping King Jarrek's cause.

"Dew yew reelly thenk that the zard-men are lizards?" the Princess asked High King Mikahl, in an attempt to change the subject.

He started to answer, but Hyden Hawk cut him off. "They are, m'lady." He gave Mikahl a wink and then focused his full attention on entertaining the Princess. "They were a prominent race once. According to the writings of one Urfell Nevlen, the Westlanders attempted to kill them off a few hundred years ago. Up until recently, it was believed that they had succeeded. They ride big four-legged lizards called gekas, and they train long beaked swamp dactyls to fight and spy for them."

The Princess's expression showed the distaste she held for such slimy scaled creatures.

"Between the zard-men and the breed beasts, taking back Westland will surely be some bloody business," King Mikahl said, more to himself than to anybody else.

"No less so than freeing my people from that slaver, Ra'Gren," added King Jarrek with a nod.

"Now, now, sirs!" Queen Willa interjected herself forcefully into the conversation. "I will not have such talk at my table. The Princess was merely musing on the existence of those creatures. All of this blood talk can wait until later. I assure you that there will be a time and place for it, but that time and place is not here, nor is it now."

Like two scolded boys, the kings mumbled apologies to Queen Willa with chastised looks on their faces. The sight was humorous to some of the ladies at the table, but the subject matter of the previous conversation kept them from doing more than eyeing the two men.

"I understand that you're leaving on your treasure hunt soon," someone said to Hyden.

"Aye," Hyden started to respond, but then remembered his manners. "Um, I mean yes, sir, we are." It had been the Lord Mayor of Xwarda who had broached the subject.

"Pirates' treasure is it?" the pudgy, half-inebriated man asked. "It seems to me that, with the people of Wildermont enslaved, and Westland overrun with skeeks and beasts, the timing of this adventure is... well ...well it's just odd."

Hyden looked at him coolly. There was a gravy spill on the man's collar where his second chin mushroomed up out of the straining garment he wore. Hyden pointed at the stain conspiratorially as he responded.

"The amount of wealth that was supposedly on that ship is more than enough to buy back every single one of King Jarrek's people," said Hyden. It was a lie, but it sounded good. "Not that I would recommend buying them back. The High King and King Jarrek need the coin though; Highwander as well. Soldiers, carpenters, and lumbermen all have to feed what is left of their families while we rebuild."

Queen Willa rescued Hyden from having to dig himself further into the conversation. "Lord Mayor, do not forget that Hyden Hawk is not a kingdom born man," she scolded. Her narrowed brows and severe tone cowed the man, but she went on anyway. "He has already bested Dahg Mahn's tower, saved Xwarda from the dragon's wrath, and helped High King Mikahl destroy that foul wizard Pael. I think that if he wanted to build a ladder up to the moon it would be none of our concern."

Silence again.

"Yeer Highness," the Princess gamely tried again to gain the High King's attention. "Deed you reelly fight the daemon-wizard from the back of a magical horse weth wings of fire?"

Hearing it from the mouth of the dreamy-eyed girl made it sound absurd, but it was true. Mikahl did fight the demon-wizard and his dark minions from the back of the bright horse. Humble by nature, Mikahl couldn't find words. What was worse, the table had gone quiet in expectation of some boasting tale. He fingered his dragon bone medallion, trying to avoid the Princess's gaze because he didn't want to flush with embarrassment in front of the whole table. Knowing that she'd seen him naked as a jay this afternoon was too much at the moment. Luckily he was saved from having to respond to her awkward question by the arrival of a train of servants bringing in the desserts.

*

All along the front face of Queen Willa's Xwardian Palace, starting above the second floor's row of arched windows, had once been a row of forty-foot tall stained glass depictions. All the glass was gone now. High King Mikahl, King Jarrek, Queen Willa, and Hyden Hawk stood in one of the open balcony-like spaces that remained, looking out across the moonlit rubble Pael's wrath had caused. The horror of the site was displaced by fragments of the stained glass that had been blasted out from the castle wall, leaving the destroyed city looking as if it had been frosted in gems.

In the foreground, below them, the fountain in the middle of Whitten Loch danced and played. The ripples reflected the light of the torches that ran along the top of the castle's inner wall. The air was still chilled and Mikahl had placed his lion-skin cloak over Queen Willa's shoulders, but it was King Jarrek who stood closest to her.

"When are you leaving?" Mikahl asked Hyden.

"Two days, if nothing diverts me," Hyden answered.

"Brady Culvert is a strong sword and a good man, Sir Hyden Hawk," King Jarrek said. "His father died beside me at Castlemont and was my dear friend."

"Aye, and I hope we have no need of swords," Hyden nodded. "The island we're headed to will most likely be deserted. On the maps I've seen, it doesn't appear to be big enough to sustain much life, but I'm honored to have him along, just in case."

"Salazar is a tricky place to lay-over," King Jarrek pointed out. "Brady's presence will dissuade the alley thieves if you display him properly. It's the Dakaneese pirates you've got to watch out for."

"Captain Trant is a master seaman, and the *Seawander* has a most capable crew," Queen Willa said. She had donated the use of her royal ship as a token of thanks to Hyden Hawk for the deeds he had done to save her kingdom.

"I can't believe that I used to think that you were a witch," High King Mikahl laughed lightly. "In Westland, they said that you once turned a man into a pig, and fed your Blacksword army the flesh of your enemies."

"And I did nothing to make them think any different," she boasted. "Fear of Willa the Witch Queen has kept many a man from crossing me. I learned that from my grandmother. Rumor and gossip, and sinister legends can sometimes be a weapon far greater than steel."

"I'm not so sure that she isn't really a witch," King Jarrek said with a grin. "She's been match-making and meddling so much as of late that it wouldn't surprise me to see her pouring love potions into the Princess and the High King's cups."

"It was Hyden Hawk doing the meddling and match-making, from what I hear," Queen Willa defended with a devilish look at Mikahl.

"I was just trying to show Princess Rosa the High King's sword—I mean his swordsmanship," said Hyden.

Mikahl's glaring eyes spoke volumes about the quality of the revenge he wanted to exact on his friend.

"Nevertheless," Willa went on, hiding her blush in the mane of the lion's fur. "I do think she's taken a liking to you Mikahl. She is smart, very pretty, and it's obvious that she has caught your eye as well."

"We're riding in the park tomorrow," Mikahl said. "If I could get some time with her, without all of you meddling and eavesdropping, I might be able to have a conversation with her. Until I've done that much, she is just another pretty girl to me."

"I believe you're right, Queen Willa," said Hyden with a nod. "He has fallen for her."

The clang of Mikahl's steel on the practice yard the next morning was louder and sharper than usual. Hyden came down with the elven longbow Vaegon had given him, and could tell immediately that Mikahl was hammering out his frustrations on some unlucky opponent. Since the day their friend Loudin of the Reyhall had died, Mikahl had risen every morning and put himself through rigorous drills with his sword. The feel of the longbow in Hyden's hand, and the ringing intensity from Mikahl's blade brought back a memory of the four of them on their trek through the Giant Mountains. This in turn spurred an even earlier memory of Hyden and Vaegon competing in the archery tournament at the Summer's Day Festival.

Either he or Vaegon would have won. The winner's name would have been carved on the Spire at Summer's Day with all the other champions of the realm, to be seen ever after. That seemed like a life-time ago to Hyden, but it had been less than a year. It was a shame that they never had the chance to finish the contest.

This morning he was unintentionally giving a demonstration on packing the wizard's eye full of arrows. He could get four of five in the center, but hadn't found a way to squeeze the fifth one in yet. But it wasn't for lack of trying. It wasn't his aim, it was the size of the wizard's eye. The center of the target was just too small to take five arrow tips completely inside its circumference.

"What you need is smaller shafts, Sir Hyden Hawk," Brady Culvert said from behind him.

Hyden turned and smiled at the strapping young man. Brady was tall and bulky, but hardly any of it was soft. His unruly dark curls left him with a boyish look. "No more of that 'Sir' crud. Not if you're going with me, Brady," Hyden said matter of factly. "We travel, we fight, and we work together as equals on our quest."

"What should I call you then?"

"Hyden, or Hyden Hawk is what my friends call me, and any friend of King Jarrek's is a friend of mine."

"Hyden Hawk it is then," said Brady with a nod. "My father used to buy hawkling eggs from your people at Summer's Day. He said they were the best for sending important messages, such as troop orders and other royal documents."

"Don't let Talon hear you say that," Hyden joked as he began unstringing his bow. "I use to climb the nesting cliffs in the spring to fetch them down." He thought of his younger brother Gerard then, and the ring Gerard had found among the nests up there. Sorrow threatened to take hold of him.

The loud clashing of Mikahl's sword filled the silence. Hyden forced Gerard and his terrible fate out of his mind. "You'll not need your plate armor; chain mail might even be inappropriate. Good leather with rings should do. I have a feeling that we might have to do a bit of sneaking about, maybe some climbing as well, and a lot of walking." Hyden paused to look over at a commotion that had broken out. Apparently Mikahl had dislodged an opponent's sword and it had flown into a bystander.

"I pity his sparring partners today," Brady said with a grimace of understanding. "He seems exceedingly aggressive for some reason."

"He's riding with the Princess this afternoon. All of this royal hoopla is keeping him from being himself." The concern in Hyden's voice betrayed how deep his friendship with Mikahl had become. "He wants to go with us more than you could imagine."

"He's the High King. All he has to do, is what he wants to do." Brady scrunched his face up in confusion. "Besides all of that, who'd rather go sailing after pirate treasure with a bunch of louts than ride with Princess Rosa?"

Brady pulled his chin in and gnashed his teeth together in a regretful cringe when he realized he had just called Sir Hyden Hawk Skyler a lout. But to his surprise Hyden was grinning at him.

"You'll do just fine, Brady," Hyden spoke his thoughts aloud. "And it takes a lout to know one."

Phen was waiting in the tower study when Hyden came down the next morning. "I can go!" The boy yelped excitedly. At his feet lay a big burlap sack full of his personal belongings and his extra robe. "When do we leave? What should I bring? What texts are we taking? Master Sholt said that I have to keep tutoring you, so I know we should at least bring three or four books. How about *Tales of the Sea*? How long do you think we will be gone?" All of Phen's questions were asked with one breath. Hyden chuckled as the boy inhaled deeply. He was about to begin again when Hyden stopped him with a question of his own.

"What did you learn about the Silver Skull?"

Phen looked at him with a perplexed expression for a moment. "How do you know that I know anything about the skull?" Phen asked.

"I am a great wizard," Hyden said sarcastically. "How else?"

"I'm starting to see what Master Amill meant when he said that you were a natural," said Phen with a shake of his head. "Without even casting a spell you got me to scour the books for you."

"You're just extra curious, Phen."

"I am, but you made Princess Rosa fall in love with the High King yesterday afternoon when you tricked the two of them. At least that's what the gossipers about the castle are saying."

"I just gave her a little more to think about is all. Not much more, I assure you. Besides, I had to get him back for that Yule gift he gave me."

"He said it wasn't him," Phen said.

"Just... He and I are even for the moment, and that's that. Now tell me about the skull."

"The Silver Skull of Zorellin is the artifact's proper name," Phen started. "I only found one listing about it in the Great Tome of artifacts. Darin wrote that the skull could be used to speak with the dead, the undead, and some of the more intelligent demons. But," Phen strode over to the table and pointed at the exposed page of the topmost text lying there, "In Dahg Mahn's untitled journal, the one that speaks about the Seal and other things relating to demon kind, it said that the Silver Skull of Zorellin can be used to transport items, and people, to and from the Nethers."

"Does it say how?"

"Wait, Hyden, I'm not done," Phen's voice was sharper than he intended it to be, but he didn't stutter or stop his lecture. "In a book called *Zorellin*, that I got from the master's library last night while all of you were at the feast, I found a bit… Hold on." Phen went to his bag, rummaged through it a moment then came up beaming. In his hand was an ancient text. He held it up as if it were a great prize, which in this case, it was.

"In here," Phen tapped the cover of the book. "It tells how the wizard Zorellin made the skull, and how he used it to enslave the demon of Krass, who he eventually used it to kill King Baffawn the Bloodthirsty for the good of all mankind."

"Very good, Phen," Hyden said. "Now the masters have loaned us the very book that gives away what it is we are really after."

"No, I sort of borrowed it," Phen smiled. "You know, just until we get back. I left the *Index of Known Forest Animals* in its place. They'll never know."

"That was my favorite," Hyden said.

"Aye," Phen said, emulating Hyden's response to almost everything. "But I also have in my sack *The Index of Known Marine Creatures*. I figured that, since we're going on a ship, you'd want us to have it handy."

"See, Phen, that's exactly why you're going with us." Hyden put his arm across the growing boy's shoulders in a brotherly fashion. "Have your masters freed you of all your other duties yet?"

"I'm yours to command, Sir Hyden Hawk," Phen stepped away and bowed with a flourish and a grin. Only the excitement he had felt when the late Master Targon and Queen Willa had plucked him from the orphanage in Xwarda City and made him an apprentice could compare to the level of exhilaration he was feeling now.

"Good," Hyden said. "I want you to use some of that energy to go find Brady Culvert at the East Gate Barracks, and also Dugak's nephew—I can't ever seem to remember his name. It's…It's—"

"Oarly," Phen remembered.

"Yes, Oarly. I want you to tell the two of them to meet us at the Golden Griffin tonight at dark fall." Hyden was starting to get excited as well. "Tell them that the meeting is mandatory, but the food and drinks are on me."

"Aye," Phen called as he tore out of the tower room to find them.

Chapter Five

Lord Gregory sat atop his mount cursing his fortune. Before him, where he would have crossed the shallows to the western bank of the Leif Greyn River, was a stretch of raging rapids that churned and thrashed with the full force of the spring thaw behind it. He was left with two choices now. He could either backtrack up into the mountains and go west, crossing the hundreds of streams, trickles and creeks that combined to make the powerful flow before him, or he could go south into Wildermont and hope that Harrap and Condlin Skyler had been exaggerating the amount of death and destruction they had found there. Even as that thought formed in his mind he dismissed it. He knew that Harrap and Condlin had most likely told him exactly what they had seen and heard. He also knew that, if the bridge that crossed over into Westland was really destroyed, his decision here and now would determine how long it would take him to finally make it back home. *If I even have a home left*, he thought to himself. Had he been younger or even healthier, he would have already been working his way back up into the mountains. Maybe it was good that he was half crippled and weary of backtracking. If Westland really had been taken over, he knew he would find no welcome there, but still he had to go look for his wife. Finding her was all that he lived for.

He took a deep breath and spurred his horse southward along the eastern bank of the churning flow. He knew that there were a few smaller towns and a dozen villages south of Castlemont along the river—Low Crossing, Seareach, and others. The Leif Greyn River split at Seareach. Maybe he could find a boat there and take the Westland flow to Settsted stronghold. There he could at least learn of his friend and peer, Lord Ellrich's fate.

Lord Ellrich's stronghold held the main barracks for the river guard. If the zard had come up from the marsh, Settsted would have fallen first. Maybe he should try to find a boat to Southport instead. No king or queen or invader of any sort would destroy the trade center of the kingdom they were taking over. Southport was Westland's biggest port. Shipping trade with all of the east, the Isle of Salazar and the other southern islands took place there. It was also a place where Lord Gregory could probably blend in with the populace.

A boat from Seareach to Southport then, he decided. He had enough gold in his saddlebags to buy his own ship. A chunk of raw gold ore the size of a man's head was left in one of Mikahl's packs, along with a fat sack of Westland coin. He'd taken the coins and with a dull axe, had broken a fist sized chunk off of the other. What he'd left behind was easily twice as much as he'd taken. Mikahl and Hyden would understand, he knew, so he didn't feel guilty for helping himself.

A day later, he saw the tip of the Summer's Day Spire jutting up over the ridge ahead of him. That afternoon, when he topped the ridge, he saw the whole flooded bulk of the Leif Greyn Valley. The Spire looked to be rising up out of a great lake.

"It's cleansing itself," he said aloud, and with some amazement. All of the dead bodies and burning wagons and deserted pavilions that he had seen as Vaegon the elf and Hyden Skyler helped him away from his routed camp were under water now. Hopefully the carnage was being washed down the river into O'Dakahn or the marshes.

It took the rest of that day, and two more, to get to the city of High Crossing. Normally it would have only taken a day, but he had been forced to skirt the flooded valley. At least the High Crossing bridge was still intact. It didn't cross the Leif Greyn River, though. It spanned the Everflow River as it came out of the Evermore Forest to join with the Leif Greyn.

No toll-taker stepped out of the little house on the other side of the bridge when he crossed it. That alone confirmed most everything that Halden Skyler's sons had told him. He didn't have to look upon the nearly deserted rows of buildings that lined the streets beyond the bridge. He didn't have to see and smell the bones and thawing remains of the corpses that had been haphazardly put into piles and burned before winter set in.

He felt eyes upon him as he rode through the empty town. Suddenly a sharp squeal filled the air and a thin filthy boy came chasing a healthy looking piglet into the road. The boy couldn't have been ten years old, and he froze in place when he saw Lord Gregory coming. Tears of terror welled up in the boy's eyes as he darted back into the evening shadows, his piglet forgotten. From somewhere in that direction came a woman's hushed, but scolding voice. Lord Gregory, saddened by the sight, but uplifted to know that there were some survivors about, spurred his mount onward.

As he left the town of High Crossing behind him, the sun was starting to set. At an abandoned farm set a short distance from the road he holed up in a barn for the night. There was no telling what sort of pilferers and bandits were about. He didn't want to spend the night out in the open. He thought about sleeping in one of the abandoned inns he had seen, but he would have had to leave his horse outside. What people remained here were desperate and would probably have the poor animal gutted and cooked in the blink of an eye.

As he lay in the barn struggling to find sleep, his heart grew heavier. Throughout the day the signs of war had become apparent, making him wonder just how bad off his homeland might be. Was Lady Trella even alive? He had to find out.

Westland couldn't be as desolate as High Crossing, could it? It could, he decided, but he knew that it wasn't. Instead of being empty and void of life, it was now full of skeeks and barbaric breed giants. The strand of hope he held for his Lady Trella was growing thinner, but he refused to let it go.

He could picture her in his mind as she had been when he'd left her at the stronghold in Lake Bottom: the yellow dress with the sky blue ribbons, the sparkling of her sapphire eyes as she kissed him goodbye.

King Balton had called on him. It was supposed to be a relatively short journey, a trip around Lion Lake to Lakeside Castle, then two weeks at the Summer's Day competition, but when Lord Gregory arrived, King Balton was on his deathbed. He'd been poisoned and knew exactly who his murderer was. Secret orders were given, then at the festival all the hells broke loose.

Lord Gregory had wanted to stay with his king, root out those responsible, and deliver them to the noose, or better yet, to the headsman's axe, but King Balton had told him no.

"Go to Summer's Day," he'd said. "Take good men, men that you trust. Mikahl will need you. You know who he truly is. He'll have my sword, and he'll be scared. You'll find him in the Giant Mountains looking for the Southern Guardian, but go to the competitions first and participate as if nothing is amiss. It's imperative that the cause of my death remain between us. If they know that you know I've been poisoned, they will try to kill you too, and Mikahl needs your help far more than the rope needs necks."

Lord Gregory had passed Mikahl in the hallway outside the King's chambers after that conversation. The young man looked troubled, as if he already knew some of what was happening. Lord Gregory remembered looking into Mikahl's eyes then and seeing King Balton in them. He understood now that Balton had known that his son, Prince Glendar, would bring the kingdom down. There was no way Glendar could ever have Ironspike. Mikahl was the intended heir to Westland. Mikahl's heart was true, and humble, and fierce. Mikahl would have to pick up all the pieces now. Lord Gregory only hoped that the boy was still alive. Why the Giant King had sent him off to Highwander where the Witch Queen ruled, he couldn't understand. He could remember clearly her Blacksword warriors cutting down his men while he lay helpless. If he couldn't find Lady Trella, Highwander was his next destination.

In the morning, while rummaging through the barn, he found a crossbow and a handful of dull, but usable steel-tipped bolts for it. Before he had taken his injuries, he had been quite handy with the sword, but now his body felt a hundred years old. He could wield his blade if he had to, and he still wore it at his hip, but the crossbow would make even a well armored bandit wary of him.

He saw no bandits that day. He did see a herder with seven goats out in a soggy green field, and a man on the wall of a keep that sat a good distance off the road. He saw a few folk who looked to be planting corn or maybe wheat behind a mule-drawn plow too. When he passed they huddled together and stared at him as if he had a golden horn sticking out of the top of his head. When he finally came into the outskirts of what used to be the city of Castlemont he saw nothing but destruction.

Half a hundred proud towers had once reached toward the heavens from the base of the city. Now there was nothing but ruin, a stubbed tower here, the taller stump of one over there, and a few other broken structures jutted up from the rubble like broken teeth. Lord Gregory figured that winter had preserved some of the meat of the dead, for hundreds of thousands of carrion birds swarmed over the piles of brick and stone and fractured wooden beams looking for another meal. It was the idea of what had happened here, more than the smell of rot in the air that made his stomach turn. He couldn't understand how Pael and King Glendar could have orchestrated such total destruction.

He had no doubt now that Valleya had fallen as well. Dreen had naught but a clay brick wall around it. If that's where the Westland army had gone, then they had taken it.

Why would they sack Wildermont and not try to hold it, though? Glendar probably had no idea that Westland would fall behind him, so he hadn't been concerned with guarding his rear. But still, any good military tactician would want to hold the source of more than half the realm's supply of iron ore. It just didn't make any sense not to.

Thoughts of King Glendar, and more specifically of his beloved Westland, began to consume Lord Gregory. He spurred his horse southward, stealing glances across the river between the crumbled buildings on his right. In places he could see the wide, powerful flow and his homeland across its span.

A wooden tower rose up from the Westland bank where the destroyed crossing bridge still stuck out like some fancy half-finished dock. Men were pulling lines in from it as if it were just that. Other men were on the tower, and there were people moving about beneath it as well. Behind them, the city of Locar seemed to be carrying about life as if nothing had changed. Dull gray smears of smoke still lifted toward the sky, and the occasional clang of tack and the faint smell of cooking meat carried in the air. It all looked pretty normal and hopeful, but only for a moment. Lord Gregory then saw a giant breed beast being pulled in a huge wagon carriage by a dozen men. Climbing to the top of a pile and squinting with his hand visored at his brow, Lord Gregory watched as the driver, a man, lashed at the pullers with a whip until they quickened their pace and disappeared beyond some buildings. Fluttering up on the wooden tower, and from several other places across the river in Westland, was an unfamiliar banner: three yellow lightning bolts crossing in the middle on a field of black. Lord Gregory reckoned it looked like a wicked golden snowflake.

Enslaved Westlanders, breed giants loose in Westland, and under the banner of some self-proclaimed Dragon Queen. Lord Gregory shook his head in dismay. King Balton would roll over in his tomb if he knew of this—if he even had a tomb. Lord Gregory, however, was filled with a newfound hope that Lady Trella might have actually survived the Dragon Queen's invasion. He had to get home and find out if she was all right, but there was no way to cross here. He needed to go south to where the river widened and split, then he had to find a boat to get across.

When he topped the hill that led down into the town of Low Crossing he saw a dozen men loading a flat barge with crates. Suddenly he was feeling uneasy. The pings and clanks of a few smiths' hammers could be heard, but Lord Gregory didn't dare stray from the road. On the southern side of a small bridge that crossed a tributary just before it met the main flow, he hurried past four well tended horses tied to the post of a fully operational tavern. As he was about to leave the town behind him, a pair of horsemen came out from behind the last riverfront building and blocked the road. By the insignia on their breastplates he knew they were Dakaneese sell-swords. He had run into them before on the docks of Southport and Portsmouth in Westland, but this wasn't Westland. Here he was nobody; his lordship meant nothing. He found, as he brought his crossbow to bear on one of the men, that he was more than just a little afraid.

The man he was aiming at spat a thick brown wad of slime from his mouth. "Let him pass," he said gruffly. "He's no absconded slave."

"But Dreg said to stop anyone that looks suspicious," the other man argued. The conviction in his voice fled when the crossbow moved from the first man to him.

"Look there, Lem, at his hilt. That sword's worth more than all of your sisters in a bundle. This man ain't suspicious, Lem, he's armed," the first man said. Then to Lord Gregory, he said, "What're you doing passing through here?"

Lord Gregory's heart was hammering in his chest. He could barely breathe, but knowing that these men were only second-rate sell-swords he said the first thing that came to his mind and hoped for the best. "Is Dreg paying you enough to mind my business?" He asked the question in a way that suggested not only that he knew who Dreg was, but that he was in the man's favor. He hoped that the extreme quality of his nervousness didn't show through his façade of annoyed confidence.

A moment of silence ensued, then the man spat another wad of brown slime from his mouth. He grinned with rotten teeth as he backed his horse away from his companions. "See, Lem," he said as he motioned for Lord Gregory to pass between them. "He's not suspicious."

"Nay, he's not," the other man said, his eyes never straying from the crossbow that was still trained on his gut.

As soon as Lord Gregory was out of their sight, he spurred his horse and rode at a mad gallop for a good long while. He thought that this man Dreg might send somebody snooping after him and wanted to put as much distance between him and Low Crossing as he could. He doubted that the two men guarding the road would even say anything about his passing, but he couldn't be sure. If they did, the fact that they'd noticed the value of his sword meant that men would surely come looking for him sooner or later.

Just before dark he spotted a wagon train approaching from the south. There were three horse-drawn wagons surrounded by at least twenty mounted men. Probably just more sell-swords guarding a cargo, he thought. Not knowing what else to do, he left the road for the hills that rose up off to the east. He hated to leave the road. He was so close to Seareach he could smell the marshes already. Even so, he needed to come up with a story, or a plan, or both. He needed to know what the sell-swords were about, who had hired them, and what the political climate was between the Dragon Queen, the Dakaneese, and those Westlanders who had survived, but he didn't want to get robbed, captured or killed doing it.

Seareach was the last place he could find a boat to take him swiftly across the river to Settsted. It was less than half a day south. If he had to go farther south than that to find transport, he would have to travel all the way to O'Dakahn and catch a sea ship. That could take weeks.

He found a low place in the hills and dared to light a small fire that night, for it was still chilly, even this far south. The beginnings of a plan began to form in his mind and he fell asleep turning the ideas over and over again.

He woke to the sound of voices—voices far too close to him. He reached slowly—as if he were just shifting his sleeping position—to where he'd lain the crossbow before he'd fallen asleep. It wasn't there. Panic shot through him, but he didn't overreact. He saw that the sun had barely reddened in the sky when he cracked open his eyelids. He felt a heavy booted man step close to his head, and could see three others. Two of them had longbows drawn and trained on him.

"Come on man, wake up," a voice said. "We'll just have a word or two with you."

The accent was Dakaneese. The way the man spoke told Gregory that he was no lackey; this was somebody who had authority.

"Who are you?" Lord Gregory asked as he sat up. He was glad he had used his saddlebags for a pillow. Had these men found all of his gold he would already be dead. The thought of the wealth in his packs gave him an idea that added well with the story he had come up with last night.

"You don't recognize old Dreg?" the man's tone was full of irony. "My men said that you told them you knew me."

"You need to hire better men," Gregory calmly replied. Though he showed no fear outside, inside he felt as if his heart might fail him. "How did you track me at night? My fire was too small to be seen from the road."

"With sorcery of course," Dreg said with a nod toward the silhouette of a robed and hooded figure who was sitting on a horse near the other men. "What were you doing up north?"

Gregory sighed. *Here it goes*, he thought, *all or nothing*. "I escaped the Dragon Queen's breed beasts through the Reyhall Forest and wintered in a cavern up in the foothills."

"You're high-born, don't deny it," accused Dreg. "Is there a reward for you?"

"Reward?" Lord Gregory chuckled nervously. "If there is, it's not a big one, I assure you."

"The quality of your steel says otherwise," Dreg's tone had become curious. "Where did you come by such a piece?"

"I pulled it off of a body at Summer's Day," Lord Gregory lied. In truth his father had given the sword to him, as his father had done before that. It had been in his family since it had been forged nearly three hundred years ago. He didn't want to lose it, but it wasn't worth his life.

"I'm a man of inspiration, and I have a weakness for survivors," Dreg said coolly. "Inspire me to leave you to your fate and I may do so, though I doubt it."

Dreg would probably let him live if he gave him the sword and some coin, but Lord Gregory had a better idea. "Get me on a boat to Settsted or Southport over in Westland," he said. "If you do, I'll make you rich—rich beyond imagining."

"Granddad's coin chest? Mam's jewelry box?" Dreg smirked. "You'll pay me when we get there? I said inspire me. I've heard this drivel hundreds of times. Just last week a man offered me an entire herd of goats to spare his young daughter from my men's lust. I agreed, and being a man of my word my men never touched the girl. I did though, and after I killed her, we feasted."

"Still eatin' them fargin goats," a man chuckled. Another laughed with him from the darkness.

Lord Gregory reached behind him and pulled his saddle bag to his lap. He heard the laughter suddenly stop as the men around him resituated the aim of their bows. He didn't stop what he was doing, though, because he knew that Dreg wouldn't let them shoot him just yet.

"Slowly, man," Dreg cautioned. "Itchy fingers all around you now."

"You'd be wiser to let me show you what I've got in private," Lord Gregory said with enough confidence that he saw Dreg considering it.

"And be pricked by some poison dart, or caught up in some ludicrous charm spell. I think not." Dreg trotted his horse up a little closer. "I could just kill you, fool, and take what you've got. Now out with it."

"Kill me if you like," Lord Gregory replied boldly. Most, if not all of his confidence had returned. "But if you do, you'll never know where this came from." He pulled the fist sized chunk of raw gold ore out of his pack and held it to where it caught the breaking light of dawn. All around him the gasps of Dreg's men could be clearly heard. Dreg himself let out an audible "Ooh" and his eyes grew as big as coins.

"It appears that I owe you an apology, sir," Dreg finally said, with some sincerity in his voice. "I have indeed been inspired. Now what was it you said you needed? A boat to Southport? Is there anything else?"

Chapter Six

Shaella, the Dragon Queen of Westland, daughter of the recently deceased demon-wizard Pael, carefully tipped the vial she held until a single drop of glistening crimson fell from it. The blood landed with a 'plop' in the clear water basin cradled in her lap. She stirred the concoction with a finger, sucked the liquid, then sat perfectly still until the swirling calmed.

On the surface of the stuff in her bowl she saw her reflection first. Her dark eyes contrasted with the angry pinkish-red burn scar that started at her temple and ran back over her ear, leaving one side of her head hairless. The rest of her thick, black mane could be laid over the ugliness so that it didn't show, but she chose to let the ruined flesh be seen. A dragon had made that scar, the dragon that she tricked and enslaved, and then used to take over the biggest kingdom in the realm. Another scar, from a knife fight that had happened long ago in a Dakaneese tavern, ran down her cheek like a permanent teardrop. The scars were nothing to be ashamed of. Though they marred her beauty, they reminded those who came before her of her violent past, and her vast capabilities. The scars made it easier for her to be taken seriously, and she displayed them like badges of honor.

The people of her new kingdom, the struggling humans, the slithery zard-men, and the huge hairy breed beasts, all thought that the dragon was still hers to command. They didn't know that she had lost her controlling collar, and thus the ability to command the great red wyrm. She didn't discourage the notion that she could call it forth on a whim, though, and her appearance kept questions from being asked.

She mumbled a few words in a musical hum and the face in the water's surface shimmered into that of another woman. This woman's features were rounder: slightly chubby cheeks, framed by blonde curly ringlets, pale blue eyes speckled with green and gold, and a smile that spoke of true innocence. She looked stunning for the hundred and twenty year old marsh witch that she really was. Shaella remembered the woman's ample bosom and wide curving hips from the visions they regularly shared together. All of Queen Willa's Xwardian court had been, and was still, completely fooled by the powerful illusion that had changed the old witch's appearance. In fact General Spyra, the aging head of the entire Highwander Blacksword army, was in love with her.

"What does our General have to say today, Mandary?" Shaella asked.

"Mastress, the hawk-man departed the palace here at Xwarda yesterday on his quest for the pirate treasure," the plump woman said in a girlish voice.

"Did you place the *finding stone*?" Shaella asked.

"Yes Mastress. A boy—an apprentice—travels with them. The stone is hidden among his things. Queen Willa has an odd interest in the youth's safety. So I doubt he'll be abandoned or thrown overboard. And none of those seamen will dare to rummage through his duffels."

"Good, good, Mandary. What else?"

"King Jarrek is still rigorously preparing his men to try and free his people from King Ra'Gren's slave pens. The General told me that they will all be leaving soon."

"And the High King?" Shaella interrupted. "When will he attack?"

"There has still been no talk of attacking Westland, my Mastress," the witch woman said. "I have wheedled the General's mind well. If it is to happen, as you fear it will, then General Spyra knows nothing about it."

"What is it that he is waiting for?" Shaella asked aloud, but rhetorically. Before her spy could answer, she asked another question.

"What does the young king do? He has the power of Ironspike at his hip. Is he daft?"

"He is far from daft. Apparently he is trying to unite all of the Eastern Kingdoms." The woman in the reflection looked away quickly. The alarm that came across her face faded as she continued. "As you know, Queen Willa and King Jarrek have bowed to him. Now King Broderick of Valleya is supposed to join them, and as soon as High King Mikahl weds Princess Rosa, her mother, Queen Rachel, and all of Seaward will no doubt do the same." The plump woman looked away again; this time the alarm stayed in her expression. In a quick whisper she went on: "He seems content to leave you be while they rebuild what your father destroyed." The last was spoken almost inaudibly, and before Shaella could respond, the woman's face backed away from the reflection and a pair of plump hands came reaching in to disturb the surface of the liquid in Shaella's bowl. As the vision shimmered away with the ripples, Shaella could still hear her spy's girlish voice talking to the intruder.

"Oh, Marial dear, you startled me. You really shouldn't enter unannounc…" Then the spell was completely broken.

My father, thought Shaella, *the mighty wizard Pael*. He had spent Shaella's whole lifetime molding Prince Glendar into his puppet. To him, she had been nothing but an afterthought, or so it had seemed until he more or less handed her Westland on a silver platter. All of his bribing and scheming had been so that they might take over the realm together. It was a shame all that planning had gone over the sill when part of the demon Shokin had found its way into him. Pael's thirst for power had caused him to rush into Highwander seeking the magic stored in the Wardstone bedrock of the place. Had he been patient and content with his original plan, he might not have been killed.

Shaella learned from her father's mistakes, though. She'd learned that lust and greed and power could spoil a near perfect plan. She was just glad that she had followed through with her end of things. Love had nearly led her conquest into ruin, but now that her hold on Westland was secure, she had the time, and the means, to communicate with her beloved Gerard. It was time that she might not have had if she'd done things differently. It was only a temporary inconvenience that Gerard was sealed in the Nethers with all of demon kind. At least she kept telling herself that. Together they would find a way to breach the magical bonds that held him in that dark place. It was that hope that drove her, the very reason that she spent nearly every waking hour in Pael's tower scouring his books in search of another way in and out of the Nethers.

There was another way. She knew this for certain. Long before Pavreal had created the Seal that he used to banish the demons back to their home, there had been a way. How else could there have been demons loose for him to banish? They had to have gotten out somehow.

The demon Shokin had breached the Nethers in those ancient days when he was just a man. He had wrought so much pain, destruction, and death in the world that the Abbadon, the Dark Lord himself, had turned him into a demon as his reward. Shokin had then terrorized demon kind until he rose above them all. Somehow he escaped the Nethers and brought his dark hordes with him. The great hero Pavreal eventually sent Shokin back to the Nethers through the Seal he carved into the Dragon's Tooth Spire with the sword Ironspike. That Seal was destroyed by Hyden Hawk Skyler and the dragon, but there was another way. There had to be.

Pael had recently used Pavreal's Seal to call Shokin back into the world, but something had gone wrong. Shokin was torn in half when Pael's sacrifice wouldn't die. Shaella's lover, Gerard, had been that sacrifice. He crawled down into the Nethers with half of Shokin's essence clinging to existence inside his mind. The other half of the demon filled Pael with the very power that eventually brought about his demise. Gerard's older brother, had somehow forced the demon out of Pael and back into the Seal, thus condemning his sibling to the horror of the darkness forever. Or had he? Now both halves of Shokin had rejoined in Gerard. Gerard held them apart, and kept them from taking over his mind with the fiery will that burned deep inside him. When he had been at death's door, alone and in the Nethers, he had eaten the yolk of one of the dragon's eggs he had stolen. It changed him completely. More dragon-beast than man now, and with the two powerful halves of Shokin bickering in his brain constantly, he fought every day to stay alive, trapped in the demon-filled darkness.

Gerard was still weak, but he was growing stronger and was starting to tap Shokin's power and knowledge. He had gleaned from the demon that Shokin had once used the Silver Skull of Zorellin to breach the Nethers. Shaella found an entry in a diary from her father's library about the artifact. A raving mad man who'd been abandoned on an island by the brutal pirate Barnacle Bones had spouted on and on about a silver skull that conjured forth a demon wind that would carry the pirate anywhere he wanted to go. After leaving the man, Barnacle Bones was never seen or heard from again. He never made port with his treasure. Shaella had searched and searched for a clue to its location, but she found nothing. The fact that Gerard's brother, Hyden Hawk, was going on a mysterious quest for pirate treasure could mean only one thing, though. He too was after the Silver Skull.

Already, Flick was manning a party and a ship to track down Hyden's group and take the skull. With the *finding stone* hidden on Hyden Hawk's ship it would be impossible for them to get away. With a few words and a sparrow's heart she, or Flick, could cast a spell that would reveal the exact location of the *finding stone*.

Flick was a capable wizard. Once one of her father's apprentices, he was loyal to Shaella's cause and always eager to please her. The two breed giants he had chosen to accompany him on his mission, Drolz and Varch were both fierce fighters. The zard called Slake was a most competent captain. He had pirated several barges full of weapons and supplies that had been instrumental in Shaella's taking of Westland. He was highly feared and regarded among his kind. The mixed crew of his sleek ship, *Slither*, were loyal and tested. As soon as Hyden Hawk found the skull, they would help Flick take it from him.

With those thoughts on her mind she rang a bell to summon her zardess attendant, Fslandra. A moment later the door to her chamber crept open and the young lizard-girl stepped in and bowed with a hiss.

"How may I serves yous?" she asked.

"Find Cole, and have him meet me by the turn of a glass in the old gathering hall, the one with the map table in it." As she gave the order she rose to her feet, went to a closet and began searching for a particular garment. "And Fslandra," she called out as the lizard-girl's tail flitted out the door. "Have Lady Able fetch me up a hot bath immediately."

"Yes Mastress," came the fading reply.

It entertained Shaella deeply to watch the Lady Able carrying bucket after bucket of hot water up all those stairs. It thrilled her even more when she made the high born woman wash her naked body. It wasn't the sexuality of it. It was the disgust and contempt that radiated off the woman as she lathered the rags with scented soap, and the way Lady Able had to clinch her bottom lip in her teeth to remind herself not to scrub too hard; the way her entire upper body glowed red with a mixture of embarrassment, anger and shame as she toweled Shaella dry.

Before Shaella took Westland, Lady Able had been waited on hand and foot in the luxury of her husband's stronghold. She'd been the ruler of her roost, so to speak, and had never kept less than three personal attendants. In her day she had humiliated, overworked, and disrespected at least half a hundred young servant girls. She'd made the mistake of demanding that she be treated like a high born lady in front of Queen Shaella's entire court.

"I will treat you exactly how you treated all those ladies that served you," Shaella said. Then she added, "Now go fetch me a tray of fruit from the kitchens and be sure not to meet the master chef's eyes."

As a queen, Shaella was merciless, cleverly ruthless in her punishments, and more than a little dark in her deeds, but no one could say that she was unjust. She showed no favoritism to the zard-men, the breed giants, or the humans. High born, or low, covered in scales and hatched from an egg, or birthed from a mother's womb meant nothing to her. A person was judged and rewarded or punished by their actions alone. The common folk had seemingly accepted her after she'd flown on her dragon's back over Portsmouth and Crossington and driven the savage breed giants out of the streets and back into line. Little did those people know that she had sent the breed to terrorize them in the first place. When she began knocking the Westland nobles, who hadn't escaped, off of their pedestals, some of the commoners began to really like her.

During King Glendar's short and brutal stint as the king of Westland, he had rounded up nearly every able bodied man and boy and marched them off to their eventual deaths. Before he'd done that, he had decorated the bailey yards of Lakeside Castle with the piked heads of hundreds of men—Westland men. Suspected conspirators, men so loyal to his father that they tried to oppose his succession to the throne, even the common gossipers who whispered the wrong thing in the wrong ear, ended up with their heads displayed on pikes. The good people of Westland had been scared to death, and rightly so.

None of the people knew that Pael was Shaella's father. Had they, they might not have been so accepting of her rule. The belief that it was Queen Willa's Blacksword army, the Valleyans, and King Glendar's evil that had taken away their husbands and sons was now prevalent. This played perfectly into Shaella's hands because she had forbidden all trade with the Eastern Kingdoms, save for Dakahn. With all borders closed, the people were starting to feel safe again, especially since Queen Shaella was now publicly punishing the zard, and the breed, when they attacked any of the humans.

As she made her way to the map-room to meet Cole, Shaella passed a group of young merchant-men in an open corridor. They all bowed graciously to her.

"You're looking radiant today, my queen," one of them said as she moved past.

When the men were long behind them, Shaella spoke. "Fslandra, do you think I look radiant?"

The lizard-girl knew that Queen Shaella was mocking the young man, and she made a gurgling sound that passed for zardian laughter.

Cole was waiting for her in the map room with a silver goblet in his hand. Cole was Flick's brother, and both of them emulated Pael just a little too much. Shaella's father had been their mentor and teacher, and they both kept their heads free of hair and their skin as ghostly white as Pael had. Cole was the eldest. He was taller and thinner than Flick, but not by much on either count. From a distance they could easily pass as twins. They had been instrumental in the taking of Westland, and in her heart Shaella considered them as her dearest friends.

Cole started to bow to her but she waved it off. "We're not in public, Cole. You know better."

"Just showing my queen her proper respect," he replied evenly.

"That's enough, Cole." She motioned for Fslandra to go. The lizard-girl shut the door behind her, leaving Shaella and Cole to themselves.

The room was paneled in deeply varnished oak. Along one wall there were wine-rack shelves holding hundreds of rolled maps. The opposite wall was glazed and a grand view of Lion Lake spread out before them. Expertly etched into the surface of the great oval table that filled the room was a map of the continent and its kingdoms. Shaella deftly plucked the goblet from Cole's hand and sipped from it. She made a sour face then circled the map-table, studying it as she went.

"I hope I didn't disturb your day," she said, "but the idea that struck me was too marvelous to contain."

"I've been dealing with reports about your Lord of Locar. It seems that Bzorch is bringing in Wildermont slaves to help build his watchtowers along the river." Cole heaved a sigh of exasperation. "I've gone over seventeen different grievances concerning your pet breed giant's conduct. Truthfully, I'm glad to be away from the mess."

"Seventeen is too many to ignore. I'll set out for Locar myself with a troop of zard on the morrow and settle the matter. I don't want slaves in Westland. Bzorch can pay his laborers like everyone else."

"You are the nicest evil sorceress queen I've ever met," Cole jested. He was glad that the words Dragon Queen hadn't slipped out of his mouth. Since she'd lost her dragon, Shaella hated the term. "Now what is this idea you can't keep to yourself?"

"I'm driving myself crazy waiting on the High King to attack us. He has to try to get his father's kingdom back or no one will really follow him. What good is a king who cannot hold his own kingdom? The problem is that every day he waits, he gathers more allies." Shaella hopped up, sat on the map-table and tapped Seaward City. "I want to provoke him, force him to come at us, before he gains too much."

"How do you want to do that?" Cole asked, his curiosity piqued.

"He's going to marry Princess Rosa soon," Shaella grinned. "I say we find out if High King Mikahl has enough honor to come rescue a damsel in distress. I'd like you to go to Seaward and invite Princess Rosa here for a visit." She gave Cole a sinister wink and chuckled deviously. "Well, maybe *invite* wasn't quite the word I was looking for."

Chapter Seven

Had to be that fargin dwarf, thought Hyden, as he darted to the bushes for the fifth or maybe the sixth time that afternoon. *Phenilous wouldn't dare betray me.* Brady Culvert was a possible suspect as well, but not a likely one. The Wildermont guardsman's sense of duty was second to none. Hyden knew that someone had betrayed him though. Someone had conspired with High King Mikahl to get the squat weed into his cup or his canteen. *Maybe it was the wagon driver, or one of his two helpers; or was it someone else in the escort?*

"It's like traveling with a wee little girl," commented Oarly the dwarf from the top of his mule. His legs weren't long enough to get around and over the back of a horse, so rather than teeter to and fro like a child's toy, he chose a narrow-backed mule that his stumpy body could manage. On top of the hairy little man's head was a pointy-topped, wide-brimmed hat that had long ago flopped over in the middle.

"I have to admire King Mikahl's mode of revenge. It's... It's..." Brady started to say "effective," but the moaning grunt that Hyden Hawk made from the bushes on the roadside caused him to finish with the word "brutal," instead.

"I swear by the goddess that if I find out which one of you helped him," Hyden called out breathlessly, "I will... I'll... Ooh! Ah! Oooh! Blast you!" The wet sloppy sound that followed caused them all to make sour faces and urge the horses a bit further away.

They were somewhere between Jenkanta and the High Port – Old Port split. They had crossed the Doon River the day before and camped at an often used cave called the Midway. They were on their way to Old Port to catch their ship and should have been beyond the split by now, but Hyden Hawk's condition forced them to stop every few miles so that he could relieve himself.

At first Hyden thought that he had eaten something that disagreed with him, but then he remembered Mikahl's comment as they had said their goodbyes. "Take plenty of soil cloth," the High King had joked with a stupid grin on his face. Hyden thought that he'd meant to take extra soil cloth for the sea voyage. He understood the jest all too well now. This was Mikahl's revenge for Hyden displaying him naked before the Princess, and it was, as Brady put it, "brutal."

"Should we let the wagons run ahead?" the commander of their customary twenty man escort of Blacksword soldiers suggested to Brady from a discreet distance. "Captain Trant will want to load the gear and make ready. He likes to keep his schedules."

"Aye," Hyden called from the roadside. "All of you go on. I'll catch up to you."

"Escort the wagons on to port, Sergeant," Brady said. "I'll escort Hyden Hawk."

"I'm staying with Hyden too," Phen said. His loyalty to Hyden, as well as his worry, showed plainly on his face.

The sergeant spurred his horse away and spoke to the wagon master. The procession began forming back up and eventually started away.

Oarly made no move to join them. As soon as the procession had moved on, he urged his mule toward the clump of shrubs where Hyden was now standing to lace up his leather britches.

"It was I who got ye," Oarly confessed with a mixture of pride and shame. "By the order of the High King, mind ye." He began rummaging through his pack and brought his stumpy arm out with a grin. "Here, eat it." He offered Hyden a thumb sized dried vegetable that still had the stem attached to it. It was glossy black, like a polished stone. "It might burn a bit going in and out, but it'll plug you up, if you know what I mean."

Hyden studied the dwarf's eyes, which were on a level with his own since Oarly was still seated on his mule. It was hard to read the dwarf's expression because his big silly looking hat shadowed most of his face. Hyden saw no malice or mischief in the squat man's gaze though, so he took the offering and bit off a big piece. The heat of the pepper crept up on him as he was walking back to his horse. By the time he got there his entire head was glowing red and on fire. Sweat poured down his brow and his mouth felt blistered.

"Ahh!" Hyden yelled. "Wah-er! Wah-er!" He walked, almost sprinting, over to Brady who was unshouldering his canteen. "Whaaat-er!"

"It'll only make it worse," Oarly said with a grin, but it was too late.

"AAHHHHH," Hyden yelled as he guzzled water like a mad man. When it didn't cool his mouth his eyes grew panicked and desperate. He made a pleading gesture with his hands. "AAHHH! AAHHH!" His eyes were squinted and watering. Water from Brady's canteen was running down his chin and his head looked as if it might explode.

By that time, even Brady and Phen were laughing.

A few moments later, after he'd cooled off and mastered himself, Hyden Hawk summoned what dignity he had left and climbed back up into his saddle. Without a word, but with plenty of angry looks, he spurred his mount down the road.

"What did High King Mikahl give you to do that?" Brady asked with genuine curiosity in his voice.

"For slipping him the squat weed he gave me this." Oarly reached his stumpy arm over his shoulder to his back and patted the handle of the wicked looking double-edged axe that was strapped there. "That cinder pepper I just gave him, though," Oarly chuckled, "now that was me own gag."

"He'll get you back, you know," Phen boasted in Hyden's defense. "He'll get you back good!"

"No lad," the dwarf said with a confident smile on his hairy face. "After that cinder pepper works its way out of him, he'll know better than to jest with the likes of me. Mark my words."

From Phen's shoulder, Talon the hawkling cawed out his sharp disagreement with the dwarf.

Oarly hadn't lied. True to his word, the effects of the squat weed quickly dissipated. Nevertheless, Hyden kept them trotting a few hundred yards behind the wagons and the escort just in case.

The land around them was green, but rocky. There were very few trees, but many clumps of shrubs and bushes dotted the landscape. They passed several herders whose large flocks of sheep and goats looked fat and healthy. After they took the Old Port branch of the 'Y' in the road, they began to see lively farms, and other humble dwellings out along the hills. It appeared that this part of the world hadn't been touched by Pael's madness.

As they drew closer to the ocean, Hyden grew excited. He'd never seen the sea. Berda the giantess had told him and the clan folk many a tale about it. The last few nights, at the fire, Hyden and Phen had taken turns reading from a book about tides and the moon's other effects on the ocean. This only made Hyden want to see the splendor of the sea that much more. Before he could see or hear the water, though, he could taste the salt in the air. As soon as he did, he sent Talon ahead to explore. With his eyes clenched shut, he watched as the world passed below through the hawkling's razor keen vision.

The road wound its way down among the sloping hills into a long stretched conglomeration of gray topped roofs and crowded, narrow cobbled streets. It extended southward farther than Talon could see at his present height. Hyden sent the hawkling rising in an upward circle, using the warmer air reflected off the rooftops until it was all well below him. Hyden saw through Talon's eyes that they were starting out onto a finger-like peninsula that extended a good distance into the gray-blue ocean. The road went the length of the finger, with smaller dirt and cobbled lanes cutting across it toward the white rolling shores. Ships, boats, skiffs and trawlers lined the myriad docks that extended from the western side of the formation. To the east, the finger was open and a fat dark gray line separated sea from shore. As Talon swooped lower Hyden saw that it was a crude wall made of granite blocks. Rolling white-capped waves crashed into it, sending up huge explosions of foam and spray. Gray and white gulls were everywhere calling and shrieking and diving on schools of baitfish. They scattered when Talon soared past.

Hyden urged Talon across the finger to the other side. The billowy sails of several gliding ships glowed amber, illuminated by the rays of the setting sun. All along the shadowy docks people swarmed like ants loading and unloading boxes, crates and net-loads of fish. Some of the ships looked like trees—their masts stood proud but empty like limbs that had shed their leaves for winter's coming. Farther up the docks the buildings started. There the lanes were full of carts and wagons. Swarms of people scrambled among others who were gathered in crowds to buy and sell fresh sea-fare. From above, it all it looked like chaos. Hyden couldn't wait to get there.

When he called Talon back to him and opened his eyes, he was pleased to find that the group was already a good way out along the peninsula. The bay off to his right sparkled as it reflected the light of the setting sun back at them. The gray tidal wall that ran the length of the other side of the peninsula was almost invisible beyond the buildings to his left. Torches were being lit and lanterns hung along the roads. As the sun left this part of the world behind, wells of wavering light transformed shadowy corners into welcoming points of commerce and congregation. It reminded Hyden of the crowded Ways at the Summer's Day Festival, especially the calls of the hawkers as they tried to draw attention to their particular wares.

More than a few people stopped to gawk at Oarly the dwarf as the group passed. Only a score of dwarves remained in the realm and all of them lived in or very near Queen Willa's Xwardian palace. To see one out on the docks was rare. Some of the older tavern songs said that thousands upon thousands of them lived somewhere far below the earth's surface, but when Queen Willa had blown the magical horn that was supposed to summon them to Xwarda's aid, none had come.

Oarly made silly faces at the younger spectators, which put smiles on the faces of everyone else. Before long, rumors that the hawk-man wizard who'd saved Xwarda from the dragon was in Old Port caused the crowds to grow. Luckily, Captain Trant, the captain of the *Royal Seawander* had anticipated as much and paid some men from the docks to block off the mass of people as Hyden's group gained the entrance to the yard of the Royal Seastone Inn.

"Wow!" said Phen as men came out of the shadows and took their horses away. "You're a regular hero, Hyden Hawk."

"Hardly," Hyden replied with a blush. He was starving and thirsty, but afraid to consume anything. He didn't know whether to be repulsed or enticed by the warm savory smells that wafted out of the inn's open doorway.

"Well met, sirs," a big barrel-chested man with a thick, but well-trimmed ginger beard said to them. He had a cob pipe clenched between his teeth and wore a spiffy gray and green captain's uniform.

"You must be Captain Trant," Hyden said with the slightest of nods. Mikahl had instructed him on rank and etiquette over the winter. Mikahl had explained that Hyden's role as a key defender of the realm in the battle against Pael gave him a status that was beyond rank, yet still of a knightly nature. He was more often than not addressed as Sir Hyden Hawk. Since he was not a kingdom born man and his rightful allegiance was not to any of the realm's human kingdoms, the slight nodding bow wouldn't offend anyone. Still, Hyden felt uneasy whenever someone of note was around. If it were up to him, Queen Willa would be just Willa and High King Mikahl would just be Mik, like he used to be, and all the titles could fly out the window. Yet here, the ship's captain was calling all of them 'sirs'.

"Hyden of the Skyler clan, I presume," Trant said as he reached out and shook Hyden's offered hand.

Hyden was shocked to speechlessness by the fact that the man knew how his clansmen would have addressed him. He was saved from the awkward moment when Oarly approached.

"Ah, Master Oarly," Trant reached down to shake the dwarf's hand.

Master Oarly? Hyden thought. *Master of what?* Already schemes of revenge began plotting themselves out in Hyden's mind. *It's going to be a sweet kind of revenge*, Hyden promised himself. His thoughts were interrupted when he saw Brady starting to go help the other military men of the escort with the unloading. "No, Master Culvert," Hyden stopped him. "Your sword can't protect the three of us if you're off with them."

"Master?" He rejoined Hyden. The boyish grin on his face showed that he was glad to be included. "I'm no master."

"You are now the Master of Defense for our exploratory party, Brady." Hyden informed him. "And any man who can go seven minutes against Mikahl's blade is a master swordsman in my book."

"Phenilous, my lad, you've grown some since I last saw you at the palace," Captain Trant was saying as he ruffled the hair on Phen's head.

"Aye," Phen replied. "You came up for the Harvest Ball last year. I didn't realize that it was going to be you steering the boat." Then to Hyden with excitement growing in his eyes he said, "The Captain has a blue monkey that dances on a leash. It can do flips even." Then back to Captain Trant with his eyes darting all around the Captain's feet, "Where is he? You still have him don't you?"

"*She's* alive and well and on the ship." He motioned them into the common room of the Royal Seastone Inn with a sweep of his arm. "We'll be sailing out with the tide on the morrow. Enjoy this night's feast, for it's all hard biscuits and salted meats for a long while after."

The torch-lit room was decorated with sail canvas, rope nets, tiller wheels, seashells, and all other sorts of sailing paraphernalia. There were also a few sets of toothy fish jaws mounted on the walls. One was a wide open maw that was big enough for Hyden and Phen to crawl through at the same time. The air was warmer along the coast, so no fire was burning in the hearth. In a corner of the half filled room was a small stage where a harpist prepared his notes and began tuning his instrument with sharp plunking twangs.

"It's a marsh thresher," Captain Trant told Phen who was still gaping up at the big set of fish jaws on the wall. "A small one at that."

Phen grinned at the others with mock terror in his wide open eyes. The serrated teeth in those jaws were as large as his hands. "How big do they get?" Phen asked the Captain.

"Big enough to bite the bottom out of a ship, I'd guess," the Captain winked at him.

"We're not going where them threshers live are we?" Oarly asked with genuine alarm in his voice. "It's bad enough I've got to leave the land. Sailing amongst monsters such as that is for birds and fools."

"Flying is for the birds, Oarly." Phen said. "We're sailing, and we're only going to skirt the southern tip of the marshlands on our way to Salazar Island."

"Just so," the Captain agreed with a surprised nod of respect.

"How long will it take us to reach Salazar?" Brady asked, doing his best not to let his eyes linger on the thresher jaws as he passed them.

"More than two weeks, less than three," the Captain said over his shoulder as he led them through the room. "It's getting to be true spring now, and might be a storm or two blows at us along the way." He stopped them when they reached a long empty table not far from the harpist's stage. "We'll lay over at Kahna to fill the water barrels in about a week. You might get some time ashore there if the weather looks questionable." The Captain looked sharply at Hyden, who was peering back at the entry door.

The door swung open and two finely clad men came in laughing. From behind them, Talon swooped through the opening and glided smoothly across the room to alight on Hyden's wrist. A woman gasped with fright, and a few men could be heard whispering above the sudden silence that followed. Talon sidestepped his way up Hyden's arm to the shoulder where he settled in and began preening himself.

They took seats at the table and a pretty lady dressed as a pirate, complete with an eye patch, and mummer's sword brought out a tall flagon of wine. Hyden stopped her at half full on his and Phen's goblets and ordered sweet milk for the two of them to come with their courses.

The singer started into a ballad just as hot bread and clam stew came to the tables. The man sang of a sailor who was out chasing treasure, and had left his beautiful lover back at port. There came a time when the sailor had to choose between the treasure and returning to his love. Of course he tried to have them both, and his lover ended up drowning in her own tears.

The wagon master and the commander of the Blacksword escort joined them, along with a senior member of Captain Trant's crew, who was introduced as Deck Master Biggs. They brought the news that the ship had been loaded. During all this, Oarly put away goblet after goblet of wine but showed no signs of even starting to be intoxicated. He did laugh rather robustly at some things that weren't that funny, but his speech never slurred and his wit stayed sharp.

They learned that they had suites in the inn for the night, courtesy of Queen Willa herself. Captain Trant told them this after a main course of nut crusted sea ray on a bed of rice that was smothered in mushroom sauce. Hyden was thankful to find this out, for his stomach was starting to roil. Phen was to share a room with him, but the boy wanted to stay and listen to the bard. Brady assured Hyden that Phen would be well supervised, so Hyden let Talon out to hunt, then went upstairs to their rooms to find the privy.

The singer was in the middle of a ditty about a fisherman who filled his boat full of fish and won the love of another captain's daughter when Hyden's horrid pain-filled scream cut through the whole place like a fog horn.

"That'd be that bite of cinder pepper coming out," Oarly bellowed into the hushed awe that filled the common room. The dwarf didn't care that he was the only one laughing. In fact, it made him laugh all the harder.

Chapter Eight

High King Mikahl, King Jarrek, and General Spyra rode three abreast across the wagon-bridge. Not far behind them came their squires. The Pixie River was running fat and swift through the wreckage that was once the town of Tarn. The river flowed out of the Evermore Forest southward and created the border between the kingdoms of Highwander and Seaward. The wagon bridge was wooden and strong, but not strong enough for two hundred Blacksword soldiers and three hundred archers to just come barreling across. There were a few footbridges as well. The three commanders, Mikahl, Jarrek and Spyra, found an old maple full of spring leaves and sat in the saddle under it conversing as the slow process of crossing the men into Seaward began.

"How far is it to Tip?" Mikahl asked the General. Tip was where they would cross out of Seaward into the kingdom of Valleya.

"A week at this pace."

Barely half a hundred people were left in Tarn. They stopped rebuilding and planting to watch the procession cross the river. A crier had come through earlier to make sure that the way was clear and that the good folk wouldn't be terrified. They'd been through enough already. King Broderick and Queen Rachel's combined army had first attacked Highwander here. The fight had been bloody, and ultimately had only served to add more corpses to Pael's undead army. Not much was left. Tarn had once been able to boast almost a thousand people, but no more. Those who hadn't died in the first attack were ridden over when the undead came. The ones who survived were either lucky, or fled the mayhem for the forest. The Highwander city of Plat looked about the same when the procession had passed through the day before yesterday.

"We're back-tracking the demon-wizard's path of destruction," said King Jarrek. "It looks like war tore through here, but something's missing and I just can't put a finger on it."

"The bodies are missing. No grave stones even," Mikahl said somberly. "Pael raised the dead and marched them to Xwarda to fight us."

"Seeing this is a powerful reminder of what the people have been put through," Jarrek mused aloud. "If King Broderick had a lick of sense he would have come to Xwarda so that you wouldn't show up at his door with all of this fresh on your mind."

"He's afraid that Queen Willa will lock him away in her dungeon, I think," said General Spyra.

"He is a coward. He fled his own castle at Dreen and left his people to face Pael," Jarrek reminded them. "He ordered the small folk inside the red wall and then fled south to Strond. I think that's where Brady said he went."

"Brady is your man, the one who braved the enemy lines to warn them?" asked the General.

"Yes. Targon magicked me and a few others out of Wildermont, but barely," Jarrek said. "I felt it only right to warn the people of Dreen of what was coming. I ordered Brady to ride to them. He stayed and fought with the Valleyans until the dawn broke and the dead started rising. He knew that I was headed to Xwarda with Targon so he rode ahead of Pael to warn everybody. He ran smack into King Broderick and Queen Rachel's army at Plat. He was captured, but then escaped. He showed up in Xwarda at the palace gates in the middle of Pael's attack, bewildered and half starved."

"The boy's got heart," Spyra said.

"Aye," agreed Mikahl. "Who managed to capture him?"

"Blacksword soldiers, I think," answered Jarrek. "They thought he was one of King Broderick or Queen Rachel's spies, I'm sure. I think that was why he was so confused. He was trying to warn them all that the dead were about to attack them, but no one would listen to him. His father was killed when Pael brought down the towers at Castlemont. He and I were fighting just a few hundred yards away." Jarrek paused a moment picturing it all in his head. "I don't think I want to talk about it anymore, if you'll excuse me." Before Mikahl or the General could respond he spurred his horse away.

"I don't envy that one," General Spyra said, after King Jarrek was gone. "There's a long, hard road ahead of him. And you've got your work cut out for you as well. What will you do after King Broderick licks your boots?"

"Queen Willa would have me ride down to Seaward City to swoon over Princess Rosa, but I'm not sure if I will. I have a mind to go to O'Dakahn and see what this King Ra'Gren is all about. Maybe if I meet with him we can spare some future bloodshed."

"Ra'Gren is about nothing but gold and power." General Spyra actually spat his distaste for the man into the dirt. "The whole kingdom of Dakahn is run by greedy, pitiless overlords, and their king is the worst slaver of them all. You'll have to either take Dakahn by force, or get really sneaky, unless you want to buy the freedom of the Wildermont people back. One thing about Dakahn is everything there has a price."

"I guess I haven't decided my course of action after we deal with King Broderick and Dreen." Mikahl tried his best not to sound disturbed by the

General's lack of optimism. "I know you have a new wife back in Xwarda. I won't keep you away from her any longer than I must."

General Spyra beamed at her mention. He was proud of his pretty young wife, Lady Mandary. She was half his age and pretty as a picture. Her true affection was far more than an old, balding man of his girth could have hoped for, but yet he had it. She said that he was her hero. He had fought bravely in the battle against Pael, and Queen Willa had rewarded him publicly, but being his plump little wife's hero was his favorite thing these days, that and trying to make a little baby general or two to carry on his name.

Thunder rumbled in the distant southern sky. A dark gray line of clouds had presented itself and appeared to be moving swiftly toward them. It was common enough this time of year for the sea to blow its wrath this far inland, but since they'd come all this way without bad weather they'd hoped to avoid it altogether.

"It'll catch us as soon as we get moving again," Spyra observed. He pointed to the empty dwellings around them. "We may as well spend the night here and let it pass over. If we don't, the men will just be wet and slower on the morrow."

"That's fine with me, General," Mikahl said. "I'm in no hurry to get my boots licked. You're the only one with a reason to hurry home." Mikahl laughed ironically. "By the gods, General, between you, Jarrek, and me, you're the only one with a home left."

Mikahl rode over to King Jarrek, leaving the General to call out the orders to make camp among the empty houses and shops in the little town. As he approached, Jarrek forced a smile, letting Mikahl know that his company was welcome. The two of them were silent for a while after they dismounted. It was after their assigned squires took their horses, and they were alone again, that Jarrek finally spoke.

"I'm thinking of riding on with my group," he said seriously. "We were going to split up when we get to Tip anyway. This…" he paused and indicated the Highwander soldiers who were starting to set up camp. "It's slowing us down. I have thousands of people under the whip, yet we're moving as slow as snails."

"I think that maybe you should then," Mikahl told him. "Your men are not needed here. Take them and ride like the wind. I've got five hundred of Queen Willa's soldiers and General Spyra to watch my back."

"Yes," King Jarrek grinned broadly at the High King. The smile wasn't forced this time. "We just might do that, but we'll at least ride this weather out with you before we go."

The rain came hard, and the long dreary night was filled with wicked lightning flashes and booming thunder. It reminded Mikahl of what his final battle with Pael had looked and sounded like. He tossed and turned, thinking about what he would do after he was finished in Dreen. He could ride south and help King Jarrek free the slaves, or he could ride west to the Leif Greyn River and see if he could spy out anything about his homeland, and the dragon-less Dragon Queen who'd taken it over. He didn't make a decision, and eventually he fell asleep, but not for long.

King Jarrek woke him. Outside his pavilion tent, Mikahl saw that the rain had stopped. It was still dark and cloudy, though, and Jarrek looked to be ready to ride.

"If you want something useful to do, Mik," Jarrek started in a whisper. It had been awhile since anybody had called Mikahl 'Mik,' but it didn't offend him. In fact, the use of the nickname gathered his full attention. Kind Balton and Lord Gregory had always called him Mik. Loudin of the Reyhall had as well. All those men he had loved and trusted. He felt he was safe in putting King Jarrek among them in his heart.

"When you're done with that craven king," Jarrek continued, "ditch the general, but keep thirty swords and thirty bows. Take them and backtrack Pael's path through the Wilder Mountains. You'll come out of them just north of Castlemont proper. Ride down on Dreg the slaver who Princess Rosa told us about and free those folks he's working in the mines. It'll give you a chance to get a look at Locar and the breed giant lord who is supposedly ruling there."

"Aye," Mikahl nodded, and clasped his friend's hand. "I may do just that. You be careful in O'Dakahn. That's a command."

"If I fail, Mik…" King Jarrek's voice trailed off, but his eyes met Mikahl's and the desperation in them was plain to see. The man cared deeply for his people. Mikahl nodded that he understood what hadn't been said, that if the unthinkable happened, he would find a way to finish what Jarrek was about to start. Then the Red Wolf, King of Wildermont, whirled and stalked off into the night.

General Spyra was full of questions the next day, but Mikahl just told him the facts. Yes, King Jarrek and his men rode south to O'Dakahn. No, he hadn't decided what he was going to do after Dreen. "Most likely, General," Mikahl said. "I'll send you and most of the escort back to Xwarda. I'll stay on a bit in Dreen, I think, and test King Broderick's loyalty, as well as his patience. If it comes to anything with Dakahn, I'll have what's left of the Valleyan host at my command."

His words hadn't really been intended as a jab, but they came off as one. It wasn't until five days later, when they rode into Tip under the midday sun, that the General bothered to speak to him on a personal level again.

"Since we've made exceptional time, Your Highness," the General's expression was pinched—he clearly did not want to be asking anything of Mikahl—"I ask that we let the men recuperate the rest of the day. The captains have asked me to see if they might hunt the tip of the forest so that we can all feast on fresh game this night instead of rations."

"A hunt?" Mikahl's grin was wide and genuine. "That's an excellent idea, sir. The best idea I've heard since I can remember."

Tip was located on both banks of the Southron River where it flowed out of the Evermore Forest. The forest reached southward along the banks and the town had been built at the forest's most southern finger-like point, thus earning itself the name Tip.

Like the Pixie River, the Southron River created a natural border. West of the Southron River was Valleya, and between the Southron and Pixie Rivers lay Seaward. The town sat on both sides of the bridge, but the Valleyans had swarmed in after Pael's horde had come through and taken most of the Seaward side over.

Since the Valleyans had taken over the town, it had started to be rebuilt before winter came. While Dreen, Valleya's capital city, had been destroyed by Pael's rampage, the rest of the kingdom of Valleya had been left untouched. There was no shortage of men and resources. New building had increased the place to a size bordering on city status. Nevertheless, the thick run of the Evermore Forest that clung to the river north of the city was still rumored to be a hunter's dreamland. Apparently the vast and sudden increase in populace hadn't scared away any of the game—at least that's what the locals were saying. They also warned that some dark beast had taken up residence in the woods and that a few men had gone missing because of it.

Mikahl borrowed a longbow and a quiver of arrows from one of the archers, then set out on the Valleyan side of the river with a group of Highwander archer captains. General Spyra stayed in town and kept everything moving along in an orderly fashion. The Seaward side of the forest was hunted by the remaining archery captains, one of whom boasted the official rank of Queen's Ranger. Needless to say the ranger's experience paid off. The group hunting the Seaward side of the river returned an hour before dusk with two does and a stag draped proudly across the backs of their horses.

Open cook fires dotted the night, and the smell of fresh cooked meat filled the air. The men were all in good spirits, save for General Spyra. The sun was going down and the High King was nowhere to be seen. The General was sworn to protect High King Mikahl, but couldn't do so if he didn't know where he was. One of the Valleyan horse ranchers, obviously a wealthy man by the size of his entourage, approached the General as full dark was setting in. The man had a concerned look on his face as he spoke.

"There's a devil boar loose out there, General," the man said, indicating the Valleyan side of the river where the High King and his group had gone off to hunt.

"It's as big as a wagon and evil. It's killed a half dozen men since the snows melted. It's been out there all winter. Them men of yours might have gotten into a pickle with it."

Spyra paled. He knew exactly what was out there in the forest. The demon-boar, and a few of the wyverns Pael had summoned into the battle of Xwarda, had escaped the might of Mikahl's sword. The wyverns had flown away, but the demon-boar had fled into the Evermore Forest near Xwarda. It had taken wounds from his men in the battle, and they'd assumed it found a place in the forest to die. The Queen's Rangers searched after the snows melted. It was no wonder they found no sign of the beast. It had come west.

The General took a few deep breaths, gathered his cool, and began yelling out orders in the darkness. It took a few minutes longer than it should have, due to the relaxed state of his men, but the General's Blacksword cavalry formed up as ordered, each with a torch blazing in hand.

"Where to, sir?" a sergeant at the front of the group asked. His horse was prancing and whinnying.

Just then, an explosion of sapphire light erupted from the middle of the forest to the north. It was followed by a sizzling crackling sound. The light shifted from blue to lavender then to a deep angry crimson. In the shocked silence that followed, the sound of faraway voices shouting, and a harrowing scream carried to Spyra and his men. Then the distant red illumination sputtered and failed, leaving the forest bathed in silent, silvery moonlight.

"To the High King!" the General yelled at the top of his lungs as he heedlessly spurred his horse toward the ruckus in the woods. There was no doubt what the source of the colorful light had been; all of the Blacksword soldiers had seen Mikahl's infamous sword Ironspike lighting up the night while he was fighting the demon-wizard Pael. The question was, why had the light suddenly sputtered and disappeared, and whose voice had that been screaming out in such horrible agony?

Chapter Nine

They were given the Royal Compartments on the *Seawander*. There were two sleeping rooms, each five paces long and three wide. They had side by side cushioned bunks shelving out from the walls. A net faced storage ledge ran high on the wall, and a small writing table filled the space at the foot of the beds. There was a brass oil lantern dangling from a short chain overhead, and as it swayed, the stark shadows it threw exaggerated the movements of the ship tenfold.

The two rooms were joined in the middle by a third, which was paneled with polished mahogany and had a round window that the crew kept clean enough to actually see through. The viewing portal, as it was called, was situated at the end of a booth table that could easily seat six men. There was a cushioned divan and an enclosed privy at the other end of the room. All three cabins were carpeted in plush sea-blue shag and trimmed with elegant brass works. As far as quarters on a ship went, this was the lap of luxury, but since none of the four companions had ever been to sea before, they thought it was cramped at best.

Oarly went straight to a bunk in the room he and Brady were to share and wasted no time getting rolled up in a woolen blanket. The dwarf asked that his meals be brought to him and that he not be disturbed. He then pulled the covers up over his head and lay stock still. All this he did to the amusement of the others a full hour before the ship was scheduled to depart the docks.

The other three only stayed below long enough to drop off their things. They were too excited to miss watching the land fade away as they took to the ocean. While they stood at the rail, Hyden had Brady and Phen go over the checklist of supplies for the tenth time. Rope, blankets, grappling hooks, lanterns, oil, arrows by the score. There were also shovels, axes, picks and other digging tools, not to mention the tents, field rations, foul weather gear and other necessities like soil cloth and healing herbs. They had thought of everything, or so they hoped. It was a good thing, too, because by the time they had finished discussing the supplies Captain Trant was bellowing, "All hands aboard!" The ship was departing Old Port for the open sea.

At dinner the night before the Captain had told them a little about the *Seawander*. At just over two hundred feet long she was no ordinary ship. Built to carry Queen Willa and other nobility, instead of a cargo, it was sleek and ballasted for optimal speed. She boasted three masts that reached high into the sky and the Captain promised that they could fly enough canvas to outrun any Dakaneese pirate ship they came across. What's more, the transom was lined with Wardstone, just like a river-tug, and the water-mage on board could make the ship go as fast as a double-decked rower, and that was against the wind. As proof of this, the ship lurched away from the dock without a single sail set and carved a sharp wake as it picked up speed and made its way through the harbor.

Men in fishing boats waved their hats and cheered the *Seawander* as she passed. A moment later, as she slid through the shadow of a monstrous ship, the crew of the galley called down to them in languages that neither Hyden nor Phen could name. Members of the *Seawander's* crew called back up to them in clipped but joyous shouts. The hulking cargo vessel towered over them in the water so much so that Hyden and Phen both had to crane their necks to take it all in.

Talon swooped and terrorized the flocks of noisy white gulls that were following along behind them. He rolled and spun and showed off his aerial prowess to the smaller sea birds as if he were their superior. The gulls seemed more impressed with the bits of food that were being stirred up in the ship's wake, but still kept a wary eye on him.

Deck Master Biggs called out orders, his voice booming through his thick seaman's beard. The first mate repeated them, and like monkeys, men took to the rigging and unfurled the yellowed canvas of a dozen or more sails. Soon the *Seawander* began picking up speed. As she left the protected area of the port she began rising and falling with the swells. Each time she came down a great splash of spray and foam shot out from under her and blew back across the deck. Phen gripped the rail tightly with one hand and thrust his other fist up into the air urging the ship on. Brady found the bowsprit figurehead, a mermaid of polished ironwood, and leaned out ahead of the ship with her, letting the wind blow his long brown hair back behind him.

"Look!" Phen exclaimed.

Hyden searched the sea where Phen was pointing but didn't see a thing. Then all of a sudden a delfin fish, as big as a man, sleek and green leapt out of the water alongside of them; another one shot out of the sea, then another. Soon a dozen of the smiling, snouted fish were arcing through the air racing and dancing with the ship as they went.

Talon swooped down amongst them, and through his *familiar* link Hyden could hear their joyous laughter and mirth. They were like a group of children playing in the summer sun.

Phen streaked across the deck toward the bow to tell Brady about the delfin. Deck Master Biggs caught him up about half way, flipped him around then half dangled him over the side rail. With a threatening, yet playful, look on his face, the Deck Master snarled, "There be no running on me deck, boy! No more warnings!"

When Deck Master Biggs pulled him back onto the ship and let him go, Phen's eyes were the size of chicken eggs, but his terrified grin was even wider than before.

The delfin followed them for some while, and before they knew it, land was no longer in sight. The Captain said something to the Deck Master who looked behind them through his long glass then pointed. Biggs said something to the first mate, who came over to where Brady, Hyden and Phen were now leaning on the rail enjoying the delfin show and Talon's antics.

"Keep a watchin' as you are," the man said with a discolored, gap-toothed grin.

Hyden let his eyes trail behind them to where the Deck Master was pointing his looking glass. For a moment he saw a surging swell on the water behind, then it was gone. It came again, only closer this time. There was a single sharp spiked fin as big as a man's leg breaking the water at the peak of the swell. Then it was gone again, back into the rolling sea. Then all of a sudden a fish the size of the *Seawander* herself leapt clear of the surface beside them. Its toothy mouth snapped shut on a pair of delfin as the terrified screeches of the rest of the pod caused Hyden to cringe and Talon to veer sharply away.

"Wow! It's a sabersnout, Hyden," Phen exclaimed loudly.

"Just so, lad!" Captain Trant boomed from somewhere. "Don't fall over the rail now."

Talon was so startled by the monstrous fish that he came swooping down out of the air onto the deck and landed badly among a roped down stack of water barrels.

The delfin were long gone when the sabersnout leapt through the air a second time. Its glossed black, dinner plate sized eye looked directly at Hyden Hawk. The satisfaction it felt after having just eaten a fresh meal was no less than the joy the delfin had been feeling when they were at play. If it could have, it would have eaten Hyden as it had the two unlucky delfin. *Thus is nature*, Hyden told himself as the big fish splashed gracefully into the rolling ocean and disappeared.

The Captain's table was in the galley, and that evening they were invited to eat with the officers of the ship. The fare was quite a bit better than the promised sea biscuits and salted meat. It was actually fresh venison and honey pork with hard bread and seaweed casserole. The table was treated to hilarious entertainment courtesy of Babel, the Captain's little blue-haired mango monkey. The monkey was the size of a newborn child and, as the first mate played a ditty on the flute, it whirled, tumbled, and spun across the table as gracefully as the ballerinas that sometimes danced in Queen Willa's auditorium.

They tried to get Oarly out of bed to attend the dinner, but not even the lure of wine or stout ale would get the dwarf to leave his cabin.

After dinner, back in the Royal Compartment, Brady listened while Phen and Hyden took turns reading out of the *Index of Sea Creatures*. They spent a little time reading about delfin and the sabersnout, but curious as they were, they read on. They read about the cloud fish that squirted inky poisonous fluids into the water to stun its prey. They read about the ever hungry marsh threshers and the rare flying sea turtles whose bright turquoise shells were worth a small fortune in gold. They read into the evening until eventually all three of them were plagued with yawns. Finally, long after the moon had presented itself, they all fell asleep to the smooth rocking motion of the ship as it carved its way westward through the ocean.

Phen found himself at the ship's rail before the sun was even up. He was heaving his supper to the fishes. Brady was right beside him. Oarly was sick as well, but had locked himself in the privy down in the Royal Compartments. Sick or not, the dwarf was determined to stay below deck the entire journey.

"It's not right," Phen whined. "I wasn't sick yesterday."

"Neither was I," Brady said glumly, just before lurching another load of bile out into the sea.

"I don't know where it's all coming from," rasped Brady when he was done. "I know I haven't eaten that much."

"Aye," Phen agreed then started to heave.

"Here," the first mate said, stepping out of the darkness. "Drink ye a few swigs of this, lads, and your guts'll settle."

Brady took the offered flask and was about to sip from it when the man cut in again sharply.

"Ah! Ah! Ah! Wipe you fargin mouth first," the man all but shouted. "Do ya think I wanna taste your innards?" Even in the darkness, the gaps in his teeth were visible.

"Sorry," Brady mumbled. He wiped his mouth with his sleeve then took a long pull from the flask. The burn of the liquor was harsh, especially in his throat. When it got down into his belly, though, the roiling there dispersed into a warm fuzzy pool. Phen took two quick swallows and nearly choked.

The next day, save for the crew, Hyden had the deck to himself. Oarly, Phen, and Brady were all below. Phen and Brady were sleeping soundly. Oarly was still locked in the privy, but snoring loudly between his less frequent rounds of dry heaving.

After conferring with Deck Master Biggs, Hyden scaled up the main mast's maze of rope ladders, yardarms, and rigging, up to the crow's nest at its top. From there he could see the horizon in all directions. There was no land in sight. It was a little unsettling, but not so much as when he looked down to see that the little ship below him wasn't actually below him at all. It was off to the right at the moment, riding up the face of a swell. Ever so slowly it passed under him and he felt the crow's nest swaying quickly out to the right of the ship as it eased down the other side of the wave. Not since he first started climbing the secret hawkling nesting cliffs to harvest their eggs with his clansmen had he felt such a tingling rush of vertigo.

No, that wasn't true. When he'd ridden on the dragon's back, he'd felt the same thrill, but that ride had been mostly at night. The feeling of desperation he felt during that flight had overshadowed everything. This was different. He decided he would have better odds calling the outcome of a coin flip than he would of landing on the deck if he fell. He knew he wouldn't fall, though. He had been climbing all his life.

For a long while he spread his arms out like they were wings and focused his sight out ahead of their course. Only puffy white clouds, blue sky, and the slow rolling turquoise sea were in his field of vision. He imagined first that he was once again on the back of the dragon, but then that wasn't enough. He imagined that he was the dragon, that he was gliding effortlessly over the sea, his big hind claws skimming the tops of the waves, and his wide leathery wings pushing volumes of cool salty air. In his mind he flicked his long sinuous tale this way and that to keep his balance true, then arced a swift banking turn one way, then the other.

Talon swooped in and landed at the basket's edge. The bird had to keep his wings out to maintain his balance there but he did it gracefully.

Hyden smiled at his *familiar* as the dragon vision slipped away from him. He touched the dragon tear medallion that always hung under his shirt. *If you ever have a need of me, just call me through the tear, and I will come,* Claret had said to him. She'd also said: *Remember who your true friends are. They come few and far between.* He wondered if her remaining egg had hatched yet. It galled him that Shaella had tricked his brother into stealing the other two. Gerard had paid the price for his thievery—or was still paying it. Hyden shook off the thought and tried to get his mind back on pleasant things, but it wasn't to be.

He didn't quite understand what Shaella meant that night, in the middle of nowhere, just before he threw her off the dragon's back. "You wouldn't know what's left of him," she said. "He's barely even human now."

Claret had confirmed that Shaella's words were true. The Westland wizard Pael had run a dagger through Gerard's heart, but Gerard hadn't died. The magic ring he'd found had kept him alive, but barely. Apparently he had crawled down into the darkness of the Nethers to escape Pael, or maybe to chase the power that the old crone had once foretold he would find down there.

Shaella said that he was barely human now, and Claret said that Gerard shouldn't have survived, but he had, because of the ring—the ring that Hyden was supposed to be wearing.

The goddess of Hyden's clan had told him that he must someday get the ring back from Gerard, that it was supposed to have been his. Until it was on Hyden's finger, the balance of things would remain badly off kilter.

Hyden hoped beyond hope that the Silver Skull of Zorellin might actually allow him to retrieve it, or at least allow him to go into the Nethers after it. He hoped that Gerard was still human enough to remember who he was.

Hopefully the bond they shared as brothers would be enough to allow Hyden to take back the ring peacefully and set the world aright.

Talon shrieked, bringing Hyden back into the reality of the moment. To the south, the sky was turning gray. Hyden took the looking tube from its holder in the basket and looked out at a dark place on the horizon. He decided that he could probably see better through Talon's keen vision. With his own eyes still open, he sought out Talon's sight. Now he could see a mass of churning black clouds as if they were right in front of him. Bright jagged lightning streaked up from the sea and fat drops of rain pelted the angry waves. The swells had grown huge and the wind was blowing in gusty spurts. It wasn't easy remaining calm as he climbed back down the mainmast to find Captain Trant.

"A bad storm you say?" Captain Trant scanned the sky to the south and sniffed the air. "Maybe so, maybe so. Biggs! Go get me the long glass!" the Captain ordered as he strode up onto the forecastle. A brass tube as long as a man's arm was brought up and the Captain peered through it to the south. He was silent for a long time, then he turned to look at Hyden curiously. "You saw that from the nest, did you?"

Hyden nodded. Talon flapped at his shoulder as the wind gusted and threatened to topple the bird. Captain Trant's eyes stopped on Talon for a moment.

"I'd suggest that you 'n' yer bird both get below afore long, and take this." The Captain deftly snatched the second mate's flask out of his shirt pocket as he moved by. "Your men will need it. That's not just a rain storm blowing at us, Sir Hyden Hawk, that's something a few tads nastier than hell!"

Chapter Ten

High King Mikahl saw the demon-boar just in the nick of time.

Earlier in the evening they had taken two nice does, and we're now trying for a third. Four of the archers had ridden north making a wide berth around the river. They were riding back toward Mikahl and the other three men. They were coming slowly, trying to flush a buck, or maybe even a wild sow, out into the open. Mikahl didn't find much sport in hunting this way, but when there was an army of men to feed, and the sun was setting, there was no better way to drum up a meal. The High King was positioned closest to the band of thick underbrush that ran along the river's bank. He was reminiscing about the last time he'd been on a true hunt.

His fond memory was interrupted by two dull red embers a good foot apart, glowing in the deepest shadows of the forest ahead of him. He squinted, blinked a few times. Then, just as he realized that the embers were actually eyes, the beast charged.

Mikahl loosed the arrow he had nocked, then flung the bow at the enormous beast and drew his sword. Whether from the sudden appearance of Ironspike's magical blue glow, or from fear of the huge charging demon-boar that it illuminated, Mikahl's horse reared and whinnied loudly. In Mikahl's head, the eldritch symphony of Ironspike's power blasted full force, into a glorious and triumphant harmony. Mikahl turned the horse with a yank on the reins and was ready to slash when one of the fool archer captains tried to be a hero and charged his horse right between Mikahl and the demon-boar. The boar's tusks were razor-sharp and at least the size of a young girl's forearm. The archery captain's poor mount didn't have a chance. The boar dug his head down and gored up through the animal. Then it reared back and sent horse and rider twisting into the trees.

Mikahl was awed by the size and strength of the creature. It was as tall as a man at the shoulder and was as big as a horse-drawn wagon, but low to the ground and covered in bristling hide.

The archery captain's sharp scream was abruptly cut off as his head slammed into a trunk. The disemboweled horse crashed down not too far from him with a thumping whoosh.

Ironspike's glow went from blue to lavender, then to cherry-red, as Mikahl's anger grew. When the boar came charging at him again, he sent three wicked pulsing blasts into the beast's neck and shoulder. He tried to spur his mount out of the way, but the terrified horse baulked. The last thing Mikahl sensed before his horse made a desperate twisting leap was the horrible stench of burnt hair from where his blasts had scorched the beast. Ironspike was knocked from his hand and he was smacked gracelessly out of the saddle by a low hanging limb. In the now completely darkened forest, he landed hard on his back.

For a few heartbeats he thought he might have been knocked out, but the deep grunting of the angry beast and the thrum of an arrow being loosed from nearby came to his ringing ears and told him that he was still in the realm of consciousness. As soon as he had his breath back, he scooted himself back against a tree trunk. He strained to see, but it was too dark. Men were shouting, and nearby he heard his horse crashing through the trees. *Blasted animal*, he thought, *Windfoot wouldn't have frozen up like that.* He found that he missed his horse quite badly.

Since he didn't know where his weapon, or the boar had gone, Mikahl figured that he was all right to wait where he was. Then someone fired up a torch. The red eyes of the demon-boar were coming in at him again, this time with a vengeance. He felt around him on the ground hoping to find Ironspike, but had to give it up. He barely had time to roll out of the way.

The demon-boar hit the tree Mikahl had been leaning against so hard that it shook the ground. It didn't advance after that, it just stood there. Mikahl could smell the acrid stench of the creature's wounds as it staggered in place right next to him. It was all he could do to hold in the contents of his bladder. Even in the torch-lit darkness the boar's size wasn't lost on him. He brushed against its side as he tried to get away. Its coarse bristles felt more like pine needles than hair.

Someone called for him but he couldn't find his voice to answer. He had a dagger in his boot, but he knew better than to waste the effort. A dagger probably wouldn't even get through the thick hide of something that big. The only course of action was to get away while the thing was still stunned. If he hadn't lost the sword, things would be different. As he stumbled blindly away with his hands up to guard his face from branches and thorny brambles, he couldn't help but feel naked. Without Ironspike he was vulnerable. He knew he wasn't defenseless without the sword. He was better than everyone on the practice yard. He had grown used to the feeling of invincibility that the magical blade gave him, though. He had grown used to its power. He decided that, if he lived through this, he would try to be more careful. He knew if he died, the power of Ironspike would die with him. Without Ironspike, who would unite the realm into a place of peace? Like it or not, he was the last of Pavreal's bloodline, and the sword would only recognize him as its wielder. For the first time, he actually understood why Queen Willa was trying so hard to get him wed.

"King Mikahl!" an exasperated voice shouted for the umpteenth time, as long wild shadows went flying about the area. Mikahl heard the call and responded.

"Here," he rasped back. The Captain found him quickly then.

"Where is it? Where is the beast?" the man asked in a frightful panic. As an afterthought he added a quick, "Your Majesty."

The demon-boar grunted beside them and made a low gurgling noise. The slow but solid sounds of trees being pushed aside, of fragile limbs suddenly being shaken loose, and the thump of heavy retreating footfalls followed.

"It's getting away," the Captain said. "Should I give chase?" His words sounded far braver than his voice.

"We'll track it together in the daylight," Mikahl replied.

The archery captain's sigh of relief was louder than he intended it to be. Mikahl thought that he could see the man flushing with shame, but didn't hold it against him; didn't hold it against him in the least.

A short while later, General Spyra's guardsmen came storming through the forest like a chaotic parade of giant fire bugs. Ironspike lay not three paces from where Mikahl sat, which saved him some embarrassment on the long ride back to Tip. Captain Finley died from the head injury he sustained when the boar threw him into the tree, and two other men had been wounded when they gave chase by torchlight. Mikahl learned all this by the campfire while munching on the hot greasy haunch of one of the does they'd killed. He raised a toast to the fallen man and then proceeded to down several cups of stout ale before promising the good people of Tip that the demon-boar would be rooted out before the host moved on to Dreen.

General Spyra didn't like the idea of staying any longer than necessary, but didn't voice his opinion. Instead, at first light, while Mikahl lay sleeping off the intoxication of the night before, the General organized a party to go kill the beast and get it over with. He sent two hundred men far to the north and had them form a tightly spaced line from the river all the way out to the tree line. They moved southward through the forest at a steady clip most of the morning before finally finding the creature. It was already near death from the wounds Mikahl had inflicted with Ironspike's magic.

Mikahl woke to the news, brought back from by rider just after midday. A wagon was sent to bring the carcass into town, and upon seeing Mikahl's hung-over condition, the General informed the men to take their time as they would be staying in Tip for one more night.

Later, after seeing the massive body of the dead boar, the townsfolk of Tip put on a feast for the General, his captains, and the hero of the day, High King Mikahl, who, according to the men, had more or less killed the beast single-handedly. As much as he wanted to, Mikahl didn't drink more than a goblet of ale that night. He didn't like the attention these people shoveled onto him for such a trivial deed as defending himself. It was a deed that he couldn't even credit to his own action. Everything he had done had been a reaction. Nevertheless, the people of Tip were happy and relieved, and that was enough to keep the smile on his face genuine until he found his way to his bedroll.

Five days later they passed through Kasta, a small city and fully fledged trading center that had only tasted a minimum of damage from Pael's army. "The undead just marched right through," the people told Mikahl and the General. "They killed a few, but didn't stop long enough to do much more."

Pael, it seemed, hadn't been around when his army of living corpses had passed. All of the people of Kasta knew who Pael was, though. Dreen was just up the road, and of the several thousand that had lived there, only a few hundred had escaped the death and destruction Pael had wrought. The story was that half the people of Kasta had moved to Dreen to claim the shops and farms of their dead families.

The entire two days it took for them to march the troops around Kasta, Mikahl was swamped with invitations to enjoy the hospitality of every noble, and some not so noble, house in the city. Both afternoons were spent wading down the avenues with a small detachment of Blacksword soldiers, through the sea of gathered crowds that just wanted to see and cheer the great young king who had defeated Pael.

In the evenings they went out of their way to avoid the persistent city folk, but it didn't matter. The crowd came to them. The last time Mikahl had seen this many Valleyans gathered in one place, they had been living corpses, wielding everything from farm implements to two-handed swords, trying to kill him and Queen Willa's soldiers. Now they were wielding the Valleyan banner, a dark shield on a red and yellow checked background, and they were cheering the very people they had been trying to kill. The Valleyans had been attacking Queen Willa and Highwander even before Pael had come along. It amazed him what a common enemy could do to get folks on the same side.

Besides being accepted by the Valleyan people, the only good thing to come of the attention Mikahl's arrival was generating was the young, proud, and fully trained destrier that was presented to him that second evening. Thunder was the beautiful animal's name, and Mikahl graciously accepted the horse. He had a squire get the information of the house that had given him the gift and hand wrote a letter of appreciation.

Thunder had the ill luck of being owned now by Mikahl. Thunder had heavy horseshoes to fill. Mikahl would take excellent care of the creature, but he would also compare the horse's every action and detail to Windfoot. Mikahl had already vowed to retrieve Windfoot from the Skyler Clan village when he had the time. Thunder would never find a more caring owner, but when Windfoot came home,

Thunder would probably spend a lot more time in the stable than he was used to. Windfoot and Mikahl had survived a lot together.

Mikahl was glad to get Kasta behind them. The road to Dreen seemed to be as crowded as the city had been. Many a cart and wagon was passed on the way to the Red City. Swine herds, goat herds, people making the journey on foot as well. Nearly all of them stopped to cheer Mikahl as he and the Blacksword detail rode past. When they finally reached Dreen, an escort of Valleyan cavalry led them from the outskirts of the fringe settlements into the big red clay brick wall that surrounded the capital city itself. Beyond the city, to the north and west, the Wilder Mountains rose up out of the arid plain.

When they approached the wall Mikahl was awestruck, not by its height, but by the amount of space it enclosed. It was said that, on foot, a man might take most of a week to walk the top of the wall all the way around the city. Mikahl didn't doubt it. The main gates and the sections of wall to either side of them had been newly rebuilt. The fresh clay brick was a lighter shade of pink than the weathered brick around the gates. And the thick wood planks that had been bolted to the old rusty iron bands of the gate itself were still fresh and white. All that could be seen rising above the thirty foot wall were two crenellated towers that were set deep into the city.

When they passed through the gates, Mikahl saw that the wall was half as wide as it was tall. Clanking iron portcullises were being raised on the inside. Once clear of them he found that the Red City was not misnamed. Nearly all of the well-spaced buildings were made of the same clay brick as the outer wall. No building was higher than two stories save for the twin towers, which reached up out of what could only be King Broderick's modest castle. The streets here were not crowded, and every other building appeared to be empty and abandoned. Most every structure boasted a fenced corral; some held prized Valleyan horse stock, others held sheep or goats. There were a few head of cattle here and there and more than one weary looking bull, but mostly there were horses ranging in the pens. The clay streets were wide and pocked with the hoof prints and cart tracks of the millions of animals that had been driven through over the years. The bulk of High King Mikahl's host made an encampment near the east gates where they entered the city. King Broderick's cavalry attachment led the others—King Mikahl, General Spyra, two archery units, and Spyra's fifty man guard attachment—through the city toward the castle. They had to stop for the night before reaching it, and it was well into the afternoon the next day when they finally came to the unimpressive head-high wall that surrounded Broderick's abode.

A pair of full-size stallions rearing to fight decorated the ornate double gate. They were a study in detail and craftsmanship. The dark stone they were carved from was veined with blood red and pinkish white. The color went well with all the red clay around them. Mikahl found that he wanted to get out of Thunder's saddle and examine them closer, but decided against it. General Spyra eased close to him, and as they waited for the gate guards to announce them to the castle, he spoke.

"Notice that the people who live inside the red wall are a little quieter about your arrival?" The General grinned. The sun reflected off of his bald head into Mikahl's eyes. Mikahl had to squint when he looked back at him.

"Aye. Days of being cheered, then all of a sudden only stares and nods inside the wall. Why?"

"Outside the walls," the General leaned in close so that he could whisper, "the craven king's power is thin. They would put you in his seat in a moment, I assure you. But here, inside the walls, Broderick has thousands of ears and a much stronger base of support. He'll lick your boots, but he'll do it in private."

If the capital of Valleya was unimpressive compared to Xwarda or Castlemont (before Pael had destroyed them), then King Broderick was a total letdown. The large, fleshy man was robed in wrinkled layers of golden cloth trimmed in red. His black hair and beard were thick, curly, and unkempt, and the people who were gathered around him at the top of the castle's entry stair looked about as happy to be there as they would at their own execution.

Mikahl had an urge and followed it. Before the craven king could say a word, he spurred Thunder forward and quickly closed the space between him and the foot of King Broderick's entry stair. The Valleyan King's Guard was surprised by the move, but more than one of them stepped up, with hand on hilt, ready, if a little reluctantly, to defend their big sloppy king. Mikahl drew Ironspike and the purplish glow of its blade was clearly visible in the midday sun. The people around Broderick, guardsmen included, instantly shrunk back from him. It was as if they all half-expected Mikahl to take off the man's head in that instant. King Broderick himself seemed only slightly impressed by Mikahl's display. Still, he was more than a little nervous as he glanced over at his court announcer and gave a sharp nod. "Thump! Thump! Thump!" sounded the butt of a staff on the sun-baked clay surface. "All hail High King Mikahl Collum, the Blessed Uniter."

Reluctantly, King Broderick went to a knee. Every person in sight of the scene followed suit, save for one, a slim man who was dressed quite regally and standing in the castle's entry way behind King Broderick's retinue. Mikahl's eyes met his and the man gave a nod of respect, no more, no less. Mikahl smiled and returned the gesture.

At least there's one here not ready to lick my boots, Mikahl thought, and found that he had more respect for the one in the doorway than anyone else he'd met here so far.

"Rise," Mikahl commanded with forced authority in his voice. He had to bite back a laugh when he heard General Spyra mumble under his breath, "He might be too fat to get up."

General Spyra was correct, for two men quickly stepped up on each side of the Valleyan king and helped him to his feet. All around them, the Valleyan people started to cheer. The look on Broderick's bright red face showed that this wasn't the introduction he had envisioned, and that he was none too pleased about the situation. The smiles on the faces around the King of Valleya showed Mikahl that it was an introduction they had enjoyed, though. King Broderick had been put in his place swiftly, and publicly, right from the start, and those who'd seen it, especially the curious man in the doorway, had enjoyed it immensely. Mikahl wasn't really amused, though. In fact, he found that he was disgusted by the way Broderick carried himself.

Chapter Eleven

The boat Dreg loaned Lord Gregory was as small as a watercraft could be and still be considered a boat. It was nothing more than a child's skiff, with two oar locks, a rudder for steering, and two bench seats. With Lord Gregory and the man Dreg sent to escort him both sitting in it, the boat sat so low in the water that the slightest ripple threatened to wash over the sides.

The deal was fairly simple: Dreg would keep the chunk of gold, the horse, and Lord Gregory's sword until he returned with or without his wife. If he did indeed return, they would travel to the cavern Lord Gregory said he had wintered in, where he had supposedly found the nonexistent deposit of gold. From there it would be an equal split. Lord Gregory had no choice in the matter that he could see. He hated to give up his sword, but it was only an object. His wife's well-being was far more important to him than the blade.

Dreg was a snake, a slaver, and an opportunistic thug. There was a time when Lord Gregory would have imposed justice in King Balton's name, and taken the man's hands off, or worse. As it was, Dreg had the boats, and the men. Lord Gregory was nothing but a broken down cripple who was patiently bailing water from the boat as Dreg's man, Grommen, cursed and pulled on the oars.

The flow of the river channel was carrying them in the right direction, but the boat kept drifting into the deep swamp grass along the edge of the marshes. It was a repetitive pattern: row over close to the western bank and then drift down river and back across the channel toward the swamp grass for most of an hour, row back, and start all over. By working the rudder to maximum effect, the crosscurrent drift could be delayed, but not avoided. They had taken turns rowing at first, but Grommen saw the pain in Lord Gregory's face when he tried to work the oars. He'd taken over then. Not so much because he was chivalrous or kind, mind you, but because of the bugs. The western bank and the main flow of the channel were relatively free of them, but along the marsh grass of the eastern edge there were swarms upon swarms of flying, stinging, itching things that Grommen couldn't stand.

Lord Gregory had a mind to get them deep in the grass, thinking that while Grommen was fighting the bugs, he might be able to get him over the side of the boat, or possibly even get his dagger into the man's neck. If he thought he had the strength in him to manage the boat by himself, he might have done it. He didn't, so he patiently bailed the water that seeped and slopped into the craft and watched with a sinking heart as they went floating by the upriver outposts of Settsted Stronghold one by one.

The single towered, squat gray stone buildings were manned now by glittery green-scaled, bug-eyed, lizard-men wearing mismatched pieces of armor. Lord Ellrich's proud river guardsmen used to have that duty. What bothered Lord Gregory the most was the banner flying in place of Westland's prancing lion. The bright yellow trio of crossed lightning bolts on the black field was irksome. The zard-man sentries, and their huge geka lizard mounts, weren't even necessary at the outposts. There was no threat of attack from the swamp now.

The zard were natural creatures of the marshes and they came and went across the river freely into the endless expanse of muck that stretched from Westland's border, south and east, all the way to Dakahn.

It was surprising that the boat went along unmolested. Not once were they hailed or stopped as they drifted down the channel. They passed a few fishing boats and were waved at by the human boys and zard working together in the nets, but not much else. His worries were blanked out of his mind when he got his first glimpse of Settsted itself. The ancient stronghold had fortified all of the men who manned the outposts along the marshland border. It had stood longer than Westland's history had been recorded. Now it was nothing more than a crumbling ruin. The great green moss covered stones of its outer protective walls and main structure were scorched black and caved in.

The village that stood between the stronghold and the river was alive with humans and zard-men alike. Many of the old dwellings still lay in piles, but plenty of new ones had sprouted up. And the dock, an over long wooden intrusion out into the river channel, was as crowded and alive as Lord Gregory had ever seen it.

It was an eerie feeling, seeing the familiar place under such unfamiliar conditions. The blasted golden lightning-bolt banner rippled and furled from the stronghold's remaining tower, from the masts of the larger vessels tied to the docks, too. The strange lizard-men, with their fist-sized black eyes and their long tapering tails, moved and worked amongst the young boys and older human men as if they'd been doing so forever. To Lord Gregory, it was as fascinating as it was sickening.

He had no doubt now that Lord Ellrich had fallen. Either here, or in the battle for Wildermont, he couldn't say, but he knew that his oversized friend would have rather died than allow the land they both loved to be taken over by skeeks.

As Settsted faded behind them, Lord Gregory hit on the hardest question about the situation. How could you take Westland back? The people seemed content with the conditions. If this so-called Dragon Queen was fair and just, who would help Mikahl reclaim his birthright? Who would want to? Obviously the land was doing better than it would have with Glendar running it. Lord Gregory wasn't too quick to judge the situation, though. Things might be going smoothly along the marshes where there was more work to do in a day than a man could get done, but what of Lakeside Castle, or the city outside its gates? What of the men who were being whipped to pull that breed giant up and down the streets of Locar? No, those with the strength to rise up against these things that had taken over would most likely do so, if they had leadership. The problem was, there was no one left here but old men and young boys. It made Lord Gregory's blood boil. There was no honor in marching over the helpless, and he found himself spitting the taste of it over the side of the little boat into the river.

"Strange to look upon, eh?" Grommen said. He was manning the tiller now, trying to slow the boat's way over toward the swarming swamp grass.

"Very," Lord Gregory replied. He turned his gaze on the man in the boat and studied him.

Grommen was a barrel of a man, stout and hard, but not quite as tall as Lord Gregory. His studded and ringed leather armor vest was well worn and boasted several battle scars on its finish. Grommen had a square face with a prominent jaw covered by ginger whiskers. The hair on his head was a few shades lighter. He was a handful of years younger than Lord Gregory, and his dark eyes were stern, but not too serious. The man's accent was a mixture of Valleyan and Dakaneese. All in all, he was built like a rounded block of stone. It was clear that the sword at his hip was no stranger to him. He was there to make sure Lord Gregory returned to show Dreg the location of the nonexistent cavern full of gold, yet Lord Gregory sensed an air of defiance about the man. He hadn't made even the slightest of threatening moves toward him since they had left Dreg back in Low Crossing. In fact, Grommen had barely said a word until now.

"We'll make camp after we pass the next outpost," Grommen said. "I know a place where we shan't be hassled."

"Whatever you say," Lord Gregory agreed sarcasticly.

"Look man," Grommen started with narrowed brows. "I know, and you know, that you'll not be coming back to show that donkey where the gold is, if there even is any. This..." He pounded at his chest, at the insignia of the mercenary company he worked for embroidered upon it. "This is our only pass key. I might kill for coin, but I'm no slaver like Captain Dreg. Give me an unruly lordling to fight in a field of battle, or a troubled patch of road where I can kill bandits, or be one, but I'm no slaver. I don't deal in human flesh." He cursed then, and let go of the tiller. He swatted at that gnats beginning to swarm around his head then took the oars up again and started desperately rowing them away from the marsh grass.

The sun was getting low in the sky. Lord Gregory imagined Grommen was tired. He had rowed them back across the river's hardy current at least a dozen times. Lord Gregory wasn't sure what Grommen's little speech was leading to, so he chose his words carefully, but before he could open his mouth, Grommen looked up and began speaking between his heavy pulls on the oars.

"I seen ya… Ungh! Seen you take the Valleyan fighter down… Ungh! I lost a fat purse that night a few years ago, Lord Lion. I know who you really are." He stopped rowing and met Lord Gregory's eyes. "You did right back there. He would have killed you had you not told them lies. From now on, I'm your paid escort. You're a merchant, come to Westland from Dakahn and you're going to pay me good, Lord Gregory. My treachery is most expensive."

Lord Gregory could find nothing to say to that, but he found a huge smile on his face. Of course, sooner or later, someone had to recognize him. How could he have thought differently? He was a renowned champion of Summer's Day. His name was etched into the Spire itself. His only regret at the moment was the fact that Dreg had his sword.

At the fire that night Lord Gregory learned of Mikahl's triumph over Pael. A load was lifted off of his heavy heart. From what Grommen was telling him, Mikahl had Willa the Witch Queen's armies behind him now and was working on rebuilding and uniting the eastern kingdoms. It seemed amazing to him— Ironspike's power being wielded by young Mikahl was an incredible thought. Mikahl, when he had been Lord Gregory's squire, had been the talk of the training yard. By the time he started squiring for King Balton he was recognized as the best young swordsman in Westland. King Balton had kept Mikahl out of battle, though, even at Coldfrost. Lord Gregory had never understood why until King Balton died. King Balton hadn't wanted Mikahl to draw any sort of attention to himself.

With the good and welcome news of Pael's defeat and King Glendar's demise came some bad news, though. Most anybody of note in Westland, be they lord, lady, or wealthy merchant, had been sold cheaply to King Ra'Gren of Dakahn, who was now ransoming them to anybody who would pay. More than one Westland lady was now a pet, or a slave to a Dakaneese overlord who could afford such an exquisite trophy.

The idea of his Trella being forced to service some greasy old Dakaneese bastard sickened Lord Gregory. He had sent young Wyndall off to warn her when the fighting first started at Summer's Day. He hoped and prayed that she understood the warning, and somehow made it out of Westland before the zard attack. He had friends, many of them older men who would not have been drafted into Glendar's military campaign. Hopefully some of them had survived and would know of Trella's fate. And what had become of young Lady Zasha? Lord Ellrich's daughter was a budding girl, the apple of her father's eye. Lord Gregory owed it to his friend to try and find her as well. If he had to, he would buy them from the Dakaneese slavers. There was no price too high. He would find the coin one way or another.

Just before midday the next day, they came upon the last of the Settsted watchtowers. Here the river split yet again around the heavily wooded island of Salaphel. Salaphel had a small port on the far side where they shipped out barges full of timbers to the rest of the realm. Grommen took the westward flowing branch that would carry them out to where the river met the sea at Southport. The going became slower, the force of the spring melt on the river's current lessened where the river was wider. Here the water was a brackish affair, and the tidal pull of the moon worked at times for the current, and sometimes against it. Lord Gregory rowed as often, and for as long as he could, but it wasn't much compared to Grommen's determined effort. The mercenary had taken a more vigorous interest in his own defection from Dreg's company when Lord Gregory had shown him the fat sack of golden Westland coins he still had in his pack. There were forty of them, a small fortune in times like these. Grommen happily took ten of them as a down payment for his services, which was twice what he'd make in half a year working for Dreg.

"I knew I was making the right choice," he said with a grin. "But know this, Lord Lion. I expect more—a lot more. After Dreg figures this out, after he knows what I'm about here, he'll put a healthy price on my head, and I'd hate not to be able to afford to return the favor."

"If you help me find the Lady Trella and Lady Zasha," Lord Gregory replied, "I'll make you a lord and personally mount Dreg's head on the gate of your keep for you."

"I'll help you do it," Grommen grinned, "but even if we don't find them ladies, you still owe me."

"Aye," Lord Gregory nodded that he understood.

It was with this stronger bond of gold-sealed promises that the two of them worked their way westward.

Grommen rode them up to a dock at the outskirts of the town of Oraphel. It was just after noon and the dock was only mildly busy.

"Why are we stopping?" asked Lord Gregory.

"You need yourself a hooded cloak for one. If I can spot who you really are, so can your countrymen. The ones that are still alive that is," Grommen said. "Besides that, you're supposed to be a wealthy Dakaneese merchant looking for wares. We can't row up to Southport in a bucket looking like starving dogs."

Lord Gregory laughed at his good fortune. He would pay this big intelligent oaf one way or the other. The man was no fool, and he was risking his life and reputation to help him.

As instructed, Lord Gregory waited in the boat while Grommen walked into Oraphel. No one bothered him. He kept his head down. Out of the corner of his eye, he watched one of the zard-men cleaning the bottom and sides of a fishing boat that was still in the water. The zard would scrub one side of the boat from the deck down then keep going under it, staying submerged for impossibly long lengths of time. The zard-man would appear again on the other side in a rush of bubbles and work his way up to the deck. Then he would move over a few feet and work his way back down, scrubbing briskly with his brush as he went under again. Another zard dove in to help him, and Lord Gregory saw how fast the lizard-men could swim. It was like watching a snake slithering across the river's surface.

"Does he get to keep the thin man?" A voice from the dock above startled Lord Gregory. He looked up to see Grommen and the man who'd spoken, along with a commanding looking zard-man whose big black eyes reflected the world around him in such a distorted way that Lord Gregory had to look away from them.

"The thin man is my master," Grommen said with a grin that only Lord Gregory could see. The other man said something in a gurgling clicking language to the lizard-man. The zard responded and the men translated for them.

"He says the little bucket is worth a silver piece at best. He'll give you seven coppers for it."

"Tell him eight and the deal is done."

The translator did his job, and after brief pause, an exchange took place. Grommen threw a wadded black cloak down to the boat. After Lord Gregory had it fastened about his neck he raised its hood and extended a hand. Grommen helped him onto the dock then bowed, as his role dictated. The zard-man took the rope that held the boat and, without a look back, strode to the edge of the pier and dove into the river. The boat was pulled away from the dock by its rope and went trailing after the lizard-man's wake.

"Fargin crooked skeeks," the translator said to Grommen and Lord Gregory with disgust. He paled, though, when the zard who was cleaning the nearby boat hissed.

Grommen ignored the exchange. "We have a wagon carriage waiting for us, Overlord. If we hurry, we can be in a Southport inn by dark fall."

Chapter Twelve

The power of the ocean storm was relentless and violent. The *Seawander* rolled and swayed, and it seemed as if it had been dark for days. Thunder crackled and boomed, and lightning streaked through the sky in wicked, jagged flashes. Several times it felt like the bottom had fallen out of the world, like the entire ship was tumbling through a great void. Then the *Seawander* would smack into the ocean, sometimes with bone-jarring force, sometimes at some off-kilter angle. The timbers creaked in protest and the constant hum of the wind blasting through the tight rigging made a ghostly whistling chorus that could be heard over the pelting of the heavy rain.

When Phen finally woke from his alcohol-induced slumber he felt much better. He and Hyden were thrilled, in a morbidly terrified sort of way, by the power of the storm. The storm had been raging for days. It had been dark so long that Hyden couldn't say how many. Phen, feeling seasick no longer, found a volume of text that was written on the subjects of whirlpools and tempests, among other forces of nature. He was reading excerpts of particularly scary content to Hyden in the common room. They were both sitting at the booth with Talon perched nearby watching water wash over the porthole and the occasional flicker of yellow lightning outside.

Phen had to re-read his text every now and then due to the crazy gyrations of the lantern swinging overhead. Hyden, at that moment, was more worried about the lantern dashing itself against one of the roof beams and showering them with flaming oil than he was about the storm, or Phen's horrors. Nevertheless, he felt a chill as Phen read about an old ship passing by a giant whirlpool and nearly getting caught in its deadly grasp.

" '... the Captain emptied a bottle of sweet brandy in one long gulp then corked the vessel and tossed it overboard,' " Phen read on. " 'I thought he was giving up, downing a bottle, a final toast to a good run at sea, but I was mistaken. The Captain watched the bottle's course as it spun away from the ship in a huge radial arc. He carefully gauged its speed as it floated around and down into the bottomless siphon.' "

"What is 'radial'?" Hyden interrupted. His eyes were glued to the jerking sway of the lantern as if hypnotized by its motion.

"It's a variation of radius," Phen answered impatiently, forcing Hyden's attention from the light. "The bottle's path moved in an arc around the center of the whirlpool away from the ship." He showed Hyden on the tabletop with his fingers.

Outside, a quick strobe of lightning flashed through the water rolling down the window beside them. Before its light had even faded, low rumbling thunder growled its way into a sharp series of cracks, almost like breaking wood. Phen gave Hyden his 'creeped out' look of mock terror, causing Hyden to laugh, in spite of his overwhelming sense of unease.

" ' The Captain,' " Phen continued, " 'watched the bottle's course as it spun away from the ship in a huge radial arc. He carefully gauged its speed as it floated around and down into the bottomless siphon. He was calculating in his head. Then, all of a sudden Captain Spratt had it. He began barking out orders to his crew. A sail dropped into place and snapped full of wind. The oar drum began a quick and steady rhythm, yet we were still drawing closer and closer to the swirling hole in the sea. More orders were screamed, more sails unfurled, and the tattoo of the drum boomed faster and faster, keeping time with the thundering of our hearts. It seemed as if we were doomed...' "

The door at the top of the stairway that let down into their cabin flung open for a moment and someone stepped in. The wind slammed the door shut with a sharp bang.

"By the gods, Phen," Brady said weakly as he sloshed in from above. "Can you not read something less frightening?" He was soaking wet and dripping on the plush carpet, but no one seemed to care. The whole room stank of dwarf anyway. Oarly still hadn't left the privy. If you had to go, you had to get wet.

"Where's that flask?" asked Brady. He still looked a little green around the gills, so Hyden reached down and pulled the tin from his boot and gave it to his friend. Brady drank from it deeply.

"Oarly likes it when I read to him." Phen nodded at the privy door with a grin. Brady sighed and slid into the booth next to him.

"Let me finish. I'm almost done with this passage," Phen said. "Where was I? Oh yes... 'It seemed as if we were doomed. For long hours the rowers pulled and pulled for their lives. It was as if we had come to a standstill. The water rushed by and the rowers rowed against it, and we didn't move any further away from the siphon, but at least we didn't get any closer to it. Captain Spratt called on the gods of wind and sea, and when they didn't respond, he cursed them and urged his men on. Then, finally, we broke the grasp of the vortex. A finger's breath, and then two. Then we moved a foot. Ever so slowly we crept away from that hole in the sea. That night the Captain tapped a cask of rum and we all drank ourselves into a merry stupor. Then we thanked the gods, and more properly the brave Captain, for our lives.' "

Phen slapped the old book shut with a boom that made Hyden and Brady both Jump. Even Talon squawked and flapped his wings at the sudden sound. "See," Phen said, amused that he'd startled them. "It ended well."

"Ah, but the very next day a giant thresher shark ate the bottom out of the ship and they fed the fishes at the bottom of the sea, like they say happened to King Glendar," Brady said.

"Could you tell if it was day when you were out?" Hyden asked Brady.

"I think daylight has come and gone," Brady replied. "It's as dark as dark gets out there."

"Aye," Hyden nodded.

The door to the privy creaked open and a waist-high jumble of wild matted hair, with a bulbous nose in its middle, peeked out. "Did I hear somebody say something about a flask?" the haggard dwarf ventured weakly.

Brady took another small sip and, after Phen and Hyden both refused it, he stood and stumbled over to the dwarf. Oarly took the flask and emptied it in one gulp. The ship swayed and rolled, sending him stumbling back into the privy. The door slapped shut and Brady stood there long moments before he realized that Oarly wasn't coming back out.

Just as Brady resumed his seat beside Phen, the door atop the stairs opened again. A moment later, a gust of rainy wind and Captain Trant came blasting in. The Captain's wet and bedraggled monkey, Babel, was sitting on his shoulder looking miserable. As the Captain gained the carpeted floor, a curious look came over him, and after wrinkling his nose a time or two, he turned to look at the privy with distaste.

"Still won't come out of there, eh?" He chuckled and shook his head in wonder. Water trailed from his matted beard. He wiped his hand across his face and plopped down onto the divan with a slosh.

"Cookie was bringing you a meal, but he lost it on that last lurch. He's gone to fetch another for you," said the Captain with a wry grin. "Quite a storm, huh?"

"Yes it…" Brady started to reply but Phen cut him off.

"Have you ever sailed around a whirlpool?" the boy asked Captain Trant.

"Nay, lad, and I hope to never have to. But I can say, and so can you, that we've sailed through a true tempest. I don't know what else to call a storm such as the one we've just bested."

Phen grinned. He couldn't wait to tell the other apprentices back in Xwarda that he had sailed through a tempest.

Thunder rumbled outside, and lightning flickered in the window again. "So we're through the worst of it then?" asked Brady.

"Just so," Captain Trant answered with a strange look at Hyden, who was staring at the lantern swinging above the booth again. "It's near to impossible to break one like that."

Hyden glanced at the Captain and flushed with embarrassment. "When will we see the sun again?"

"Not so long from now. This time on the morrow we might be able to see the Isles of Kahna."

"Are we going to get to go ashore there?" Phen asked excitedly.

"That's precisely what I came to discuss." Captain Trant leaned forward and put his elbows on his knees. His burliness made him look like a wet bear. Babel the monkey shivered away the excess water from her blue fur, crawled on the back of the divan and made herself comfortable.

"We've taken some damage..." The Captain saw Brady's look of alarm and quelled it quickly. "It's nothing to lose sleep over, mind you. We'll make the islands just fine, but we'll be ashore there for a few days while we're getting the *Seawander* right again. She's a strong ship. She got us through the storm. We just need to make her ready for the next one."

"How long do you think, Captain?" Hyden asked.

"Two days at best, but more likely four. Five if we have to cut and fit our own timbers."

Hyden nodded his understanding and Brady seemed relieved. He glanced at the privy then back at the Captain and a devious look came over him. "If we can get Master Oarly out of there while we're on the island, can you have someone affix a lock at the top of the door?"

"Yeah," Phen chimed in with a giggle. "Make sure it's high enough that he can't reach it."

The Captain roared out a laugh. "I think we may be able to do that. I'm certainly going to have to replace this shag when this adventure's through, and that smell..."

"What is there to do on Kahna Island while we're stuck there?" Phen asked the Captain.

"There's great line fishing along the landward docks, and there's those old tombs to explore." Captain Trant looked more to Brady than the others and winked. "There's also fire dancers after the sacred moon feasts. We might be in store for one. They have them often enough. They say the native girls go into a trance as they gyrate." The Captain grinned. "I seen 'em once. They were far too naked for me to notice if they were really in a trance or not. I can assure you that they know what parts to gyrate, and just how to gyrate 'em."

Hyden seemed just as interested in seeing that spectacle as Brady was. Phen wrinkled his nose. His mind was still on the tombs.

"What's in the tombs?" he asked, determined not to let the subject wander again.

The Captain sighed with an understanding smile on his bearded face. "The islands are full of primitive folk. They have juju wizards and the like. There's a cavern full of shrunken heads, and some spectacular underground lakes and tidal pools." Seeing Phen's growing interest, the Captain leaned closer and spoke in a creepy conspiratorial voice. "Legend says that there's a giant emerald hidden down there in the depths of one of those sea tunnels, but no one can find it because it's hidden by spells and guarded over by ancient juju creatures."

Hyden felt a sudden chill climb up his spine. Tempting things hidden in the depths of the earth was exactly what had drawn his younger brother to his demise. The look of excitement and determination on Phen's face was exactly as Gerard's had been after the crazy old soothsayer told them their fortunes. The resemblance literally scared Hyden to the bone. He had to forcefully draw breath and remind himself that Phen was not Gerard, and that these tunnels and tombs that the Captain was speaking of probably didn't lead down into the darkness of the Nethers. He decided that, if Phen wanted to go into them, then he would go too and make sure no harm came to him. They wouldn't waste time looking for lost jewels, though. One treasure to find was enough.

"I wonder who or what is guarding Barnacle Bones's treasure?" Phen asked out of the blue. "Actually, I guess it was Cobalt's treasure last. What sort of magics would an ancient dragon put up to guard its hoard?"

The room fell silent. Hyden hadn't put much thought into that part of the quest. Brady and Captain Trant were both looking at him for an answer. All he could do was swallow hard. A peal of deep thunder filled the silence. The sudden crack of the door at the top of the stairs being whipped fully open by the wind startled them all. The sound of the rain and the ghoulish chorus of the wind whistling in the rigging came to them. Talon awkwardly leapt from his perch and glided through the air to land on the table between Hyden and Phen. The bird wasn't at ease being inside the cramped cabin for so long. Knowing this, Phen ran his hand lovingly over the hawkling's feathers and cooed softly.

The room filled with the savory smell of fish stew and hot bread as the cook and his helper eased carefully down the steps. Apparently their arms were full, for the door stayed wide open as they descended.

Hyden was glad for the intrusion because he was hungry, but more so because he had to think about Phen's question. What would a wise old dragon do to guard its hoard? He should have asked the White Goddess when she shared her knowledge of the Skull of Zorellin. He really should have asked Claret. Captain Trant and Brady would both want an answer sooner or later, especially when they drew closer to Cobalt's lair.

Later that evening they sailed out of the storm and into relatively calm waters. Behind them, the nasty wall of gray churning clouds and rain-streaked violence moved northward toward the rocky Valleyan coast. Even Oarly came up from below to see the sunset. He didn't stay long, and barely spoke. When he did, he asked Master Biggs to fill the flask he'd taken from Brady. Once it was full, he eased back down to the cabin and found his bunk.

Phen made the rounds, quizzing every man on the *Seawander*, from the Captain to the cook's assistant, and every hand in between about the tombs of Kahna. Only six men on the ship had ventured through them. To Phen, the tombs sounded like nothing more than a distraction for kingdom folk whose ship had to lay over on the island, but all the men he questioned agreed on one thing: that there was a great emerald down there somewhere in those depths, and you could find it, and death, if you dared to go looking for it. Phen, as it turned out, was planning on doing just that.

Hyden didn't like it, but his objections got caught in his throat when Brady began helping Phen prepare. It was Brady's reasoning that brought Hyden around. "We can feast and watch naked girls gyrate then go on a fool's quest for a few days, or we can sit around in an inn, bored silly, and listen to Phen read about the same sort of things and pester us until we're crazy."

Hyden conceded that was the truth of things. So the next afternoon, when the call of "Land ahoy!" came, Hyden joined in the preparations for Phen's little adventure. He decided that Phen should have probably been more involved in the planning of the greater quest that they were on. The boy did his job well. Phen questioned the seamen again, eliminated the tombs and tunnels that they'd seen already from his list, and planned his itinerary so meticulously that, by the time they had rowed to shore, Hyden found himself believing they might actually have a chance of finding the legendary jewel.

Chapter Thirteen

The solitary man who hadn't bothered to bow to High King Mikahl turned out to be Prince Raspaar of Salaya. His father ruled the tiny, little-known, island kingdom that was stuck between the much larger island of Salazar and the southern tip of Westland. The Prince's dislike for King Broderick was only surpassed by the love he had for his people, which was exactly why he was in Dreen to begin with. Over several morning sessions in King Broderick's grazing pen turned private practice yard, the Prince and Mikahl discussed several subjects while they sparred. Mikahl had to go easy to keep the Prince from being discouraged, but he did so politely, and discreetly. Mikahl learned that Shaella, the Dragon Queen of Westland, had raised tariffs on all shipping trade, which, due to her destruction of the bridge in Locar, was the only type of foreign trading that Westlanders could do.

Prince Raspaar's people were dependent on importing several staple items from Westland, such as wheat, corn, and firewood in the winter. In the past they had purchased those items with the only real valuable resource that Salaya had: jade. Now, since the bulk of the noble folk from Westland and Wildermont had been killed or sold to the Dakaneese slavers, the demand for jade had dropped to almost nothing. So many animals had been ridden out of Westland with the army before Queen Shaella had slithered in that Westland had a severe need of horses.

Prince Raspaar's father, King Raphean, was prudently trying to get a foothold in the business of filling that need. He wanted Salaya to act as a middleman between the Valleyan horse lords and Westland. With horses to trade, the people of the little island could keep the flow of necessities they were dependent on steady. Of course, King Broderick had been all for it. He loved a profit. The craven king didn't want the Dragon Queen for an enemy, and dealing with her directly might offend Highwander royalty, more precisely, Queen Willa and High King Mikahl. So a go-between was necessary. Now King Mikahl was seething mad at King Broderick's insolence and trying his best not to be angry with the young Prince, who in all truth was just looking out for his own kingdom's welfare at his father's request.

"If it's not my Salaya then it will be Telgan, Borina, or even Salaphen or Salazar that will assume the position of broker," Prince Raspaar said after pressing a better than average attack of slashes. "It would be far better for you and the alliance of eastern kingdoms if it were us," he continued. "My father and I will be doing the dealings, and I assure you that we feel no particular loyalty to Westland, not since King Balton was killed. When one of the eastern countries can fill our need in Westland's stead, we would be glad to divert our business from the west entirely."

Prince Raspaar was forced to stop speaking and had to use all his concentration and skill as a swordsman to defend against Mikahl's next attack. Thankfully, the assault only lasted for a few minutes. It ended when Mikahl toppled the man and then hurled his own practice sword into a thicket. Mikahl huffed out a heavy sigh of frustration and started walking toward the bushes to get his weapon. His mind was churning with angry, but hopeful possibilities. The Prince was talking again and the words he was saying we're like slow fertilizer to Mikahl's ideas.

"Of course," Prince Raspaar continued. "We cannot rely on goods from the east sent by ship at this time."

Mikahl stopped, picked up the practice sword, then asked, "Why not?"

"Dakaneese pirates are as thick as carrion after battle." Raspaar had the courtesy to wince at his bad choice of comparisons, but he continued anyway. "It's well known that Queen Shaella is half Dakaneese and somewhat particular to King Ra'Gren and his kingdom. They say that she despises his use of slaves for labor, but that didn't stop her from selling the noble folk of Westland to him. The Dakaneese pirates seem to avoid any ships flying her lightning star banner. All other ships sail at their own peril. It's nearly impossible to avoid the murderous scavengers along the coast between O'Dakahn and Southport. The Salazarkians have worked out an extended sea route to Seaward City, a credit to Queen Rachel's cunning, I'm sure. They seem to be able to elude the pirates, but the cost effectiveness of a lesser island kingdom like ours using the Salazarkian ships is counter productive."

"So you're telling me that, if and when the trade routes are free of Dakaneese pirates, your kingdom will start trading with the eastern kingdoms for your needed goods?" Mikahl didn't wait for an answer, but stepped closer as he pressed on. "What if I..." He darted quickly then and went into an attack with his sword. This press was a little more forceful than the Prince was accustomed to. In the span of three heart beats Prince Raspaar's sword was spinning across the yard. After it clanged to the earth, Mikahl only shrugged with an innocent grin on his face.

"So you could eventually sail a ship full of horses right up into Southport or even Portsmouth in Westland?"

The Prince glanced at his sword lying several feet away in the trampled grass. He had heard rumors of Mikahl's true abilities with the blade, so he wasn't surprised, or offended, by the sudden defeat. He had come to like Mikahl's straightforward attitude and the way he cut through the formalities of his position to get right to the point of things. The possibilities that King Mikahl was just now beginning to see had been in Raspaar's mind all day along. Raspaar felt in his gut that Mikahl would eventually bring Dakahn down and retake Westland. To have the High King as a friend was an honor, whether Mikahl succeeded in those two ventures or not, but if he did succeed, the bond would be the best thing that ever happened to Salaya. To the people Prince Raspaar was sworn to protect, that was what mattered most.

With a devilish grin of his own, he bowed to Mikahl's training yard victory, and felt triumphant with his own political score. "High King Mikahl," the Prince whispered as he rose from his bow. "Not only would ships full of horses be sailing right into Westland's harbors, but the agents of our equine importing houses could move about Westland's cities completely unmolested. Salaya is such a little non-threatening island kingdom, and King Broderick's treachery doesn't have to catch your attention, or Queen Willa's. Just think, in a matter of months, you could know every little thing about Westland's situation."

"We'll need to find you a less notable supplier of horses than the King of Valleya," Mikahl said. "He won't be available. It shouldn't be hard, though, every other man in Dreen is a fargin breeder."

"I see," the Prince replied curiously, wondering what exactly it was that Mikahl had in store for King Broderick.

Two days later, General Spyra started back toward Xwarda with one hundred and one less men in his host than had come. Thirty archers, thirty infantry, and forty cavalrymen stayed behind with the High King. The day after Spyra marched back east, Mikahl took his little army out of Dreen's north gate on a northwesterly course up into the Wilder Mountains. King Broderick lent fifty of his specially chosen blue-cloaked pikemen to the group.

Mikahl didn't hurry them, even though he felt a certain desire to do so. They took their time going through the mountains and stuck to the trampled path of the Westland army's passage. That host had numbered nearly ten thousand, and almost a year after they had come through, the evidence of their passing was still quite clear. Like a well-travelled road a lane of dirt and destruction wound its way over the rocky ridges and down into the green valleys. Where the forest infringed upon the way, it had been hewn down by the Westlanders' axes. Where the way had been rocky, boulders and other scree had been cleared to the side. Deep ruts, where hundreds of supply wagons had rolled through, gouged the earth, and the stone rings of a thousand campfires dotted the landscape.

They made good time even at their relaxed pace. For three days their movements were slowed even further by heavy rainfall, but Mikahl didn't let them stop. Not even when they were forced to wade waist deep, with their horses in tow, through a flooded valley while lightning flashed all around them. Mikahl had left his fancy pavilion tent behind and was using a standard issue canvas just like the others. His only luxury was that he didn't have to share his lodgings with three other soldiers.

The last night of the rain storm a rider came into the encampment bearing messages for Mikahl. He had been expecting one message, but was handed three. The first was from General Spyra. It was the one he had been expecting. After dismissing the messenger to the mess kettle, he broke the General's seal and unrolled the scroll. It read:

I've done as you asked, and things are in order as you hoped for. A message quite unexpectedly arrived bearing the Prince of Salaya's seal. I've enclosed it, and his messenger is still among my men. I thought it the best course of action to take due to his unexpected arrival. The third message, I fear, is dire news, but unless I receive a command from you ordering a change in my plans, things will go as we discussed.

Your humble servant,

General Thomas Spyra

It was good to know that the General was ready, but it must be truly grave news for Spyra to think that Mikahl would change his plans now. He could guess what Prince Raspaar's message said. King Broderick had betrayed him to King Ra'Gren, or something similar. Mikahl was glad to know that Raspaar was truly on his side. The young Prince would make a great king some day. He didn't bother to break the seal on that message yet. He went straight to the third message. The seal on it, the seal of Xwarda, had already been broken as it was addressed to both Mikahl and General Spyra. It was from Queen Willa, and the news was staggering.

Mikahl had to put the damp parchment down and catch his breath. He understood why Spyra might think he would change his course of action now. Maybe he would eventually, but not until he handled the matter of Dreg for King Jarrek. He couldn't afford to dally with Broderick anymore, and a few more days of his absence wouldn't affect the new situation much, if at all. Queen Willa would know what to do until he was done scouting. He would try and figure out a way to get Princess Rosa back from the Dragon Queen while he did it. The fact that Queen Shaella was bold enough to carry out Rosa's capture and now demanded Mikahl's head in return for the girl, made his blood boil. He was so mad he cursed Hyden Hawk for letting the bitch live.

At least Hyden took her dragon from her, Mikahl thought. No doubt Princess Rosa's mother, Queen Rachel, was at this very moment contemplating the value of his head. Surely her daughter's life had to be more valuable. With King Jarrek in O'Dakahn, and Broderick working against him, what Queen Rachel chose to do here could very well turn the bulk of the east against him. He was at a loss. He wished for his father, or Lord Gregory, or even King Jarrek's advice. They were all experienced diplomats and strategists. He was nothing but a squire with a magical sword.

He spent long hours that night, and every waking moment of the rest of the journey to Castlemont, turning over his possible courses of action. None of them seemed appropriate. He didn't give up, though. King Balton had always said there was a way out of every situation, a way to turn every wrong into a right. Mikahl wasn't sure he believed that at the moment, but he knew his father's favorite saying: 'Think, then act. If you aren't doing either of those things then you're really not doing anything at all.' He scoured his brain like it was a cook's dirty pot, searching for any idea he could think of that might help him save Princess Rosa. As the empty, ruined outskirts of Castlemont came into view, though, his mind began to grow numb.

The mightiest castle in the land was wasted. The city around it was a ghostly desolation of nothing but shambled ruins and burned out shells. He spied a company of men up high amid the wreckage of the castle's main structures and sent some of King Broderick's mounted blue-cloaks to investigate. He knew what they were though—scavengers, grave robbers, looters of the dead. He figured they were working for somebody, maybe even Dreg. The idea of being enslaved and forced to pick through your own people's corpses for valuables with a man behind you holding a whip made Mikahl sick with rage.

He rode farther, spurred onwards by some unseen gut-clinching force that had him tasting bile in the back of his throat. Then he topped a small rise and saw what was left of the Locar crossing bridge and was even more taken aback. Across the river, the Westland city of Locar was bustling and had been fortified with wooden watchtowers along its side of the river. Queen Shaella's black and yellow lightning star emblem flickered from a dozen banners, both near and far. Mikahl had to force his tears back. King Balton had been the proudest, most honorable man that had ever lived. The golden lion banner should be dancing in the wind here instead of the mockery before him.

"As you said they would, Your Highness, the Valleyans have disappeared among the ruins," one of the cavalry captains said.

"Tell your men to be ready for an ambush," Mikahl replied without looking at him. "Gather them quickly and we'll ride in a tight group down toward Low Crossing. I think that is where it will happen."

"If I may be so bold, Your Highness, why are we going to ride into an ambush?"

"In life, sometimes the rabbit is really a lion in disguise," the High King said softly. "Have faith, Captain, I would not lead you blindly to your death."

"I'm sorry, Your Highness. I didn't mean to offend."

"Your wariness is wisdom," Mikahl turned to face him and the sadness was instantly gone from his face. Now his expression held only checked fury and determination. The High King's eyes were oceans of confidence and the Captain's concerns were swallowed up in their depths.

"As you command, Highness." The Captain bowed his head then spurred his mount away to gather the men.

Mikahl didn't hide amongst them as they slowly worked their way southward. He led them. He put himself out in front of them and had Thunder prancing his most cocky strut as they went. Behind him, his men had their bows ready or their swords drawn. The men in the rear kept glancing back, trying to see where King Broderick's blue-cloaks had gone.

It was on the outskirts of Castlemont City that Dreg presented himself. Easily as cocksure as Mikahl, he sat upon his horse alone in the center of the road and waited for them to come to him. He wasn't alone for long though. From out of the nooks and crannies of the city, the empty buildings and alleyways, Dreg's sell-swords, and his fully-armored Dakaneese soldiers began to gather behind him. It didn't take long for a force as large as Mikahl's to gather. The only thing that surprised Mikahl was the lumbering breed giant, and the score of scaly green zard-men that came up behind them and were now blocking any chance they had to retreat.

Once Mikahl and his men came to a stop, Dreg rode forward.

High King Mikahl turned to his captains. "When it begins, charge the sell-swords," he said loud enough for all to hear. "Make a way for me. I'll take the breed myself."

"Brave words for a dead man," Dreg said as he reined up a few dozen yards ahead of Mikahl.

Mikahl turned Thunder to face him. His eyes caught on something that was as out of place as a fish on a tree branch. His eyes narrowed and he looked to Dreg, then back to the sword hanging at his hip. There was no doubt that it was Lord Gregory's sword. How it had gotten from the Skyler Clan village where they had left Lord Gregory to die last summer was a mystery.

"You look like you've seen a ghost, boy," Dreg mocked. "Am I the first real man you've ever seen?"

"Tell me where you got that sword and I won't kill you when this battle's over," Mikahl said. His rage, at the moment, was barely containable. "It's my only offer."

Dreg laughed. "A crippled fool searching for his wife left it for me, boy. Who said that you'll live through this battle to kill me when it's done?"

"You misunderstood." Mikahl rolled his shoulders. "I said that I wouldn't kill you when the battle was over, you fargin slaver..."

There was a sharp ringing hiss as Ironspike came free of its scabbard. The blade was radiating white with Mikahl's rage. It was so bright that it threw shadows in the broad daylight. Its magical symphony filled Mikahl's head, and the tingle of its power flooded through his veins.

"...I'll kill you before it gets started," Mikahl finished. Before Dreg could even draw breath, a sizzling streak of yellow lightning blasted from Ironspike's blade into his chest sending him whirling backwards off his horse, feet over head, over feet.

Chapter Fourteen

Mikahl reined Thunder around and yelled, "Charge!" Then he spurred his eager mount back through the narrow corridor his parting ranks of soldiers made for him. Over Ironspike's symphony he heard the thrump and thrum of his archers loosing arrows into the Dakaneese. The thunder of hooves and boots pushing forward, and the sound of ringing steel filled the air. As soon as the archers loosed their second volley, he called for them to turn around and fire at the zard-men who were closing in behind. A few of the foot soldiers, and two of the cavalrymen who had been forced to the rear of the charge turned to aid Mikahl. Their courage was welcome in the fray, but the riders only served to keep some of the archers from having a clear line of fire at the closing enemy.

Many of the fierce zard-men already had arrows sprouting from their fronts, leaving them looking like scaly porcupines. Thunder leapt into their midst and Mikahl swept Ironspike in a gleaming, blood-slinging arc through anything in his path. The breed giant stepped clear of the blade and brought around his tree-trunk club into Thunder's unprotected side. Mikahl was thrown from the saddle as the horse leapt and churned in the air from the force of the blow. Mikahl landed awkwardly, but rolled quickly to his feet. The zard-man before him was as surprised as Mikahl was, but Mikahl put his blade into the zard's neck before it could blink. As it hissed and gurgled away its life, Mikahl was relieved to see Thunder bucking and kicking at the zard nearest him. Mikahl barely dodged the huge club then. He found himself looking straight at the rock-solid chest of the half-breed beast. Had it been a full blooded giant, such as Borg, or King Aldar, he'd have been looking at a crotch instead of a chest, but this was a wild and savage thing that had never fully evolved. With a quick thrust he jabbed Ironspike's white-hot blade deep into the breed giant's thigh then dove away. The beast roared out in agony as its flesh sizzled and smoked where Ironspike had stabbed it.

Mikahl hoped that, once he'd reduced Dreg to a smoking corpse, the sell-swords would have turned and run, but they hadn't. It was probably because of the Dakaneese soldiers that would witness their desertion. King Ra'Gren was notoriously merciless to any who betrayed him.

The knot of battle in the streets was fierce. Steel rang upon steel and the air was saturated with the spray of sticky blood and cries of agony. Some of the Highwander archers threw down their bows and resorted to their short swords and daggers. In most cases a clear shot with a bow was impossible now. Some of the better marksmen waited and loosed with expert precision, finding an enemy's exposed neck or ribcage.

An orb of orange swirling flame came down among the men from a balcony. Dreg's wizard was joining the battle. Another orb exploded among the archers. The streaks of iron-tipped death they were loosing into the Dakaneese all but stopped. The survivors of the initial blast fought the scorching wizard's fire that clung to their skin and armor like feathers to tar. The few that had escaped the magical blaze held their ground and continued to fight.

The zard used short swords to some effect, but became most deadly when they were weaponless and fighting with only tooth and claw. They could drop to all fours and were quickly under the blows thrown by Mikahl's men. Their powerful jaws were filled with sharp tiny teeth and they could use their tails to sweep men off balance and to divert otherwise lethal blows. Mikahl saw this, and while the breed giant limped awkwardly at him, he sent an array of sizzling crimson pulses into the zard from Ironspike's magical blade. The breed giant's club came down at him and he caught it with his sword in midair. Ironspike went right through the wood and Mikahl was brutally cracked in the side of his shoulder by the log that came free from its handle. His ear felt as if it had been ripped from his head, and he stumbled away from the battle clutching it, and cursing his lack of foresight. In a rage, he charged back at the breed giant, and as the monstrous savage committed to the swing of his shortened club, Mikahl spun into the blow and brought Ironspike around in an overhead chopping arc. It wasn't the breed giant's head he was aiming for, though, it was its forearm. The white-hot blade cleaved through flesh and bone so smoothly that its heat nearly cauterized the wound. The breed screamed in agony as its weapon, and part of its arm, went tumbling into the muddy street. The breed giant backed away then. Mikahl feigned a charging step after the creature and it broke into a run. Mikahl saw, not too far behind the fleeing beast, a large group of men on horseback all with bright blue cloaks billowing out behind them. He could only hope that General Spyra hadn't let him down.

An explosion of crackling lightning erupted in the middle of the fray in the street. Clods of smoking dirt and debris flew out from the impact. An empty helm tumbled through the air and what might have been a hand clutching a short sword clattered down not too far from where Mikahl stood. An arrow streaked upward from the knot of men. He followed its path. It deflected away a few feet in front of a man in a black robe who was looking down from a balcony and gesturing frantically.

"Got you," Mikahl whispered as he pointed Ironspike at the robed figure. He found the melody for lightning and let it rise above the rest of the chorus. A bolt shot forth from the blade into the unsuspecting mage. Mikahl held it there for long smoldering moments then finally, when the smoke was rolling up from the man in a thick black cloud, he let it go. The wizard's sizzling body crumpled to the deck. Mikahl turned to see the approaching blue-cloaked riders. A few of them ran the wounded breed giant screaming into the river. The rest kept coming. Mikahl was heartened to see swords coming out of scabbards and being raised high. These weren't the traitorous pikemen that King Broderick had sent to betray him to Dreg. These were General Spyra's men. He looked back to the battle in the street. The sell-sword's and the Dakaneese were pulling back, thinking that surprise reinforcements had come.

"Break!" Mikahl yelled above the din. "To the roadside, to the alleys. Break men, break!"

· Those that heard, repeated the call, and the Highwander men darted out of the lane into alleyways, or out toward the docks and the fishing houses on the river's side of the road. The Dakaneese were shocked when the blue-cloaks rode right into them and began cleaving and slashing away.

Mikahl hoped the long double-time march General Spyra had imposed on his men hadn't been too hard on them. They had turned north out of Dreen and trekked through the lower Evermore Forest around the passage that Mikahl's men had taken. Mikahl was glad to see them. Keeping his men moving slow enough for General Spyra to keep up had been taxing.

Mikahl gathered some of the men from the roadside and put them to the task of taking prisoners while the rest came into the dwindling battle to help finish the Dakaneese soldiers off. To Mikahl's surprise, General Spyra had come himself. The man fought brilliantly, just like he had against Pael's undead army. He seemed dissapointed when Mikahl called him away from the butchery to speak with him.

"Well met, General," Mikahl grinned. "What of the real blue-cloaks?"

"Stripped naked and under guard just north of Castlemont," the General reported. "Most of them laid down their arms freely and swore they would kneel to you. They seem to dislike King Broderick's treachery as much as you do. I still put them under guard, though. So that's the zard, then?" the General asked, directing his gaze over to a twitching green-scaled mass at the roadside. "They don't seem as deadly as the rumor-mongers would have us believe."

"Aye," Mikahl agreed. "It was easy for them to take Westland while the whole of its army was here in Wildermont fighting, but don't underestimate the scaly bastards. They're tough." Mikahl pointed to the river where two of them were swimming like snakes against the Leif Greyn's powerful current.

"We'd better hurry ourselves out of their sight then," General Spyra suggested. "They seem to be able to cross the river at will. We could be swarming with them if we're not careful."

"Finish this then. I want as many prisoners as possible, especially Dreg's men. A close friend of mine may have passed through here and I hope to learn as much of that as I can."

The General gave a curt nod and rode off toward the jumble of his men who had surrounded the surviving Dakaneese soldiers and sell-swords and were awaiting an order. Mikahl sought out Lord Gregory's sword in the muck and gore that was spread about the street. It took some effort, but he found it. Amazingly, it wasn't badly damaged—just a few missing jewels and a gouge in the gold-chased hilt. The blade was still sharp. Mikahl ordered a soldier to find Dreg's corpse and retrieve the scabbard.

He found Thunder limping and whinnying in pain among a group of other riderless horses. Pulling Ironspike free of its scabbard, he saw that its blade radiated a soft blue glow now that his rage had subsided. With a pat on the destrier's rump with the flat of the blade, Ironspike discharged its restorative power into the steed. Thunder snorted his relief and nuzzled Mikahl in thanks. Mikahl gave the horse a pat on the neck then went off to lend Ironspike's power to the injured. He'd done the same thing after he'd recovered from his terrifying battle with Pael. He was glad to help those in need, but Ironspike's healing power was a double-edged sword, so to speak. If its healing powers were tried on one who was wounded beyond the sword's power to heal, the sword instantly took that life to ease the suffering. Mikahl found that he had no taste for that sort of thing. Many men who lay dying wanted a priest, or a friend to hear their last words no matter how much pain they were feeling. Mikahl didn't feel right about taking that little bit of life from them. So he used the blade selectively, on those he felt it could help, and left the others to Spyra's company cleric and the few godly knights that traveled with the special cavalry.

It was well after dark when they finally got all the prisoners and the injured inside an abandoned stronghold just outside of what used to be Castlemont proper. They were far enough away from the river, and the view of the new Westland watchtowers, that they felt safe from an attack. The stronghold's outer wall was made of thick stone blocks and easily defendable. They had too many men to put all of them inside the place, though, so many of the uninjured camped outside the walls. Watches were set, and the gate left slightly ajar so that if the zard or the breed did come across the river they could crowd all of the men inside quickly. It wasn't the perfect place to hole up a makeshift army for the night, but it would do. They still had over three hundred men and fifty prisoners camped a day's ride to the north at High Crossing. Even if the zard did try to come and surprise them, they could mount a formidable counter-attack.

Mikahl let General Spyra worry about the details of the defense. He had every confidence in the man's abilities. Mikahl was more worried about Princess Rosa, and how he was going to find a way to get her out of the Dragon Queen's evil grasp. While that ate up the back of his mind, he was eager to figure out how Lord Gregory's sword had come to be in Dreg's possession. He was in no mood for pandering or parley when he went and found the sell-sword prisoners tied up and guarded in a lower chamber of the keep.

There were eighteen prisoners who were not dying or severely injured, eleven of whom were sell-swords. Of these eleven, only seven were involved in Dreg's mining and slavery enterprise. Mikahl pulled them out for private interrogation. He found a pantry on the same floor as the prisoners. It had a stairway that led up to the kitchens, and that gave him an idea.

The first sell-sword said that a man came through from the north with a big chunk of gold and traded the sword and the gold for a boat, but he didn't know where the man was going. Mikahl put the tip of Ironspike's blade to the prisoner's throat. The man's eyes went wide, and he began to sweat profusely, especially when he felt the hum of the powerful magical weapon vibrating against his skin. Once Mikahl was certain the man had told him everything he knew, he told him to scream out in agony. When the man was done he sent him up to the kitchens where some soldiers were waiting to watch over him.

The next man to be interrogated had been waiting right outside the door under guard and heard the cries of the man before him. When he came in he was terrified and ready to talk, but to Mikahl's disappointment he knew less than the first man. His yelling and screaming however, sounded far more agonized and convincing than the first man's had. The third man named a prisoner who knew the details before Mikahl had even finished the first question. Maxrell Tyne was the name, and he was one of Dreg's captains.

Maxrell Tyne was frank with Mikahl. He was loyal to the coin, not to Dreg, or any other man.

"You'll never spend another copper if you don't tell me everything you know about the man who carried that sword." Mikahl's gaze left no room for argument. "You'll not leave this room."

Maxrell didn't disappoint. He told Mikahl everything. "The man with the gold took a boat with a mercenary named Grommen. They are headed to Southport to search for the man's wife and niece. The man said he found the sword on a body at Summer's Day. I heard him myself."

Mikahl was ecstatic. It had to be Lord Gregory. The Lion Lord hadn't left his sword at Summer's Day, he had taken it into the mountains. He asked Maxrell for the name the man had given, and when he heard the answer, he was sure beyond all doubt that Lord Alvin Gregory was alive and well, and seeking Lady Trella and Lord Ellrich's little daughter, Lady Zasha.

Mikahl happily corrected his thought. Zasha wasn't so little any more. She was a beautiful young lady. He hoped that she and Lady Trella had survived the madness. "You could recognize this Grommen?" he asked.

Maxrell Tyne nodded. Mikahl then made his prisoner an offer that couldn't be refused.

Mikahl told General Spyra most of his newest plan and the man laughed a deep laugh of joyous mirth. General Spyra was unbelievably happy about his part in the things to come. When he and forty five of his best men rode back into Dreen wearing blue cloaks no one would suspect a thing. The gates to the city would open right up for them. King Broderick would think that his soldiers were home from their treachery, at least until General Spyra took him into custody. After that happened, General Spyra would become the acting ruler of Valleya. He could send for his new wife, Lady Mandary, and she could come live like a queen until Mikahl finished what he was going to do. She would love him for it, he was certain.

Chapter Fifteen

Hyden couldn't say which smelled worse, the cavern they were in, or the dwarf. Oarly was still drunk from the previous night's feasting. Brady was as well, but Oarly had apparently bathed in spirits of some sort. He smelled like a monastery's brew barn—like fermenting fruit and yeast. The cavern, on the other hand, smelled of brine and rot. Something had died down in the passageway and Hyden could tell by the sickly sweet odor that the death had been relatively recent.

Hyden's head was pounding, more from the heady smoke the bonfires had bellowed out late last night, than from the few goblets of ale he drank. He didn't know what green plant it was that the painted Ja Jebba sorcerers had thrown on the fire, but its smoke had been uplifting, to say the least. It still amused him that Captain Trant called the Ja Jebba village sorcerers 'juju wizards.' Their language fit his mocking description well. Every other word they spoke sounded like "ju", "ja", or "jo". Their almond skin and wickedly painted faces made them seem to turn into fantastical things as the pungent smoke took effect on the people gathered around the fires. Their honey-skinned half-naked women had, as Captain Trant promised, known exactly what parts of their bodies to gyrate and exactly how to gyrate them. The only negative aspect of the whole experience was the fact that no one in the group had been allowed to sleep off the haze of the evening.

Before dawn broke the horizon, Phen was raring to go. As soon as they landed on the island, the eager young mage purchased a map of the tombs. He discounted it entirely. It showed the same caverns that the sailors he'd questioned had visited. He knew there was no teasure in them. While the others drooled and drank and floated on the smoky high, Phen was busy. He bribed a native who worked at the inn they were staying at, and learned of an ancient tribesman whose daughter sold love potions, charmed trinkets, and curses. He had to buy a sackful of useless crud to learn what he wanted, but after spending enough coins and teaching the woman a minor spell of finding, she let him speak to her father. The old man had cackled with delight when his daughter told him that Phen was searching for the real tombs of the Jakarri.

"Who knows?" the woman translated the old man's words to Phen. "The Jakarri have been dead for two thousand years, but there is a place on the island where you might find something very interesting." The woman looked at her father with more than a little concern showing when he named the place. She didn't seem to like the idea of translating its location to Phen, which made Phen all the more eager to learn it.

"The Serpent's Eye," she finally said with a voice full of reluctance. She showed Phen its general location on the map she'd sold him. It wasn't labeled as such—it was just a cove on a stretch of rocky shore. "You'll have to enter at low tide and by boat," she told him. "The eye closes when the tide comes up. But be warned, none who have ventured there have ever returned."

Now here they were, still reeling from the night before, hunched in a low-ceilinged cavern watching the tide close up the only way out. Deck Master Biggs had let them off and rowed out of the cavern some hours ago. Talon was outside as well. The hawkling was hunting the glade of windblown trees at the top of the rocky formation they were inside of. Hyden wanted his *familiar* close so that he might send him for aid if the need arose.

They had already followed one of the two passages that led away from the entrance. It terminated in an ancient pile of bones, many of them human. They were scattered about a long abandoned nest of some sort. Phen found a rusty shirt of chain mail, a broken dagger, and a chain made of fine silver with an ornate key dangling from it. In a dried out oil cloth sack, he also discovered a small journal. The pages were brittle and the wire-thread binding was ruined, but the strange text that had been expertly scribed within could still be made out. Phen carefully wrapped the old volume and put it in his pack. Then he put the silver chain over his head with a proud grin of accomplishment.

Phen was so pleased with what he found that he already agreed to return to the inn without exploring further. The others wanted to sleep off their agony, but there was a problem: the tide had already risen past the point of no return. Now they were stuck in the cavern until the tide withdrew. After coming to terms with their plight, the others agreed to explore the other passage with Phen just as soon as they had a meal and a took short nap.

They ate dried salted meat and cheese, with fresh bread Phen purchased from the inn's cook. After they had eaten, Oarly and Brady both lay back and rested. Hyden used the time to practice a simple illumination spell that Phen had already mastered. When it was cast properly, a small fist-sized ball of yellow radiance, about as bright as an oil lantern, would appear in the caster's hand. It would rise above his head and hover there, following him wherever he went, until he broke the spell with a gesture and a spoken word.

Hyden had managed it a few times, but more often than not, his sphere appeared too small or misshapen, and the light was some strange mixture of green and orange that barely lit his hand when it formed.

"Your problem is your pronunciation of the words in the spell," Phen scolded him. "You can't speak like a village hick when you're using magic. Very, very bad things can happen."

"The boy found, and looted, a dead man," Oarly grumbled between snores. "Now he's grown bigger than his britches."

Brady laughed. "No, Oarly, he's right. Hyden Hawk might turn one of us into a goat by accident if he gets his words wrong."

The dwarf didn't hear. He was already snoring again. What Oarly referred to as peaceful sleep sounded more like a cavern full of angry bears. Oarly was happy to be off of the ship, and ecstatic to be underground. He had said so at least a hundred times while they were exploring the first tunnel. The quality of Oarly's snoring shifted and began to sound more like a trapped and wounded animal bellowing for its life. Hyden tried to blame the terrible sound for his mispronunciation of the spell words, but Phen wasn't buying it.

"If you can't say the words with Oarly snoring," Phen lectured. "How are you going to be able to say them when arrows are flying at you?"

"All right, Phen," Hyden sighed and tried again. This time the orb appeared in the correct shape and with the proper amount of yellow light emitting from it, for its size. The sphere was only the size of an acorn, though—far too small to light anyone's way.

"You're getting closer," Phen encouraged. "It's more in th—"

"Shhh!" Brady hissed suddenly. "Can you hear that?" he added in a whisper.

The light in Hyden's hand dissapated, leaving them in relative darkness. The sloshing water surging in and out of the cavern's mouth had a blue-tinged glow deep within it. It kept the space swirling and drifting in a perpetual glimmer of subtle illumination. Over the sound of the ocean, a long deep hissing sound could be heard. The shimmering of the water played on the stalactites crazily. Hyden could barely see Phen, who was sitting only a few feet away from him.

"What is it?" Phen whispered. The sound was growing louder.

"Look," Brady pointed toward the black gaping maw of the tunnel they hadn't explored yet.

They could barely see what he was pointing at. A faint green glow was flickering slowly along the tunnel walls. It was growing brighter, as if someone were carrying a green-tinted lantern out from the tunnel's depths. The hissing sound came again, and this time the fact that it was coming from something very big and very alive was unmistakable. Oarly's snore rumbled through the cavern over the hiss, then stopped abruptly as Brady cuffed him in the side of the head.

"What... what?" Oarly grumbled angrily.

"Shhh!" both Phen and Brady hissed in unison.

A soft "Ooh," was all that Hyden could manage to get out of his mouth as the thing came into view.

With eyes the size of chicken eggs, Phen quickly scrambled to Hyden's side.

The huge eel-like thing undulated forward. None of the companions dared to move for fear of alerting it to their presence. Its slimy, scaled skin radiated a phosphorus green glow. It turned its hovering head toward them and a long purple-black tongue flickered forth. Hyden couldn't judge how big it was until it lurched swiftly at them and put its head close enough that it nearly licked his face.

Its milky white eyes had no pupils and were as big as Hyden's head. At least twenty feet of the thing was out of the tunnel now. The creature's head was viper-like and swaying sinuously above the rough floor. The underside of its body was lined with row upon row of palm-sized suckers. Its mouth was wide enough to swallow a man whole. Hyden felt the strangest sensation as the serpent weaved in place, tasting the air around them.

Hyden's chest began to tingle. When he looked down, he saw that it wasn't actually his chest, but the medallion that hung there. Tiny little sparkles of light were jumping from the teardrop shaped jewel mounted in the disc. They weren't alive, but the prismatic flashes of pink, turquoise and lavender light resembled fleas or fireflies shooting out like a fountain. The strange emissions faded after they went more than a foot or two away from the jewel.

The serpent hissed, and Hyden sensed its disapproval of them trespassing in its home. He tried to speak with it in his mind, as he had with the dragon, Claret, and King Aldar's great wolves, but the scaly creature's only response was to flick its tongue at the dragon's tear hanging around his neck.

Hyden could hear the breath trembling in and out of Phen's lungs, and he smelled something rancid. After a moment the serpent eased away from them and slipped itself headfirst into the water. The eerie light of the distant sun shining through the submerged cavern mouth died out as the creature filled the hole. Hyden counted his heart beats as it slithered past them. He was at ten when Phen broke his concentration.

"What was that?" the boy rasped.

Hyden figured that he could have gotten his count up to as many as fifteen or even twenty before the serpent's tail finally disappeared into the water, taking its phosphorus glow with it. By Hyden's estimation, the thing had to be nearly a hundred feet long.

"I don't know what it was, lad," Oarly murmured in a shaky tone. "But it made me shit me britches."

"I thought that was its breath," Brady said with a gagging cough. "Make some light, Phen."

Almost instantly a globe appeared in Phen's palm and ascended to a spot about a foot over the boy's head.

"It's going out to feed," Hyden said after taking a few deep breaths to calm himself. Oarly's stench was foul.

"Let's go see what's back there while it's gone," Phen suggested.

"You go, I'll stay," said Oarly. The look on his hairy face was a comical mixture of disgust, embarrassment, and relief as he stood and unsnapped his belt. He waddled gracelessly to the water and waded into it until he was standing waist deep. The water clouded around him, causing the others to retch and turn away.

"If you stay with the dwarf, Hyden," Brady said between heaves, "I'll go with Phen. That way we will both have light. The smell is killing me."

"I don't think you should go in there," Hyden told Phen. "What if it comes back?"

"You just want to go yourself," Phen argued. "Besides that, it will take a long while to fill that thing's belly. You said it went out to feed."

"Aye," Hyden sighed. Phen was right, he did want to go himself, but someone needed to stay with Oarly. "Go then, but straight in and out. Brady, if you don't see anything after awhile just drag him out of there. If that thing comes back, you'll be trapped."

"Yes, sir," Brady replied.

Hyden was glad to see Brady's gleaming sword come out as he and Phen started down the tunnel. To his surprise, he managed to get his little orb of light to appear on the first attempt, and this time it was the correct size and brightness.

"Most things with a glow like that are night feeders," Oarly said from the water's edge.

Hyden glanced toward the dwarf to respond, but found him on the bank bent over bare-assed and ringing out his clothes. The sight of the Oarly's furry little rump caused Hyden to bite back a laugh. If the dwarf hadn't so brutally tricked him with the squat weed and the cinder peppers, he might've felt sorry for him, but after that horribly painful night at the Royal Seastone Inn, when the peppers made their way out of his system, he just couldn't find any mercy for Oarly in his heart.

"Well, it's not night time and the thing is off to feed," Hyden replied.

"Maybe it's because it lives in a cave underground, or because it's always dark in the depths of the sea," said Oarly. "But my gut tells me it might be guarding something back there—probably a nest."

"Why would it leave if it's guarding something, especially when strangers like us have shown up?" asked Hyden. He was starting to think that maybe the dwarf was a little bit daft.

" 'Cause with the water up, no one can get in," Oarly replied. "Which also means we can't get out of here with its prize—whatever that may be. It knows we will be stuck here when it gets back."

Hyden realized that Oarly was probably right. The dwarf wasn't daft—he was just extremely strange.

"What do you think we should do?" Hyden asked.

"Well, I think we would be in its belly already if your charm hadn't dazzled it." Oarly paused and grunted as he pulled his wet britches back on. "We could wait for it to come back and try to slay it, which I'm not sure we could do with the weapons we have. Or we could swim for it, which is probably the best idea for the three of you, but I can't swim, so I'm not recommending that plan either."

"So what do you suggest?"

"I think that, if Phen and Brady don't disturb whatever it is the serpent is guarding, we can hide in that first passage until the tide is right for us to leave. It's too narrow for that thing to fit into. You could have your bird get us help then, like you said. At least enough men to keep it scared back up in its hole till we get out of here."

It was a sound idea, except for two things. "Phen will meddle if there's anything back there to meddle with," Hyden said. "And Talon can get Master Biggs's attention to come get us, but can't tell him to bring extra men."

"Well, we better go keep Phen from stirring up trouble then." There was very little enthusiasm in Oarly's voice.

The dwarf fastened his belt and, with a pained look, started down the tunnel after Phen and Brady. Hyden, with his magical orb bobbing over his head, was right on his heels.

After a long, twisting jaunt through the rocky tunnel they came upon Phen and Brady. They were standing at a point where the tunnel seemed to drop away and open up into a vast cavern. Both of them were standing stock-still. When he gained their side, Oarly froze as well. Hyden's jaw dropped to the floor when he saw what had stopped them.

The bowl-like bottom of the cavern was full of clear water. Swarming in the water were thousands of serpents, all about three feet long and glowing the same eerie shade of green as the giant one. A glittery island rose out of the churning moat of eel-ish things. The cavern's high ceiling was dripping with vicious looking stalactites and Phen and Hyden's orbs of magical light caught on the treasure and sent sparkling shapes dancing and reflecting through the shadows overhead. On the island, there was a pedestal held up by three kneeling, life-size rusty statutes of skeletons. On the pedestal was a rather large emerald. Sprinkled about the island were dozens of smaller emeralds and a scattering of golden coins.

Oarly, who was the one who recommended that the treasure not be touched, started forward with a will. Hyden caught his shoulder and stopped him before he could get more than a step away.

"Not a chance!" Hyden's voice was flat and full of authority. He had to admit that it was tempting, though. "If you made it past all those little sea vipers, the juju wizards' skeletons would get you before you could return."

"You think the skeletons are real then?" Phen asked in a shaky voice.

"Enchanted, or whatever you call it, most likely." Hyden replied. "That's what the legend says right, that Jakarri juju wizards guard the emerald? If this much of the legend is true, I'm not about to doubt the rest of it."

"I think the old man who sent us here was trying to feed the snakes, Phen." Brady's voice was grim as he continued. "I want to be away from this place before Momma comes back home."

"Aye," Hyden agreed. "Let's go."

"Wait!" Phen said as he skirted over to the edge where the tunnel met the cavern. At his feet the water churned and splashed. Out on a shelf of rock overhanging the swarming serpents sat a small ornate wooden box. "The symbol on the lid looks to be the same as the one on the key I found in the other tunnel."

"I'll get it," Hyden snapped as he edged past Phen. Just like he had done hundreds of times on the hawkling nesting cliffs back home, he eased out along the wall toward the ledge. Below him the water began to boil with hungry little serpents. Luckily they couldn't get a good enough hold to slither up the side of the slick mossy pool.

Once he was at the ledge, Hyden grabbed the wooden box. It was light in his hands. He would have thought it empty if something hard hadn't been rattling around loose inside it. He tried the lid with his free hand but it was locked. Just as Phen had hoped, though, it had a little silver clasp and lock that had obviously been crafted by the same talented smith that had forged the key.

"Here," Hyden called and tossed the box to Phen.

Brady reached out as Hyden came across and pulled him the last few feet back on to solid ground. After he wiped his hands off on his pants, he urged them all back down the shaft.

"Let's go, Oarly." Hyden turned the dwarf gently around and got him moving in the right direction. "Like you said earlier, we're not equipped to get at that sort of treasure, or fight iron skeletons and giant sea serpents today. But believe me, man, there will be another day for it."

We can come back someday with Mikahl and Ironspike to help us, Hyden thought to himself.

"I'm in!" Phen exclaimed. He was gleefully skipping and sidestepping down the tunnel, causing his orb of light to sling shadows along the mossy walls.

"I never doubted that for a minute," Hyden laughed. "But we've had enough adventure for this stop. We've still got the Silver Skull of Zorellin to find."

"If you do come back to get that emerald someday, I'm in as well," said Brady with a little more confidence than he was showing a few minutes ago.

"I'll come," Oarly said.

"Only if you shit before you leave the inn!" Brady said.

"Come now, my fierce friend," Oarly jested back to him. "Don't you know that it was my stink that kept the beast from eating us earlier."

"Aye," Hyden chuckled. "Probably so."

Later, when the serpent returned, it paused only briefly before the smaller tunnel. It flicked its tongue half a dozen times as far into the depths as it could reach, and Hyden's dragon tear medallion sparkled to life again, but only for a moment. The serpent soon disappeared back into its lair and, a few minutes later, the whole of the cavern was permeated with the smell of fresh raw fish.

It took all the patience and reserve that Phen could muster to keep from opening the box while they waited for Deck Master Biggs to come and get them, but he managed it. Once they were safely back behind a locked door at the inn, though, he wasted no time cracking the lid. All four of them had agreed not to speak of the treasure they had seen down in the Serpent's Eye cavern, but the little jeweled ring that was in Phen's box was another thing altogether.

Hyden couldn't help but think about his brother, Gerard, and the horrible fate that a similar ring had brought him. It was all he could do to keep from snatching the prize from his young friend and hurling it into the sea.

Chapter Sixteen

So far, his trap had worked several times. Hell-born minotaurs, wyverns, and several fat gristly borusks couldn't seem to resist the tiny twinkling light that his magical ring could emit.

Gerard Skyler, if he could still be called that, hunched his slick, hard-plated body. He wrapped one arm around his spiked knees. The other, he held palm down on the smooth black endless floor of the hell that he was trapped in. His growing wings wrapped around his once human features, making him look like a glossy jagged boulder of coal, or maybe a large fractured piece of onyx. The glow of the ring on his clawed finger was like a firefly's light in the depths of space, a single star in a whole galaxy. Its magic was strong, though, far stronger than Gerard could comprehend. It drew lesser demons to it like a bucket of blood might draw sharks in the sea. The two halves of the demon Shokin injected thoughts of malice in Gerard's mind, terrible ideas of horrific destruction and consumption, all at random. Gerard had come to like them. It had been just him and his painful transformation, and this endless blackness, for so long that the intrusions were welcome.

For a long time after the freed half of Shokin had returned from Pael, it had tried to pull itself together. It was no easy task, but Gerard mastered them. His changes weren't just physical. The dragon's yolk was transforming his mind as well as evolving his body. Now he was more creature than man, part dragon, part demon, and part human. His skin turned scaly, and at his elbows and knees, dagger-like spikes formed. His chest and stomach turned into steely plates, and a row of triangular fin-like platelets ran down the back of his head to the tip of his tail. His fingers had turned into claws, and his heels and toes grew into sharp spikes. He had grown taller as well, twice the height of a normal man, with thick thighs, and a long torso. His head was still relatively humanoid in shape, which made his visage all the more alien. His brows were thick platelets and his nose was elongated with open nostrils. His teeth had turned into finger-long fangs and his hair hung in thick ropey strands. His eyes, though, his eyes hadn't changed. They'd grown larger to fit the sockets that they were in now, but they were still the eyes of Gerard Skyler, son of Harrap, brother of Hyden.

Those eyes were sometimes fierce and determined like they had been on the hawkling nesting cliffs; like they were at the moment. Sometimes his eyes were full of love and longing. Those were the times when Shaella visited him through her Spectral Orb. Sometimes they were sad and empty as he wandered alone in the Nethers where there was no sun, no light at all, save for the tiny glimmer of his ring.

His attention turned to a shadowy form that was coming closer to investigate the light of his ring. He was surprised to see that it wasn't a lesser demon this time. It was an Oragod, a hulking greater demon that was so malignant it could sap the will-to-live out of anything that stayed too close for long.

"*Kill it!*" part of Shokin hissed gleefully into Gerard's brain.

"*Yes! Yes, so we can feed,*" the other part of the demon added.

Gerard was still alive and he needed to consume flesh to sustain his growth and existence, but Shokin was demon kind. It fed on fear and hate. This Oragod, if they could kill it, would satiate their gnawing hunger for a good long while.

The Oragod lumbered closer. Its skin reflected a grayish hue when it caught the light of the ring. It was a four-legged beast that moved low to the ground. It had two wicked looking horns sticking up from its head, and it was easily three times Gerard's size. This would be no easy kill, especially since Gerard had to do it quickly or risk the demon enslaving his will.

Gerard felt his molten pulse quicken.

"*Wait till it gets closer,*" Shokin whispered.

"*Yes, then blind it with a flare of the ring's light,*" Shokin's other voice added.

Gerard felt the urges of the dragon's fire burning in his veins as well. The plethora of instincts that came over him was like a tidal wave of predatory acid that ate down into his very bones.

The thing was closer now. Glossy saliva dripped from its disfigured ram-like head and sizzled where it hit the floor. Its body was wolfish, but it moved with serpentine grace. Neither hair nor scale covered its thick pocked skin. Its teeth and talons were as big and sharp as swords, and evil magic radiated from it like a stench. Gerard sensed it all in his blood, and a pulse of desire pounded through him.

With a tentative sniff at the air, the Oragod came into the light. It looked curiously at the slick rock sitting so out of place on the smooth expanse of floor. It couldn't smell evil, nor could it smell the brimstone that all demons emitted. Cautiously, it reached out its fore claw and, with the tip of one of its talons, touched the source of the magical light that had drawn it there.

With a guttural, primal roar, Gerard leapt up and spewed a streaking blast of dragon fire into the beast's eyes. It shrieked and writhed, blinded by the flame's scorching heat as much as by the sudden brightness. The instinct of the dragon's predatory bloodlust burning in him took over Gerard. He didn't have to think. That was a good thing, because the two halves of Shokin were cackling with gleeful malice all through his mind.

Gerard leapt to the back of the writhing thing and didn't even bother to dodge the sharp claw that raked harmlessly across his steely chest plate. The bigger creature arched its back and howled, twisting in vain as Gerard drove his toe claws and fore claws into its flesh for traction. He crawled right over onto its back, and an orb of purple static swelled out around them both. It felt like lava on Gerard's skin, but he drove the Oragod's magic from his mind. With unbelievable speed, Gerard crawled up its back, clinging to it with his claws like a squirrel clings to a tree. He made his way over its shoulder. Another blast of fire across its face made the thing scream and howl out in rage. The radiant protective spell it had cast flickered away. It thrashed and bucked and shivered every which way it could, but it couldn't throw Gerard off.

Gerard tore into its flesh with a ravaging hunger and within moments found the thick pulsing arteries there. Like a wolf trying to tear a troublesome piece of meat from its kill, Gerard reared back with straining muscles. The thick jugular pulsing through his teeth ripped, then tore, gushing out and bathing him in warm sticky blood.

For long days, that might have been weeks, he feasted on the devil's flesh. It filled him with more than sustenance though. The devil's evil boiled inside him. Its essence tingled through both his body and his mind. By the time the feast was done, Gerard understood much, much more than he had before. Shokin's power, the Oragod's power, and even the power of the dragon's fire inside him were his to command, not the other way around. The more demons and devils he consumed, the stronger he would grow.

Shaella called out to Gerard from the world above. In her bedchamber, the depths of the Spectral Orb swirled with pastel shades of powdery blue and lime. The head-sized crystal sitting atop the ornate wooden staff she'd had crafted for it was the centerpiece of the room. The staff stood with its silver heel socketed in a hole in the center of the floor. Shaella sang the chant her father had taught her as she paced slowly around it.

Inert, it looked more like a fancy post lantern than a powerful prismatic artifact. Activated, its power radiated through the room with tingling heat and dazzling refractions. The cloudy swirls inside the crystal sphere turned purple as Shaella's chanting melody was joined by the chilling chorus of the sphere's magical voice. Then, all at once, the image of Gerard came into view inside the orb.

Shaella felt no disgust when she gazed upon the sight before her. She sought out Gerard's familiar eyes and locked onto them. He was still in there, and she loved him so much that, as long as she could see him, nothing else mattered. It was hard this day, though, not to let her gaze stray to his harsh toothy maw. A long, ragged piece of dark meat dangled from where it was caught in his fangs and drew the eye. Its presence was a strong reminder of the changes Gerard had been through. Not the physical changes mind you, but the primal ones, the ones Shaella tried not to think about.

"I've missed you my love," she said. She was wearing a white gown and nothing else. She sat down on the edge of her bed and lay out sideways in a seductive pose that pronounced the heavy shape of her breasts.

In his mind's eye, Gerard could see her, and the longing lust he felt for her forced Shokin's pesky voices from his brain completely.

"Shaella," he rasped. "Are you well?"

"Yes, my love," she whispered, letting a finger trail down her belly. "Much has happened since we last spoke."

"Tell me," he said, savoring the sight of her.

"I've stolen a princess," Shaella said. "Cole is bringing her to me. I will trade her for the head of the High King, or maybe for his sword. With either, I gain the power to rule the entire realm. And if those fools are afraid to cross him, then I'll dangle her as bait and draw him into a trap. Either way we will win."

"You cannot underestimate the power of his blade, love," Gerard rasped, not sure how he knew to give the warning.

Shaella cocked her head. Gerard had been weak and barely alive for so long that she'd once thought he would die in his hellish prison. Now, though, he had grown into something huge and powerful. He wasn't scrabbling to survive anymore, he was thriving. The proof was hanging from his bloody mouth. She knew from his previous ravings the demon that had possessed her father was now somehow inside him, but she could tell that the demon was no longer in control. Gerard was mastering what he was, and that made her curious as to what he might have learned that could help her. She wanted to rid the land of the young king who had killed her father and would soon come to reclaim his Westland throne.

"Is there nothing that will help me defeat the blade's power?" she asked. The hem of her gown had inched its way up to her belly and her fingers were now probing her depths for her lover's eyes. Her breasts heaved and strained against the silky material of her gown as her breaths quickened.

"The priests of Kraw," Gerard rasped. The knowledge came from the memory of the devils he had consumed, or maybe from Shokin. "On the Isle of Borina, Kraw has a sect of priests. Their knowledge of necromancy and sorcery might help you." Gerard's voice was harsh and deliberate. "I will find Kraw in this blackness. Once I've questioned him, I might be able to tell you more. I will try to persuade him to guide the priests in the direction you desire." His voice became a low primal growl as Shaella arched her back and bucked with the power of her passion. Through husky breaths, Gerard continued. "Seek them out and let them set a trap with the bait you've taken."

Her moans of pleasure sent rippling tingles through Gerard. He wasn't quite human enough to be physically aroused by her anymore, but in his mind and heart she filled him with a certain kind of satisfaction—a feeling that he could never find anywhere else. She was his, and he loved her. If this so-called Kraw wouldn't help Shaella, he would devour it and anything else he came across.

"My love," she whispered. Sadness had come over her now that her lust had been quelled. "Your brother dallies in his quest for Zorellin's skull. If I knew where it was I'd have it already, and you could kill King Mikahl yourself."

"Hyden will find what he seeks," Gerard rasped with absolute confidence. Fleeting memories of his brother danced across his mind. They were so strong that, for a moment, they even obscured the vision of Shaella in his head. Only a strong jealous feeling, the knowledge that Hyden wanted to take his ring from him, could force the joyous thoughts away.

"When he does find it, take the skull from him any way you can," he growled. "Be patient, love. Soon I will be strong enough to take on the entire world, and when I am, I will conquer it and give it to you."

Shaella felt the heat rising in her belly again. Her sadness evaporated as the warmth spread through her thighs. Gerard, it seemed, had come into his new self. His words, and the confidence behind them, made her body purr with delight, but more than that, the look of sincerity and longing in his eyes cut right through her.

"I love you," she gasped as she tore her gown from her body. "Give me the world, Gerard," she said as she opened her legs to him. "Come give me everything you have."

Shaella's sweating body glistened as she slowly brought herself to climax again. She found her herself fantasizing about Gerard's huge misshapen member thrusting painfully inside her, and the hot breath of his hideous face on her neck.

"Soon," she heard him rasp huskily. "Very, very soon."

This time when she came she was engulfed in an explosion of ecstasy. She slipped away into a dreamy blackness, leaving Gerard thirsting to seek out Kraw, and maybe even the Lord of the Hells, the Abbadon himself.

Chapter Seventeen

King Ra'Gren sat upon his throne seething. His bulking muscles clenched, unclenched and then clenched again. His normally almond-skinned face was a deep crimson and his thick white brows were split by a throbbing vein on his forehead. His hair and goatee beard were long, wavy, and white as snow. The golden spiked crown atop his head was heavy with gemstones. Diamonds, rubies, and sapphires all sparkled with the light of the dozen torches that lined each long wall of his crudely opulent, high-ceilinged throne room. Like the crown, the throne was made of solid gold, but it was hard to see. It was draped with the furs of several different wildcats. Black and red striped tigren fur, and the bright yellow spotted hide of a rare marshland saber cat, was prominently visible underneath the well-built king.

To any of the few subjects who were standing in his hall, he could've passed for forty years of age, but he was nearer to sixty. A half dozen golden chains hanging around his neck, and the size of the jewels dangling from some of them, kept the eye from noticing the wrinkles on his weathered face. He wore a white, sleeveless shin-length robe fastened at the waist with a golden chain, and leather sandals that laced up to some point higher than the hem of his robe. In his clenched right hand he held an ancient iron trident, oiled and black; it was the only thing near the man that didn't appear to be worth its weight in wealth. Being that it was the generational symbol of his house, it was probably worth more than all of the precious jewelry he wore combined. The rumor mongers said that at least a hundred men had felt its three not-so-sharp tines inside their bodies since Ra'Gren ascended the throne. Ra'Gren knew the truth: ten times that many had died by his trident in private.

Before him lay an old wooden chest. It was a gift from King Jarrek, the third of its kind to arrive in a handful of days. Inside the chest were the heads of three of Ra'Gren's overlords, bringing the total to seven. The message that came with the chest was the same as the others: 'Release all the citizens of Wildermont from their bonds of slavery or heads are going to fall.'

The group of six concerned overlords who carried the chest into the room was standing nervously behind it. They were obviously worried that the Red Wolf would come for them next.

"Who were they?" Ra'Gren asked.

"Overlord Ra'Estes of Kahndan, and two of his six underlords, Ta'Ligad and Am'Estal, I believe." Overlord Ta'Ken bowed, and added a "Your Majesty," for good measure. "Kahndan is rather close to O'Dakahn Your Highness. Some of us are starting to worry. Already Overlord Pa'Perryn of Oktin, and his brother

Pa'Pallyn have been shortened. And as you know, just last week the overlord of Lokahna was killed as well."

"Do I need you to advise me, Ta'Ken?" King Ra'Gren snapped. "I asked you whose heads are in the box, not for a list of the dead, or where they're from. The towns these dead men were from all sit along the Kahna River. They all border Valleya. Obviously King Jarrek survived the fall of Wildermont and thinks he can scare us into freeing his people." Ra'Gren took a deep angry breath.

"Odava will be next, if the pattern holds," the King growled. "Bring me the witness to this absurdity, the one who was there when these heads came off."

Ta'Ken motioned at the door. The guarding soldiers opened it and an old crooked-boned man in drooping shackles limped in. He was followed by one of Overlord Ra'Estes' surviving underlords.

Ta'Ken hadn't wanted to become the spokesman for his peers, but since his stronghold lay at the northeastern most outskirts of O'Dakahn, the duty had fallen on him. As the slave and the underlord eased by him to stand before the King, Ta'Ken winced at the sight of the slave's lumpy, misshapen forearm. It looked like the bone was about to burst through his skin. A long ill-sewn cut ran the length of the hump. The underlord kicked the slave behind the leg, causing him to fall to his knees. Then, he too bowed before King Ra'Gren.

"You are?" the King asked the underlord, ignoring the slave completely.

As per custom the underlord resumed standing, but kept his head bowed as he spoke. "Your Highness, I am Underlord Pa'Tally. I was the first to find the bodies of my overlord and the others."

"When was this?"

"Early yesterday morning, Highness. I rode here as fast as I could."

"Describe what you found."

"Kahndan Keep was empty," Pa'Tally answered. "Fourteen guards were dead, all of them killed by dagger or sword, save for the gateman. He took a crossbow bolt to the neck. Overlord Ra'Estes was sprawled atop his harem bed naked and headless. The others were found in their night clothes in the guest quarters in similar poses."

Ta'Ken dropped his eyes when the King glanced his way. He was relieved when Ra'Gren continued questioning the underlord.

"What of his possessions?"

"The slaves are all gone, but his horses and sheep are still there. His jewels and other valuables were left in place as well."

"How many slaves?"

"Seventy-eight women, and sixteen men."

"For Wildermont!" the witness screamed as he lunged up at the King. In his hand he now held a blood-drenched dagger. Its tip found the skin over Ra'Gren's heart, but only nicked the flesh before Overlord Ta'Ken saw two of the three tines of the King's trident burst out of the slave's back on either side of his spine. The third tine missed the flesh due to the slave's emaciated condition. The sparsely filled room exploded into an uproar and several soldiers stormed out of the shadows and gained the King's side.

With a sudden lurch the slave came over backwards as the King kicked the body off of his weapon with a sandaled foot.

"He had the dagger sewn into his skin!" Ta'Ken exclaimed when he saw the gaping slash on the slave's forearm. Ta'Ken was aghast. He looked at the King with wide eyes and repeated, "It was sewn into his skin."

"Silence!" Ra'Gren roared. The quiet that followed was absolute until the slave moaned miserably. Ra'Gren stood and strode down the three steps of the throne dais and slammed the butt of his old iron weapon through the slave's skull with a crunch. Then he turned and threw it as if it were a spear back up toward the throne. It stuck deeply into the soldier nearest the King's seat, the heavy tines piercing through plate armor as if it were as thin as papyrus.

"Captain Em'Dep is relieved of duty," Ra'Gren snarled at the second commander of his personal guard. "Em'Tally, you are to take command. If an enemy's blade ever gets that close to my heart again I will kill you all and sell your children to the fargin skeeks."

Another silence followed in which two offended zard merchants sitting in the back of the chamber rose and eased toward the door. The only other movement was King Ra'Gren reclaiming his trident and then resuming his position on the throne.

No sooner did he get himself situated than a fierce looking young man stepped up, forcing his way through the shocked group of overlords to take a knee before the King.

"What is it?" the King asked harshly. He had a look on his face that could freeze lava.

Ta'Ken took an unconscious step away from the newcomer, knowing that a single ill-spoken word could end any one of them. To his surprise, the man now rising before the King had a look of disgust on his face.

"I want the honor of bringing you King Jarrek's head." The man nearly spat the words. "Pa'Perryn, Ra'Estes, and these..." he gestured at the group of overlords standing behind him like cornered goats in a pen. "...these pitiful men have no spine," he continued. He flexed his ample arms and chest. "An overlord should be proud and strong. He should be able to defend himself from kingdomless men."

Ta'Ken managed to look the man in the eyes even though he could feel his cheeks burning. The others were looking elsewhere.

"I have men that are capable, and it would be my honor to remind these overlords of what they seem to have forgotten."

Ra'Gren didn't seem very impressed with the young man. "What do you want in return for bringing me Jarrek's head?"

"Your Highness, three of your river towns are without leadership now. To be called overlord of any of them would please me." The man looked up at the King with a slightly defiant look on his face. "Though I will gladly bring you Jarrek's head just to remind these so-called overlords how to be men."

"You've got iron balls, man," the King said with a dry laugh. "But, if you think my lords are not capable, then take a moment to imagine what kind of price they can afford to put on your head. Though these cowering stalks lack muscle, they fill my coffers with coin. Year in and year out they do. If you think you can do that, then by the gods fetch me Jarrek's head and take your pick of river holds." The King eyed the overlords standing behind the braggart. "This one has offended you, no? If Jarrek's head is not in my lap before long, I assure you that this man's contempt will be punished publicly. Until that time he is to be given your full cooperation." Ra'Gren sighed and looked down at the man's now uncertain expression. "What is your name?"

"Krenson Rhone, Your Highness." he answered cautiously.

"Jarrek should strike Odava soon. Go there. See if you can't keep Pa'Stryn's head attached to his shoulders. You have put yourself in a position that should keep you properly motivated. Either you will succeed and rise, or you'll fail and die."

The King pointed at the body on the floor. "Ta'Ken will make sure your group is properly outfitted. Take this wretch with you as you go."

Dismissing Krenson Rhone as if he were no longer there, King Ra'Gren turned to his overlords. "How many slaves was it?"

"Seventy-eight women and sixteen men," Overlord Pa'Tally answered with a nervous glance at the body being dragged away from his feet.

The King stared blankly at the crimson smear left on the floor, scratching his beard as he thought about the situation. After few moments he sighed again. "Lord Pa'Tally, you are appointed as acting overlord of Kahndan. Do not get comfortable, and try not to lose your head." Turning away from the men, the King took a goblet from a tray that a trembling slave had been holding throughout the ordeal. After a long sip of wine he asked, "Lord Ta'Ken, what is it you suggest we do about King Jarrek? You all have plenty of coin. Hire someone to hunt him down, or get rid of your slaves if you're afraid of his wrath. I've sent Krenson

Rhone to dispatch the nuisance." Ra'Gren laughed then, his mirth was full of irony. "If you do not think that is enough answer to the problem, then do what you will."

Later, while Krenson Rhone was riding as swiftly as his horse would carry him to Odava, Lord Ta'Ken was debating with the other overlords, and a few of the more prosperous slave traders, about which mercenary company to hire. The debate ended with them all agreeing to put a bounty on the King of Wildermont. Fifty thousand golden fangs would be paid to who ever brought in Jarrek's head. It was enough coin to build a castle and retire knowing that for generations your descendants would live well. Ta'Ken imagined that it would only be a matter of days before he could give his king a chest that held a head he wanted to see. He thought the irony of paying for the assassination with Wildermont minted coin was a statement unto itself.

Krenson Rhone, tired and weary from his two day ride, came to the gates of Odava's keep with high expectations, and even higher hopes. It didn't seem to bother him that no one asked who he was as he entered. The men there greeted him pleasantly and escorted him to the overlord's dining hall. It came as a great shock to Krenson that Lord Pa'Stryn's headless body sat at the head of the table.

King Jarrek promptly stepped out of the darkness with a malicious snarl showing beneath his red-wolf skull helmet. He chuckled just before he hacked off Krenson's sword hand. After gathering as much information as he could, Jarrek took his head too. He put the body with Pa'Stryn's men's corpses in the cellar. By dawn the keep was empty save for the carrion. The hundred and thirty-five slaves that had been held there were escorted into Valleya and freed. Then, Jarrek and a few of his men delivered their fourth chest to King Ra'Gren.

Ta'Ken just happened to be at court the day the fourth chest arrived. He was in the middle of telling the King about his consortium's generous bounty. Ta'Ken almost laughed when Krenson Rhone's head was pulled from the chest. His amusement ended when Lord Pa'Stryn's came out next. In fact, he was appalled. Knowing that his own keep was now the closest to the Valleyan border and the farthest from O'Dakahn, he decided to up the bounty to a hundred thousand golden fangs.

The whole situation was getting out of hand. O'Dakahn was the profitable seaport cesspool city it had always been, but the other cities of Dakahn were getting edgy. The good folk, the merchants and crafters, the barrel makers and farmers, and especially the river men, were starting to wonder if they were truly protected by the lords they paid their tariffs to. Even the gambling and prostitution rings were losing custom. Ta'Ken had no intentions of losing his slaves to the Red Wolf. He hired a dozen bodyguards and two dozen more men to fortify his keep. Then he left O'Dakahn to go protect his home.

If Ta'Ken could have seen the look on King Ra'Gren's face three days later when he pulled the tenth head King Jarrek sent him from the chest, he would have been mortified.

That day Ra'Gren began to fear. Holding Ta'Ken's severed head in his lap, and hearing the state of disarray his kingdom was descending into, he decided to make a statement that even King Jarrek and his vigilantes could not ignore. It would be a statement that would put an end to all of it.

He summoned the main slave traders in the kingdom to his throne room and personally purchased from them a hundred of the youngest and most innocent Wildermont slaves available. The next day, in the vast trading square near O'Dakahn's shipping center, King Ra'Gren had his hundred Wildermont innocents form a line. Every day, thousands upon thousands of people gathered there to hawk and trade their wares, but they were all cleared back for the spectacle. One by one Ra'Gren had his new slaves beheaded. After the last terrified little girl's body collapsed at his blood-spattered feet, Ra'Gren had the hundred heads piled into a wagon and then staked a Wildermont flag in the mound.

"Leave this in the square as a reminder," he ordered, as he and his retinue rode back toward the castle. "Anyone who tries to move it will join them."

Chapter Eighteen

" '... when Sorgisee first landed his ship at the mouth of the Pixie River, he thought his crew was the first to set foot in that land,' " Hyden read to them. They were sitting at the booth table in the ship's little common room. Brady was lounging on the divan barely listening, and Oarly was in his cabin under the blankets. It had been a long two weeks at sea since they left the Island of Kahna. All of them, save for the dwarf, were getting restless.

" 'After exploring up the river Sorgisee found that he was wrong. A village of dwarves greeted them kindly, and though their languages differed, they communicated with hand signals and crude gestures. Further north they found the elves, who could speak to them in the common tongue of the age. The little folk danced at the elves' feet and fluttered around them like butterflies. The elves told them that there were other men, far to the west, harsh and pale men who sought to own the land instead of share it. The elves also spoke of giants, men as tall as trees that ranged as far south as the Willdee... Willda...' "

"Wilder Mountains," Phen said. "Your reading has improved," the boy added encouragingly. "But could you read to yourself for a while. This is tedious work, especially on a rolling ship."

Phen wasn't being rude on purpose. Captain Trant had given him an old unused logbook. With his tongue held at the corner of his mouth, Phen was meticulously copying the foreign text of the old book he had found in the serpent's lair into it. He wanted a copy he could look at and study that he didn't have to worry about damaging.

"I think I've had enough reading for the day anyway," Hyden said, not offended. "How many more days?" he asked Brady. Hyden had asked the question a dozen times already that day, and both Brady and Phen answered in exasperated unison.

"Four more days!"

Hyden laughed aloud, as much at himself as at them. "I'm going up," he said. "Talon wants to stretch his wings, and I might just tag along."

"Braggart," Phen huffed jealously, but with a smile. "If you would let me wear my ring, I might just be able to see through the eyes of a hawk like you do."

"Aye," Hyden ruffled Phen's hair. "And you might turn into a fat hairy gruek and try to bed Oarly as well."

"Ewwww!" Phen made a sour face. "I'm not Gerard you know."

"Aye," Hyden responded seriously. "But I love you as if you were my brother, and if I would have kept the ring he found when he offered it to me he wouldn't be where he is now."

"Aye," Phen dropped his head, now sorry for bringing up such a subject. The truth was he was sort of afraid of the ring he had found. Not afraid to keep it dangling next to the key on the silver chain around his neck, but afraid to slip a finger through its inviting hole.

"If Captain Trant is right, then in a few days, you might be able to start deciphering your book," said Hyden as he started up the stairs.

"Do you really think it's pirate code in the book?" Phen asked before Hyden could get out the door.

"It's probably recipes for old fish wives," Hyden said letting the door slam shut behind him.

Brady laughed from the divan. "Or it's directions on how to get eaten by a sea serpent," he said.

"I hope it's a spell that tells me how to turn my wise ass friends into toads," Phen said with a hopeful grin on his face.

"It would probably turn Oarly into a prince, then," Brady joked.

They both laughed at that.

After the chuckle, Phen dipped his quill and went back to work. Brady resituated himself on the divan and went to sleep.

Hyden deftly climbed the mast. He shooed Babel out of the crow's nest and made himself comfortable. The strange blue monkey hung around in the rigging for a while but soon disappeared from view. Talon was gliding alongside the ship and Hyden closed his eyes, seeking the hawkling's vision. After a moment he changed his mind and tried to find Talon's sight with his own eyes open, like he had been forced to do in Dahg Mahn's trial. The sensation came to him easy enough and the spectral image of the world spread out before him. He could see more than was physically there. He could see the nature of things, their power, and their essence. In the depths of the sea ahead of them he made out a swirling school of little fish and the dark intent of the larger ones darting in and out of the cluster to feed. On the horizon he saw the colors of the wind and the different layers of warmer and cooler air. Out of view to the right of the ship, he knew lay the vast swampy marshlands. They separated Dakahn and lower Westland, and somewhere in those deep marshes was Claret's abandoned lair. He looked to his left where the maps he'd studied showed nothing but an endless expanse of sea. To his great surprise, something revealed itself out in the beyond. The prismatic color of slow pumping wings soared over the sea on a course parallel to the ship's. Whatever it was, it was powerful and full of both good and evil intent. Its aura was that of a great predator and full of wild powerful magic. As it noticed Hyden's magical vision, or maybe the radiant power of the dragon tear hanging near his heart, the thing veered its course closer to the *Seawander.*

Long before the men of the crew saw it, Hyden knew it was a dragon. Young and lean, and full of life, it flew through the air with such powerful sinuous grace that even Talon felt inferior at the sight. It was aquamarine in color, and its glittering turquoise scales reflected the afternoon sun like a pile of polished gemstones. It made no move to attack, and it didn't venture nearer then an arrow shot. Hyden could sense its reluctance to be so close to the destructive humans. It feared them. It was probably twenty paces long from tip to tail, but Hyden knew that someday it would be big enough to grasp a ship the size of the *Seawander* in its claws and carry it away just like the great blue dragon Cobalt had done with Barnacle Bones's ship.

Someday this dragon would know no fear. Hyden wondered what that would feel like. To be the greatest creature in the land was beyond his fathoming.

After awhile the dragon trumpeted a shrill warning and veered away back to the south. Hyden watched its aura fade into the wind, and finally caught his breath. Talon fluttered down onto the lip of the crow's nest and cawed his satisfaction to Hyden. The bird also perceived more when they shared their vision. As he climbed back down to the deck, Hyden wondered just what it was that Talon sensed through their bond.

Phen and Brady stood near the mermaid bowsprit figurehead grinning at him as he approached. Word of the dragon flying alongside the ship had reached them and they dared not miss such a sight.

"Did you speak to it?" Phen asked excitedly. "Like you did with Claret?"

"Aye," Hyden nodded. "I told it if it got hungry we would throw a young mage overboard for its supper."

Phen's expression went blank for a moment then he slugged Hyden in the arm. "Really, did you speak with it?" he asked again.

"It was young and wary of us," Hyden answered. "It was only curious, I think, but no Phen, I was too mesmerized by its grace to find words."

"Aye," Phen understood that feeling completely.

From somewhere toward the middle of the ship a loud bell clanged twice.

"That'll be our supper," Brady said flatly. "Hard biscuits and even harder meat."

Three nights later the cry of "Land Ahoy!" woke them with a start.

The lighthouse of Salazar was on the distant horizon, and the welcome idea of being on land again caused Oarly to make his way up to the ship's rail. The dwarf was standing on tiptoe peering into the night for a glimpse of the great magical fire that burned to guide ships in to Salazar's port. Without the added height of the crow's nest, it was impossible to see, though, so Oarly begged a pint from the Deck Master and grumbled his way back down below to drink it. The others couldn't have slept if they wanted to. They stood at the rail feeling the warm ocean breeze and speculated on what Salazar might be like.

When dawn broke they were rewarded with a grand sight. The greenish beacon of the fire had topped the horizon and guided them through the early hours. It was an odd feeling having land to their left now.

The tower stood over four hundred feet tall. Its base was as big around as four or five of Xwarda's great towers, and it gently tapered as it rose.

"It's huge," observed Phen.

It was made of grayish-white granite blocks that sparkled in the sunlight, as if the tower were coated with frost. At its top, a green-tinged blaze fought the bright light of day in order to be seen. The tower jutted up from an uninviting rocky shoreline that was infested with screeching sea birds. Strange looking fanged creatures lazed about the rocks bellowing their irritation at the birds. The ship didn't pass too close, for fear of the unseen reefs hidden under the water. Talon shot out toward the swarming army of birds with excited vigor, only to pause and hover about halfway across the expanse of emerald sea. A great winged shadow leapt from the shore. A long, sharp-beaked sea dactyl, with a wingspan of maybe fifteen paces flew out toward them, calling out a warning cry. "Cooo Cawww! Cooo Cawww! Stay Away!" Hyden heard its intent. Talon quickly found the ship's rail near Phen and hid the embarrassment of his fear by preening himself as if nothing had happened.

Soon the rocky shoreline grew greener and softer, eventually turning into a beach of silvery sparkling sand. They passed several fishing vessels and a pair of cargo ships that seemed to be undergoing modifications while at anchor. The land beyond the beach was a rolling green that was speckled with lush patches of forest. Herds of great brown furred beasts roamed aimlessly with their heads down in the grass. A few modest homes, built of stone, with red tiled roofs could be seen here and there. As they sailed further around the northeastern face of the crudely triangular shaped island, the evidence of people grew more frequent. The size and height of the homes and stonewalled keeps grew as they went. Many of the roofs here were tarnished copper. When the shoreline broke so that they were sailing due west, the group was awe-struck by what revealed itself before them.

Ships, hundreds of them, both big and small, and a few that were enormous, littered the bay. Some of them flew the black sword banner of Highwander like the *Seawander*. Others flew the rising sun of Seaward, or the red and yellow checked shield of Valleya. Many of the ships flew an unfamiliar black banner with a wicked looking yellow lightning star emblazoned on it, and even more ships were anchored there under the Dakaneese trident.

The island lay to their left, but ahead they could see a long stretch of built up land that extended north for a great distance. It curved back toward them, off to the right, wrapping the bay on three sides. The mass of buildings, dock-houses, and towers was easily three times the size of Xwarda. The sheer immensity of the place left them all speechless. Phen tried counting all the towers he could see rising above the warehouses and packed together homes, but lost interest when he reached a hundred and could tell that he wasn't even halfway through them.

"I never knew it was like this," said Brady. "My father came here once and said that the city of Lazar was bigger than two Castlemonts, but I thought he was just teasing me. It seems it's thrice that size, if not bigger."

After ordering the sails to be rolled, and giving the water mage the helm, Captain Trant joined them at the rail. Babel the blue monkey was perched on his shoulder fiddling with the Captain's hair intently.

"It's a hell of a place," the Captain said. "They make everything a shipper needs here on this island, from boxes and crates, to water-tight barrels, or wooden packing drums. They build the greatest ships that sail the seas," he chuckled sourly. "With the great forge fires of your people temporarily extinguished, Brady, the price of metal work is higher than the clouds."

"My Wilder Mountains are full of iron," Brady said proudly. "We will rise again. King Jarrek will make it so."

"The guilds of ship builders here will be thankful for it," said Trant. "Every nail, clamp, davit bracket, and fitting on the ships you see is made of Wildermont steel, even the bands on the barrels crowding the decks."

"Does Salazar openly do business, dark business, with Dakahn?" asked Hyden. An idea had formed in his head out of nowhere. It was a powerful idea, one that might go far toward King Jarrek's cause.

"The trade? Slaves?" Trant asked.

Hyden nodded.

"Not that I know of," mused Trant. "Maybe in an oblique sort of way they do. The Dakaneese, like all of the kingdoms of the realm, buy their ships from Salazar. Dakaneese pirates steal a lot of them from the trade routes and re-fit them for resale at O'Dakahn. Dakahn is less dependent on Salazar's work than others."

"Do you know anyone with authority in the ship-building guilds?" Hyden asked.

"Of course, of course. I think if you'd like to meet some of them while we are here I can arrange it. They would love to meet the man who stole the Dragon Queen's dragon."

Hyden's mind was churning with possibilities.

"When will we get to see if your pirate friend can read my book?" Phen asked excitedly.

"Sooner than you think, lad." Trant laughed at the boy's eagerness. "If Sir Hyden Hawk will allow it, you may accompany me to the office of the harbor master as soon as we're secured. The Rulers of Salazar are wise men. The harbor master here is an old sea dog. He was a grand scoundrel in his day. What better way to keep your harbor safe from pirates, than to have a pirate running the harbor?"

The wink Trant gave them, and the look on his face, left a lot unsaid. After the Captain returned to the bridge, Phen turned to Hyden with a whisper. "Do you think Captain Trant was a pirate too?"

"It takes a pirate to know a pirate," Hyden answered. He gestured at the floating city of ships, and the mass of hustle and bustle going on all across the bay. "I imagine that a lot of those people are pirates."

A few minutes later the Captain ordered the anchor to be dropped. He came back down to the rail then. "Get your things, Phen," he said. "Leave the book with Sir Hyden Hawk, but bring the copy you've been working on." Trant snarled roguishly. "If it turns out to be some great valuable bit of information, we don't want the old bastard to steal the original from us, do we?"

Phen giggled and felt an eerie sensation in his gut. Nearly three weeks of anticipation while on the ship had him giddy with expectancy. He couldn't wait to find out what the ancient book said. He was glad, though, that he, Hyden, and the others had agreed to keep the secrets of the Serpent's Eye to themselves. The crew of the *Seawander* thought that the old wooden box had been empty. Only the four who went into the cave knew of the jeweled ring that was dangling from Phen's neck.

Chapter Nineteen

The harbor master's office wasn't very roomy, Phen observed. It stank of pipe smoke, and the desk before him and Captain Trant was overcrowded with logbooks, scrolls, and other loose pieces of parchment. There was a great oak table in the middle of the room behind them. It was covered with documents. Maps, charting tools, and open volumes, all held in place by matching fist-sized brass bells, covered its top. Beyond the table was a big window that looked out over the bay. On either side of the window decorative nets full of rare shells, dried spider-fish, and other ship's paraphernalia hung from the ceiling. Behind the harbor master's desk was a series of shelves with even more stuff piled on them, including a perfectly replicated miniature of a six-masted cargo vessel that kept drawing Phen's eye. The harbor master himself, Phen decided, had probably been a real pirate at one time. He wore a patch over one eye, and had a knife scar that ran from his gnarled ear down to his throat. He was an old man. If asked, Phen would have guessed him to be a hundred. Nevertheless, he was sharp, grouchy, and talked like a proper pirate should talk.

"...fourteen barrels o' water, and three o' rum," he read Captain Trant's list of needed provisions back to him. "...eight o' salted beef, and how many rounds o' cheese?" He peered closer at the parchment, scowled, then looked up at Trant. "Where you going from here, Captain, that you'll only need two weeks' worth of rations? They told me your hold was near to empty. You're not planning on going to old Westland are you? I can tell you, you'll find no welcome flying the Blacksword there."

"No, sir," Trant answered. "We're going south to a little spring island that's off the charts." After he said it, he realized that he probably shouldn't have, but there were a dozen islands too small for human habitation about two days south of Salazar. He hadn't said which one.

"What in all the hells for?" the harbor master asked with eyes full of genuine curiosity.

Trant wasn't sure what to say. He had thought about this conversation at sea, but his respect for the man before him wouldn't allow him to even try and deceive. Phen noticed the Captain's hesitation and spoke.

"We're searching for a rare plant called *silverleafed skullrella*. My master wants to find a new source of it. It's used in casting spells."

"And you think this plant grows on the Pirate Isles?" the harbor master asked.

"The pirates are all Dakaneese," Phen said. "Master Sholt used to buy our silverleaf from the Isle of Borina, but the Red Priests have gone crazy since Pael called up his demon. The plant grows in the warm humid climate of the islands."

The harbor master looked at Phen for a moment then burst into laughter. "Where did you get this little turd, Trant?"

He stamped Trant's request, still chuckling. "What a bunch of nonsense. The pirates are all Dakaneese..." He was laughing now. "If it's not my business, boy, just say so. You can't lie to the devil."

Phen grinned sheepishly. "Sir, can you tell me whose banner is the eagle holding the snake? Their ship is huge. And who flies the lightning star?"

"The eagle is from the land of Harthgar. It takes more than a season to sail from here to there, and it's open sea the whole way. They say that there be walkin' talkin' people covered in fur, with tails like a cat's livin' in the hills there, but I ain't never seen one." He paused and handed Captain Trant his approved loading ticket. "The lightning star is the Dragon Queen of New Westland's."

"She's not a dragon queen anymore," Phen said with pride. "Hyden Hawk stole her dragon and set it free."

"Yes, well, try telling her that, lad. She's a tariff-happy witch is what she is. They have all the good lumber, and most of the good meat in Westland. Dragon or no, she's not afraid to make us pay for it all."

"Off the record, Ralphal," Captain Trant interrupted and changed the subject, "do you still have those old code legends you used to keep. Show him, Phen. Show him the transcription you've started."

Phen took out the log book he had been copying and handed it to the harbor master. The old man squinted his good eye at the page, turned it, and squinted some more.

"This is old script," he muttered. "Not pirate, but Elvish... Amazing. Where did you come across it?" he asked Trant, then turned his gaze on Phen.

"It's from an old text I purchased from a juju wizard on Kahna," Phen lied.

The old man laughed again. "Juju wizard..." he was still chuckling as he rose and hobbled across the room to a shelf on a wall that Phen hadn't noticed earlier. "I don't know how much use this will be to you. The dwarves used to inhabit all of Highwander. Old Port was a dwarven port long before the humans came along. Them short bastards never could get the hang of the sea. The elves used the port more than any. This is an old dwarven, elven, human translation. It was popular before the common tongue of man replaced the other languages. It's a rare volume and I covet it, but if Captain Trant will guarantee that I'll get it back when you return from your hunt for magic plants, I'll let you borrow it."

"He will," Phen said over Trant, who had started speaking.

"I can guarantee that, I think," the Captain glared at Phen. After a moment, he added: "I can assure you, Ralphal, your text will stay in my cabin exclusively. Our young turd can use it there, where I know it will remain safe."

"Very well," the old pirate said in a way that told them he had other matters to attend to. Captain Trant took the translation and said his goodbyes, then Phen thanked the harbor master for his help and they were on their way.

Once they exited the building and started back toward the docks to find Deck Master Biggs and the crew, Trant cuffed Phen on the back of the head. Phen didn't like it, but he knew he deserved the correction.

"*Silverleafed skullrella?*" Trant asked incredulously. "You must be daft. What were you thinking? And that talk of Borinian priests... Bah!" He shook his head, but there was a smile on his face.

That evening they all dined in a place frequented by captains and lesser lords. The fare was fantastic and the drink strong. They roomed at an inn called *The Sword of Salt*, in a section of the city where people, mostly from the eastern part of the mainland, caroused. The Captain explained that there were Dakaneese, and Westland sections of the city as well, but that they wouldn't be welcomed there. "You might find yourself among a crew of inked up Seawardsman over here, even a Valleyan horse trader or two, but that's far better company than you'll find anywhere else on the Isle of Salazar."

Phen didn't doubt it one bit. He had seen the aggressive looks that some folk gave them as they made their way back to the ship earlier.

The whole of the next afternoon Phen was in the Captain's quarters translating. Hyden invited Brady, and Oarly to take a walk through the trading lanes. It took only a short while for them to realize that Oarly was a spectacle for the sailors to jeer at. To avoid trouble, they made their way back to the inn and proceeded to get drunk in the common room.

Hyden didn't overdo it. In the morning, they were to leave port for the little island that lay four days to the west and south of Salazar, the island where Claret had told him they could find Barnacle Bones's ship. Then the Captain appeared and told him that, later, the two of them would be dining at Lord Buxley's manor with a couple of notable ship builders. Hyden had no idea who Lord Buxley was, but Trant spoke of him as if he were a powerful man in the greater scheme of things.

It gave Hyden a chill just thinking about what he had to do after they found the skull. If it was up to him, Zorellin's gourd could stay where it lay, and the ring Gerard took into the Nethers could stay where it was, as well. The goddess of his people had told him to go after the ring, though, and to do that he needed the

Silver Skull. She had helped him and Mikahl destroy the demon-wizard Pael and his minions. There was no way he could deny her. If she said that it must be done, then he would do it. She was a goddess after all.

Phen came down late in the afternoon looking for something to eat. He was excited to see Hyden there, and as soon as he asked for some meat and bread, he took a seat next to him and started telling what he had learned so far.

"The dead man in the cavern, the skeleton with a key around his neck, was an elven consort, whatever that is?" Phen said quickly. "His name was something like Heart of Leafy Oak, or Leafy Oak Heart, in our language. The ring he was carrying was a gift from the elven king or queen of the time."

Hyden nodded in appreciation of Phen's efforts as much as at the royal nature of the gift.

"The book is his journal. He started it the day he left the Heartswood. I guess that's where the elves used to live."

"Still is," Hyden explained. "The Heartswood is a forest that lies in some secret elven land, but it's magical. When the elves are in the Evermore Forest, it's because the whole Heartswood is in the Evermore." Thinking about elves made him sad, leaving his expression uneasy.

Sensing Hyden's discomfort, Phen picked up where he left off, just as cheerily as ever.

"He wrote his name, and his family lineage, which is two whole pages long. Then he wrote what his mission was—all on the day he started the journal. I haven't gotten to how he ended up in the serpent's lair yet, but I skipped forward and found a little bit about the king he was delivering the gift to." Phen stopped as his bread and meat, and a big goblet of ale arrived before him. Hyden poured most of the ale into his own cup then sent the barmaid after some fresh milk.

"You have to stay alert for these two," Hyden indicated the weaving form of Oarly perched next to Brady at the bar. Brady was sitting with his face down, passed out on the planks. "Deck Master Biggs will be around tonight, but Captain Trant and I are having dinner with a shipbuilder." He turned to Phen and grinned. "You and Talon get to watch over the drunks while we're gone."

"I'll be in Captain Trant's room working," said Phen through a mouthful of bread. "Master Biggs can watch 'em."

"Aye," Hyden laughed at Phen's studiousness. "At least keep an eye on Talon, then. Take a chunk of meat for him when you go."

"Aye," Phen replied. He took a long sip from Hyden's goblet when Hyden was looking away. When he had Hyden's attention again he told him he should probably take a bath before he went to a formal dinner.

Hyden laughed, but left to find the innkeeper. Phen took a few more sips of the ale. He was too intent on learning everything he could about the ring and the oak-hearted elf to let himself get drunk, but the fact he had distracted Hyden enough that he could get drunk if he wanted pleased him to no end.

*

Lord Buxley's table was set with golden dinnerware in a dark, candlelit, wood-paneled room that sported several grand seascapes and a fireplace the size of a small cottage. Hyden thought it was silly drinking from a golden cup and eating with solid gold utensils. It was nerve-wracking for him. He found himself worrying about proper manners with every word he spoke. Phen always called him a mountain clan hick, but hadn't taken the time to instruct him on etiquette. What few manners he did possess, he learned from Mikahl, who had been raised in a Westland castle, and Queen Willa, who, like an overly concerned mother, seemed to correct his every public move.

The fare was freshly killed game hens and honeyed pork with butter-soft rolls and vegetables. The wine was sweet, smooth, and very potent. Hyden managed not to embarrass himself through the feast and was glad when the conversation turned from technical shipbuilding jargon and general news from ports afar, to him.

Four men, all important to the shipping industry in one form or another, shared the lord's table with him and the Captain.

"So, they say you stole away Queen Shaella's dragon," the pudgy, but kind lord of the manor said to him. He obviously wanted to hear the story firsthand.

"Aye, uh, yes, sir," Hyden stammered. "The dragon—Claret is her name—wasn't serving her by choice. Shaella tricked her into a binding collar. She controlled the dragon through a similar collar that she wore." Hyden leaned back in his seat feeling awkward. "It was just a matter of getting the collar from her neck to mine."

"How, pray tell, did you do that?" another man at the table asked.

"I shot it from her neck with an arrow," answered Hyden seriously. "Of course, I asked the dragon to keep still when I did it."

"Of course," Lord Buxley shared a glance with Captain Trant and the others that showed his disbelief.

"Impossible," one of them said.

"Preposterous is what it is," suggested another.

Captain Trant shrugged. He was beginning to see that this dinner was not going as planned. He hadn't realized how out of place Hyden would be in a formal situation. An idea struck him. "You have a bow or two about, don't you? Let us see just how good our hero is with one."

An hour later Hyden was amazing them all with his talent from a balcony that overlooked the well-kept wooded garden at the rear of Buxley's estate. The sun had set and it was growing dark outside.

"Three this time," Hyden said confidently.

"Three?" Lord Buxley exclaimed. "And in the moonlight no less." He looked over the rail, down at a young boy who was just catching his breath from his last retrieval. "Keep your eyes peeled, Dannor. He's going for three this time."

Behind him, Hyden heard Captain Trant making another wager. He had won several already, but none as large as the one he was making now.

"Are you ready?" Lord Northall asked from beside them. Northall owned a company that specialized in making barrels, crates, and other containers for shipping.

"Aye," Hyden said, feeling completely at ease now.

Lord Northall threw one apple, then another, and a final one into the air, high over the garden. An arrow loosed as soon as the first apple was away. Hyden pulled his next arrow from where he had lined them across the flat top of the balcony rail. He nocked it quickly, then drew and fired high into the air. The third arrow he loosed at a downward angle as the last apple fell into the trees.

Captain Trant, who had seen Hyden Hawk successfully pull off this very feat from the rail of a rolling ship, had wagered a sizable purse against two of the shipbuilders this time.

"Go, Dannor," Lord Buxley ordered like an excited boy.

The young cook's son tore off across the lawn toward the woods to search for the fallen apples.

While they waited, Lord Northall brought up the subject of conversation they had all been waiting for.

"Captain Trant tells us you have an idea that might help us get the iron work we desperately need back under way. As you know, production has all but stopped here on the island."

"Aye," Hyden nodded. "It's simple really. Start buying back the Wildermont slaves from the Dakaneese."

"We're not slavers man!" Lord Buxley said indignantly. "We're honorable men."

"Let him finish, Morgan," one of the others demanded.

"Found one!" Dannor called up in a thin voice. "It's cored."

One of the gamblers moaned.

"Still two to go. He couldn't have gotten all three," muttered the other.

"Go on," Northall urged Hyden to continue what he was saying.

"There are so many Wildermont slaves that, if you bought them from the slavers in quantity, you could get them quite cheaply."

"We have been hearing that a mercenary named Dreg is already trying to use slaves to mine the Wilder Mountains and work the forges," Northall said kindly. "And as Morgan just said, Sir Hyden Hawk, we are not slavers."

"Dreg won't be in business much longer, I assure you," responded Hyden confidently. "I doubt he will live to see midsummer. He is too far away from Dakahn, and King Jarrek is deadly determined." Hyden unstrung the bow and leaned it against the rail as he continued. "I don't want you to be slavers. I want you to free the slaves you buy. Give them the coin to get to their homes and back to work. They are the miners and smiths you need. It won't be long before your supply is restored and they would owe you their freedom. Your investment would be returned, men would be freed, and without bloodshed."

"I found another!" a voice carried from the edge of the woods. "The arrow is still in it!"

"Haw!" Lord Buxley laughed.

"Start stacking it," Captain Trant told the men he'd wagered against.

"Not just yet," one of them grumbled. "There's still another out there, he may not have gotten it."

"Just start counting," the other gambler said dejectedly. "Don't you know when you've been had?"

Lord Northall was staring intently at a place in the moonlit sky. His expression showed that he was contemplating Hyden's idea. "We would need protection for those we freed so that they could work without being molested by sell-swords from Dakahn or skeeks from Westland." He turned back to Hyden. "This High King, is he a good man?"

"Mikahl is as honorable as they come," answered Hyden. Though he spoke with a proud reverence for his friend, he couldn't forget the incident with the squat weed. "He will find a way to protect those you free. I'll arrange it myself when I return from this trip. But I'm thinking King Jarrek will have it worked out long before then. If the rumors are true, he has already killed half a dozen Dakaneese overlords and freed thousands of his people."

"You're a rare kind of man, Sir Hyden Hawk," Northall said. "Most men would be trying to turn a situation like this into a profit for themselves."

"Found it!" Dannor yelled breathlessly. "It's hit. That's three for three!"

"Scoundrels like Captain Trant here are always trying to make a profit off of a poor fellow," one of the reluctant losers smarted as he started adding his coins to his fellow's pile.

"The man drank wine from a golden goblet this night, and he fancies himself poor," Trant shot back.

"The miners and smiths you so desperately need are all spending this night under a Dakaneese whip," Hyden reminded them. "Don't you forget it." After a beat his scowl turned into a grin. "Shall we try four?"

Chapter Twenty

Flick stood, with a long brass looking tube to his eye, watching from the prow of the zard ship *Slither* as the *Seawander* eased out of the bay of Salazar under the power of its water mage. The hood of Flick's plain black robe had blown back with the breeze, revealing his slick white-skinned head. He was glad to have the ship in his sights. He had used a dozen sparrows in the last few weeks keeping track of their location, and the cage was nearly empty. Each time he cast the spell to find the locating stone that was hidden aboard the *Seawander* he had to drink fresh sparrow's blood. He had no idea if he would be able to obtain more of the birds from the island. If he lost sight of them again it could become a problem.

"Keep us well behind," he told Slake, the sarzard captain of the ship. "But don't lose them." He handed the telescope back to the glittery green scaled lizardman.

The morning was bright and Flick pulled his hood back over his head to keep the sun from burning his scalp.

Down below, Drolz and Varch, Flick's two breed giant fighters, were snoring away. The whole ship vibrated with the irregular rumbles. The two primitive half-breeds were so big that they had to have special hammocks made to sleep in. They had to stay on separate sides of the ship too, otherwise it would list with their weight. Both were well over eight feet tall and together they weighed more than a wagon load of granite blocks.

Flick was glad that this would be over in a few more days. One of Slake's human crewmen had been sent to the inn called The Sword of Salt to spy on the hawk-man's party. The dwarf and the Wildermont soldier had been overheard saying that the island they were searching for was only four days south of Salazar. Flick hoped that it was so. If they lost the *Seawander,* and ran out of sparrows, he would be forced to go skulking back to Queen Shaella looking like an incompetent fool. He didn't want that to happen. He didn't want to kill Hyden Skyler either, but she had ordered him to do so. Flick had become Gerard Skyler's friend during the days of planning the theft of the dragon egg. It had been Flick who'd rowed Gerard through the marsh to the Dragon Spire. To kill his friend's brother would be hard, but he would do it. He wasn't exactly sure why, but he knew that he would do anything Queen Shaella asked him to.

Bzorch, the lord of Locar, was thinking deeply.

In a recent visit, Queen Shaella had told the breed giant that he could no longer have human slaves pulling his wagon-chair about the city. She told him he could no longer have human slaves at all. He didn't dare continue, but his cousin, Cozchin was trying to explain to him that, if he paid the humans to pull him about Locar, they wouldn't be slaves: they would be employees. Bzorch wasn't sure if Queen Shaella would approve. As much as he was growing to dislike her and her skeeks, he was still afraid of her considerable power. Tempting her wrath might jeopardize the little empire he was building just across the river from Castlemont.

Before the great bridge to Wildermont was destroyed, Locar had been the main center of land trade for Westland and most of the continent. Now, it was the one civilized place for the breed giants to live. Only a few hundred of their kind had chosen to remain in Westland. Men inhabited the city of Locar too, but the zard stayed well away. There was a base sort of revulsion there. The zard hated the breed almost as much as the breed hated the zard. If not for Queen Shaella's demand that they leave each other alone, Bzorch would have had zard-men pulling his wagon long ago.

Sitting in a big wooden throne in the lobby of a commandeered manor, Bzorch was contemplating why his kinsman, Vachen, had recently crossed the river to fight with the skeeks against the Valleyans. He had already dismissed the idea of having men pull his wagon chair around. As usual, Cozchin was thinking a few moments behind him.

"Is he going to live?" Bzorch asked as he rose to his feet.

The question threw Cozchin off for a few moments because he was still turning arguments for keeping the human wagon team in place through his primitive mind.

"Vachen?" the bewildered brute asked.

Bzorch was nearly ten feet tall, and as intimidating as a breed giant could be. He was the alpha of his kind and exuded dominance. The title that Queen Shaella had bestowed upon him, for his help destroying the bridge to the east, had little to do with the firm control he asserted over his people. Cozchin, at just over eight feet tall, was trembling as he looked up to meet his brooding lord's gaze.

"Yes, Vachen!" Bzorch snapped. His one, long caterpillar-like eyebrow formed a sharp 'V' over his deeply set eyes. One of his lower fangs was jutting up over his upper lip when he wrinkled his snout into a snarl.

Cozchin took a reflexive step back and spoke more quickly than he would have liked. "Lost his arm. He swears that the sword that wounded him was the same sword that old King Balton used to banish us."

"The rumors are true then," growled Bzorch. "Shaella said Ironspike found an heir." He started striding back and forth before his wooden throne while he continued to think. If he could capture the sword and its wielder he could increase his favor tenfold. If he presented Ironspike to the Dragon Queen, he was quite sure she would let him hand-pick a team of bug-eyed skeeks to pull his wagon cart anywhere he wanted to go. The idea made him smile and growl with mirth.

"Go find that big sneaky bastard Graven and send him here," Bzorch ordered. "Then see if Vachen can get one of his skeek friends to swim a trolley rope across the river north of Castlemont. After that's done, kill Vachen and those nasty skeeks he brought back."

"What are you going to do?" Cozchin asked, now enamored with the prospect of killing zard-men.

"I'm going to send Graven over to Wildermont to sniff around. Put the tower men on alert. I want all movement across the river reported. If Ironspike is really over there I will have it."

"Wheen the High King heers of thes ye'll find yee're in a fix," Princess Rosa chirped indignantly. "He well come for me, you knew."

"My dear Princess, you've hit the anvil squarely," Cole responded with a hint of mockery in his tone. "The High King is exactly who my queen hopes to attract with such lovely bait."

"Wheen he comes, yee'll regret thes affront."

Cole laughed, poured a dollop of water haphazardly over her face, and then tied the filthy sack back over her head. He gave a whistle and the covered tinker's wagon they were riding in lurched forward.

It's just a dream, Rosa said to herself as she sat up. Looking around, she realized that it had been just a dream. She wasn't jostling along in the back of the wagon with a pale-skinned wizard, but neither was she lying in the down four-poster bed in her mother's Seaward palace. She was in a circular chamber at the top of one of the Dragon Queen's lofty towers—the same place she had been for days and days on end.

She had all but given up on High King Mikahl's rescue. The first few days she half expected him to come swooping in on his magical horse to save her, but night after night she cried herself to sleep, each tear carrying away with it a small amount of hope.

He was afield in Valleya, she knew, dealing with her uncle, King Broderick. She understood that he might not even know she had been taken yet. If he did, he couldn't possibly know where she was being held. These realizations became clearer as the days wore on. It occurred to her that, if she really was bait, then Queen Shaella would eventually have to dangle her in front of her prey in order to draw him there. The longer Rosa spent in the tower, the less she was sure she wanted that to happen. Even without her dragon, Queen Shaella was a powerful force. Rosa didn't want Mikahl to become a victim too.

A soft humming sound told Rosa that the strange lift was coming up through the hole in the center of the plank floor. Food and wine would be on it. She would have to get it from the lift quickly or it would go back down, and she would go hungry. Several times she had been tempted to climb onto the platform and ride it down, but fear had kept her from it. Surely the Dragon Queen had her slimy lizards guarding the tower's exits.

To her surprise, it was more than just food on the lift this time. The hard but beautiful looking woman who'd tricked a dragon and stolen the greatest kingdom in the realm was standing there looking at Rosa with a curious smile on her scarred face.

"He's going to keel yew, jest like he deed Pael," Rosa snapped, surprising herself with the heat of her voice.

"I'm sure he will try, love," Queen Shaella responded. In her hand she held a pair of heavy shears, the kind saddlers use to cut through thick leather strapping. The jab about the demise of Shaella's father didn't seem to faze her.

"He's close, you know," Shaella taunted. "Your hero and that kingdom-less fool Jarrek have been harassing King Ra'Gren as of late. Ra'Gren had to kill a hundred of his Wildermont innocents to quell their meddling. He beheaded them himself, right in the market square at O'Dakahn." She spoke of these things as if she were talking about a poorly chosen gown that a rival lady had worn to the ball. "The question is will this glorified squire come for you at all?" Shaella stepped off the lift and strolled her way around the ill-kept room where her father used to keep his messenger hawks and pigeons. "A king has to think about his people first, you know," she laughed. "If he has a kingdom left to rule that is. This one might just decide that your life isn't worth it."

"Yeer wrong!" Rosa shouted, with new tears rolling down her cheeks. She hoped Shaella was wrong, but couldn't find much confidence in the thought.

"Don't worry, dear," Shaella said, taking Rosa's hand in hers. Before the young Princess could pull away Shaella cut half of the little finger from Rosa's right hand off with the shears. Rosa squealed in agony and clutched at the missing digit. Blood surged freely out of the wound and down her arm. Shaella laughed and quickly pocketed the finger she had snipped. "With this little bit I'll make sure he comes and finds you."

Rosa retched while trying to wrap part of her dress around the bleeding stump. She'd never felt this helpless in all her life. The room began to spin around her. Pain throbbed through her arm into her shoulder. Then her eyes rolled to the back of her head as she fainted on the floor.

In the empty plane of blackness that held Gerard, he savored the taste of the creature known as Kraw.

Days ago he had approached the great hell-born demon and was mocked when he asked for its help. Gerard's pent up hate, and his ill-formed dragon-born instincts overwhelmed him then. He attacked Kraw viciously. The devilish thing rained blow after blow down upon Gerard's plated skin to little or no effect. Kraw's demonic spells of hellfire and lightning did even less damage. Gerard tore into the demon like a starving dog into a plate of fresh beef. His own magical attacks of blinding white light, and his terribly sharp teeth and claws overcame the devil in a matter of moments. Soon, Gerard was wallowing in a great lake of thick black blood, and relishing the feel of the tingling power his soul was absorbing.

He was Kraw now. He was Gerard too, but Kraw was a part of him. Each and every bite of the devil's flesh he swallowed increased his strength. No longer just a disfigured dragon-blooded beast with a demon trapped in his mind, he was now a force to be reckoned with. He was as much demon as he was man, and as much dragon as he was demon. As his power grew, so did his thirst for it. He wanted to be free from this hell. Kraw's dark knowledge flooded his mind and filled his molten veins with raw power. There were places down here where Gerard could feast, he learned from the hell-born essence. Places where he might gain the power he needed to escape. There were lesser demons he could send to the world above to help Shaella. There were so many possibilities that he found himself tearing savagely into what was left of his meal so that he might move on to another. Already the red-robed priests who worshipped Kraw were on their way to Westland. They would do Gerard's bidding now. They would do all they could to help him and Shaella be together again. He would expend everything that he was to make sure of it, and he would devour anything that got in his way.

Chapter Twenty–One

Mikahl couldn't believe he was actually back in Westland. It would have been an emotional moment had he not been so wracked with nerves. He couldn't understand how the people of Southport were going about their business as if nothing were amiss. There were scaly green zard-men working among the humans, and no one seemed to mind. They were doing the harder labor that the men who'd been drafted into King Glendar's army had once done. The bustling city seemed to be thriving, and everywhere Mikahl looked he saw the yellow and black lightning star banner fluttering in the breeze.

Mikahl, Maxrell Tyne, and four Highwander soldiers, all dressed in the garb of Dakaneese sell-swords, only garnered the occasional glance from the people. Mikahl was torn between finding Lord Gregory and searching out Princess Rosa. He knew that if he could find Lord Gregory he would gain an adviser who understood both politics and strategy. Lord Gregory could also help him figure out what to do about Rosa, and the Dragon Queen. He had no idea where the Princess had been taken, but he had some information about Lord Gregory's whereabouts from the mercenary, Tyne, so his course was decided for him. He wasn't sure Princess Rosa was even in Westland. With Queen Shaella wanting his head so badly, he was keenly aware of his surroundings. He only hoped the Lion Lord hadn't been caught by the Queen's soldiers while snooping around looking for Lady Trella.

According to Tyne, if Lady Trella wasn't a Dakaneese captive, she was most likely a refugee on the Isle of Salazar. A few dozen nobles and merchants had gotten word before Shaella's attack and had fled Westland by ship. Salazar had taken them in. The Westland nobles that King Ra'Gren successfully ransomed had been sent to the island as well. Tyne knew this because he had escorted a few of them there himself.

Tyne spoke to a man who saw Grommen riding around in a fancy carriage with a secretive person of wealth. The two had stayed at an inn that Mikahl remembered as the Golden Lion, but was now called the Dragon's Doorstep. Tyne said he hoped to find them still there, but if not, he assured Mikahl he would gather as much information as he could. Mikahl saw no sign of a fancy carriage as they approached the upscale place. When they gained the entrance, Tyne suggested that Mikahl and the other men wait outside. Mikahl had been the King of Westland's personal squire for several years, and Lord Gregory's before that. He didn't want to be recognized. Against his better judgment, he agreed, knowing that if Tyne decided to betray him, he would be in a serious bind.

For a long while they waited near the entryway trying not to look nervous or suspicious. The Highwander soldiers looked as out of place as Mikahl felt. Their fidgeting and pacing seemed to betray them as impostors. The truth was it made them appear angry and impatient. This wasn't the section of the city where idle sell-swords were welcome, and a nearby candlemaker soon started complaining.

From down the street a sarzard grumbled something in his tongue to a human underling who translated the question to the candlemaker. "What is the issue? These men are obviously waiting for their employer who is inside the inn."

"They're scaring away my custom is what they're doing!" the man responded indignantly.

Mikahl heard the man's voice over the din and saw the sarzard, and the others gathering around him, staring back at them curiously. Instinctively, his hand reached over his shoulder and fingered Ironspike's hilt. He didn't dare pull the sword here. Its powerful magic would draw unwelcome attention to him and his men. Casually, he moved his hand to his hip where Lord Gregory's sword hung in its scabbard. It was all he could do to keep from drawing it to try and fight his way out of this predicament. The Highwander men were alert now too, but none drew steel. Mikahl's only comfort was that he knew all it would take was a word for these men to follow his lead.

As the sarzard, and his group, approached, a few possibilities ran through Mikahl's mind. If they were forced to fight, he thought they could make quick work of the zard-man and his troop. Hopefully they could do it without attracting much attention. They would have to silence the loud merchant who was now pointing and gesturing angrily, pulling passersby into the ordeal. They could make a run for it, but there really was no safe place to run. A human wearing a guard uniform similar to the sarzard listened to the lizard-man hiss and growl something that none of them could understand. He then stepped forward and spoke.

"Sarzard Askolzz said you have to wait somewhere else," the man said with more than a little uneasiness in his voice. "You're scaring away the custom."

Mikahl was relieved that none of his men had drawn a weapon. "But our captain is inside," Mikahl replied, easing his hand away from Lord Gregory's weapon. "He should be along soon."

The man gave him an odd look. Mikahl realized that his accent wasn't even close to Dakaneese. If anything, it gave him away as a Westlander. The man spoke to the sarzard in a growling series of hisses and spurts. The lizard-man shook his head and replied. The man translated. "He says there are several taverns in the immediate area. One of you can stay and wait for your captain. The others must get out of the street." The man looked to the sarzard as he clicked and hissed some more. "He says that if you were not here on business he would take your weapons." The translator swallowed hard then looked Mikahl directly in the eyes. "I would go to the Otter's Den if I were you. It's just around the corner there." The man pointed up the street away from the candle maker's shop.

Mikahl noticed a crowd gathering at the other end of the block. He nodded and asked one of the soldiers to stay, and then with a nod to the guardsmen, and the sarzard, he led the others up the road to find the Otter's Den.

The guardsmen had recognized him as a Westlander, he knew, and the look they'd shared conveyed that it was all right. There was something more to the look, and for the first time since being back in Westland, Mikahl got the sense that not everything was going as smoothly as it appeared in the city.

Maybe the people were just bustling along as usual, or maybe they were just pretending to.

The looks they received from the customers at the Otter's Den showed that their presence was both surprising, and unwelcome. Apparently, Dakaneese sell-swords had the favor of the zard, but not the Westland men. Mikahl could imagine that many of these people's liege lords, and maybe some of their family members, had been captured for ransom, or sold to Dakahn as slaves. Mikahl took a chance and loudly ordered a round for him and his men. His obviously Westland accent threw the people staring at them out of kilter, but not for long. A pair of intoxicated men started toward the bar with a look of ill-intent in their eyes. Mikahl cursed Maxrell Tyne under his breath. The last thing he wanted to do was get into a brawl with his own people.

"There you are, my lumps!" a loud Dakaneese voice blared out angrily from the open door of the tavern. Mikahl gave a sigh of relief. "There you are searching for the bottom of a cup when we've a package to retrieve from Lake Bottom." The gleam in Tyne's eyes told Mikahl that his statement wasn't just intended for the customers of the Otters Den. The man had found out something, and Mikahl felt a glimmer of hope surge through his body.

Grommen couldn't believe he allowed the Lion Lord to talk him into breaking into the old stronghold at Lake Bottom. Yet here he was, in the late of the afternoon, standing in a darkened chapel, waiting on Lord Gregory to finish a search of his former home's interior. To Grommen's surprise, it hadn't been hard to get in. There was a secret door hidden behind a section of wall that ran double for a short way.

Footsteps sounded outside the chapel and Grommen dropped between a pair of pews and lay still. The door opened and a harsh orange glare shone in for a moment. The torchlight receded as the door closed.

Grommen feared they were already looking for the Lion Lord. His golden cow was probably hiding in an attic, or scooted up under a bed awaiting capture. No, he decided. He had to give the broken down brawler a little more repute. This had been his home since birth. No doubt he knew every crack and cranny of the place. He—

"Hey," a voice whispered, just above Grommen's head, causing him to jolt.

The door hadn't opened again had it? No, not since the torch-light had come through. He would have known by the shadows if someone came in then. His heart was hammering in his chest as he quietly reached for his dagger.

"Where did you go?" the voice whispered again.

Grommen relaxed, it was the Lion Lord, but how had he gotten back into the chapel without alerting him? "I'm here," he groaned as he got back to his feet. "How did you get back—"

The Lion Lord shushed him. "Follow me."

They exited the way they came in and, to Grommen's surprise, two horses waited patiently outside the hidden entry. He could hear shouts and hisses of alarm around the building. A feeling of dread came over him. "What did you do?" he asked.

"I set the barn on fire," Lord Gregory laughed.

He was in such high spirits that Grommen thought he might have gone mad. "What would you do that for?"

"To cover the escape of a few old friends," Lord Gregory grinned. "She escaped them Grommen," he laughed out loud. "She, and Lady Zasha, got away."

"We're likely not to get away, man," Grommen grumbled. "We need to move."

"Aye," Lord Gregory nodded. "Follow me."

To Grommen's disappointment, instead of going back south into the woods, the Lion Lord headed around the wall toward the front of the keep. Reluctantly, Grommen spurred his horse to keep up with the Mad Lion. He wasn't about to let a bunch of skeeks kill or capture his monetary future. His blood ran cold when he saw Lord Gregory stop in front of the main gate tower and begin yelling and screaming up at the zard-men posted there. He could tell by the surprise on his companion's face that Lord Gregory hadn't expected the gate to open so quickly. The two of them had to dance their horses around the crossbow bolts that were suddenly flying at them. Grommen heeled his horse and caught up with the Lion Lord. He whacked Lord Gregory's mount on the rump with this meaty hand, but the horse reared up instead of bolting, nearly flinging the Lion Lord to the ground. Lord Gregory's experience showed through as he held on and soon they were in a headlong gallop that seemed futile at best.

A pair of zards riding one of their huge geka mounts was almost on them, and another geka with four zard-men on its long scaly back wasn't far behind. Grommen was glad that they ended up fleeing southward. The last thing he wanted to do was go farther into Westland. They ran the horses as fast as they could gallop for a long time and managed to put the scene behind them. Only then did they stop and walk the animals for a while.

The road they took led toward a town called Midway. It edged the western coast of the continent. On their left side was a line of a dense sea-blown forest; on the right, a vast expanse of cobalt and gray that smelled of brine. They stopped and rested in the darkness, but eventually they heard the shouts of the pursuing zard-men calling and they were forced to mount up again. The horses were tired, and the gekas were gaining on them. When dawn finally broke, a glance behind told Grommen they would soon be overrun. Already an errant crossbow bolt had nicked his shoulder. It seemed hopeless to continue fleeing, but neither they, nor the horses, were ready to give up. It wouldn't matter, he decided. They had little chance of getting away now.

"Look," Lord Gregory shouted. He was pointing up ahead.

In the distance, a small encampment of men looked to be stirring to see what the mad approach of hooves and claws was about. The lookout was standing and pointing back at them while calling out to his companions. The look of bewilderment on his face turned to drop-jawed shock as Lord Gregory and Grommen raced right past him. Lord Gregory recognized the man, but was so astounded that he didn't stop until a radiant blue glow lit the morning like a beacon. By the time they reined their horses to a stop, the sound of battle coming from behind was clear.

Maxrell Tyne had gotten the horses and some supplies from the merchant who was unfortunate enough to still honor Dreg's company some credit. From what the innkeeper had said, the merchant Grommen was escorting was named Ellrich Alvin and he had enquired about the state of affairs at Lake Bottom far too many times for his interest to be just curiosity. It amused Tyne that the sarzard had become so lax in their duty that their queen's greatest enemies could pass under their slimy noses like they were just sell-swords and merchants.

The group rode out of Southport toward Midway. They could have forced their pace and found an inn at the little town that stood halfway between Southport and Lake Bottom, but they decided to camp along the way instead.

Mikahl chose the last watch of the night because he liked to go through his ritual series of exercises with his sword in the predawn light. Out on the road, away from civilization, he wasn't afraid to draw Ironspike and work through his positions and repetitions. This was a time of clarity and peace of mind that he couldn't seem to find elsewhere. That first morning, going through his routine on Westland soil, had been fulfilling. Just knowing that he could get this close gave him hope. Thoughts of how to take his homeland back from the zard began to form. It could be done, he finally decided. And with that certainty came confidence.

They rode through Midway that afternoon and made camp just before dark. Watching the sunset on the Western Sea again, after so long, filled Mikahl with resolve. It was the very same sunset he had seen a million times from the wall of Lake Bottom stronghold, and from the tops of the many towers at Lakeside Castle where he had grown up.

The next morning, after his routine, he'd just finished washing the sweat from his skin when the approach of galloping horses caught his ear. He was glad Ironspike was in its scabbard now, and half thought that maybe its glow had attracted whoever it was that was riding down on them. That wasn't the case, he learned, when he saw the two men being chased toward the camp by several armed and angry zard-men riding their huge lizards. When he recognized one of the men as Lord Gregory, he decided to end the chase on the spot. Without hesitation, he drew Ironspike and poised to attack.

Chapter Twenty-Two

The island was far bigger than Hyden imagined it would be. He had envisioned this part of the quest as being the easiest. He figured he would have Talon fly over the whole landmass. He would look through the hawkling's sharp eyes and locate the decaying ship. Then they would retrieve the Silver Skull and be on their way. After seeing what the lay of the land was, he knew it wasn't going to be that simple. But he found that, after the monotony of the long voyage, he wasn't disappointed.

While Brady and Oarly supervised the transfer of supplies from ship to shore, Phen explored the beach. Through Talon's vision, Hyden surveyed the island from overhead. It was nothing more than a roughly circular crown of jagged rocky hills that jutted up out of the ocean around a bowl-shaped valley. The density of the foliage in the valley made it nearly impossible for Talon to see what was below the canopy. Nothing resembling a decaying ship revealed itself in the hills around the shoreline, so Hyden assumed that what they were after lay somewhere in the jungle of the island's interior. Seeing that it might take weeks to search the area on foot, Hyden tried a different approach. With his eyes open he sought out Talon's vision and made several passes over the valley. He was pleased to find a faint aura of magical power radiating from an area not far from the jungle's edge, at the base of the steep section of the surrounding hills. What he saw was an oblong glow with a crude trail that tapered from it like a teardrop in the jungle floor.

Hyden had to close his eyes to see the terrain through his *familiar* more clearly. The shared vision was not necessary anymore. Talon worked his way down, fluttering from limb to branch to vine under the canopy. With the hawkling's large wingspan, sustained flight under the trees was nearly impossible—there were just too many obstacles in the way. From a perch just over where Hyden had seen the larger portion of the aura, he was now looking at a great oval mound of overgrown earth. The trail that tapered away from the mound ended at the gaping mouth of a dark cavern right where the forest met the surrounding up-thrusts of rock.

Hyden judged the location to be a little more than a day's hike from their landing point. He was glad they'd anchored where they had. Captain Trant had chosen the spot because of the shelter provided by the shoreline.

Out on the sandy beach it was only slightly breezy. Hyden decided that they would camp on the island for the night and start out in the morning. Seeing that it was already getting late in the day, he asked Oarly and Phen to seek out some firewood while he and Brady finished the task of unpacking the supplies.

Several of the Seawander's crew came ashore to stretch their legs. Deck Master Biggs was ordered to take three of his men and accompany Hyden's party on their journey. Biggs brought with him a bottle of brandy, and after the rest of *Seawander's* crew had returned to the ship, he passed it around the fire. Neither Hyden nor Phen drank, but Brady took a sip, and Oarly and the four seamen proceeded to get good and drunk. While Brady sharpened first his sword, then a machete, Phen told them what he had learned from the elf's journal over the last few days.

"The ring was for King Chago," he said. "From what I remember from Master Lunkle's history lessons, King Chago was a tyrant. I can't figure out why the elves would have wanted to give a gift to one of the worst rulers the realm had ever known."

"Maybe they sent the gift before he became that way," Brady suggested.

"No." Phen shook his head. "I thought that a possibility at first, but Loak, that's what I call the elf, Leafy Oak Heart, wrote about some of Chago's horrible deeds, like when he had his men ride down and kill all the people from the village of Ultura, or when he had half the people at Summer's Day put to the sword."

"I thought Summer's Day was considered sacred ground?" commented Brady.

"Not then, only after Pavreal trapped Shokin in the Seal with Ironspike." Phen spoke matter-of-factly. "The pact that made the Leif Greyn Valley sacred ground was the pact Pavreal made with Claret to guard the Seal."

"That's true," Hyden agreed. The great red dragon, Claret, had told him as much.

"But the Spire has stood there longer than man can remember. That makes the Leif Greyn Valley a special place. That's why no kingdom has ever laid claim to it."

"Aye," both Hyden and Phen agreed at the same time, as they often did, resulting in a laugh.

"It doesn't say why the elves were giving the ring to the tyrant?" Hyden asked.

"It may, but I haven't gotten that far yet. Loak details each day meticulously. I'm a quarter of the way through the journal and they've only been at sea a week."

"Just skip through it," Brady suggested as he studied by the firelight the edge he'd honed on the machete. On the other side of the bonfire Oarly and the seamen all burst into laughter at some joke one of them had told. From beyond them came the sound of the waves rolling in and the faint creak of the *Seawander's* rigging.

"Would you skip through your training drills?" Phen asked Brady. Then to Hyden he added, "He probably does. I haven't seen him practice once this whole trip. No wonder he can barely last five minutes with High King Mikahl."

"Anyone who can last a full minute with Mikahl is either extraordinary with a blade, or just plain graced," said Hyden reverently. "I've seen Mikahl dance with a demon and send it skulking away like a scolded cur."

Brady gave Phen a satisfied grin that turned into a silly smirk.

Hyden looked up at the starlit sky and watched Talon circle down and land by Phen. He was thinking of the day Loudin the hunter had died in the Giant Mountains. Through Talon's vision he'd watched Mikahl cut the hind legs and tail off of the hellcat that killed their friend. That was also the day Hyden found his magic. He'd healed a mother wolf that had broken her pelvic bone in a fall. Weeks later her two pups led Hyden from the dying tree in Dahg Mahn's trials to the door of the old wizard's tower. Trying to keep Loudin's memory from ruining his mood, he turned to Phen.

"Teach me a new spell—that scrying spell." His chest swelled as he continued. "I've learned the light spell, the flaming finger, and the jolting grasp." He leaned closer and whispered, "I'm going to get Oarly with that one soon."

Brady laughed at them.

"I've almost mastered the vanishing object," Hyden said, "but half the time I can't make the item reappear." He gave Phen a serious look. "Where in all the hells do things go anyway?"

"Another dimension, I think," Phen said. "Work on that one until you have it mastered both ways before we start another."

"Aye," Hyden nodded reluctantly then picked up a small sea shell to practice with.

"I'll be over here," Brady said. He looked more than a little nervous as he crept over to the far side of the fire with the others. Already he had seen Hyden make one of Oarly's old boots go away never to be seen again. He didn't want to be next.

Morning brought with it a sense of excitement. Hyden was glad for the men Captain Trant sent with Deck Master Biggs. They loaded up all the packs, ropes, and digging tools they could carry. Brady took the lead with his machete. Hyden followed with the elven longbow Vaegon had given him held at the ready. Phen was next, carrying a long steel dagger that he'd gotten in his dealings with the juju wizard who'd sent them into the Serpent's Eye. The three deckhands were next. They were too weighted down to carry a weapon in hand, but each dangled a well-kept short sword at the hip. Oarly and Master Biggs took up the rear; Oarly, with his wide, double bladed axe slung over his shoulder, Master Biggs with a heavy crossbow wound and ready to fire.

The passage through the humid undergrowth was far slower than Hyden expected. Brady had to hack and slash every foot of their path. Birds, and other things, cackled and cawed from everywhere. Undergrowth shook violently as large creatures fled their intrusion. Clouds of yellow flies swarmed around their heads, and sweat poured from their bodies by the bucketful.

"This is not as fun as it sounded like it was going to be," observed Phen.

"Aye," half of the group said in unison, but nobody laughed.

Hyden didn't have it quite as bad as the others, at least not when Talon was perched on his shoulder. The presence of the hawkling seemed to deter the pesky flies. Phen noticed this, and with a piece of dried meat devilishly lured the bird to his shoulder for a while. Behind them, the sound of Oarly's labored breathing, and his constant grumbling competed with the buzz and hum of the insects. A persistent cry, shrill and angry, resounded from somewhere above. Whatever it was kept shaking the tree limbs, but was never seen.

Around midday they came across a clearing that had been formed by a fallen tree. They stopped and rested, eating a meal of dried beef, sliced cheese, and sea biscuits. All of them drank plenty of water, enough that Hyden began to worry if they carried enough. They didn't stop very long. The persistant yellow flies seemed to like them even more when they were still. A few grueling hours later the flies suddenly went away. Phen was the first to say something about the welcome relief.

"Oarly must have shit," he called to Hyden and Brady ahead of him.

"What?" Hyden chuckled back over his shoulder.

"The flies have gone," Phen giggled. "Oarly must have shit his britches again and fogged them away."

"I heard that," the dwarf said behind them. "It's more likely that your foul breath grounded them."

Phen, and a couple of the seamen laughed, but they were all startled to silence when Brady shushed them.

"Can you hear that?" Brady whispered at Hyden.

A deep buzzing sound was resonating up ahead of them. It sounded like a swarm of something far larger than the yellow flies. Talon leapt from Hyden's shoulder and flew ahead. All eyes watched Hyden's concentrated expression, searching for a hint of alarm or fear.

Hyden saw the same thick jungle flora ahead of them: huge heart-shaped leaves, long dangling vines, and clusters of bright blue flowers that grew out of patches of thorny brambles. Talon followed the sound, fluttering from branch to branch as he went, taking it all in. Subtle alarms were going off in the hawkling's mind, the instinctual warnings that all creatures seem to have built into their consciousness, but so far curiosity was dominant. Hyden felt the alarms too, like tiny voices saying, "Not good. Fly away. Go around." The hawkling ignored them bravely, and eased forward as Hyden bade. Then from a stone's throw away they saw the source of the sound. Talon perched on a limb and froze in place just long enough for Hyden to see what it was. Then he fled back to the group, as quickly as he could fly through the dense jungle.

It was a nest of hornets, Hyden saw in that moment. Not ordinary flower-buzzing bugs, but huge red hornets the size of cucumbers, with finger-long venomous stingers sticking out of them. The nest was the size of a pavilion tent, and thousands of the creatures buzzed here and there through the trees. The skeleton of something lay near the hive. Another hump of something even larger seemed to undulate with the wasps as they swarmed over, feeding on its flesh. Hyden hadn't been able to make out any more. Talon's instincts had thankfully taken over and forced him to fly away.

Trying not to alarm the others, Hyden pointed to the left of the line they had been traveling, and spoke in a near whisper. "Let's go that way for a while," he suggested. He ignored the barrage of hissed questions from the others. He didn't want to tell them that no bow or sword would save them if those things set upon them. He doubted there was even a spell that might let them escape so many poisonous flying things. There was no other choice but to skirt well around the nest. Later, he might tell them exactly what he'd seen.

After a long while, he had Brady circle them back around toward their original course. He kept Talon ahead of them, searching for signs of anything that might be a danger.

"Look," Phen exclaimed, pointing off into the trees. When Hyden saw it, his heart nearly stopped. A lime-green snake, as big around as a man, and easily thirty paces long, slithered away through the lower branches just beside their trail. When it was about a hundred strides away, it startled something in the undergrowth. Whatever it was growled fiercely and rattled shrubs and leaves as it darted away from the snake directly toward them. Phen stood open-mouthed and wide-eyed as a dark shadowy form bounded straight at him. He raised his dagger feebly when the cougar-like creature revealed itself. Teeth bared, it leapt at him. It was covered in quills like a porcupine, and Phen could do nothing as it pounced. Just before tooth and claw found Phen's flesh, the creature sprouted two more quills, each with fletching on the ends. The alert seaman behind the boy booted him to the ground just in time to avoid disaster. Both Hyden and Deck Master Biggs had loosed arrows at the creature. In the leafy shrub where it crashed down, a wicked-looking spiked tail thrashed about a moment before stilling.

"Well theres be fresh smeat for sssupper," Oarly said cheerily. The slur of his speech betrayed the fact that he had taken more than a sip or two of Biggs's brandy during the day.

"It's a blasted overgrown lyna," one of the seamen said as he looked closer at the kill.

"Could be," Master Biggs nodded.

"I'm not sure we want the smell of fresh meat close to us in this place," said Hyden as he helped Phen to his feet.

" 'Tis true, Hyden Hawk," Oarly replied robustly. It was obvious that he had overcome his seasickness. "These Island creatures won't be smelling fresh meat around this dwarf, lad. They'll be a smelling scorched meat, from a raging fire, and they'll fear the smell of it too."

Hyden had to agree that the smell of scorched flesh and a huge fire would most likely dissuade anything from snooping too close to the camp. It would probably keep the bugs away too. The thought of the huge hornets swarming them in the dark made him shudder.

With speed, and precise skill, that seemed as out of place as it was surprising, Oarly beheaded, gutted, and skinned the creature. Within moments the feline thing was tied by its legs to a limb that the dwarf cleaved from a tree with his axe. Phen took it upon himself to put one end of the spit on his shoulder while Oarly took up the other. It was an awkward looking rig, as the dwarf was easily a head shorter than the boy.

"You'll want to pick a campsite well before dark, lad." Oarly told Hyden. "We'll need plenty of time to find wood and set up alarms."

Alarms? Hyden asked himself as they started back under way. He found himself wondering, not for the first time, how Oarly had earned the title of master, and what he might be a master of. He was finding himself glad to have the dwarf along, though. He would never have thought of setting up alarms around the camp, and if he had, he wouldn't have had the first idea of how to go about it.

Later, when Oarly suggested they stop, Hyden didn't argue. It wasn't a clearing by any means, just a place where the trees were farther apart than elsewhere. The group was surprised when Oarly shrugged out of his packs and went to work.

"Stand back," he said. He sipped from a flask, put it away, and wiggled his brows cheerily at Phen. With his axe held out he began spinning around and around in counterbalanced lurches of speed. Teetering and tottering as he went, he used his sharp blade to mow down the undergrowth to a manageable level. When he was done, he leaned on the haft of his weapon and stumbled in place for a moment. When his eyes rolled back out of his head he pulled a small shovel from his belt and threw it three feet wide of Hyden. "Dig us a fire pit. I'd let Brady do the honors, but he's wore from swing'n that machete all day. You two come on," he barked at a couple of the seamen, and off they went into the jungle. The two men took turns carrying back armfuls of dead fall that Oarly was chopping into manageable chunks. After a fire was going, and the meat was spitted over it, Oarly took out a pack that contained a sizable ball of twine and what might have been a dozen little bells.

"Come on, Phen," Oarly ordered. "You'll have to get up on my shoulders to help me get our web strung over some of these branches. I learned this trick from the Spiderton Tinks and it has to be done just so."

"Who are the Spiderton Tinks?" Phen asked and Oarly obliged him with the tale as they went about stringing twine.

"Amazing," Brady commented to Hyden as they watched the dwarf show Phen how to make a silent approach on them next to impossible. When his tale, and the rigging, was done, Oarly took a piece of sizzling meat from the thing roasting on the fire, sniffed at it, then wolfed it down.

"Mmmm, that's tasty," he said as he cut another piece. "Master Biggs, pass me that flask." Then to Hyden, "You'll want three two-man watches tonight. Me and the boy done did our part." Oarly swigged deeply from the tin container a few times, and passed it back to the Deck Master, who passed it on to his men. No sooner had the dwarf lain back on his bedroll, than he started to snore.

"That right there," Brady said. "That sound alone will keep the fiercest of creatures away from us."

Hyden nodded his agreement with a distant smile, remembering Mikahl and Vaegon making almost the exact same comment about the sounds Loudin of the Reyhall used to make while he slept. He couldn't help but remember the fine times they'd spent around a fire very much like this one. Neither could he forget that most of them never made it out of the Giant Mountains.

Chapter Twenty-Three

At the last possible moment Mikahl rolled into the direct path of the lead geka. The creature was moving too fast to snap at him with its needle-sharp teeth. Neither it, nor its riders expected anyone from the party on the roadside to intervene in their chase. The cold-blooded beast leapt over Mikahl intending to avoid the glowing blue blade he carried. As Mikahl hoped, it hadn't leapt very high. With an upward heave of such force that it made Mikahl go to his knees he thrust his sword into the creature.

The geka shrieked in pain as its own momentum dragged its body across the razor sharp steel. It churned at the end of its leap, knocking Mikahl farther into the road, but the beast was dead before it found the earth again. The force of its limp impact with the rutted dirt threw the two zard-men riding its back over its head. They landed badly and before they were done tumbling Grommen was hacking into them with his heavy sword.

Mikahl didn't get the chance to regain his feet before one of the zard-men riding the second geka leapt from its back down onto him. The geka's driver reined the creature headlong into the camp and let its gnashing jaws go to work. Two of the Highwander soldiers were caught off guard by the attack. One of them was bitten almost in two. The other, who had been attempting to shove his companion out of the way, had his arm chomped off at the elbow.

The horses picketed at the forest's edge brayed and bucked wildly. Maxrell Tyne charged toward the road to help Mikahl, drawing his blade, and cursing their sudden involvement in a battle with the skeeks as he went. It was only then that he realized one of the men who was being chased was the one they were seeking. One of the fleeing riders, brandishing nothing more than a carved walking stick for a weapon, was now charging his horse back toward the road. With a violent swing, he clouted the zard-man that had tackled Mikahl in the side of its green-scaled head.

In the middle of the camp, the other two zard-men were dismounting their geka; one with a short sword raised high, the other with a long barbed pike in its clawed hands. The geka driver stayed on his mount and fired a crossbow at Grommen. The bolt struck the big fighter, leaving the wicked missile protruding from his shoulder.

Tyne saw that Mikahl had found his feet and started toward the unprotected flank of the thrashing geka. The remaining Highwander soldier put a serious gash across the big lizard's snout and was now ducked behind a tree near the horses, waiting for help. The geka lunged and snapped at him with futile effort. Finally, it screeched and hissed, and latched onto the nearest horse. It shook its head violently back and forth. As big as the geka was, it couldn't sling the horse around, but it did lift the screaming steed off of its hooves, snap its tether, and tear a huge chunk of flesh away. The horse half bucked, half fell sideways into the trees with a loud crash, thrashing and whinnying pitifully. The geka, after several jerking chomps on the horsemeat, raised its head high and chugged the substantial morsel down its gullet.

Unable to keep the big lizard from exposing itself, the geka rider hissed a curse and leapt from its back. The Highwander soldier charged from the trees aiming his sword at the geka's chest just as Maxrell Tyne ran a sword into the creature's gut. Both blades struck deeply. The geka reared in pain and twisted its tail around, knocking Tyne to the ground. The Highwander man barely got his sword free and dove out of the way. The zard who had been riding the creature had no intention of continuing the battle and broke into a tail-slinging run back up the road the way they'd come.

"Stop him!" Grommen yelled to whoever was listening. He wasn't close to his horse, and he was in terrible pain, or he'd have chased the zard down himself. Tyne heard him, and stumbled from the trees to get mounted, but when he started to climb on a horse, a fierce grinding in his knee dropped him.

The zard-man before Mikahl looked at him with its blank black orbs and hissed menacingly. Then it glanced at Ironspike's glowing blade. It started toward Mikahl, feigned a claw one way then rolled around twisting to rake its claws from the other. Ironspike whistled as it cut through the air. Mikahl dropped to knee level and the zard-man tried to leap back, but it was no use. A deep furrow across its scaly upper thighs opened up. Mikahl stepped out of range of its thrashing claws and tail and glanced up the road at Lord Gregory. Beyond his friend he could see the fleeing zard. The other pair of Highwander soldiers were engaged with the remaining zard-men in the camp. Tyne was trying to get there to help them, but limping badly.

Mikahl pulled Lord Gregory's sword from his hip and hurled it at him with a grin. "Lose something?" he yelled. He didn't even look to see where the thing ended up. Instead, he started off toward the Highwander men who were fighting desperately to defend themselves.

Mikahl held out Ironspike's tip, and in the symphony it sent coursing through him, he found the single melody he was after. Sharp red darts of magical force shot from the weapon into the zard wielding the pike. The thumping impacts sent the lizard-man sprawling across the roadside.

"Clear out!" Mikahl yelled. The Highwander men wasted no time falling to the ground and rolling away. A streaking blast of lightning consumed the remaining zard. Before it could register what happened it was charred to a husk.

Seeing his own sword twisting through the air toward him filled Lord Gregory with a surge of uplifting energy. He spurred his mount to meet the blade, and with effortless grace snatched it out of the air by its hilt. As if it knew what he intended, the horse under him turned and lurched forward after the fleeing zard. Lord Gregory knew that, if they let it get away, a hundred more would be on their trail. There was no telling what sort of system the skeeks used to deliver messages, but all it would take was a single bird to Southport and half of Queen Shaella's army would be looking for them. He gained on the fleeing creature, but had to rein his horse toward the side of the road to avoid a whizzing crossbow bolt. After it loosed at Lord Gregory, the zard-man tore off into the forest. Lord Gregory drove his mount headlong into the trees after it. He ducked and twisted in the saddle, narrowly missing a low hanging branch and took a whipping snap across his face from a smaller limb, but he didn't slow his pursuit. His horse leapt a chunk of dead fall then darted around a gnarled old stump. Just as he caught up to the zard, it looked back with fear showing in its black eyes. Lord Gregory's horse stepped on the zard's tail just as the Lion Lord's blade swept down. The result was the lower half of the zard-man being trampled under the horse while the upper half rolled away into a tree trunk where it smashed to a halt with a wet crunch.

Lord Gregory trotted back out onto the road rubbing the welt on his face. He was bloody from the branches he'd ridden through, but he didn't care. He was hefting the familiar weight of his father's blade in his hand and feeling more hope than he had in ages. Lady Trella had escaped the invasion of Westland with little Zasha, and Mikahl had found him and returned his treasured heirloom. The Lion Lord of Westland couldn't help but let out a roar. To his delight, his primal call was answered by the roar of another young lion. Mikahl was feeling it too.

The Highwander soldier who had lost his arm was so near to death that Maxrell Tyne pushed his blade quickly into the man's throat and walked away. The man had been semi-conscious at best, and they were in no position to give proper aid. Mikahl saw the deed and swallowed his anger. Tyne had done what he couldn't have, and it was probably for the best. They pulled the barbed bolt from Grommen's shoulder and patched the wound as best as they could, then the five of them rolled the big geka carcasses to the forest's edge and dragged them out of sight. It wasn't easy. They were as big as three horses each, but it had to be done. After that they dragged the rest of the dead into the forest too. This part of the road wasn't heavily traveled, but all it would take was one passerby to raise an alarm they couldn't outrun.

As soon as the road was cleared they started back toward Midway. The first ship out of Westland might get them out before queen Shaella learned of the mess Lord Gregory had left back at Lake Bottom Stronghold, but if they lingered they were done. There was no time for reminiscing. In spite of everything Mikahl wanted to say to his one-time lord and mentor, he held his tongue. Lord Gregory did the same. There was plenty he wanted to learn about the state of affairs abroad. Neither could suppress the joy of being reunited, though, especially since the last time Mikahl had seen Lord Gregory, the man had been one heartbeat away from death, and Mikahl had been nothing more than a frightened squire.

Lord Gregory, before Queen Shaella's invasion, had been the liege lord over most of Southeast Westland. With his hood down he might be recognized in Midway, but in his defiant mood he didn't care. The people of Westland had always loved him and he knew they wouldn't betray him to the zard. He hoped to use his status to get a fishing captain or a small cargo ship to sail them away from Westland as quickly as possible. They could easily find a ship if they rode through Midway and continued on to Southport, but the extra day on the road would put the group, and more importantly High King Mikahl, at great risk. Lord Gregory had taken the knee before Mikahl just before the hellcat had attacked them in the Giant Mountains. He had known all along that Mikahl was King Balton's intended heir. His duty to protect his king overrode all other thoughts in his mind, save for those of getting to his lady wife.

He told Mikahl his thoughts as they galloped into the outskirts of Midway. Neither of the two sell-swords, nor the Highwander soldier could offer a better plan, so Mikahl agreed.

The people of Midway were wary of the travelers. The road suddenly cleared as the bloodied group came passing through. Lord Gregory and Mikahl both looked on in sorrow at the emptiness and gloom that hung over the once lively town. The people were still there, they were just hiding. The smell of cook fires was in the air. The fall of peaked curtains was seen as they made their way toward the wharf. Fresh laundry hung in the late morning sun and a few older men labored away with their heads down and eyes averted.

"Look," Mikahl pointed down the way toward the dock as it came into view. Only one ship was tied to the moorings. It was a large two-masted vessel with a double row of oar portals along its side. It was a slave-powered galley, and Lord Gregory's heart sank when he noticed the banner flapping lazily from its mast: the trident of Dakahn.

Just then the door of the tavern beside them burst open, and a young, shabbily dressed woman hurried away with tears in her eyes. A drunken man stumbled out after her. Gregory put a restraining hand on Mikahl when he started to intervene. The man was wearing fairly new studded leather armor, and the fancy hilted sword strapped to his belt spoke of either authority or experience. He paused when he noticed them looking down at him from their horses. He half growled, half laughed then stepped back into the doorway.

"Captain Konrath, we've got company," he said with a heavy Dakaneese accent.

Maxrell Tyne eased his horse up between Mikahl and Lord Gregory. "Pirates," he said under his breath. "Follow my lead."

Under normal circumstances Captain Konrath would have ignored the men outside. They posed no threat to him. He had eight men on the ship watching over his supplies and the slave rowers, and six more men were not too far away enjoying the hospitality of the Midway tavern girls. These waters had been picked clean, had been for a time. He was of a mind to hire out to Ra'Gren, and a few more men behind him would increase his leverage. Looking through the tavern door, he could tell that the men outside were armed. A half dozen ways to either hire them, or cheat them of their belongings, passed through his head.

He gave a nod, and a pair of his unoccupied men followed him out. Like the Captain, they were well armored and carried quality steel. The Captain though, standing well over six feet, with legs as big as tree trunks, and a leather mask plate that covered one of his eyes, was by far the most imposing of the three. When he stepped out of the doorway and the morning sun caught his grisled visage, even the horses backed away. There was a hole in the mask to accommodate the covered eye. The white of that orb seemed far larger than normal, like there was no skin around the socket. It was unnerving to look upon.

"Seeking work maybe?" he asked in a gravelly voice.

"What sort of work?" Maxrell returned. His Dakaneese accent was as pronounced as the pirate's.

"Ra'Gren's hiring all the swords he can gather," the pirate captain said, putting as much promise as he could into his voice. "Could be steady through the summer they say. It seems that King Jarrek and that so-called High King have been causing the old bastard some trouble along the Valleyan border. Killed a handfull of overlords and cut loose their slaves."

"Guarding land borders then?" Tyne asked with distaste showing plainly on his face.

"Some of it," the Captain took a pull from the bottle in his hand. "But from what I hear, he's gonna try and take all of Wildermont while it sits near to empty." The man leaned in and lowered his voice, his one brow narrowing conspiratorially. "My man said there be plenty of valuables to pick through. Slave whores aplenty too. That fool Glendar left behind as much as he stole. And those that stay around and fight for Ra'Gren are 'sposed to get a bit of Wildermont land as payment for the service."

"I'll fight for gold," Tyne responded with a smirk. "I got no need for land or trinkets. Besides, we have business on Salazar. Might be we could find you when we're through." He paused for effect, and gave Mikahl and Lord Gregory a knowing glance. "If we still need any coin then."

At the sound of the word 'coin' Captain Konrath pricked his ears up, wondering what sort of business these men had in Salazar that might afford them the luxury of turning down months of good paying work. Salazar wasn't even out of his way. Maybe a day, but he could provision his ship there instead of in Southport and save a handful of coin by avoiding the Dragon Bitch's tariffs. Even if these men didn't sign on with him, he could fatten his purse and save some expense by taking them to Salazar on his way back to Dakahn.

"Salazar is where you're headed then?" the pirate gave a gap-toothed grin that combined with his menacing face plate to make him look utterly insane. "If you've a few coins for passage, the *Shark Tooth*'s your ship, and I'm your captain."

"If you can pull anchor right now, I'll fill your fist with coin," Tyne jingled his belt pouch and glanced at the two zard-men sitting just inside the tavern's doorway.

Captain Konrath's grin vanished. He elbowed the man beside him and mumbled an order. A moment later the call for "All hands!" was ringing through the tavern. In less than a turn of the glass, Lord Gregory, High King Mikahl, Maxrell Tyne, and their two men were on the *Shark's Tooth* under sail for Salazar.

Chapter Twenty-Four

Morning came all too soon for Hyden and the expedition. He and one of the seamen had taken middle watch, and though nothing had tripped Oarly's alarm, a large shadowy form had paced the undergrowth at the far edge of the camp. When Hyden looked at it with Talon he could see its aura and knew that it was a predatory feline creature, possibly the mate to the lyna beast that had been their supper. It didn't linger, but sleep was a long time coming for Hyden. Between Oarly's snoring, the alien sound of the island jungle, and the whispering of the last watch he didn't sleep at all.

While Oarly and Phen rolled up the twine and stowed the little bells, Hyden investigated the jungle floor where their nocturnal visitor had been. Prints as big as his open hand, and similar to the paws of the creature they had killed, were plain to see. Hyden wondered if the huge hornets had been feasting on a similar creature. Then he wondered if the porcupine-like quills that coated the animals were some sort of natural defense against the flying insects.

The things that had shaken the lower tree limbs and shrieked at them the whole of the day before were apparently busy elsewhere. Morning passed in relative peace as they worked their way through the jungle. A smaller cloud of flies found them, though. The steady buzz droned on and on, not succeeding in drowning out the clanking, grumbling sounds of their passage.

Near midday they came upon the mound that Hyden had seen. It humped up nearly twenty feet, was easily as wide, and probably sixty feet long, by his best guess. A little hump tapered away from the main mass in a nearly straight line toward the cavern. It corresponded with the aura Hyden had seen when Talon flew over. Up close it looked far less like an overgrown ship's hull than Hyden thought it would. Oarly paced down its length and then climbed over it. He kicked at the ground with a look of deep concentration on his face.

After a while, during which time the others drank water and munched on dried beef, the dwarf eased up to Hyden. "We found your dragon," he said. "Maybe the ship's not far away."

"The dragon?" Hyden asked.

"It is," said Oarly. "That's the bulk of its body there." He pointed to the mound. "And this long tapering roll is its tail." He trailed his finger down the long hump that pointed toward the cavern. "And that, I suppose, was its lair." He grinned and shrugged. "It must have crawled out to die. At least it looks that way. It was a big mother in its day. Must've been near three hundred feet from tip to tail." He turned and pointed out into the jungle. "I'd bet that old boot you made vanish, that not too far out there you'll find its skull." Oarly glanced back at the cavern and seemed eager to be into the earth. "Can't wait to see what's down there. Might be the big blue bastard dragged the ship down to its hoard."

"Might be something else has taken up residence in there, Master Dwarf," said Deck Master Biggs as he stepped up amongst them. He corked his flask after a quick sip and handed it to Oarly. "Might be all kinds of things living in a hole that big."

Oarly swallowed. "Aye," he nodded. "But we got a couple of half-arsed wizards, a few swordsmen and some arrows. And I got me axe. All we need now is some torches and we are off."

"We're not going to go traipsing in there yet," Hyden said, thinking of the giant serpent that had slithered in on them back on Kahna. "It'll be dark soon." The thing that had stalked the shadows last night crossed his mind as well. "Let's make a camp here first, and then a few of us will take a look and see how far back it goes."

"Bah!" Oarly growled, but he still stomped away and went to work. "Anything to keep a dwarf from getting under the ground."

Hyden chose to build the camp near the dragon mound. Something about the area felt safe to him. Maybe because it was relatively free of trees, or maybe because of the magical aura he'd seen radiating from the earth that covered the wyrm's carcass, he wasn't sure which. While the area was being cleared and the fire pit dug, Phen ranged off and found the mound that presumably held the dragon's skull. When he told them of the discovery, Hyden could see the raw excitement in the boy's eyes. He hoped he hadn't brought Phen into too dangerous a situation. He had been planning on leaving Phen at the camp with Master Biggs and the seamen while he, Brady, and Oarly ventured into the cavern to look around. After careful consideration, he decided that Phen's spells might come in handy in a pinch. That, and he couldn't bring himself to disappoint his eager young friend. He could remember being Phen's age, and he had been allowed to hunt the formidable Giant Mountains and scale thousand foot-high cliffs for hawkling eggs.

"Should we set up the pavilions?" Master Biggs asked once the fire was roaring in the pit.

"Aye," Hyden said. "I have a feeling we'll be here a day or two. There is no sense in letting the bugs have a free meal while we're here."

One of the seamen who had been off gathering wood with Oarly came hurrying back. "We found some flowing water," he called out as if they had found a treasure trove. "The dwarf sent me back to gather up the empty skins."

"That's one less thing we have to concern ourselves with," Hyden said more to himself than to anyone else.

Before long there was nothing left to do but explore the cavern mouth. Oarly was as eager as Phen to venture into the imposing looking hole. Brady had long since donned his chain mail shirt and strapped a packful of torches to his back. Oarly carefully stowed his battle axe and took out a heavy pick that looked no less deadly in his hands. He slung a coil of rope over his shoulder then dangled some smaller rock-chipping tools from his belt. When he took a torch from Brady and made to light it in the fire, Phen told him that he and Hyden could make all the light they needed with magic.

Oarly lit the torch anyway then looked Phen in the eye. "If the ceiling caves in and separates us, or if a giant bat flies down and tries to eat you for dinner, lad, I'll not be finding my way back in the dark."

After hearing that, Phen decided to keep his suggestions to himself.

Hyden strung his bow and strapped a full quiver of arrows to his back. He gave Phen his long dagger to carry. Phen dutifully strapped its sheath to his belt and fixed his brown mage robe so that it wouldn't interfere with the handle if he needed to draw it.

From above, Talon shrieked out a call and circled them. In his mind, Hyden told the bird to hunt itself a meal, but to stay close to the entrance. He wanted a pair of eyes outside as well as in. After that, they started into the darkness.

Oarly led, followed by Hyden and Phen. Brady, with his sword in one hand and a torch in the other, took up the rear. Oarly's brand wavered and threw wild shadows back across the dirt floor, but the flames were not bright enough to light all of the cavern. They could have been standing in a field. Phen cast his orb light spell and remedied the problem. The cavern was about twenty paces across, and easily as high. It was relatively clear of debris and the stone was worn smooth from countless years of the great dragon sliding in and out.

Within moments they came across some long exposed bones. A fairly neat pile lay to one side, the skeleton of one of the dragon's meals, by the powdery yellow looks of them. The walls were patched with a furry gray mold, which hung down in beard-like dangles here and there.

"Look," Oarly said, pointing to a track that had been pressed into the dusty floor. It looked fresh. The huge paw print was sharp and defined, and a lot bigger than the one Hyden had studied outside the camp. Its shape was similar, though.

"Won't kill that bastard with an arrow," Oarly said, before moving on.

They could feel a breeze from overhead. The air was warm and salty, but once they passed the natural vent, the cavern took on a dank musty smell.

Hyden glanced back. The opening of the cave looked like nothing more than a distant rabbit hole from where he stood. He decided there was still a bit of daylight left, but as they moved deeper into the lair he told himself that he wanted to be back in the camp by full dark. He leaned his bow against Brady and cast his orb of magical light into existence with a proud grin. Brady gave him a nod of approval as Hyden took back his weapon.

"Pretty good, huh?" Hyden asked.

"When you get the dwarf's boot back from wherever you made it go, I'll be impressed," Brady joked.

Phen moved past Hyden during the exchange and was now easing up behind the dwarf with a mischievous look about him. The radiance from Hyden's magical orb made the shadows thrown by Phen's light far less noticeable. Oarly was oblivious to the boy's approach. Hyden saw what was about to happen and prodded Brady to get his attention. Phen had a handful of the moss he'd scraped from the wall. Hyden stifled a laugh as the boy threw it over Oarly's head and shoulders and yelled, "Spiders! Gods they're everywhere!"

Oarly yelled and spun, swatting at himself furiously. For a moment he looked like a dog chasing his own tail. He nearly set his hair on fire with the torch he held. His barks of terror turned quickly to curses as Hyden and Brady roared with laughter. Phen jumped around laughing and pointing at the dwarf. "Just try to scare me again with tales of giant bats, you old grouch," Phen threatened with mock severity.

"Ah, lad," Oarly grumbled, fighting a grin. "You got me good, lad," he chuckled. "But you don't have any sort of inkling what you just started between us."

"You'd better be wary of Hyden Hawk," Phen giggled. "He owes you a good one."

"If the scalding that cinder-pepper put on his arse didn't warn him away," Oarly gave Hyden a hard look, "then only the gods can save him."

Hyden could feel the heat on his backside when Oarly spoke the words. He would never admit it, but after the incident he had long considered letting bygones be bygones. But now getting Oarly back was a matter of pride, especially since Phen was in the game too. As they started moving deeper into the cavern, Hyden decided that he might be wise to worry about Phen as well as Oarly. The boy was clever, and wouldn't be able to resist getting him if he had the chance.

A few dozen paces later the cavern turned to the left and the air became ripe and fetid. Oarly pointed to a half-eaten carcass lying to one side of the floor, then to a respectable size of scat piled across the way. The hum of insects buzzing about the decaying meat filled their ears. Oarly turned, and was about to speak when a deep rumbling growl came out of the gloom behind the reach of their light.

"No sense in running, lads," Oarly started as he hurled his torch out into the blackness. "Might as well kill it now."

They could see the thing in the twirling light of the torch. It was another of the quill covered felines, but this one was twice as big as a horse. Hyden instinctively loosed an arrow at where he thought he'd seen its eye glinting in the darkness, but the creature was already charging. Brady ran up to meet it, with his sword held out ahead of him. Hyden stepped in front of Phen and loosed another arrow. This one struck the creature in the chest, but it didn't even seem to notice.

"For Doon!" Oarly yelled and darted with surprising quickness out of the way of a swiping claw. He swung the pickaxe at the thing's side and it struck deeply. The weapon was yanked out of the dwarf's hand and remained stuck in its flank. As Oarly growled his anger at the loss, a spiky tail whipped around, and with a deep thump caught him square in the back.

Hyden loosed again but knew that, unless he could hit the creature in the eye or the neck, his efforts were futile. With Phen behind him he backed them toward the cavern wall. Brady slashed and ducked the snapping set of slobbery teeth, then thrust his blade into the creature's chest. It left a wicked gash, but the angry beast didn't falter. A wild arcing claw caught Brady along his side and sent him tumbling toward the far wall. Had he not been wearing the chain mail shirt, he would have probably lost his guts. Instead, one of the creature's claws was torn from its paw when it got caught in the links. Brady's head was gashed wide and he didn't seem able to get up when the creature started at him again.

Oarly, with two spikes sticking out of his back, and blood flowing freely from the wounds, managed to shrug out of the rope coil. As the creature closed in on Brady, the dwarf ran up behind it and chopped at the root of its tail with a shovel that had been dangling from his belt. He struck true and the tip began curling and uncurling uselessly as it trailed along the floor.

The beast roared, turning to face the dwarf in an acrobatic spin. The animal's attack was so sudden that Oarly was left defenseless. The creature swiftly bit down on his shoulder and forced him to the ground.

Hyden wasted another arrow, hoping to draw it off of the dwarf, but Phen shoved him out of the way and charged toward the mêlée.

Hyden wanted to stop him, but recognized that Phen was casting a spell. He hoped it was one that would get the thing off of the dwarf because Oarly appeared savagely wounded. He decided that he couldn't help save Oarly and protect Phen at the same time, so he sprinted toward the battle. He was moving around toward the thing's head to try and find a shot when Phen's spell took form.

All around the beast's rear legs the cavern floor began cracking and splitting as hundreds of green wormy-looking things sprouted up. They grew quickly into snaking tendrils and in a matter of seconds the back half of the animal was wrapped in a twisted tangle of rope-thick thorny vines.

The beast roared and thrashed, trying to pull free, but couldn't manage it. Hyden darted in, and with all his strength pulled the bloodied dwarf away.

Brady stumbled to his feet and, after taking in the situation, he shook the cobwebs from his head and charged in from the side. His sword sank deep into the monster's rib cage. He didn't even pull the blade free. He just scrambled back against the wall and let the thing's movement tear its insides to shreds on his steel.

"Is it dead yet?" Oarly moaned.

"No, but its well on its way," Hyden said. Already the creature was wallowing in a great pool of its own blood.

"Be getting me pack, lad," Oarly said to Phen with a terrible look on his face. He was drenched in blood and a deep black hole that Hyden could easily put two fingers in could be seen on his back. His shoulder had several smaller teeth wounds. Phen grabbed the satchel and brought it over to the dwarf.

"What, Oarly?" he asked, rummaging through the pack with tears welling in his eyes. "What is it you want?"

"Give me the flask lad," Oarly coughed and blood sprayed out at them in a froth. "I want to drink my last."

Phen twisted the lid off and handed it to the dwarf. Hyden's heart hit the bottom of his stomach and he felt tears streaming down his cheeks.

"Oarly," Phen said through his tears. "You can't die."

Oarly trembled with the effort of taking a swig of his drink. With a grasping groan his eyelids fluttered shut and his head fell limply to the side.

"No!" Phen wailed. The sheer agony in the boy's voice made Hyden shudder.

Brady staggered over and put his hand on Hyden's shoulder. He was too shocked to say a word.

"Lad," Oarly rasped in a barely audible whisper. "Come closer lad." Phen leaned down and put his ear close to Oarly's bloody mouth. "What is it, Oarly?" Phen asked through his tears.

A long silence followed, and Oarly slowly sucked in a long deep breath. Then he went still. Phen sobbed, but the dwarf suddenly jerked up, shaking Phen violently, startling the other two out of their wits.

"Ha!" he screamed directly into Phen's face as loud as he could. "You think it's that easy to kill a dwarf?"

Chapter Twenty-Five

"As gullible as a trio of beardless maidens," Oarly said, after he downed the remaining contents of his flask. "My own mam done me worse than this for getting my fingers in the mushroom pie."

Despite their anger at being had in such a horrible manner, the others were grinning. It seemed Oarly had grown on them. Phen was fuming, but Hyden thought his red scrunched-up face might be holding as much embarrassment as anger. Getting so emotional over Oarly's mummery seemed to bother the boy as much as the dwarf's gloating.

"Come on," Hyden finally said, helping Oarly to his feet. "Let's get you back to camp and tend you proper."

"Nah, lad. We're already here," Oarly said as he shouldered the rope, snatched up his pack and started back down into the cavern. "I'll let that fargin thing die a while longer before I pull my pick out of it. We can look a bit deeper while we wait."

They didn't have much of a choice other than to chase after the dwarf. Brady, whose sword was still embedded in the dead beast, looked at it a moment, then with a curse followed after the group.

The tunnel twisted and began angling downward, and before long a faint light could be seen ahead of them. As they neared the slightly illuminated area they saw that the tunnel opened up into a great chamber that was lit from above. A dying ray of evening light cut through the vast space at a nearly horizontal angle, one side of the visible line was a few shades darker than the other. A huge hole in the upper reaches of the chamber was easily big enough for the old dragon to fly in and out of. With the light of Hyden's magical orb, and Oarly's torch, there was just enough illumination to show them that they didn't want to proceed just yet.

"There's your fargin spiders, lad," Oarly said. "Red Feasters, meanest spiders a digger ever came across." Oarly was holding his torch so that the flickering flames lit up the edges of a nearby crevice that had been webbed over. The spiders themselves were bigger than a man's fist, and black with wicked red splotches. Phen winced at the sight of them.

Hyden surveyed as much as his eyes could take in. Stalactites and stalagmites reached toward each other at the edges of the main opening, but the large central area was clear of obstruction. Another, larger, tunnel could be seen across the opening, leading downward and away from the vast space. The opening was mostly covered by another web. The black and red-colored spider resting at its center was as big as a water barrel. When Oarly lit a second torch, and hurled the one he had been carrying out into the cavern, more webs could be seen further down the shaft. A good way up above them there appeared to be a scallop of shelf where a third tunnel possibly led away. Neither place could be investigated without provoking the severe looking arachnids, and Hyden found that a relief.

"From midmorning to just after midday," said Oarly as he looked up at the opening above them. "That's when the light will be best for us. We'll have to burn them out, lads." He turned toward the companions. The blood that ran from his mouth, and the gash on his chest, had matted everything from his beard down and made him look very near to death. "Unless you want me to go take care of them now?" The determined grin on his macabre visage held no hint of jest.

Brady shook his head in disbelief.

"Nah, nah," Hyden said with a shiver. "Let's go get your pick, and Brady's sword, and we'll burn them out on the morrow."

Hyden studied the layout of the cavern a moment then started back out of the tunnel after the others. He would do some exploring with Talon later, he decided. There was plenty of room for the hawkling to maneuver. He'd eliminate a whole lot of wasted effort if he could find a sign of Barnacle Bones's ship without putting the others at risk.

Back at the camp, Phen used a minor healing spell to close up the gash on Brady's head and bring the swelling down. Phen tried to work the spell on Oarly, but the now thoroughly intoxicated dwarf wouldn't have it. The two wounds on his back were not as bad as they had originally seemed. The thick padded leather vest he always wore had taken the brunt of the damage. The tear in Oarly's shoulder looked terrible though. It was deep, and it wouldn't stop bleeding, even after they compressed it with cloth for a time.

Oarly almost came to blows with Master Biggs when the seaman poured a good dollop of his liquor into the wound. They all assumed that the anger was from the pain until Oarly swore that if the man ever wasted that much drink on something as trivial as a minor injury again, there would be a scuffle. Oarly then proceeded to take a dagger, the blade of which had been heated to a glowing red in the campfire embers, and with a grunting huff, laid it across the wound. He seemed more concerned with not burning his beard than he did with the searing heat, at least until his flesh sizzled. He slung the dagger away then, and gave a primal yell. Then he gave Phen a curious look, grunted something no one could understand, and passed out completely.

Hyden was thankful when Biggs ordered the three fidgeting seamen to stand guard over them for the night. Oarly and Brady were already asleep, and Phen was yawning between his dozing nods. Hyden was as nervous as the crewmen, which was just as well, because before he went to sleep he wanted to fly with his *familiar*.

A half-moon lit the night sky to a silvery blue. The the area around the dragon's remains was the only place Hyden could see that hadn't been overgrown. He was glad for it. He climbed to the top of the dragon's mound and sat down, marveling at the liveliness of the stars until he was relaxed enough to seek out Talon's vision. Then he took flight.

The hawkling was circling high overhead. Hyden felt the sated sensations the bird was feeling, and the added weight of the meal it had eaten. Talon's presence in his mind was welcome and comforting. The encounter in the tunnel had been terrifying. He hadn't thought about it much yet, or said anything to Oarly about it, but the dwarf's charade hadn't been appropriate. Hyden had buried many close companions in his short time, and he found no humor in that sort of thing. He would tell Oarly what he thought, but he would do it when the time was right. At the moment he was curious about what they had seen today.

It didn't take Talon long to find it. The gaping hole was midway up the far side of the rocky hill that rose out of the jungle beside them. As Hyden hoped, the cavern opening faced the southwest. Oarly was wrong: It would be midday or after when the sunlight lit the chasm best.

Talon spied a steep fall of rock near the cave mouth. At the bottom was a dark jumble of broken trees and scree. The stuff would have continued falling into the sea had it not wedged itself in to a section of narrowly formed rock.

Up the slope from the cave mouth there was a scattering of wind-blown trees clinging to the rocky soil with all they had. Above that, ominously silhouetted in the moon's light, was a jagged looking ridge. If he could have stood at the base of the cave looking south, Hyden knew that all he would see would be ocean. Far below Talon, the sea churned and sprayed as it slammed into the rocky shoreline.

Eventually the hawkling flew into the opening. The side of the mountainous formation that faced the sea seemed to be only twenty or thirty feet thick. Talon felt as if he were flying into a hole that had been chipped into a giant egg. From what Hyden remembered of the inside of the great cavern, the spider-web tunnel led back toward the middle of the island. The scallop higher up had to be fairly shallow. No light had crept through that area when they were inside, so he was certain that it was nothing more than a suspended shelf. It occurred to him, as Talon circled back up out of the opening and perched on the lip, that it wouldn't take much to fracture and crumble that whole side of the cavern. What bothered him most, was that looking down through Talon's eyes, he could tell the area they had been standing in earlier was a good bit below the level of the sea. If the rock ever did collapse, the ocean water would come rushing in and flood everything inside.

He doubted any of that was going to happen, so he sent Talon soaring down into the maw to search for signs of the ship. Talon wouldn't go near the webs, and saw nothing resembling a pirate ship anywhere else. Disappointedly, Hyden decided that they would have to burn the spiders out, as Oarly had suggested, and then see where the lower passage took them.

Talon was growing weary, and Hyden still intended to use his minimal magic to heal the dwarf while he was asleep. Calling Talon back to him, he opened his eyes and made his way back to the camp. Inside his tent he fondled his medallion and noticed the same strange tingle it had given off in the serpent's lair. He watched as the prismatic leaps of light swirled and darted away from the jewel. They seemed to flare to life, and burn out, all within a foot of the dragon's tear. Some leapt in arcs, some in zigzagging streaks, others in curling loops. It was hypnotizing, and it didn't cease as he made his way into his bedroll.

He had meant to tend Oarly, but found himself in a mesmerized trance. When he lay down he held the medallion out in front of his face. He watched it until it carried him into a dreamy state where the static hum of magical energy seemed to surround him as if he were submerged in it. Out of the dancing lights a familiar figure began to form, just as it had formed out of the great water fountain at Whitten Loch. With a sad smile, and wide open arms, the White Goddess turned to face him and spoke.

"Hyden Hawk," she started in her sweet musical voice. Hyden found that, even though she was made of nothing more than a swirling white mist, her full, voluptuous figure flustered him. "Be wary Hyden," she warned. "When you recover the Skull of Zorellin you will find great danger with it. Be very careful." Her image began to fade back into the cloudy whirl.

"Wait!" Hyden yelled, but his voice turned into a thick oily smudge that spread across the surface of his vision. The ripples it caused soon wavered into a pair of sparkling glimmers. They formed into great yellow orbs that were split by sharp sword-like pupils. The hot smell of brimstone and sulfur filled his nostrils. The eyes he was looking at blinked from the bottom up. They were dragon's eyes, and they were familiar.

A deep voice that sounded like shattering boulders filled his ears.

"Hydensss," the great red dragon Claret hissed to him. "Not all dragons are scapable of understandingss. Some dragons do nothing but hatesss. Do what you must. My tear will sprotect you, but you smust protectss your friends. Do you remember who your friendsss are Hydensss?"

"Always," Hyden heard himself gulp the response.

Claret's voice wavered. "Doos not hesitate Hydensss." The vision began to fade. "Do what you mussst."

"You *must* get up," Phen was saying. Hyden woke with a start as Phen nudged him with his boot. "It's almost midday Hyden. Even Oarly's up and about."

A sharp call came from somewhere above the tent. Talon's crying shriek conveyed Hyden's mood.

"All right," Hyden managed, but the blanket of sleep that was still lingering over him was thick and heavy, so Phen shook him again.

"All right, all right," Hyden forced himself up onto an elbow. Through the fabric of the tent it was clear that his young friend hadn't been exaggerating. It was bright outside. Probably near midday. He noticed that Phen, as usual, seemed to be on the edge of bursting with excitement.

"I'm not leaving until you're out of that bedroll," said Phen. "On Oarly's orders."

"Aye, then," Hyden huffed and rolled to his feet. Phen eased out of the tent while Hyden readied himself for the day.

Phen also had a dream, a revelation about the ring he found in the Serpent's Eye. The discovery made clear why the elves were going to give it to the tyrant. Loak hadn't been an emissary, he'd been an assassin. It wasn't the ring he was going to give the King. He was going to use the gift to get close enough to kill the man. The ornate wooden box, the story of the gift, was all a charade to get Loak close enough to do the deed. King Chago, Phen finally remembered from a history lesson, had killed a pair of elves for nothing more than chasing an arrow-shot stag out of the Evermore into the kingdom lands. Once Phen remembered that, the rest fell into place. The question he had debated all morning, while the others slept, was how the ring would help Loak assassinate King Chago. Phen finally came to the conclusion that Loak would need no help killing the tyrant, but he might need help escaping after he did.

Phen, so excited that his promise to Hyden was forgotten, slipped the ring on his finger. He didn't feel a change, but he knew he had guessed correctly. A quick trip around the camp, where he paused to make faces in front of the seamen and feigned a punch at Master Biggs's face, with absolutely no response, not even a flinch, confirmed it. The ring made him invisible. To further test the ring's limits, he loomed over a sleepy-eyed Oarly. The dwarf grunted and grimaced with pain as he worked to pull on the new boots Hyden had purchased in Salazar. Phen took a flaming brand from the fire and lifted it before the dwarf. He expected Oarly to see the branch he held, but all the dwarf saw was the fire hovering in the air by itself.

Phen had to laugh. Even now, almost two hours later, Oarly was trying to convince Brady that a fire nymph had come to him.

"...ball of flame as big as a melon, I tell you," the dwarf was saying. "Lifted right out of yon fire and hovered before me. It's a sign," Oarly declared with wide eyes. "Burn the spiders out as soon as possible. I tell you it's a sign."

"What's a sign?" Hyden asked as he came squinting out of his tent.

Phen wanted so badly to tell him of his great discovery, but he remembered his promise, and was ashamed since he had broken it.

Hyden noticed the wave of visible unease that passed across the boy's face. "What gives, Phen?" Hyden asked, ignoring Oarly's recounting of the fire nymph story.

Phen looked away from Hyden's gaze and shrugged, feeling even worse now for not answering truthfully. "Oarly saw a fire nymph," he said. "We've been waiting for you all morning."

"It's a sign, Sir Hyden Hawk," the dwarf broke in. "We've got to get back down there and burn those feasters out."

"If we don't," Brady chimed in with a wary glance at the stumpy-legged dwarf, "this fargin lump will never shut up. I think he took an injury to the skull yesterday."

Hyden laughed and directed his attention from Phen to the others. "How do we go about it then? I've never burned out spiders before."

Oarly's plan was simple. Hyden agreed to it, and not long after, the four companions, along with Deck Master Biggs and one of his men, stood at the point where yesterday's exploration had ended.

The two seamen carried buckets of water and extra torches. Hyden's part was easy. All he had to do was fire arrows wrapped in oiled cloth into the spiders and be ready to assist the dwarf if he needed it. Oarly had the hard part. How the dwarf was up and about and so ready to take on the spiders with the pain of his fresh wounds, was beyond any of them. He supposed it was a testament to the potency of Master Biggs's liquor. Nevertheless, Oarly insisted on being the one to douse the webs with lantern oil.

They counted three spiders. Oarly raced down toward the webs on his short stumpy legs calling out, "For Doon! For Doon!" as if he were charging headlong into a battle. He slung the highly flammable liquid onto the first web and its maker, and himself as well. Then he ran back and huddled behind a rock formation.

Hyden lit an arrow and loosed it at the huge spider then readied another. Phen stood dutifully with the torch waiting on Hyden's command.

The web went up in a great whoosh of flame. The spider wiggled and rolled crazily, but finally curled up into a charred ball. As soon as the smoke cleared, Oarly ran in and began dousing the second web. There were two spiders there, and one of them came after Oarly with surprising quickness.

"Light it," Hyden said and Phen reached out touching the wrapped arrow tip with the torch. The arrow arced out over the cavern floor and came down just over Oarly's shoulder. It missed the spider, but the sudden appearance of the flame startled the creature. No sooner had it returned to its web than Hyden's second arrow ignited the lantern oil. Oarly darted away from the blaze with a wild grin on his face and started dancing a jig and howling. At least that's what it looked like he was doing. In truth the dwarf's arm had caught fire and he was wheeling around trying to put it out. Master Biggs started after the dwarf with one of his buckets and ordered his man to follow.

"But the other spider's not dead," the seaman said fearfully.

A glare from the Deck Master replenished the man's courage, and a few moments later they were heaving their buckets at Oarly. Master Biggs finished the task by dousing the last spider with oil and tossing the dwarf's torch at it.

After Oarly calmed down, they wandered cautiously into the cavern shaft. It narrowed considerably and seemed to end, but the light of Phen's magical orb revealed another opening higher up in the rock.

It took all of a moment for Hyden to climb up and look. He stood there in awe for a long time. Golden statues from ages past grew like mushrooms out of piles of coins. A gleaming sword, and a half dozen chests bursting with gold and jewels littered the cave. A giant jeweled collar with a smaller collar dangling from its clasp leaned against a broken piece of ship's mast that was laying under a half-eaten fish the size of a man.

A chill froze away Hyden's amazement. He could see a pair of jade eyes peeking out of a busted chest. They were staring directly at him, and he knew he had found what he was after.

"Oarly," Hyden called out. The dwarf had crawled up and was peeking over the edge of the rock, but was too stunned to respond.

"Oarly," Hyden yelled again, thinking that the dwarf was still down with the others. Hyden suddenly remembered the words of the White Goddess from his dream. *When you recover the Skull of Zorellin, you'll find great danger with it.*

"What is it?" Oarly responded as he pulled himself over the edge.

"How long does it take one of those spiders to spin its web?" asked Hyden as another thought occurred to him.

"The turn of a glass, or two," Oarly answered absently. "There's no need to worry about them webbing us in, lad. I can tell ye firsthand that our fire was plenty hot." He held up his charred sleeve as proof.

"I'm not worried about the spiders," Hyden said in a voice that carried his fear with it. "I'm worried about how soon it's coming back."

"How soon what's coming back?" Brady asked as he joined them.

Phen crawled up, followed by Master Biggs who answered for Brady. "Whatever was eating that godsmackerel?"

"It's, it's... It's still fresh," the seaman stated the obvious with a whimper.

Phen was too excited to be afraid, and as soon as he'd finished speaking, he realized he should have kept his mouth shut, but it was too late.

"Hyden look," he pointed at the huge half-eaten fish. "Look at the size of the bites that've been taken out of it!"

Chapter Twenty-Six

Hyden investigated the teeth marks in the dead fish and decided they were left by a dragon. Luckily it wasn't an older one. He judged by the size and spacing of the marks that this wyrm would be around sixty feet from tip to tail, with a head the size of a mule cart. Claret's hissed warning from his dream the night before echoed through his head. *Not all dragonss are scapable of understandingss. Do what you mussst.*

She was telling him that their friendship was between the two of them, he decided. He thought he understood. Just like she might destroy a village and its inhabitants, he might have the need to kill this young dragon. She wouldn't hold it against him if he did. He was glad for this insight, for without it he might try to find a way to spare such a beast, if it could be done. He was glad that it wouldn't matter in this case, not if they got what they were after and hurried out of there.

"Grab the Silver Skull, Brady," he ordered. "It's there in that chest." He pointed at it. "Get it, and let's be gone before our host returns."

"Are ye daft, lad?" asked Oarly. "Here is freedom for all of King Jarrek's folk." He indicated the treasure. "There's enough to buy all of the slaves back, and then some."

"Aye," Hyden agreed. "And what are you gonna do with it? Are you going to swim it off of this island? Grab a handful each of you, then come on."

"He's right," Master Biggs agreed, as he shoved jewels and coins into the water bucket he was still carrying. "The *Seawander's* not the ship to haul this load. We'll have to come back for it."

Since Phen made no move to pick anything up, Brady handed him the Silver Skull. The boy didn't seem to care about the value of the treasure around them at all.

Brady waded through a pile of gold and silver coins over to the gleaming sword that was jutting majestically out of the pile. Grinning ear to ear he pulled his old blade out of its sheath and slid the pristine piece of well-forged steel into its place. It fit well enough, he decided, and he tossed the old weapon away. Then he went for a decanter full of diamonds. These he gathered not for himself, but for the people of Wildermont. Each one he shoved into his pouch was freedom for two or three of his countrymen, and it appeared that he was trying to get them all.

"Enough!" Hyden finally yelled. He was getting an uneasy feeling. "Let's be gone before it returns."

Reluctantly they agreed. Oarly let Hyden lead the way to the lip they'd climbed. The dwarf was burdened with the jewel encrusted statue of some strange looking animal that he had heaved onto his shoulder. It looked as if it weighed as much as Phen.

The seamen were no better off. The water buckets they carried were overflowing with sparkling gems and heavy gold coins, and Phen was struggling with the weight of the wicked looking jade-eyed skull he held cradled in his arms.

Hyden and Brady had their weapons out, but Brady's sword wasn't being held at the ready. He was just using the light from Hyden's magical orb to study its jeweled hilt. Had he been ready to defend himself with the priceless blade, he might have been alert enough to avoid the young black dragon's streaking blast of sizzling breath. As it was, the Wildermont fighter was caught off guard and lashed out awkwardly in terror and pain. The clothes and skin of his left arm quickly foamed into a soupy pink froth, exposing meat and gore. Only the quick instinctual swipe of his sword, that barely nicked the creature's nostril, saved the others from a similar fate.

The dragon withdrew its head back into the darkness, but it hadn't fled. Its angry growl filled the tunnel like a rumbling quake.

"Back!" Hyden screamed, as he loosed arrow after arrow at the shape looming in the darkness. "Go back. Run!"

He kept loosing arrows until the sound of feet behind him had retreated. Then he turned toward Brady and winced at what he saw.

"Go," the Wildermont King's Guard managed to say through gritted teeth. His left arm and shoulder were nothing more than dangling sloughs of sinew and bone now, but he still stood with the fancy sword held out before him. "Help my king, Hyden Hawk," he said as he stumbled off toward the beast.

Hyden felt a deep pang of sympathy and respect as he charged back toward the others. Brady was a good man. He couldn't let the loss overwhelm him, though. He had to think.

An idea began forming itself even as he ran, and when he burst into the treasure cavern, a glance at Phen's tear-streaked face strengthened his resolve. He snatched something from the nearest pile of loot and began calling out orders like a battlefield general. Out in the tunnel, a primal battle cry arose from Brady, but it was cut short with a sickening crunch and a growl that shook the rock around them.

It was all the others could do to keep up with Hyden's sharp commands, but they somehow managed it. Hyden only hoped that everything Claret said was true. If the magic of her teardrop dangling from his neck didn't protect him, then his plan was a waste, and his life would be over.

As the growling hiss of the angry dragon came near to the entrance of the treasure cave, Hyden realized that it was far too late to wonder about it now. Already, the dragon was peeking in to get a good look at its next victim.

Off to Hyden's right, the terrified deckhand shifted, causing a golden goblet to tumble down a pile of coins and clank into an ornate candelabra. Hyden's anger flared at the fool as the dragon lunged its head into the room and blasted the area with its corrosive breath. As if the man had been made of sand, and the dragon's spew merely jet of water, the gurgling seaman melted away into a grisly pool of gore.

Hyden's eyes darted around the mess. He was terrified for his young friend. Phen had just been over there. Hyden couldn't see him, or anything that might have been him, but it was no relief. He knew that if the boy had been near that blast he would have at least been spattered. Even the jewels and precious metals that had been doused by the black dragon's breath were now hissing and bubbling away. Tears welled up in Hyden's eyes at the thought of losing the boy.

"Over here you little black wyrm!" he yelled at the top of his lungs.

Oarly and Master Biggs were in position by the door, but the dragon's head was still too far into the chamber for the plan to work. Seeing this, Hyden threw his arms up as if to cast some powerful spell and started striding at the dragon fearlessly. As he had hoped, the beast pulled back and started sucking in the breath that it would use to melt him into the floor.

Before the dragon finished inhaling, Hyden yelled, "Now!"

Oarly was standing against the wall beside the entryway. The dwarf threw a rope over the top of the dragon's neck to Master Biggs, who was waiting on the other side. With the precision of a veteran seaman, the Deck Master pulled the end of the rope through the buckle of the great collar that was laid out across the floor and took off running with the rope in tow. Hyden saw the collar leap from the floor as the rope pulled it up. It looked like the noose was going to close, but he never had a chance to see the rest of what happened.

A huge spray of hot liquid washed over Hyden as the dragon unleashed its acidy spew. His vision was wiped away and the breath pulled from his lungs, but, to his surprise, a pulse of radiant energy erupted from the medallion at his chest and engulfed him. He heard Phen scream out in anguish and was thankful to know that the boy had survived.

"For Doon and Brady!" he heard Oarly yell.

Then the dragon's gigantic roar filled the chamber. A moment later Hyden's head slammed full of chaotic thoughts of hate and destruction. The dragon was more than a little angry. Hyden commanded the thoughts to cease and sent out a shocking reprimand to their source to establish control.

A muffled roar erupted then, a long howl from Oarly that seemed to pass over Hyden's head. The dwarf's yell ended in a tinkling crash of coins and a sharp, "Ooof!"

As the bright dancing sparkles of energy that had engulfed Hyden twinkled out of existence, he found himself on his knees before the seething maw of the young black dragon. All around him metal and rock hissed and smoldered.

He looked around the room and saw Phen huddled in a sobbing crouch over Oarly's splayed body. The Deck Master was standing as still as a statue, as if he were frozen in place. His mouth was a perfect 'O.' The rope he had pulled the dragon collar closed with dangled limply from his hand.

"You didn't have to kill my friends," Hyden said to the dragon harshly.

The sound of his voice caused Phen and the Deck Master to gasp in surprise. They thought Hyden had been melted by the dragon.

"You tricked me," the dragon growled more into Hyden's mind than aloud.

"You tricked yourself with your eagerness to destroy us," Hyden spat. "Now go skulk around in the bigger cavern and think about your new situation."

The dragon hissed and hesitated. Through the smaller collar on Hyden's neck he sent a sharp shock of persuasive punishment through to the beast. The dragon trembled visibly with the sensation, but resisted the urge to roar out. The idea of the dragon's collar sickened Hyden, but after what this dragon had done to Brady and the deckhand, he found he could stomach using it. Reluctantly, the wyrm withdrew its big head from the chamber and eased back out of the tunnel.

"How did you survive that?" asked Phen. He started to say more, but the memory of Brady's fate, and the sight of the puddle of remains of the deckhand overwhelmed him. "Get up, Oarly," he sobbed and shook at the dwarf's shoulders.

Oarly groaned, and Phen hugged him fiercely. A pudgy fingered hand came up and patted Phen's head reassuringly. "I'm all right, lad," he said. "Was that Sir Hyden Hawk I heard ordering the dragon about?"

"Yeah," Phen said. "But Brady didn't make it."

"Aye," Oarly sighed. "Sometimes this be the way of things, lad."

"Aye," Phen sniffled and helped Oarly to his feet. Tears flowed freely down his face.

Hyden learned from Phen that Oarly had leapt onto the dragon's back to fasten the collar and had been slung across the chamber during the skirmish. Battered and bruised, the dwarf was content to haul out the dead seaman's bucket of jewels instead of the encumbering statue.

Master Biggs hadn't spoken since the dragon blasted his man away. He was alert, though, and answered the enquiries about his condition with grunts and nods. He started to leave his bucket of wealth behind, but thought better of it. Too many slaves could be freed for him to just abandon it.

The three men and the dwarf made their way out of the lower tunnel warily. As they emerged into the great cavern, the dragon was lying up on the scalloped shelf with its head hanging down glaring at them. Hyden shifted the weight of the Silver Skull to one arm and put the other around Phen protectively. Through the collar he told the dragon to lie still until they passed. He kept a mental thumb on the beast's neck until they were well on their way into the long passage that led toward the camp.

When the light of day could clearly be seen ahead of them, Phen hurried toward it. Hyden didn't stop him. He couldn't blame the boy for wanting to be out in the open again. He was glad the ordeal was over, and for the first time since the dragon attacked, thoughts of Brady filled his head.

All of Hyden's life, death had been near him. Hardly a year passed that one of his cousins or uncles hadn't fallen to their deaths from the hawkling nesting cliffs where his brother had found Talon. Then Mikahl's friends, Lord Gregory, and Loudin the hunter had been mauled by the hellcat up in the Giant Mountains. His friend Vaegon had been killed by the Choska in the battle of Xwarda. He found that he couldn't shed a tear for the Wildermont King's Guard, but he held a place of respect for the man in his heart. Brady had traveled across the continent warning people of the demon-wizard's army of undead, and the final stand he made had gained them the time they needed to set their trap. Hyden knew that King Jarrek loved Brady like a son. He didn't relish the idea of telling the Red Wolf of Wildermont of his man's death.

Talon's fierce shriek broke Hyden's reverie and the alarm his hawkling *familiar* sent through him grabbed his full attention. *Intruders in the camp*, he gathered from the sound. "Come on, Phen's in trouble," he said as he took off at a sprint toward the cave mouth ahead of them.

Master Biggs followed, but Oarly couldn't find the strength to run. His body had been bruised to the point of breaking when the dragon slung him into the wall. The dwarf set his bucket to the side and took off in a hop-step after the other two. Oarly decided that, if young Phen was in trouble, he could suffer the pain of a short jog. The scene he found when he emerged out of the tunnel was startling, and a little confusing.

Oarly had never seen a breed giant before, and the pale bald man wearing wizard's robes looked eerily like the demon-wizard Pael. Oarly soon saw why Hyden Hawk and Master Biggs weren't trying to fight the new arrivals. Another giant had Phen by the collar and held a wicked looking blade to the boy's throat. Not too far away lay the bodies of the two seamen who had been posted to watch out for them. Oarly could see, by the way the blood still oozed from the stumps where their heads had once been, that they had only just been killed.

"I'll take the skull," the bald wizard said in a menacing voice. "And the controlling collar," he added before Hyden could command the dragon to come to their aid.

Hyden sat the skull down in the thick grass before him and started to take the collar off.

"Let him go," Hyden indicated Phen, before he loosened the collar. "Or there is no bargain."

Flick made a miniscule gesture with his hand and half a dozen crossbow bolts came whizzing down among them. One of them hit Master Biggs in the back and sent him sprawling to the ground. Oarly looked back and saw a scattering of lizard-men high up on the hill. Some were reloading; some had their weapons still trained on the group.

"You're in no position to bargain, Hyden Skyler," Flick said. "My queen ordered me to kill you, but I grew to respect your brother before his demise. For that reason alone I'll spare you."

"Take the skull and the collar," Hyden pleaded. "But leave him. He's just a boy."

"He is our guarantee that you'll not pursue," Flick said. "But as Gerard's friend, I give you my word that once we are on our ship I will let him go. Once I put on the collar, the dragon will keep you from following us."

"And if I refuse to give you the collar?" Hyden asked. The last thing he wanted was for that bitch Shaella to get control of another dragon. It was bad enough that she was going to get the Silver Skull. Hyden could only imagine what sort of trouble she would cause with it.

"Then you order the dragon to attack," Flick speculated. "You'll all die in a flurry of arrows and steel long before it can get here." Flick's voice was smug and impatient. Hyden could tell he was nervous. "By the time it arrives, I will be wearing the collar."

"Who do ye think you are?" Oarly barked angrily. "Some sort of imitation of that madman Pael?"

The jibe struck a nerve in Flick. He had apprenticed under Shaella's father and had idolized the ambitious wizard.

"Kill the dwarf!" he shouted up to the zard on the ridge.

"Wait!" Hyden yelled before they could loose. He unbuckled the collar from his neck and threw it at the wizard's feet. "You gave your word you'd let the boy go. If you break it, I'll track you far beyond death."

"Your brother told me once how much respect you commanded," Flick said, unable to suppress his victory grin. "I will keep my word, even though Shaella won't like it. Hopefully the surprise of gaining a new dragon will help her forget my insubordination."

"Hopefully the dragon will turn on you both," Hyden spat. Then to Phen he said, "When they let you go, stay where you are. My eyes will be on you the whole way."

Phen's gaze locked on Hyden's then. He was trying to will his thoughts into his friend's mind. "Finish Loak's translation, Hyden. Try to see what's been invisible to us."

"Enough," yelled Flick. "Get the skull," he ordered one of his breed giants. The big brutish man-beast picked the artifact up with one hand as if it were a piece of fruit. Then Flick turned and led his group into the jungle.

Chapter Twenty-Seven

It didn't take Captain Konrath long to realize that the small group he had taken aboard was no ordinary mercenary crew. It was also clear that they had no intention of sailing on to O'Dakahn with him. The decidedly western accent of the two men who carried jewel-hilted swords spoke of nobility. The one they called Grommen had the look of a Valleyan horse hand, and the quiet, dutiful man was obviously from Highwander. Maxrell Tyne, though, he was all Dakaneese, from his fast talking hard-edged negotiating skills, to his crafty purchasable loyalty.

Konrath sensed that he could buy Tyne and use him to strip this strange lot down to their skin, but he also sensed that he couldn't afford Tyne's price. What he would get out of the fancy swords wouldn't satisfy two greedy bastards, and he guessed that there wasn't much else of value that they carried. He knew that he didn't need Tyne to rid his ship of trouble, though. Dakaneese or not, the bastard Tyne could swim with the fools if he got in the way.

The *Shark's Tooth* was an able craft. Its crew was well seasoned and the Captain had a firm grasp of control over them. Thirty-six slaves on a lower deck manned the twenty-four oars in shifts. They were well fed and bore few scars from the oar master's whip. Their presence still sickened Mikahl, but as Lord Gregory reminded him, they were at sea. If something were to be done to help them, it had to be done at port in Salazar. Not here, not now.

Mikahl accepted Lord Gregory's wisdom as if it were set in stone, even if he didn't like it. The two Westlanders caught up on most everything they could think of, but Mikahl did the majority of the talking. Lord Gregory had been unconscious for the duration of the war that Pael waged on humanity. Most of the details Mikahl revealed were new to the Lion Lord's ears and he listened raptly.

It was their third evening on the *Shark's Tooth*. They were standing at the rail looking out over the sea. The sun was about to set and the slow rolling waves were tipped in molten gold. They were speaking quietly to each other about the political situation in Valleya when Captain Konrath decided to make his move.

"Turn around now," Konrath ordered in his grisly pirate voice. "Nice and slow or my men will get you where you stand."

Mikahl turned to see three of the pirates standing before them with their wicked curved blades held only inches from him and Lord Gregory. Atop a lidded bin, behind the three men, the half-masked Captain grinned smugly down. A shuffle of movement down the deck revealed that Grommen, and the Highwander soldier were in a similar predicament.

Mikahl searched the ship for Maxrell Tyne, but didn't see him. He was surprised that his first thought was that the mercenary betrayed them. His instincts told him that Tyne was either being held at sword point somewhere, or had brokered a deal where he might play both sides of the fence. After all, both he and the Captain were Dakaneese.

"Crossbows in the timbers," Lord Gregory said under his breath.

"Waves," was Mikahl's reply. "Give him your knee now."

When Lord Gregory dutifully dropped to his left knee and ducked his head, Captain Konrath's laugh was cut short. Mikahl used the step the Lion Lord's leg created to propel himself up into a somersault over the startled seamen. Ironspike came out with a ringing sing and a bright purple glare threw shadows across the evening. The thumping of half a dozen crossbow bolts into the deck and the cry of one of the seamen who'd been struck by his own man's bolt filled the dusk. Mikahl's world was consumed with a different sound, a symphony of powerful magic.

After Mikahl launched himself, Lord Gregory simply fell over and rolled. While Mikahl's radiant acrobatics drew the seamen's attention, the Lion Lord drew his blade, and as quick as lightning, put its tip through the bellies of two of them. The third pirate was cursing and reeling away, holding the bolt jutting out of his neck.

A sizzling dart of red streaked from Ironspike's tip toward the men in front of Grommen and the Highwanderman. They used the moment of shock it caused the seamen to get clear and draw their own weapons. It wasn't necessary, though. The next sound that echoed through the evening was so blood-curdling that even the ocean stood still for a moment.

Konrath's yell was gut-wrenching. With pain-filled eyes, the Captain of the *Shark's Tooth* lay on the deck fumbling at where his lower leg used to be. A glance at the foot lying nearby in a growing pool of blood made him gulp and begin to sob.

"I told you not to challenge these men," said Maxrell Tyne from the top of the wheelhouse overlooking them. Then the mercenary turned to the first mate. "I suggest you tie that stump off before your captain bleeds to death. My friend won't want to kill him just yet."

"I won't?" Mikahl asked, keeping his eyes on the agonized Captain.

"If you did, he would be dead, no? This is a pirate ship, King Mikahl," Tyne said matter-of-factly. "We cannot just sail it into the trade port of Salazar. The Captain here knows where we will be able to land unmolested. I don't think his men know the lantern shutter codes. That's one of the bits of knowledge that a good pirate captain hoards."

Lord Gregory kicked Captain Konrath's booted foot over the side of the ship into the sea. The first mate edged nervously over and put a belt around the Captain's stump then cinched it tight. The scream that everyone expected to hear never came. Konrath passed out from the pain. Then, as if nothing had ever happened, Lord Gregory put his elbows back on the ship's rail and resumed his conversation with Mikahl.

"So, King Broderick will be in Xwarda now under the witch's guard?" he asked.

"She's not a witch, I tell you," replied Mikahl. "She is a fine and noble queen. She's not afraid to get her hands bloody either. When Hyden, Vaegon, and I were bringing Ironspike to its cradle, she met us in the Evermore with a group of her rangers. She had dreamed of our coming and was dressed for battle. I think she thought we were King Broderick and Queen Rachel's spies or something. That's when the Choska and the horn-helmed rider attacked."

"The thing that killed Vaegon?"

"Aye, but it didn't kill him then." Mikahl pinched the bridge of his nose as it was an unpleasant memory. "That day in the Evermore, Grrr, the pack leader of the Giant King's great wolves, died to save me. Queen Willa carried me back to Xwarda and her healers kept me alive. When I came around, Pael was knee deep in Xwarda."

"And now Hyden is off chasing a silver skull?" Lord Gregory looked mystified at this. He would have expected Hyden to be aiding Mikahl or King Jarrek directly.

Mikahl shrugged a "what-can-you-do" shrug. "He speaks to a goddess sometimes," Mikahl explained. "The goddess of his people. She told him he needed to use this skull to retrieve a ring that his brother took into the land of demons. The ring is supposed to balance some great scale of power. I don't understand any of it." Mikahl sighed. "I envy him. He is freer than the rest of us somehow. I cannot explain it."

"Everyone has a duty, Mik," Lord Gregory said solemnly. "Don't think for a moment that Hyden doesn't have his. Traipsing into the land of the demons sounds unfathomable. I doubt he would do this if the goddess hadn't given him the task."

"Aye," Mikahl conceded.

"This General Spyra, who you stood with at Valleya, he's capable?"

"He can fight both as a leader and as a warrior. He fought bravely against Pael's dead men, but that doesn't make him a good candidate to run a kingdom. He was the most stable figurehead that was available to me." Mikahl shrugged again. "That, and I trust him."

Lord Gregory nodded. "We need to find out who is King Broderick's true heir," Gregory said after a long bit of thought. "That is the starting point to fixing the Valleyan problems. As for Seaward and Queen Rachel, I think that there is only one solution."

"What's that?" Mikahl asked hopefully.

"You will have to sneak back into Westland and free Princess Rosa. You'll have to get her to safety, and then marry her."

"That's a lot harder than it sounds."

Gregory laughed at the look on Mikahl's face. "It sounds impossible. What's harder than impossible?" As he had done hundreds of times when Mikahl was a fumbling page growing into a capable squire, Lord Gregory ruffled his hair. "You have the Prince of Salaya to spy for you, and his trade ships will help you in and out of Westland. You know the inside of Lakeside Castle as well as any man alive, probably better, since you caused so much mischief there in your youth. You have Ironspike, and all the power that comes with it. It won't be easy, Mik, but unless you want Princess Rosa to wither away in some dungeon cell, it's the only option." Gregory smiled a sad, yet reassuring smile. "We will spend a day or two on Salazar searching for Trella and Zasha. Then, either way, we will go to the Isle of Salaya and find out what knowledge Prince Raspaar has gathered for you. We can make a plan then. From what I've seen, Queen Shaella has only a loose hold over our kingdom. There was no resistance when the skeeks invaded. They're not battle tested."

The fact that Lord Gregory was already thinking about such things filled Mikahl's mind with some comfort, but the idea that he might have to go back into Westland alone to rescue Princess Rosa was daunting at best. He began stealing his resolve to do what Lord Gregory felt must be done. He wasn't sure what he felt emotionally for the Princess, but he was certain that he didn't want her to come to harm. The semi-private carriage ride they had taken the day after the introductory feast in Xwarda had revealed a lot about her that he liked. Once they were alone, her pretext of formality had fallen away and they had spoken as Rosa and Mikahl, not the High King and the Princess of Seaward. Deep in his heart he'd known as soon as he'd found out that she'd been taken that he would go after her. At least now he wouldn't be doing it blindly.

He trained with Ironspike each morning they were at sea. The symphony of the sword was a soothing and welcome distraction from the uneasy worries that clouded his mind. Not only did the sound comfort him, it revealed aspects of its own power that he hadn't yet perceived. Each session gave him a little more understanding of Ironspike's nature, and revealed ways that he might use it better. By the time they reached the Isle of Salazar he had done more than resign himself to the fact that he had to go into the Dragon Queen's castle alone to save the Princess. He found he was looking forward to it. If he could find out exactly where Rosa was being held, then Mikahl thought he could actually save her.

Ironspike was far more than just a magical weapon, Mikahl figured out. It was a tool, and the skills he was learning presented endless possibilities and filled him with confidence. Tricking, or even killing Queen Shaella while he was in Westland was a possibility as well. After all, it's not like she still had a dragon to defend her.

When the ship docked in a fishing village called Rydia, only King Mikahl, Maxwell Tyne, and Lord Gregory left the ship. They learned that the Westland settlement was a bit further south down the coast, and forced the feverish, yet recovering Captain to land them there. The refugee settlement was called Balton, named after the last king that had ruled Westland honorably.

Just stepping onto the shore filled Mikahl with pride. Though he hadn't known King Balton as his father, he had loved him as a king. Mikahl noticed that Lord Gregory was trembling. If Lady Trella wasn't here, then he didn't know where else to look for her.

"Come on, M' lord," Mikahl put his arm around his friend's shoulder. "Let's go find your lady."

An inn called the Lost Lion seemed the place to start their search. The two Westlanders made their way there, both noticing the stares and awed glances they were getting as they passed through the growing town. The place reminded Mikahl of Portsmouth, one of Westland's greatest cities, as it might have been a few hundred years ago. Proud, sturdy, and clean, the settlement of Balton was small, but every bit of it spoke of determination, pride, and persistence.

Lord Gregory sat on the stoop of the inn, too nervous to go inside. Mikahl strode into the common room not knowing what to expect and was caught off guard by the sharp voiced woman standing at the bar.

"About time you came around," Lady Zasha said with a bit of heat in her tone. "Has the mighty High King returned to his people?"

Mikahl was speechless. Lady Zasha was extremely pregnant and looking as beautiful as ever, but he couldn't tell if she was really angry with him or not until she scowled his way. He was saved by a most welcome sound.

"Oh Mikahl," Lady Trella burst out as she charged from the kitchen doors over to him. She hugged him fiercely with tears running down her face. "Oh, if my Lord might have lived to see you come into your own."

Mikahl realized then that she didn't know her husband had survived. "Come, m'lady," he smiled down to her, and took her by the hand.

He was almost as surprised as she was at what awaited them outside the inn. A few hundred people had gathered in the street, and as Lady Trella and Lord Gregory embraced in a joyous torrent of tears, the crowd bowed to their true king.

"All hail King Mikahl," one of them said.

"Hail King Mikahl," the others shouted back.

From the doorway behind him, Mikahl heard Lady Zasha say, "I suppose that since you brought Lord Gregory back from the dead you're off the hook."

Chapter Twenty-Eight

"If anyone can get Rosa out of Westland it's the High King," Queen Willa said in a vain attempt to comfort Queen Rachel. Princess Rosa was Rachel's only child and had been the sole subject of conversation since she'd arrived in Xwarda.

"Am I a prisoner here too?" Queen Rachel asked through tear-filled eyes. "Oh, how the gods punish us for our folly," she blurted. Then she began sobbing again.

"No, Rachel," Willa gave an exasperated huff. "Your cousin is being held for a more recent treachery than last autumn's attack on my people. As I told you, Broderick recently consorted with the Dakaneese and the Westlanders to betray the High King. These are the very same Westlanders that kidnapped your daughter, I might add. Nevertheless, Dreg was killed, and quite a few of Jarrek's people were freed. I sent them as many men as I could spare, and King Mikahl has requested that you do the same. I think that, since he has gone off into Westland to find your daughter, you should comply."

Queen Willa wasn't sure that Rosa was the reason why Mikahl had snuck into Westland, but she made it sound that way. Queen Rachel came from Seaward as soon as she heard Broderick was a prisoner. She'd come seeking information, a terrified mother whose daughter had been taken for motives beyond her reckoning. Queen Willa gave her a shoulder to cry on, and for the last two days had come to realize that the treachery of last year was more of Broderick's design than Rachel's.

General Spyra hadn't known Mikahl's motives either. The General's message made it sound like he wasn't sure where Mikahl had actually disappeared to. Mikahl's message to Willa, though, had made his destination, if not his motives, clearer.

"How many men?" Rachel sobbed. "Would five thousand be enough?"

Now we're getting somewhere, thought Willa. "I think five thousand well armed, and well provisioned men would show the High King that his efforts to save your daughter are greatly appreciated."

"Where should I send them? Under whose command?"

"To King Jarrek in Wildermont," Willa answered as she thought of something that made the corners of her mouth turn up into a devilish smile. "Have them march right through northern Dakahn to Seareach. That's where they will be needed the most."

"Through Dakahn?" Rachel's sobbing ceased. "But that's... that's..."

"This is what Ra'Gren needs to see. He needs to see firsthand our support for Wildermont. The sell-sword army he is putting together to defend the mines won't dare attack five thousand me—"

A sharp knock at the door of the sitting chamber interrupted Willa's words. She excused herself, wondering what was so urgent that someone would disturb her private meeting. Her advisors all knew the importance of this discussion.

As her hand moved toward the polished brass handle of the heavy wooden door, the knock sounded again. As she thought, it was Dugak. Only a dwarf's knock came from that low.

"What is it?" she asked rather sharply as she yanked open the door.

Starkle, the little blue pixie, fluttered around the excited dwarf's head. Obviously something extreme was happening. Still, Willa held out a hand to stop Dugak from coming in. Once the door was pulled shut behind her, she motioned for him to speak.

"Droves of dwarves," the pixie said in a voice far too big for its size.

"It's the might of Doon, Your Highness," Dugak cut in over the fluttering blue gnat. "It seems they've come to answer your call after all."

What in all the gods is he talking about? Is he drunk again? Willa wondered. Starkle must have seen her perplexed look and began trying to explain.

"Thousands of dwarves have come down out of the hills north of Jenkanta. They're armed and prepared for battle."

"Where did they come from?" Willa still didn't grasp it. "There's not a hundred dwarves left in the realm."

"Oh, but there are," Dugak said with a grin. He did a jump-skip in place, trying to contain his excitement. "Don't you see? They came because you blew the Horn of Doon. They've come to answer your call for aid."

Understanding replaced her confusion. Almost a year ago, when Pael's undead army was standing outside the gates of Xwarda, she had blown the Horn of Doon, hoping to summon the dwarves to help them defend the Wardstone that the city is built upon. "They're really late," Willa said with a smile at the wonder of it.

"What should we tell them?" asked Starkle. "That we've no need of them. Should I send them back underground?"

Dugak swatted at the pixie as if he were a pesky insect. Luckily for Starkle the dwarf missed.

"Just because that battle is over doesn't mean that there isn't a need." Dugak looked to his queen. Under his thick mass of beard, his chest was puffed out proudly. "Us dwarves are the ones who built this city in the first place. Who better to rebuild it?"

"I'm not going to put them to work, Dugak, unless they offer," Willa said with a giggle at the silliness of the dwarven army coming out of the earth a whole year late. "Go welcome them, Dugak. That is an order. Explain to them what has happened and arrange a feast. No matter their tardiness, the return of the dwarves of Doon to Xwarda is a reason to celebrate."

With an elaborate bow the dwarf turned and started away.

Starkle, now flying just out of arm's reach, said, "The elves built Xwarda with the aid of the giants you dimwit dwarf. That was long before a dwarf ever set foot in this land."

Queen Willa suppressed her amusement at the strange turn of events and retreated back into the sitting room. She thought it best to get Queen Rachel's five thousand men committed as soon as possible. Maybe, just maybe, she could get some of the dwarves to go and help Mikahl and Jarrek too. Their legendary skills as fighters and builders would go far toward helping Wildermont raise itself out of the rubble. She would start working on that at the feast. Right now she still had Rachel's offer to seal, and by the sound of the woman's new sobbing, tactfully bringing the subject of soldiers back around wasn't going to be easy.

General Spyra couldn't have been more content. His young wife had arrived from Xwarda with the new troops Queen Willa had afforded the effort, and now two thousand men were on their way through the mountains to help King Jarrek. Dreen was as occupied as a city could be, and no viable threat was known. He didn't have a concern beyond the lovely woman beside him.

Lady Mandary's sparkling blue eyes twinkled, and her straw-colored ringlets dangled like ribbons of gold in the afternoon sun. The carriage ride had been her idea. She wanted to see as much of the Red City as she could. Spyra tried to explain to her that it was the same throughout the interior of the great red wall that surrounded Dreen. There were low, red block buildings surrounded by corrals and sheering yards, and as many grazing lots as there were homes. There were no towers or cathedrals, no spectacular landmarks, just wild-smelling functional stock pens and a few large taverns.

Spyra still found her interest in his work a pleasant surprise. She had always asked him of this and that, but now she seemed to want to know every detail of the High King's plans. Spyra didn't find this suspicious because Lady Mandary expertly catered to his ego. She kept him boasting of this, that, or the other. He found himself almost seeking her approval of the ideas that he and King Jarrek had been tossing around in Mikahl's absence. When she learned that Mikahl might actually be in Westland, she hurried the tour, feigning lightheadedness. Of course the General rushed her back to the modest palace of Dreen. He hoped to get reacquainted with her in a more personal way after dinner, and getting her comfortable was of great importance to him. He had no idea that, once she locked herself in her chamber, she was going to use her witchy magic to confer with Queen Shaella. After all, Lady Mandary was one of the Dragon Queen's favorite spies.

"Leave me for a while please," Lady Mandary ordered her attendant when she was finally in her chamber. "I will be taking a nap and I do not want to be disturbed until dinner."

"Yes, milady." The servant woman had some doubts to her mistress's sanity. Already she had seen the woman speaking into a bowl and had overheard several peculiar conversations when the lady was the only person in the room. She expected one of those to take place now, and hurried out to her own quarters. She didn't want the ravings of the General's wife to be any of her concern.

The single drop of blood that dripped from the vial into the basin of water seemed to stain it with abnormal potency. The liquid went from clear to pink to a deep thick crimson color in only a matter of moments. Once Lady Mandary was satisfied with the texture and color of the glossy red surface, her eyes rolled back into her head. She began to chant in rhythmic musical repetition while her hands danced at the ends of her outstretched arms. This would take awhile, she knew. Her queen wouldn't be expecting this call.

The arrival of the red-robed priests of Kraw at Lakeside Castle in Westland happened with little fanfare. The four priests had little use for courtly pleasantries, and less for feasts and celebration. It was good that they didn't expect much of a welcome, because Queen Shaella hadn't bothered to prepare as much as a goblet of water to refresh them from their travels. The priests didn't complain, but it seemed they didn't understand why they were there. They didn't know that Gerard was Kraw now. All they knew was that to serve their master, they had to serve her.

There was a bit of disagreement over this, but after the first prayer session, the priests began to understand. Gerard answered their questioning calls with perfect clarity by sucking the life out of one of them and commanding the others to follow Shaella's every whim. It was impossible to argue when the dried up husk of a man was lying on the floor.

"Already one of my wizards has the Silver Skull of Zorellin in his possession," she told them. "It is on the way here as we speak, and when it arrives we will use it to bring your Kraw out of the Nethers so that I can have my Gerard. But I do have another agenda that needs looking into while we wait."

The priests' first task was to make the High King aware of Princess Rosa's presence in Pael's tower, and set a trap for him. The trap, they determined, was the easiest part. They tried using Rosa's fingertip to cast a drawing spell on Mikahl, but it didn't work. Then they unpacked the library of spell books and journals they'd carried with them from the Isle of Borina, and spent the night scouring them for another way to draw their bait in. They didn't find what they were looking for, but they settled their things into the comfortable gathering chamber they had been allotted and learned the reason why their first attempt had failed.

There had been an assumption. It had rendered the main component of the spell useless. It was this very component that they were now speaking about to Queen Shaella.

"What is it that you need to cast this spell?" asked Shaella. "I was told that the Princess's finger would do."

"We need a piece of her to mark her as the bait," one answered.

"And a piece of someone that he truly loves," added another. "It seems we misjudged his feelings for her."

"And the finger I already gave you?" Her tone had an edge to it. "You told me that you could draw him with that alone."

"That was our mistake, Queen Shaella," the third priest said. "We assumed that the High King loved Princess Rosa, but apparently that is not so. As it is, we need another piece of her, and a piece of someone he truly loves, to correctly cast the drawing spell."

"Find another way then," she spat. She could think of no one that Mikahl might love. The only one he was close to was Gerard's brother. Hyden was at sea, still alive because of Flick's weakness. She wasn't that angry with Flick, though. He had served her cause for years and was bringing her a grand surprise. Even evil queens like to be surprised every now and then. She was a woman after all.

An itch presented itself in her mind, like an insect crawling across the inside of her skull. It was insistent. She hadn't been expecting anyone to reach out to her, and thoughts of Flick's spinelessness caused her to think that maybe he had lost possession of the skull. She knew firsthand that Hyden Hawk Skyler was the trickiest of bastards. Flick should have killed him when he had the chance.

"A bowl of water!" she ordered the nearest priest. He grabbed the finger bowl from the table and set it before her. It was small, but it would do. She snarled at another of them. "Come now, a drop of blood. I know you can recognize a simple spell of seeing."

One of the priests nicked his finger with a dagger and let a few drops fall into the bowl. Shaella's deft chanting turned the dingy liquid into the distorted image of Lady Mandary.

It came as a relief that it wasn't Flick, and Shaella couldn't help but smile at the plump girlish image of the old marsh crone that was looking back at her from the surface of the water.

"My Queen," Lady Mandary said reverently. "I only disturbed you because there is something you should know."

"What is it, love?" Shaella asked sweetly enough to put the woman at ease. "I have a bit of a problem here that you might be able to help me with anyway. Tell me what you've learned."

"It's the High King," Lady Mandary said with a bit of alarm in her voice. "He is in Westland as we speak. He has been for some time, though my General has no idea why."

"How many soldiers are with him?" Shaella asked suddenly. *How could he have invaded without me hearing of it?* It made no sense at all.

"No troops, my Queen. Only a handful of men are with him."

"Maybe our spell worked after all," one of the priests said to his fellows.

"Who was that?" Lady Mandary asked with concern. If she was found to be spying for Queen Shaella, even in a roundabout way, she could lose her head. She had a good reason to worry about whose ears might hear her words.

"Just a Borinian priest," Shaella said. "I assure you, the last thing on his mind is who, or where you are. Is Mikahl after the Princess?"

"The General isn't sure why he's there."

"Tell me, dear," Queen Shaella said, "who does that glorified squire truly love? We've learned that he doesn't love the Princess just yet."

"He hardly knows the girl," Lady Mandary replied. "How could he love her? He loves his friends dearly, and King Jarrek too. No doubt he cares about the boy, Phenilous."

"Wait!" Shaella snapped so loudly that the priests, as well as her spy, jumped from the sharpness of her words. "Oh, Mandary," Queen Shaella giggled. "I think you've helped me more than you'll ever know. You'll reach me again if you hear anything else, won't you?"

Shaella didn't even wait for a reply before tapping the bowl of bloody water, causing a ring of ripples to evaporate the image on its surface.

"So you require a component that is a piece of someone he loves?" Shaella asked the priests with a smile on her beautiful scarred face.

"Yes, yes, Queen Shaella, we do."

"And once this piece of that person is taken from them, it no longer lives. Is this correct?" The priests glanced at each other for reassurance, but finding no flaw in her reasoning, they nodded.

"Then this piece of someone the High King loves doesn't have to come from a living body, does it?"

"There is nothing in the wording of the spell that requires the piece to come from someone alive," one of the priests answered. "We are primarily necromancers. Most of our spells deal with the dead."

"I think it's time for me to designate a royal gravedigger," Queen Shaella gave a haughty laugh. "For everyone who has heard Mikahl's tale knows that there is no one he loved greater than his father. We will just have to dig up old King Balton's corpse and take a piece of him."

"And another piece of the Princess, Queen Shaella," one of the priests reminded eagerly.

Chapter Twenty-Nine

It was hard for Talon to follow Phen and his captors through the thick overgrowth, but the hawkling managed it. Hyden watched on in helpless fury as Flick's party made their way toward a part of the island that was nowhere near where the *Seawander* was anchored. He let Oarly lead them. They were headed back to the *Seawander* so that they could sail around the island and pick up Phen. Hyden didn't want to lose sight of the boy for a single second. He was concentrated on Talon's vision. It was up to the dwarf to get them through the jungle. Deck Master Biggs followed them. Oarly had removed the crossbow bolt from the man's back, but the traveling was taking its toll on the seaman, as was the humidity. The Deck Master's breath was coming in great heavy gasps.

To Hyden's great horror, just as the sun was beginning to set, Flick and his troop of grumbling freaks came out of the hills onto a gravelly shoreline. Their ship was anchored a short way from the island and a long gang plank led from it directly into the shallows. A dozen zard-men, all armored in studded leather vests emblazoned with Queen Shaella's lightning star, scurried about. Hyden's heart sank. He, Oarly, and Biggs still had a long hike between them and the *Seawander*, and that was only if the Deck Master could keep up.

A commotion at the zard ship drew Talon's full attention, and Hyden watched. A streaking bolt of jagged yellow light leapt from Flick's hand toward one of the breed giants. *Was Phen trying to escape?* Hyden wondered. He couldn't tell what happened next due to the flash burn the wizard's spell caused in the hawkling's eyes.

Shouting and hissing from the ship could be heard, and then a painful shriek of boyish terror that could have only come from Phen.

Talon made out the stumbling shape of the breed giant that had been holding Phen. The man-beast staggered into the cover of the jungled hillside. The other breed giant was lying sprawled across the rocky beach. Hyden was confused. He couldn't see Phen anywhere, but the bloody twisted form of a lizard-man lay not too far from the smoldering breed giant's body. *Were they attacked?*

Talon's flash blindness was clearing, but the boy was still nowhere to be seen. Not on shore, not on the deck of the zard ship that was starting to ease away from the island now; not anywhere.

In the dying light of dusk, Hyden could see Flick standing on the deck, fastening the dragon collar around his neck with smug satisfaction. The wide eyed-expression that came over the wizard's face told Hyden that the link between man and wyrm had been established, and he warned Talon to be wary of air-born threats.

The Silver Skull had been quickly taken below deck. Talon followed the ship for a short way as it headed out to the deep sea, but since Phen didn't appear to be aboard the craft, the hawkling circled back and began searching the shoreline and the edges of the foliage. Hyden's heart was clenched with fear. To his utter dismay, not a single sign of Phen could be found. To make things worse, when the moon was high in the sky, a storm came blowing in, and a heavy tropical rain began to fall.

Hyden had Talon fly from the shoreline around the island in the rain to find the *Seawander*. Once it was located, he explained to Oarly how to direct Captain Trant to the site of Phen's disappearance. He wanted Oarly and Biggs to go on to the ship while he went back the other way and searched for the boy.

"What was it the boy said about finding what had been invisible to us in his books?" Oarly asked while Hyden was lightening his packs. Hyden took his elven longbow and a small pack of supplies, but that was all.

"I'm not sure what he was talking about," Hyden said absently. His thoughts were fixed on finding Phen. If the boy was alive, Hyden was determined to locate him. If he was dead, then Hyden would lay eyes on the corpse before he gave up.

"If he lives…" Oarly started, but stopped himself before he could finish the sentence. After a tug at his beard he spoke again. "Phen is a smart lad. He will find shelter and ride this storm out. You should rest, Sir Hyden Hawk. You've been through an ordeal. Your clearest wit would serve you better than this haste. You'll not find anything but trouble traipsing across this strange island in the dark."

"Aye," Hyden agreed. " 'Tis true I could use some sleep, but even if I lay down and closed my eyes, no sleep would come." Hyden wiped the rain, or maybe a tear of worry, from his eyes. "I'll not let him sit out there shivering in the cold, alone, and possibly injured, Oarly," Hyden said as he started into the dark wet tangle. After a few paces he had disappeared completely. Oarly heard Hyden's voice calling back to him, "Just get to the ship and have Trant set sail as quickly as you can. Talon will let you know if I find any trouble."

"I will!" Oarly called back, but he was certain that the sound of the storm had swallowed his voice before it reached Hyden's ears.

Hyden set a crisp pace for himself and charged on through the night. Talon had to land frequently, so that he could shiver the accumulated wetness his feathers absorbed as he flew around the area where Phen was last seen. Hyden cursed the rain. Any tracks the youngster might have left would be washed away. He turned the scene over and over again in his head. *Why had Flick struck down the breed giant with his lightning spell? Had the breed tried to protect Phen?* A horrid thought crossed his mind then. *What if the breed giant had tried to hurt Phen?* To keep his word, the wizard Flick might have killed his own man. Mikahl had told him that the breed giants were notorious eaters of man flesh. Nothing made any sense—the dead zard-man, the other giant staggering into the foliage.

He eventually decided not to dwell on anything as he jogged on toward the rocky shore. Twice he went off course because he let his thoughts wander to the darker possibilities. If it hadn't been for Talon's persistence, he'd have been wasting his time, but just before dawn the hawkling's keen direction led him right to the bolt-riddled body of the breed giant that had staggered away from the shore.

Eight crossbow bolts, the same as the one the zard had sunk into Master Biggs's shoulder, jutted up out of the huge corpse's back. This breed giant hadn't been the one handling Phen, but Hyden searched all around him anyway, for any indication that the boy had been there. After finding nothing, he rolled the breed over for a closer look. The sound of the quarrels breaking as the giant's great weight snapped them off startled Hyden. A great three-clawed gash ran across the breed's lower abdomen, probably from the claw of the dead zard that lay beyond the edge of the jungle.

"Phen," Hyden called out as loud as he could. "Where are you Phen? It's me, Hyden."

There was no response, save for the roar of the storm-born waves as they crashed into the rocky shore not far away.

The scene at the shoreline was the same as he had seen it before. A mangled zard that had seemingly been torn in two lay on the rocks just above the tide line, and the breed giant with the great black char mark on his chest was rolling to and fro in the shallows. It was hard to see in the rainy gloom, but Hyden used Talon's eyes and continued anyway.

"Phen!" he yelled what could've been a thousand times over. "Come out, Phen! It's all right." Hyden didn't even notice the sunrise, or the way the storm rolled past the island leaving the shoreline a vivid world of lush green foliage, dark rocky crags, and bright blue sea. Hyden's eyes kept finding the crimson stain of the lizard's lifeless body, and the puckered black char that covered the breed giant's chest.

"Phen!" he screamed and screamed some more until he finally collapsed on the rocks. His voice had turned to a torn and raspy wheeze. Even Talon's piercing shriek had lost its resonance. The two of them were completely spent, overcome with the realization that Phen was nowhere to be found.

"Lord Bzorch," Cozchin said with a smile that revealed his long wicked-looking lower teeth.

The Lord of Locar was sitting on his wooden throne doing absolutely nothing, but breathing heavy. All of the duties of running the city had fallen on Cozchin as of late. He didn't mind it too much because he got plenty of boons out of the deal: an occasional woman to rape and eat, and plenty of extra coin. It wasn't that hard to scare the human inhabitants of the city into compliance anyway. And it was entertaining.

"What is it?" Bzorch snarled, revealing teeth easily twice as deadly as Cozchin's. The breed giant Lord had been thinking a lot lately. His spy, Graven had been reporting things that caused him to think in a more diplomatic manner than what he was used to. Despite all of his instinctual primitive urges, he wanted badly to be a good leader for his people. He was the Lord of Locar, and he was starting to take the title seriously.

"Graven has returned from Wildermont again," said Cozchin with a look of distaste on his apish face. "He has news and says that it is important."

"See him in," Bzorch ordered. "Then, my dutiful cousin, I want you to find out if the dragon gun he brought back last time has been successfully replicated."

"Yes, Lord," Cozchin almost spat the response.

Graven had stolen his place as Lord Bzorch's favorite. Cozchin didn't like it at all. All Bzorch ever worried about now was what was happening in Wildermont, and how to mimic the pitiful humans' mechanical forms of defense. Cozchin didn't understand what use there was for a giant spear-launching weapon. The idea that once a working replica was perfected, Bzorch wanted one installed on every single watchtower around the city was preposterous. And now a wall. Why was Bzorch having a wall built around Locar?

Cozchin let Graven into the lobby then went off to check on the dragon gun with the hot fire of jealousy burning in his primitive mind. Half of the Reyhall Forest would be gone before Bzorch was done, figured the disgruntled half-breed as he went. Not that Cozchin cared about the trees. He was starting to think that Bzorch had gone mad with paranoia. Trenches, towers, dragon guns, and defensive walls— it was as if Lord Bzorch was expecting an attack soon.

"Lord," Graven growled with a bow after he heard the door close behind him. Bzorch waved the supplication off. "What news?"

"It's as you feared, Lord Bzorch," the big man-beast snarled. "Many hundreds of men, dozens and dozens of them, are coming into Wildermont from the mountains. They are building defenses to the south."

Bzorch understood that Graven could hardly understand the concept of numbers. Bzorch could read, and count, and reason as good as any man. A few hundred men, he figured, was likely a more accurate count. This only strengthened the idea that was forming in his mind.

"They're not fortifying along the river?" Bzorch asked. This still surprised him. He was sure the other humans were going to come for Queen Shaella soon. He had figured out that the Shaella that had stolen Westland wasn't as strong as she first appeared. He'd also figured out that she lost control of the great red wyrm somehow. The dragon had not been seen or heard of for many long months. Until he had become the Lord of Locar, Bzorch's access to books and maps had been limited to what the breed raiders had taken from the humans in the months before King Balton had imprisoned them on the Island of Coldfrost. Now, though, he had access to recent maps that showed the kingdoms to the east, and the many islands that littered the southern coast. Bzorch's one simple idea of finding Ironspike's owner and giving him to his queen had evolved into a plan that was almost the complete opposite of his original intent. Already Graven had identified the banners of Highwander, Valleya, and Wildermont amidst the growing number of men gathering across the river. Bzorch had seen for himself from atop one of his watchtowers, through his sailor's looking glass, the green and gold lion of Westland flying atop a stronghold's tower over there.

He wasn't sure what to do, but he wanted to hold Locar for him and his people. Of that he was certain. But he was growing less and less attached to the idea of fighting for Queen Shaella with each passing day. It was with this in mind that he started building the timber wall around his city. He was also having a great trench dug just inside the barrier. He wanted to be able to fill the trench with diverted water from the river if an attack came. The whole defensive plan was already underway. Now he was contemplating parleying with the humans across the river. Their might was beginning to show itself, and he was quite sure that thousands upon thousands more men from the east would eventually be brought to bear against Shaella. He would rather bargain for Locar and an allegiance, maybe even aid an attack on Westland, but only if Locar remained under breed giant control. Such was the reasoning that had him brooding on his throne.

"I want you to find a man," Bzorch said after long deliberation. "A native Westlander, whose loyalty to us can be trusted." He paused again, searching for someone to use as an example. "Farlanod, the logger we've made rich, or one of his braver men, someone like that. I will prepare a written message for whoever you choose. You'll escort this person across the river into Castlemont. I want the message to reach the High King, or the at least the Red Wolf, if he is truly alive."

"What will the message say?" Graven asked.

"I think the contents of the message..." Bzorch started with an angry look down at his spy's questioning. "This will determine the future of our people. I'm not sure yet of the wording. You need not concern yourself, Graven. Your safe return will be guaranteed. One thing that I've learned about humans who call themselves noble is that they are mostly honorable. Killing a messenger, and his escort, goes against everything they believe."

Graven didn't believe it, but after the look he was given, he didn't dare argue.

*

For a full day after they found Hyden sitting in a daze along the rocky shore of the island, the crew of the *Seawander* scoured the area, looking for a sign of Phen. It was as if he had vanished. The only conclusion was that he could have drowned, unless he was still on the zard ship headed for Westland. Captain Trant ordered the men aboard and set sail for Salazar's great port of Sala. There he would commandeer a ship to come retrieve the vast fortune they'd found on the island, and begin using the procedes to finance King Jarrek and the High King.

There was no doubt that Hyden was now planning to go off into Westland to find Phen and get back the artifact he needed. He now was of the belief that Phen had been taken onto the zard ship. From Sala he could find passage on a cargo vessel to Westland easily enough. As much as any of them hated to admit it, that was all they could do. Despite the great discovery of Cobalt's hoard and all the freedom its value might purchase, a dark cloud of defeat hung over the *Seawander* as it worked its way out to sea.

Only Oarly seemed interested in what Phen said when Flick was taking him away. Instead of locking himself in his cabin, or the latrine, the dwarf locked himself in the Captain's cabin. With careful attention to subtle detail, he began going over the work Phen had done translating Loak's journal. Oarly was certain that there was something there Phen wanted them to see, something that had been 'invisible to them.'

Chapter Thirty

"Someone once said that a dragon could lay waste to all of Salaya with a single breath," Prince Raspaar said with a chuckle. The island was small, but it boasted a sizable city at one of its two approachable ports. Being that it was nothing more than the tip of a mountain jutting up out of the sea, it was completely surrounded by rocky shoreline. There was no need for defensive walls or archer towers here. Only the lower portion of the island could support roads, and Salaya was surrounded by wicked coral reefs that would shred the hull of a ship unless navigated correctly.

King Raphaen's immaculate, yet modest, two-story home was far from being a castle. It was built on the crown of a hill overlooking the city that shared the island's name. Save for a somewhat famous garden at the top of the mountain, the terrain above couldn't sustain effective farming. The rocky mountainsides barely held enough greenery to feed the goat herds. The few sections of the island that did allow for agriculture were devoted to growing a rare herb that was in high demand throughout the realm. There were jade mines here too, but the entrances were hidden.

A great counter-weighted tram that clanked up and down the mountainside on a set of iron tracks was powered by two huge oxen walking in a circle around a spool of chain. The contraption lumbered up and down, carrying people, goods, and small animals in cages. The whole time he had been in it, Mikahl half expected it to go sliding back down the mountain into the city below.

"It is a small island," Lord Gregory agreed with the Prince.

"But it's beautiful." Lady Trella's elation was palpable as she nestled against her husband.

"You're too kind, my lady," the young prince of the island kingdom said with a smooth regal bow that caused Lady Trella to giggle.

They exited the tram and stood at an ornate wooden rail that surrounded a well-tended garden. It seemed as if they were riding on the bow of some colossal ship. From their vantage they could see the ocean in every direction save for behind them. There was a monastery somewhere below, and the monks who resided there tended the place called the Fairy Garden. The board walkway they were on wound its way around the bowl-shaped mountaintop. Clouds of white and sea-blue flowers, and ornately trimmed shrubbery surrounded small copses of perfectly formed miniature trees that were barely chest high to the High King.

The only tree able to sink its roots here, the fairy tree, was like any other tree, save for the fact that, at its full height, it would be barely as tall as a man. Bright green leaves the size of fingernails covered the branches. Looking at them,

Mikahl remembered the little man dressed in frog skin that had tricked him, Hyden, and Vaegon in the Evermore. He half expected to see a handful of the little people walking around the miniature forest.

"Dugak and Master Oarly would feel like giants in that wood," Mikahl observed.

"Who?" Lord Gregory asked. Mikahl smiled at his old friend. "Dwarves from Xwarda that I know." Lord Gregory actually heard the answer, which surprised Mikahl. The Lion Lord's head had been in the clouds since he'd found his lady wife.

"You've met dwarves?" Lady Trella asked curiously. Prince Raspaar seemed interested in Mikahl's story now, as well.

Lord Gregory slipped behind his wife and put his arms around her gently. He breathed deeply the scent of her hair, seemingly uninterested in anything Mikahl had to say.

"Aye, m'lady, I have." Mikahl's smile was wide. "And elves, and even a blue-skinned pixie that would fit this forest well. The dwarves are..." he paused in search of an appropriate description of his hairy, usually drunken friends. "Unique," he finally said, remembering Dugak's sweet bearded wife, Andra.

"And giants," Lord Gregory added with his chin resting on Lady Trella's shoulder. "Don't forget the giants."

"Not just giants—King Aldar, the king of the giants," Mikahl said proudly. He reached into his collar and pulled out the piece of bone that the Great King had carved into a lion's head for him. "It's dragon bone," he boasted. "It was supposed to be for my father, but, well, you know."

The sudden thought of King Balton triggered a memory of the dream he had been having for the last few days. He wasn't sure why he started dreaming of his father, but he had. He'd never dreamed of King Balton before. He decided that it was because of the familial feelings he held toward Lord Gregory and Lady Trella, and the memories that being around them evoked. They had raised him in his awkward years while he squired for the Lion Lord and struggled to become a man. Still, the image of his dream—his father, half-decayed and worm-ridden, telling him to save the Princess of Seaward, while Rosa screamed in terror in the background, was an unsettling thing to recall so suddenly.

Lady Trella, noticing Mikahl's loss of color and the change in his demeanor, put the back of her fingers against his cheek. "You're fevered, Mik," she said in a motherly tone. "You should rest."

"Aye," he replied, unable to shake the morbid picture his mind was displaying. He had the strange feeling that he had been magicked in some way. Instinctually, he stepped away from his companions and pulled Ironspike a few inches out of its sheath. The sword's radiant blue glow brightened the leaves of the fairy trees near him and as soon as the symphony of the sword's magic was in his ears the eerie feeling left him, but not the memory of it.

A monk in black robes who had been silently meditating nearby at one of the many altar-like shrines that were spread around the gardens, came upon them with an excited look on his face. The man was plump and bald, save for a thin horseshoe of graying hair that ran around the back of his head from ear to ear. The circle of his wide open mouth could barely be seen through the silvery gray mustache and beard that ran down to the rope that held his robes closed at the waist.

"Look!" he gasped, pointing at the fairy trees nearby. "It's miraculous!"

When they turned to see what the man was so excited about, they were treated to one of the rarest sights to ever been seen in the realm. Everywhere Ironspike's magical light had touched the leaves of the fairy trees, crimson flowers were blooming before their eyes. They appeared like droplets of blood, and after a moment a bright yellow and red explosion of needle-like pistols formed at the center of each flower. As they bloomed further, the yellow and red combined into a flaming orange that made the trees look as if they were catching fire. A light breeze ruffled the flowering leaves, and the phenomenon began to spread across the entire copse to the other trees until soon the whole grove had bloomed.

Mikahl and the others were left speechless. Only Lord Gregory braved the silent awe to speak.

"M'lady," he whispered softly into his wife's ear. "It seems the local foliage has grown jealous of your beauty and is now trying to compete."

Mikahl's dream had been wiped completely from his mind by the sweet fruity smell of the blooms. At Lord Gregory's words he glanced at Prince Raspaar and rolled his eyes. Both of them gave Lord Gregory a look and they eased away from the newly reunited lovers. The monk moving around the walkway was watching with shocked fascination. As the blooms matured he started to join them, but a look from the Prince sent him scurrying around to study elsewhere.

"There's no doubt what they will be doing tonight," the Prince said to Mikahl with a laugh. "I do believe that, if he hadn't had his arms around her, she would have melted into the earth."

"He does have a way of speaking to her, doesn't he?" Mikahl said. "Even the most prudent of maidens couldn't have resisted a compliment like that."

"As you mainlanders always seem to say," the Prince said in agreement. "Aye."

News of the High King's arrival at the Westland settlement on the island of Salazar traveled swiftly. When the *Seawander* anchored in the great port of Sala, the Harbor Master sent word to Captain Trant immediately. Hyden was pleased to hear that Mikahl was just a short sail away, visiting the island of Salaya. He, Oarly, and Trant traveled by carriage to the Westland settlement called Balton while Deck Master Biggs went about finding a ship to haul the dragon's hoard.

Hyden Hawk needed Mikahl's advice, and he had to let his friend know what sort of damage he had done by letting the black dragon fall under the control of Queen Shaella's wizard. He didn't relish telling Mikahl the news. Already Mikahl was miffed at him for not killing Shaella when he'd had the chance. Shaella had truly loved Hyden's brother Gerard and for that reason he had foolishly let her live. Now his mistake might cost Phen his life. There was no guessing how much death and destruction would fall on his shoulders for letting the Silver Skull and the black dragon slip into the bitch's hands. He was in such a state that it was all he could do to keep from taking the first ship to Westland to find out what happened to Phen and kill Shaella himself. The urge to do something, anything, to help right the wrong was overwhelming. This feeling was only eclipsed by his desire to save Phen.

Oarly insisted that the High King and the Lion Lord be included in the planning of any attempt to go into the Dragon Queen's domain, and Captain Trant's conclusion that if Phen wasn't dead already then it was unlikely that they would kill him now, helped Hyden keep his cool.

They'd sent word to Mikahl and Lord Gregory by swifter hawk and Mikahl was to return on the morrow from Salaya. Then they would all sit down and figure out what to do. The fact that Lord Gregory was alive and had spent the whole winter among Hyden's clan folk hovered in the back of his mind as well. He hadn't spoken to, or even sent word to, his people since he had set off into the Giant Mountains what seemed like a lifetime ago. He decided that, as soon as he'd saved Phen and retrieved Gerard's ring from the Nethers, he would go home for a while.

Oarly was glad Hyden was remaining semi-clearheaded about the matter. He was on the cusp of finding something in Phen's translation that was just out of reach. He had seen something happen in the dragon's treasure cavern that hadn't seemed possible until Phen made the strange statement about finding something invisible in his work. Just before the dragon had liquefied the seamen, Oarly had seen Phen huddle behind an artifact and disappear. The dwarf had dismissed it as being a trick of the eye caused by the rush of fear when the dragon came in on them, but now he felt that he might have been seeing true. As they waited for Mikahl to return to the Lost Lion Inn, and enjoyed the kind hospitality of the mother-to-be who was running the place, Oarly was delving deeper into Phen's books trying to figure out the conundrum.

The tavern had long ago emptied of custom, yet Hyden and the dwarf still sat at the bar. Uncharacteristically, Oarly refused to do more than sip at a goblet of mulled wine. Beside him, Hyden sat quietly talking with the innkeeper, Zasha, about Mikahl's youth.

"He was a troublesome cuss," she said with a grin at the memory. "We all were. We caused a lot of silver hairs to grow in our time, I assure you."

"If I wasn't in such a foul mood, I would be prying you for an edge of information to use against him in the next prank I play." Hyden took a long sip from his goblet. "As it is, I feel like I'll never be able to jest again."

"Whoever she was, she couldn't have been all that."

"Nay, Zash," Hyden smiled and shook his head. "It's death that has me feeling so low. Death, and the possibility of more of it."

"Death is just part of life," she said with an innkeeper's practiced neutrality. After an uneasy glance at the big hawkling eyeing her from Hyden's shoulder she asked, "Is there anything I can get for your feathered friend, Sir Hyden Hawk?"

"Please Zash, it's Hyden, just plain Hyden." The slur in his voice revealed that he was more than just a little drunk. "A few strips of red meat, and Talon here will love you for life. He's had enough fish to last an eternity."

Zasha wasn't sure she wanted the fierce looking predator bird to love her forever, but she disappeared into the kitchen and returned with a platter of meat strips. Talon leapt to the bar with a flutter and began to consume them vigorously.

The sound of the door closing behind Hyden brought a huge smile to Zasha's face. She wobbled her pregnant self around the bar and hurried to greet a young man who looked to have spent a good deal of time laboring at some physical form of work.

"I thought you'd never return," she said as she nearly leapt into his arms. "Oh, Wyndall, so much has happened. Lord Gregory has returned, and High King Mikahl, and look." She pointed to the back of Oarly at the bar, who absently scratched at the crack of his wide, partially exposed buttocks. She had to stifle a laugh. "There's a dwarf here at the Lost Lion," she giggled.

"And the great wizard Sir Hyden and his hawk from the battle of Xwarda as well," Wyndall added with a respectful grin. "After we offloaded in Seaward, we stopped at Weir in Highwander to search for more ore to purchase. Rumors of Sir Hyden and King Mikahl's deeds are often spoken of over cups in those taverns. I think there's even a song or two about them."

Just then Hyden turned and fell from the stool into a crumpled heap on the floor. Oarly gave him a glance and returned to his reading. Talon peered down from his plate, but soon went back to his meal.

"He's drunk," Zasha said. "He just lost a few dear friends."

Wyndall nodded in understanding. He had lost everything to Glendar's insane campaign against Wildermont, but his smile didn't falter. "I bet Lady Trella is pleased." He gave his wife a long kiss on the lips.

"To say the least," she replied and pulled him closer. "Promise me, Wyndall. Promise me you'll not run off with them." Her eyes took on a fearful look. "Lord Gregory is not your liege any longer, and you're about to be a father."

"You're everything to me Lady Zasha," he reassured her with a pat on her swollen belly. "I'll not leave you for the world."

"That is the smartest thing I've heard anybody say in months, lad," Oarly said, turning from the bar with a grin. His voice was full of hope and joy, for he had just figured out what foolish young Phen had done. It was hard to have anything less than respect for the boy's idiotic action. But after traveling for so long in the company of fools like Brady Culvert, and Sir Hyden Hawk Skyler, to expect anything less from the young mage was just plain silly.

Chapter Thirty-One

"How many?" King Ra'Gren asked one of the underlords from the Dakaneese city of Owask. The title of underlord labeled a man whose station was a few steps above common. In Dakahn, if you were not a slave you were at the very least a lord. This man, Lord Antone, was Battle Lord Ra'Carr's message runner, and he was fairly nervous. "So far we are thirty-five hundred strong. That's not counting the men from Oktin and Lokahna. As far as Lord Ra'Carr has been able to tell, that is twice the number of men currently holding Wildermont."

It was late afternoon and the torch-lit throne room was stuffy with the smell of pitch and men.

"I didn't ask you for an account of our enemy," King Ra'Gren growled down from his fur covered throne.

Lord Antone visibly blanched. The last runner, Lord Archa, had been impaled by the King's trident only a week previous for arguing about Ra'Gren's attack strategies. Sadly, Lord Archa had been right, and two days after his death the King altered the plan to the man's suggestion. Remembering this, Lord Antone held his tongue. If he could keep himself alive, he would find great favor and vastly increase his holdings once Wildermont was taken.

"Where are they staged?" Ra'Gren asked. His eyebrows rose as he gazed on the nervous lord below him with a look that challenged him to say more than the simple answer to his question.

"On the border, just north of Pearsh, my King."

Ra'Gren paused, his large hand clenching and unclenching on the shaft of the iron trident standing at his side.

Lord Antone almost added, "A half day's march from Seareach," but wisely decided that the geography of the area made that perfectly obvious to his king. He was glad he held his tongue. King Ra'Gren looked as if he was eager to gig somebody this day.

Seated in the rows of pews opposite the throne were many of the community leaders of the city of O'Dakahn; the owners of the mercenary companies, the major slave traders, the men who owned the farmlands and the like. A few men from the shipping industry, and a group of builders from the Isle of Salazar were there to bargain for Wildermont slaves. Most of the Dakaneese slave merchants usually had representatives in court in their stead, but with Ra'Gren's coming attack on Wildermont on the horizon, and rumors of a huge slave purchase about to take place, they came themselves.

"Are there not more swords to be had?" Ra'Gren asked with a hard gaze out across the pews. "I know for a fact that there are more than thirty-five hundred sell-swords working in my kingdom. Why are they not in my service?"

The Dakaneese army was strong. Ra'Gren had thousands of soldiers at his command, but for some reason he was trying not to use them in this campaign. He wanted to take Wildermont with mercenaries who didn't fight under his trident banner. The idea of paying them all with the Wildermont gold King Glendar had gifted him was a pleasant irony.

An older man stood, and visibly forced one of his competitors back to his seat as he worked his way forward. "If I may?" the man said over the murmur of the attendees.

"Speak, Lord Tromas," Ra'Gren said, causing the room to silence. "You and your company have served Dakahn well. I Trust your words."

"I can offer you a few hundred more men that have just come in from the sea," he said with widespread arms. "I think I speak for all of the major companies when I say that we're spread thin. The increase in our own piracy has created the need for ships and trained fighters to escort cargoes as of late. Most of my men are still away, my King, but as they return, I will gladly send them into your service."

A man from the front row of pews stood and spoke over the old mercenary. "My King, I have four hundred trained men, and two hundred untrained men to offer immediately."

"Those aren't swordsmen, Lord Cryden, those are slaves," Lord Tromas spat at the interruption.

"Enough," Ra'Gren said with a booming bang of his trident on the marble floor. "The next man that speaks without permission will be fed to the skeeks."

Lord Tromas smirked at the upstart then turned back to his king with his chin held high, but Ra'Gren paid him no mind.

The King turned to one of the men standing patiently behind him. "I want the shifts of the city guard thinned down to the minimum. Send everyone who isn't absolutely necessary along with two thousand of our cavalry to aid Lord Ra'Carr immediately. I want..."

"My King," a young breathless boy called out loudly, just before one of the great oaken doors of the throne room boomed closed behind him. "Forgive me," the boy huffed between breaths. A clear path between Ra'Gren and the intruder had opened up. Everyone expected Ra'Gren's trident to go flying into the young man at any instant.

"This had better be extraordinary news, boy," Ra'Gren said. The vein on his forehead looked like an earthworm, and his white hair contrasted violently with the bright crimson tint of his anger.

Confused, the boy looked uncertainly at the men who had parted before him. "Lord Paleon sent me." He gasped for breath and continued. "An army of Seawardsmen have crossed into Dakahn." The boy breathed again, this time taking a few breaths before going on. "When Oktin's guard challenged them, the Seawardsmen killed them all. M'lord Paleon says they're headed to Wildermont to aid the Wolf King."

Ra'Gren turned to Lord Antone and said hotly, "Well you can scratch the men from Oktin from Ra'Carr's count. I want riders, birds, and fargin smoke signals if need be sent to warn my Battle Lord. He is to advance his men into the Wildermont hills beyond Seareach long before those tattoo-covered mongrels can get there. The maps show a narrow bottleneck where he can trap them."

When he didn't make for the door immediately, Ra'Gren stood and looked sharply down at Lord Antone. "You'd better make sure Ra'Carr gets the message soon, man," the King growled. "If those Seawardsmen get there before Ra' Carr can set the trap I will personally flay you and keep your children as pets." The look in King Ra'Gren's eyes conveyed a threat far more intimidating than the words, and with that Lord Antone was off.

"You, the man with the trained slaves," Ra'Gren called out.

"Yes, my King," the man rose and gave Lord Tromas a smug glare.

"Take your men and slow the Seaward army's passage." Ra'Gren ordered as he began to pace back and forth before his throne. "I don't care if your men are killed or not, nor you for that matter. Buy Lord Antone a day, that's all I ask. If your men fail, and you still live, I'll know you for a coward. Now go."

Lord Tromas pulled on his chin and cringed. He had expected the King to punish the man for his outburst, but not with such finality. He jerked his attention from the matter when his name was called. "Lord Tromas, I want your men on their ships," Ra'Gren's voice was harsh. "This goes for all you fargin pirates there in the back as well. Every ship flying Seaward's setting sun is to be molested. If you can take the cargo, do so; if not, they rest at the bottom of the sea. Valleyan and Highwander ships as well. I want every captain who does not fly the trident to be afraid."

With a dismissive wave to the attendees Ra'Gren turned back to the captain of the city guard who was still waiting beside the throne. Ra'Gren almost berated him for standing there after he had been given orders, but remembered that the young messenger boy had interrupted them. "Two thousand cavalry, two thousand infantry, and all the city guard that can be spared," Ra'Gren told him. "I want the cavalry riding today. They are to compress Queen Rachel's little army between themselves and Ra'Carr's sell-swords. When the infantry and the city guard arrive at the bottleneck at Seareach, I want them to find that there's no one left to fight. Do you understand?"

"I will lead the cavalry myself, my King," Captain Da'Markell said with a sharp salute.

"Good, Overlord Da'Markell," Ra'Gren nodded. The new title of overlord made Da'Markell's eyes widen and his chest swell visibly.

"We will be expecting word of your victory soon," Ra'Gren finished with a dismissive wave.

The man saluted again, and hurried off to begin carrying out his orders.

Ra'Gren turned toward the court's scribe, whose desk was at the side of the hall. "Remind me later, Brackly, to send a bird to Shaella. The Dragon Queen owes us a favor or two." The King surveyed the throne room then. It was nearly empty now, save for a few men still waiting patiently in the pews. "What else do we have today?"

"A Lord Northall and his associates from the Island of Salazar," the scribe answered dutifully. "They are seeking to purchase a large quantity of slaves."

"Lord Northall," Ra'Gren said expectantly as he sat back down on his throne. The redness had left his face and he seemed to be far calmer than he had been earlier.

Lord Northall rose and strode forward, his expression that of a nervous businessman, while inside he was torn.

He wanted to help King Jarrek, and in the process get the mines and forges of Wildermont up and running again, but he had doubts now. He didn't think Jarrek could protect the people he had released, much less any others. King Ra'Gren's attack on Wildermont seemed far more serious now than it had before. It wasn't just a bunch of greedy sell-swords now. Trained city guard, and cavalry were about to be involved.

The fact that Queen Rachel was sending men to aid Wildermont brought about another set of problems. If Ra'Gren killed her men, she would retaliate, and after all the death and destruction that Pael and King Glendar left behind, Seaward and Dakahn had taken the fewest losses. Both countries still had strong militaries. A war between them could have unforeseen repercussions for Jarrek and the slaves he sought to free. Lord Northall decided to go about his plans to purchase a thousand slaves and free them. But he needed time to sort out his company and the island's best interest in all of this. It pained him how his personal feelings had to be put aside. If it were up to him, he would buy all the slaves, and the sell-swords, right out from under the power hungry tyrant, Ra'Gren. He'd set them on the man like a pack of wolves. He took a breath, and mentally checked his expression to make sure his hatred for the King before him wasn't showing. Once he reached the foot of King Ra'Gren's dais, he bowed graciously.

"Salazarkian coins are always welcome in Dakahn," Ra'Gren said encouragingly. "But it is a strange request when the island folk want to purchase slaves. Slavery is forbidden on Salazar, is it not, Lord Northall?"

"It is Your Highness," Northall answered, and offered no more.

"Explain your need to me, and why you are choosing to break the law and custom of your people then."

"King Ra'Gren," Northall started his well rehearsed and mostly factual story. "The sudden lack of iron ore and forged products from abroad has caused the prices of those items to take dragon's flight. To compensate for the extra expense, some of the wiser builders are trying to cut down on the cost of labor. We believe the entire industry will come around to our way of thinking after they realize the losses their coffers will feel if we cannot continue to build and sell our ships."

Ra'Gren tilted his head, considering Northall for a moment. "How many do you need?" he finally asked.

"A thousand head," Northall said, hiding his disgust at the way he was speaking of human beings as if they were chattel. "Some of them need to be prime laborers. Men from thirteen summers to fifty, but we would like at least half of them to be younger, with women to look after them." Northall smiled and shrugged. "We want some of them to grow into the trades, and the women can cook and tend the others."

"Ha," Ra'Gren half laughed. "If you would have asked for all able bodied men I might have thought you were consorting with the Wolf King. Don't think I'm a fool, Lord Northall. You don't want women and children for the reasons you stated here."

Northall cringed inwardly. Were his true motives to free the slaves so obvious? He began to worry. He couldn't believe he was so transparent.

"Don't look so chagrinned, man," Ra'Gren laughed. "It is wise to think about the future."

The future, Northall thought. *What in all the hells?*

"There's no sense hiding it," Ra'Gren scolded. "You want breeders. Some men to do labor now, some youth to grow into the work, and women to breed, so that a dozen years from now you'll not need to come to us for more." Ra'Gren nodded as if he respected the plan.

With a continuous effort, Northall tried to keep from commenting out of character. "Since you do not disapprove of our intention, I think we can double our first order."

"Approve, disapprove, it doesn't matter," Ra'Gren laughed. "By the time your breeders' offspring have matured enough to perform, you'll have fattened my coffers aplenty. As it is, I will have owners bidding away to fill your order, with so many extra mouths to feed, the sellers are competing by upping the throne's take. I'd bet my crown that one of the slavers offers me half the profit just for the honor of filling such a healthy order." Ra'Gren's gaze ventured past Lord Northall to the slavers still sitting in the back of the hall. They seemed to be conferring amongst themselves. A few of them had pallid expressions on their faces. Finally one of them stood and gave a nod to the King, indicating that he would split the profit of Lord Northall's purchase evenly with the crown.

"Mortram Grail will see that your needs are met."

"Thank you, Majesty," Lord Northall said with a broad-faced smile. He bowed and made his way over to Mortram Grail. Once the great oak doors of the throne room closed behind them, the slaver sighed and turned to Lord Northall.

"It will take a few hours to ready the herd for your inspection," he said in a way that showed his disappointment at having to pay his kingdom half the profit from this sale. "I assume you'll want to pick from the lot?"

"Yes, yes," Northall answered. The relief at being out of the King of Dakahn's presence was visible on both of them. "I'll be taking a meal at the Sea Master's Inn. Do you know it?"

"Of course, excellent choice. The pen we keep the herd in is not far from there," the slaver said, nodding his approval at Northall's choice of eateries. "I'll send a man to the inn to fetch you when we're ready."

"Very good," Northall said. His group of private guards, posing as his associates, had gathered behind him.

"Come," Northall ordered his men and started out of Ra'Gren's lavish palace. As soon as they were away from the place and its many ears, Northall ordered one of his men to ride to Salazar's embassy house. He told the man to immediately send birds to Wildermont and Dreen to warn King Jarrek and General Spyra of Ra'Gren's intention. Northall wasn't sure a warning from a Salazarkian lord would prevent what was to come, but at least he would know that he tried to tell King Jarrek of Ra'Gren's intent to bottle up the approaching Seawardsmen. He could only hope that Jarrek had the men to stop the attack. If the Red Wolf couldn't hold there, Ra'Gren would be able to take Wildermont with ease.

Chapter Thirty-Two

Having just heard from Lady Trella about the death of Father Petri, High King Mikahl was in low spirits when he walked into the Lost Lion Inn and saw his good friend Hyden. The look on Hyden's face filled Mikahl with dread. A quick scan of the room explained the expression. Neither Phen, nor Brady Culvert was among them, and the reason was obvious.

"It gets worse," Hyden said, seeing the look of grim understanding come over his friend.

Talon fluttered down from a roof beam and landed on Mikahl's shoulder. The big hawkling softly cooed a greeting.

"Hey, Talon," Mikahl said softly to the bird. He took a deep breath then sat at an empty table. Talon leapt to the tabletop and began preening himself, content to just be near his old companion.

It was after dawn and the Lost Lion's common room was empty. The one other guest that had stayed the night left with the Highwander soldier and Master Biggs before sun-up. There was no need to worry about interruptions or prying eyes, which was just as well, because Lord Gregory and Prince Raspaar were laboring like commoners, trying to get Lady Trella's travelling trunk through the door.

As soon as the luggage was properly put away there would be breakfast and a meeting of minds. Until then, Mikahl reflected inwardly while Hyden tried to figure out how he was going to explain all that had happened.

"I feel like I'm in a story," Lady Trella said, trying to lighten the mood of the men around her. "Here I have a lord, and a prince carrying my things, and a king brooding in my common room. And there at the bar sits a renowned wizard and his pet dwarf."

Despite his ill mood, Hyden couldn't help but smile at the jibe. Oarly growled in mock anger, which made him seem even more like a pet sitting at his master's side. The noise Lord Gregory and Prince Raspaar were making with the trunk made it pointless to speak further, but the two men finally got the heavy box up the stairs.

"How is Jarrek?" Hyden asked, after Lady Trella had gone up to supervise the placement of her things.

"Not well," Mikahl answered. "He harassed the King of Dakahn, killed a dozen of his overlords, and freed over a thousand of his people, but Ra'Gren is ruthless. He stopped Jarrek's little war cold by executing hundreds of Wildermont innocents in the street. They say it went off like a stage show, that Ra'Gren relished the act. They said that he let the last little girl, who had watched all the others die before her, beg for mercy. He teased her with freedom, Hyden. Then he whacked off her head without a thought." Mikahl pinched the bridge of his nose and continued. "From what word we've gotten, Jarrek's war is no longer a little one. King Ra'Gren is buying up sell-swords to try and take a firm control of Wildermont."

"Willa will help Jarrek," Hyden said.

"Aye," Mikahl agreed. "And so will I just as soon as I can get Princess Rosa back from that dragonless, dragon-riding bitch, Shaella."

"Princess Rosa?" Hyden asked. *What could have happened to her?* His heart was sinking lower than it already was. The gods had made Rosa just for Mikahl, Hyden was sure of it.

Mikahl got up and strode around the bar. He made himself a mug of ale as he explained. "Rosa was taken from Seaward some weeks ago." Mikahl gestured at Oarly and Hyden, asking if they wanted some ale too.

"Who am I to turn down the chance to get served by the High King," Oarly said with a forced grin.

"Shaella's not dragonless anymore," Hyden said, almost too quiet for anyone to hear.

"What?" Mikahl nearly shouted. He'd heard all too clearly. The sound of his voice startled Talon. The hawkling flapped back up to his rafter perch, leaving a pair of feathers to flutter down from above.

"I... We... Uh..."

"Pael's fargin ghost snatched our boy," Oarly said over Hyden's stammering. "We found the Silver Skull, and enough treasure to buy all of Ra'Gren's slaves to a man. We even collared the young black wyrm that killed Brady, but Shaella's wizard snatched the skull, and the controlling collar, then he sailed away."

"Don't forget Phenilous," Hyden put his face in his hands. "They snatched him too."

Oarly hadn't told Hyden of his discovery yet. He'd wanted to research the journal further to be certain before stirring up any hopes. He went with his instinct, though, and decided that now was as good of time as any to explain. "Phen wasn't snatched away," Oarly said matter-of-factly.

"What?" Hyden's head whipped around to meet the dwarf's eyes. "Tell me what you know."

Oarly was a known trickster and Phen's fate was nothing to jest about. The dwarf had no trouble meeting Hyden's gaze, and the look in his eyes strengthened the conviction of his words.

"It's in the journal," Oarly started. He took a long pull from the goblet of ale Mikahl handed him and then licked the foam from his mustache. "Loak was an assassin sent to kill King Chago. The gift was his ruse for gaining an audience. The ring was for him to use to escape, once he had done the deed. It was ensorcelled to make the wearer invisible. Loak could kill Chago, slip on the ring, and make his escape back to the Evermore unseen."

"What are you telling me?" asked Hyden.

Mikahl was looking at the both of them as if they had gone mad. He had no idea who Loak was, but he'd heard of the infamous tyrant King Chago. His brain told him that none of it mattered. Something far more dire than the news of Shaella gaining another dragon had piqued his mind, but as Oarly spoke of Phen the thought eluded him.

"Phenilous put on the ring and somehow caused the wizard to blast the breed giant," Oarly explained. "Our boy went aboard that zard ship trying to be an invisible hero."

"What in all the hells are you two talking about?" Mikahl finally burst out. "Zard ships, breed giants, Pael's ghost, and who in all the hells is Loak?"

"An elf," Hyden answered, but was saved from having to explain further.

"I think it would be best if we all break our fast and listen to the story from the beginning, Mik," Lord Gregory said as he and Prince Raspaar came down the stairs. "Trella and Zasha are coming to fix us a morning feast. We can all tell our tales at the table. Then we can begin to sort it all out and make a plan."

The Lion Lord stopped and pointed at the young man coming down the stairs behind them. The man's hair looked like a nest and he was wiping sleep from his eyes. "Sir Hyden Hawk, Master Oarly, this is Wyndall. He is the one who saved Zasha and Trella from the skeeks at Lake Bottom."

Wyndall forced a smile and raised his hand dismissively before banging out a side door to have his morning piss with the door half open.

The Lion Lord indicated the man who had been helping him get the chest up the stairs. "And this is Prince Raspaar of Salaya. He is a friend."

While the ladies prepared their meal, Wyndall pulled two tables together then stood back as the others chose a place. He wanted desperately to join them, to be a part of the great planning that he knew was about to take place, but looks from both Zasha and the strange dwarf kept him from it. Instead, he trudged through the kitchen and began loading in wood from the chop pile out back.

Lord Gregory started by telling them all of his recovery in the Skyler Clan village, and his long slow battle to walk again. He spoke of what he thought when he first saw the rubble of Castlemont, and of his meeting with Dreg. He told of his journey into Westland with Grommen, who had recently partnered with Maxrell Tyne and taken over the *Shark's Tooth* after Captain Konrath mysteriously disappeared. He led his tale all the way up to finding Mikahl, and their arrival at the Lost Lion Inn.

The food arrived and, while they ate, Mikahl told his story as well. He told of the long slow march from Xwarda with General Spyra, and of the fight in the lower Evermore with the demon-boar. He touched briefly on King Broderick's betrayal and the battle with Dreg and the mercenaries. He told everything he could think of to tell, then sat back and listened with rapt attention as Hyden and Oarly took turns recounting their fascinating journey.

An elbow from Oarly stopped Hyden from saying too much about the Serpent's Eye on the Isle of Kahna. They had made a pact to keep that place a secret, but otherwise they left out few details. Oarly even described the grisly way that Brady and the seamen had fallen to the black dragon. Their tale, as all of the others, ended up with them arriving at the Lost Lion Inn.

All eyes fell to Prince Raspaar then, who after hearing the fantastic adventures of the others, could only open and close his mouth as if he were a beached fish.

Mikahl explained Raspaar's involvement with the group. After hearing how the Prince of Salaya had craftily used his equine importing scheme to place spies in Southport, Portsmouth, even in Castleview, the city built along Lakeside Castle's northwest wall, Hyden and Oarly both begrudged him some respect.

"It seems we have two people who need to be spirited out of Westland now," Lord Gregory observed as the food was cleared away. "And another dragon to contend with. I'm glad I missed the first one."

"As much as I hate it, my duty to the people of the realm has to come first," Mikahl's voice was soft and sad. "The Silver Skull of Zorellin must be destroyed or recovered. The damage Shaella can cause with it far outweighs the lives of Princess Rosa and Phenilous."

Hyden rose and shoved himself away from the table. His chair went tumbling over behind him with a force that startled the others. "No," he yelled. "The skull is my responsibility, and I swear I'll get it back from her." He heaved a heavy breath. Putting his closed fists on the table, he leaned over and looked Mikahl directly in the eyes. "You use the power of that sword to get Phen and Rosa out of harm's way. I will fix the follies of my family like I should've done long ago."

Hyden's sense of guilt was palpable as of late. His brother had helped Shaella collar the great red dragon Claret that had been forced to help take Westland. Now the ring Gerard had taken into the Nethers had caused him to seek out the Silver Skull's hiding place and deliver it to the Dragon Queen on a platter. He should have killed Shaella when he had the chance. He hoped to gain the opportunity. If it arose again he would not hesitate.

"If you expect to have even half a chance to succeed at any of this then you will have to work together," Lord Gregory said.

"I agree," Oarly said with a harsh tug on Hyden's sleeve.

"The Princess is being held somewhere in Lakeside Castle," Raspaar said, trying to get things moving in the right direction. "We have a ship scheduled to deliver horses to Portsmouth in a few days. We can get you there, or maybe let you off in a sturdy rower near Lake Bottom." He glanced at Lord Gregory for support.

"I'll not enjoy being in a rowboat again," said Oarly.

"You're not going with us," Hyden told him. "You'll stick out like a broken toe in Westlad."

"She is in Pael's tower," Mikahl said directly to Hyden, ignoring the others. "With the sword, and the bright horse, I think I can easily get Rosa free and away. It's finding Phen and the skull that will be the issue."

"If you find the skull, you'll find Phenilous," Oarly said. He wanted to go after the boy with Hyden, but he knew the wizard was right.

"How do you know she is in Pael's tower?" Lord Gregory asked Mikahl.

"My father tells me every night in my dreams," Mikahl answered before thinking of how crazy the explanation sounded.

"You can't rely on a dream," Lord Gregory said coolly.

"If there's anything in this life that I trust, it is Mikahl's instincts," said Hyden Hawk. "If we can get there, then Talon can help me find Phen and the skull. Without a doubt he can confirm Princess Rosa's presence in the tower. We might even be able to get a message to her."

"Now we're getting somewhere," Lord Gregory nodded to everyone. "There are arrow slits in Pael's roost."

"If Phen wasn't so foolishly brave," Oarly added, "we would have the ring to help find the skull, and only one hostage to worry about."

"Phen is capable," Hyden defended, more to reassure himself than for any other reason. "He probably already has the skull, and the collar, and is flying with Rosa toward Xwarda on the dragon's back."

"I wish it were true," Oarly said.

"Aye," Hyden and Mikahl said in unison, causing Oarly and Prince Raspaar to give them a strange look.

"So where will you want to leave the ship?" the Prince finally asked.

"There is a way into the dungeon through the wall that faces Lion Lake," Lord Gregory told them. "And also there's a way through the temple in the northeastern..."

"That will only get us inside the wall," Mikahl cut off the Lion Lord. "We need inside the castle itself. Do you know how to get from the dungeons up to the main halls?"

"King Balton showed me the way once. His dungeon was a barren place. I can try to make a map for you, but I have literally died and come back to life since then. It's been years." Lord Gregory stopped speaking and studied a point somewhere in space. The others were waiting on him to continue. Eventually he sighed away the memory and did so. "Maybe I should go with you. I spent twice as many years as Mikahl in that castle, and people I know and trust might still be around to help us gather information."

"No," Mikahl said flatly. "I'd rather be chewed up and swallowed by a dragon than face Lady Trella if something happened to you again."

"He's right," Hyden agreed. "If Mikahl and I need to get out of Westland in a hurry, we can manage it." He found his hand was fondling the dragon's tear medallion under his shirt as he spoke. "I'll not risk the happiness of your lady on it."

"You can't expect the rest of us to sit around and do nothing while you two risk your lives and the future of the realm," Gregory said, indicating the sword at Mikahl's hip. "It's a blatant waste of experience."

"I do not expect either you or Master Oarly to sit around and do nothing," Mikahl told Lord Gregory, putting a hint of kingly authority in his voice. "There's plenty to be done in Wildermont. There are ships sitting idle at the dock here. If you can find a water mage to propel you up the Leif Greyn River through the marsh channels, you can get there in a week unnoticed. Lady Trella will be safe enough there, as will you. King Jarrek could use your wisdom. Eventually, General Spyra will need to be relieved of his reign over Dreen. I can think of no one more suited to the task then you, Lord Gregory."

"What about me?" asked Oarly.

"What better place for a dwarf than the ore-rich mountains of Wildermont?" Mikahl said. "You can help King Jarrek with the slaves he has freed, and the others that Lord Northall is purchasing. It will take leadership to get the mines and forges running again."

"In all of this, nothing has been said about what to do with Queen Shaella and her new dragon," Lord Gregory said.

"Not true," Mikahl said, with a stern look at Hyden. "The great wizard Sir Hyden Hawk has already sworn to fix the follies of his family. If there is one thing in this life I know I can depend on, it's Hyden Skyler keeping his word."

Had it been anyone else speaking to him in such a manner, Hyden would have probably throttled them. Mikahl was just trying to get under his skin and motivate him for what was to come. The tactless reminder of his oath was not intended as an insult. A dozen sharp remarks came to mind for Hyden to reply, but he chose to keep them to himself. He locked gazes with the High King, and with a nod of determination he said the only thing that was left to be said: "Aye!"

Chapter Thirty-Three

Phen wasn't sure what he expected. Being a smart, well-read boy of fourteen years he obviously hoped to find adventure. The glory of success motivated him almost as much as his sense of duty. He felt that he had to stay with the Silver Skull. He had to make sure that the Dragon Queen didn't get it. Hyden needed it. The consequences of his actions were all but forgotten when he slipped the ring on his finger and disappeared.

Twice now he could have snatched the artifact and thrown it overboard. It would have sunk to the bottom of the sea, as simple as that. But Hyden needed the skull to get into the Nethers. He had admitted his true reasons for needing the skull to Phen one night on the *Seawander*. Phen knew that he would have to wait until the zard ship docked somewhere before he could get it ashore. It was the only way, save for one: the dragon collar.

If he could get that, he could put it on and have the dragon attack the ship. He could get the skull and have the dragon fly him back to the *Seawander*. That is exactly what Hyden would do, he knew. The only problem with that plan was the wizard, Flick. Flick refused to take the device from his neck. Since he was invisible, Phen wanted to try to pick it off while Flick slept, but he couldn't get past the complex magical lock the cautious wizard placed on the door to his cabin each night.

Phen was left with little to do other than hide, listen, and starve. He tried not to let the gruesome death of Brady steal his resolve. He kept his mind occupied by reviewing the spells he had memorized. The growing emptiness in his belly consumed his thoughts the rest of the time.

He eventually quelled his hunger with a brief and daring foray to the galley. There, a fat, grouchy, but luckily lazy zard-man was assisted by an even lazier young human cook. After getting his belly full that first time, Phen's visits to the galley became regular events. He was glad that there were humans on the ship. Other than meat, humans and zard-men shared completely different tastes. The zard even ate their meat raw and didn't mind if it started to rot and grow maggots. They ate beetle stew, and pickled spiders. Once, the captain let the ship drift in a school of eels. The zard dove from the ship and swam through the school with spears. They ate the eyes and the guts of the fish they brought back and left the white meat for the men. Phen had been so sickened from watching the lizards feast that he almost vomited. The sound of his retching nearly got him caught. If it hadn't been for the ship's lyna he would have been rooted out and thrown overboard, or stewed for the captain.

The zard ship, like any other ship, picked up rats where it docked and took on cargo. Zard food drew things on to the ship that were worse than rats. No typical cat could manage to keep the vermin from a zard ship. The zard used lyna, a feline creature very similar to the creature that had bitten Oarly when they first went into the cavern. These lyna weren't huge like that. They were no bigger than a typical mouser, but they had the same prickly fur and unpleasant demeanor.

Phen theorized in his idle time that Barnacle Bones's ship, and maybe some others that the great blue dragon had carried to the island, had lyna on board. On the isolated land mass, the creatures had thrived on the jungle's lavish fauna, growing larger as their predatory needs demanded.

It was easy to see how they would. The smaller ones ate spiders, snakes, rats, and just about anything else that rode in the crates and storage bundles. The lyna that saved Phen was a little smaller than an alley cat, and though its tail tip sported sharp, hard spikes, its sleek scaly hide was only prickly if you ran your hand across it backwards. Phen, being the creative boy that he was, named the creature Spike.

Apparently, Spike could see Phen even when he was invisible. The creature slept in the cargo hold with the boy, amongst the smelly barrels of stored food items and water kegs. More than once, Spike saved him from the unfriendlies.

The unfriendlies were the poisonous spiders, brazen rats, and the things that slithered close while he slept. Spike also covered Phen's noisy mishaps while he was moving around the ship. After a few days of interaction a bond had formed between the two of them. Once that happened, a link of familiarity opened up. Spike became Phen's *familiar*, just as Talon was Hyden's *familiar*. Phen relished the idea of it. After finding that Spike could halfway comprehend the zard's hissing, smacking speech, in a halting feline sort of way, he grew even more excited. Now Phen could eavesdrop on the zard conversations and make some sense of them.

He didn't learn much, only that the zard didn't like the sizable black dragon flying so near the ship when it came around. And that they and their captain, Slake, didn't really like the wizard. The zard did have a reverent sort of respect for Queen Shaella. She had placed Flick in charge of this mission and that was the only reason they followed his orders.

Phen spent some of his time exploring the link he and Spike formed. If he concentrated really hard he could see through Spike's eyes and hear what the lyna heard. Through listening that way, he didn't get Spike's crude thought translation of the zard speech, though. To understand what they were saying, he had to let Spike listen and interpret his *familiar's* thoughts. He gained the tiny bits of knowledge that Spike had in his little brain and Phen now knew the layout of the *Slither* from bow to stern and every nook and cranny in between. That was how he'd found the Silver Skull. It was in a hidden compartment in the floor of Flick's cabin. The wizard had no idea that the hidden compartment stuck down into an open hold that had been left empty for this voyage.

Once, Captain Slake had crept down below and examined the skull. Phen was in the hold looking at it himself, debating on whether or not he should sink it. Phen was able to feel the snaky thoughts roiling off of the scaly green zard-man. Slake's black-orb eyes were full of greed and lustful intention. Phen was terrified. He had to force himself back into a sticky tar-glazed corner and breathe without making a sound. The whole time his heart was pounding away in his chest like an oarsman's drum.

Slake's bulbous eyes landed on him for a moment. The sarzard froze, and a haze of fear swept across its strange gaze. The zard captain sensed Phen's presence, or maybe smelled him. A long forked tongue flickered forth and tasted the air. Then Spike appeared from the shadows and roared, as if he were chasing an unfriendly into the hold. The sound broke the chill of the moment. Not sure if one of Flick's spells, or some other strange human thing had caught him contemplating treachery, Slake hurried out, and as far as Phen knew, had never returned to examine the skull again.

Craving fresh air, and tired of crawling around in tight creepy spaces, Phen braved the open deck of the *Slither* a few times. He hoped to get a sense of how much longer the ship would be at sea. But each time he had come back down feeling as if the journey would never end. He was tired of being invisible. It made him feel like he was a ghost or a spirit. With the ring on, he couldn't even see himself. He wasn't sure he could stand the growing feelings of claustrophobia much longer. On his current journey to the open deck, he was relieved to see land on the horizon off to the right. Things would start happening soon, so he relished the lungfuls of thick salty air and mentally prepared himself to be ready for anything.

His plan was simple: if the cry of "Drop anchor" rang out, he would snatch the skull from its hiding place and try to carry it off the ship. From conversations he'd overheard, he knew that they were going to dock at Portsmouth, Westland's second largest seaport. It would be crowded, and if he was lucky, the *Slither* would tie up to a dock instead of anchoring out in the bay. Hopefully he would be able to stroll down the gangplank carrying the skull, which would be invisible when he held it. If the ship didn't dock, but anchored, he would have to deal with the opportunities that were presented. Invisible or not, he knew that he couldn't just a row a dinghy to shore unnoticed.

Spike was another problem. The *familiar* link that had been created was a permanent one. Phen couldn't leave the lyna behind, even if he wanted to. Spike was too big to ride on Phen's shoulder. Phen thought about putting the creature in his shirt, but knew that his scent would probably kill it. He smelled so sharp these days that even the dullest zard made a bitter face when their tongues flickered toward him, and some of the men on board looked back searching for the source of the pungent smell when he crept past. He decided that something had to be done about it.

Phen opened a water keg where they were lashed in the cargo hold. It was as big as him. He stripped down and used his shirt as a rag to wipe the filth from his body. Then he attempted to wash his clothes. He knew that if the open keg were found it would cause a stir, but this close to making port he figured no one would panic over it. He doubted, anyway, that they would suspect an invisible stowaway of the deed.

Later, as he gazed at the land sliding slowly by them, he began to see homes, barns, and rocky pastures. He was growing excited, thinking that they were nearing Portsmouth, but he learned from the words of one of the men that it was only a small town called Midway where there was nothing but lumber and whores to be had. Phen knew from his map studies that they would pass Lake Bottom next. Not the stronghold, but the city. Phen knew that one of King Mikahl's friends, one of the Summer's Day brawling champions, had once lorded there as well.

He wished that he could see the keep from the ship, but it was a good way inland, up the river that flowed swiftly from the base of the roaring falls below Lion Lake. On the far side of that lake, Phen knew the Dragon Queen's castle stood. His wonderment at seeing Westland for the first time was dampened by the knowledge that Portsmouth was still a day or more away. He was stuck on the *Slither* that much longer.

That night, Phen smuggled a bucket into the cargo hold so that he could wash the places he had missed. No sooner did he get started than a storm swept down upon them. The sea swelled and the zard ship leaned and twisted with the power of it. Phen had to fight to stay on his feet while trying to keep water from sloshing out of the keg he had opened. His efforts were futile.

Phen had the dagger Hyden gave him. It hadn't been of much use, except for spearing dried meat from the table in the galley, and getting into the water barrel. Now, as the ship pitched suddenly, the dagger fell to the plank floor with a loud clatter. Footfalls sounded overhead, and then more loudly from the stairway outside the hold. As the faint illumination of his magical light extinguished, Phen realized that the floor was covered in his wet footprints. He snatched up the dagger and did the first thing that came to his panicked mind.

As the door opened, and the bright yellow light of a lantern cut through the gloom, Phen's heart froze. A grisled seaman held the lantern out and squinted through the glare at an obvious trail of wet footprints that led from the now leaking barrel straight to where Phen was standing. Spike darted out of the door as the ship rolled, buying Phen a moment. He couldn't let the man call out an alarm.

Phen threw the dagger across the shadows to the opposite corner of the cargo hold, drawing the man's eyes that way. He cursed his luck because the man saw the wash barrel that Phen's shirt was still soaking in. It was halfway between Phen and the dagger now. Seeing no other resort, Phen charged.

The old sailor looked curiously at the wet footprints that appeared, speeding across the floor at him. His eyes went wide the moment he realized that something he couldn't see was making them. In a reflex, he swung the lantern just as Phen ducked a shoulder into his waist. The resulting collision caused the man to let go of the lantern as his breath was forced from his lungs. It sailed across the hold and smashed into an erupting ball of flames near the corner were Phen had thrown his dagger. The man fell back into the door and his head hit the jamb with a loud crack. Phen could tell by the odd angle of the man's neck that it might be broken. He didn't have time to think about it, though. The fire was starting to spread. More feet pounded the deck overhead, the crew on their way down to the hold.

The ship lurched and thunder cracked outside the hull. Phen fought his rising panic and charged toward the water barrel he'd opened. With all his strength he made to heave it over, but it wouldn't go. He realized the ship was leaning the wrong way and took a calming breath while he waited for the next wave. Slowly, then with alarming suddenness, the *Slither* tilted toward the corner where the flames were starting to blacken the wood. Phen pulled and heaved and leaned, and finally the heavy barrel tipped and fell, dumping its water across the floor in a great splash. In the last light of the flames Phen found his clothes and dagger and huddled in the corner shivering with terror.

He'd killed a man. He didn't have time to dwell on the deed, for several zard came storming in and began using the bucket to sling what water they could on the stubborn embers. Flick came down to investigate the ordeal as well.

"Someone left the barrels untied," a man said to the wizard. Then a zard began hissing and clacking orders at the others until the ship seemed to drop out from under them. By the time everyone recovered, Captain Slake had leapt down with unnerving reptilian grace and was easing past Flick, who was still bracing himself in the doorway.

"Tie the barrels off, fool," Slake hissed.

Phen understood the command without the aid of his *familiar*. He had been among them so long now, their strange language sometimes made sense to him.

"Why was he down here?" Slake asked. Spike darted through the doorway just then and earned a rough kick from the angry captain.

"He heard a noise," one of the human crewmen answered. "Came down to see what it was."

"Who left the barrels untied?" Slake growled.

No one answered.

"Is this a concern?" Flick asked the Captain. Slake nodded for one of his men to answer.

"One of the barrels came loose," the man said. "Probably smashed old Grady into the doorway and caused him to lose the lantern."

Just then Phen sneezed and all eyes jerked toward the corner where he was huddled. Phen couldn't help it. He had held it in as best as he could, but it didn't matter now. He was caught.

Another sneeze filled the intense silence. This one sounded so much like Phen's that Phen had to look for its source. One of the zard held a lantern up and there was Spike pawing his nose. The lyna made the sound again for good measure. Phen turned back to see that all eyes, save for Slake's, were staring at the creature. The Captain's eyes were locked on him.

The sarzard hissed long and low, his tongue flickering out toward Phen a half dozen times. Phen felt that he was as visible to Slake as he was to Spike, but when Flick spoke to the Captain again his voice was harsh enough to draw those black orbs away.

"Take us to Kingsport," Flick ordered. He touched the collar at his neck and snarled. "With this storm, and this," he indicated the scorched corner and the water-soaked floor of the cargo hold, "I think it would be wise to get our queen's prize to shore before one of your crew sinks us."

"Something came aboard with that skull," Slake hissed defensively.

"It's cursed," a human sailor added. Several of the zard hissed in agreement. One of them smacked out something that Phen understood as: "Ask the bone pirate that stole it from its temple and he will agree."

Captain Slake's response was, "Ask his spirit. It's roaming our ship."

After the exchange the crew made an extra effort to get the ship through the storm. The reminder of the origin of their cargo lent to the urgency. All sailors, even reptilian ones, were apparently superstitious. Kingsport was north of Lake Bottom, but well south of Portsmouth. Phen couldn't recall the details from the maps he had studied, but he knew that Kingsport wouldn't be nearly as crowded as the larger city. He gathered that they would be there by dawn, and after the cargo hold was left to him again, he fought the guilt he felt for killing the crewman, while trying to piece together some sort of plan for the morrow.

Chapter Thirty-Four

When Phen woke, it was well past dawn. The *Slither* was at anchor, and the Silver Skull of Zorellin was gone. The only stroke of luck that the panicked boy had was that he fell asleep in the hold under Flick's cabin. A flat barge full of barrels was tied up to the ship and the crews were exchanging kegs and crates. If he had slept in the cargo hold he would have been trampled and discovered. At least now there was a way for him to get off the ship.

Phen grabbed Spike and cradled the lyna as he eased down the gangplank that spanned the space between the two vessels. No one noticed the dipping spring of his steps on the boards. They were all too busy. A few hours later Phen stepped off the keg barge into Kingsport.

The city wasn't as small as he thought it would be. He was able to mingle into a crowd and find an alley. Once he was alone, he took off Loak's ring and, with much relief, examined himself to see if he was still there.

He'd noticed that most of the Westlander men were wearing loose fitting doe skin pants and lace collared shirts of either light wool or a canvas-like material. He wouldn't blend in with his plain brown apprentice robes, or even his under garments. Reluctantly, he pushed the ring back onto his finger, and with Spike trotting curiously at his side, he went off to find some clothes and some food.

The clothes were easy. Many a home had a line full of drying laundry, where the structures were built closely together washing lines had been strung between them. Phen shopped them until he found his fit and then changed into the garments he'd chosen. Now properly attired in an oversized, roughspun shirt and leather britches, he went in search of food. He kept the ring on, just to be safe, as he made his way through the streets looking for a hawker's cart or a table stand. He didn't find any. In Xwarda he would have come across a hundred food hawkers by now, and ten times as many people selling pottery, jewelry, cure-alls, and the like. Well, he corrected the thought, Xwarda had been that way before Pael's undead showed up. Of course, Xwarda was a hundred times bigger than Kingsport, maybe even a thousand times bigger.

He finally found some food at the Kingsport inn. In the common room, a group of men had just finished eating, and he was able to snatch a few pieces of sliced pork and a biscuit from the table. The earlier arrival of the Dragon Queen's wizard on the zard ship was the talk of the town. It didn't take long for Phen to learn that Flick had commandeered a carriage to take him and a few others to the castle through Old Town. Phen decided all he could do was follow. He was already a murderer, so being a horse thief on top of it didn't seem like that big of a deal. He hung around the common room until he gathered enough food to last, then he stole a horse from in front of a bakery and started off.

Spike fit in one of the saddlebags well enough. The lyna rode with his head poked up out of it, and curiously took in the small range of mountains that rose up to the east, and the rest of the lush, relatively flat landscape immediately around them.

At some point Phen decided to put the ring back onto the necklace he wore. Then he ran the horse for as long as he dared to distance himself from any pursuit. He stopped once to relieve himself and fill his belly. While rummaging through the saddlebags he found a blanket, a clean brown robe, a wineskin full of watered sour wine, and a pouch with three silver coins and a handful coppers in it. He hoped that it was enough for a room and a hot meal. There was also a small dress, daisy yellow and trimmed with lace. Phen dropped his chin to his chest in disgrace. It was probably a father's gift for his young daughter. He had stolen it. As the day wore on he found that the dress bothered him more than killing the seaman the night before. He tried to tell himself that, if the Silver Skull fell into Queen Shaella's hands, then the little girl might lose more than just a dress, but it didn't matter. The deed was done.

Old Town came upon him sooner than expected. It was more of a village than a town, though it looked like it might have once been bigger. As if he were nothing more than a curious boy, Phen asked a man if he had seen the wizard.

"The carriage went through around midday," the man said. "It's probably half way to the castle by now. Where you from that you talk like that?"

"I've been visiting my Aunt in Weir," Phen lied. "They all talk this way. Is there a baker in the village?"

The old fellow told him that he could get hot stew at the local inn. Phen wondered if the man really believed him. After eating the first proper meal he'd had in weeks at an inn, Phen walked the horse out of town and laid out his bedroll under some trees. He wondered if adding 'bold-faced liar' to his list of dishonorable deeds would matter. Spike curled up close to him and they slept until the birds woke them just before dawn.

It didn't take long for the Northwood to wrap itself about the castle-raised boy. The road picked and twisted its way between the forest's edges and the foothills. The Northwood was dense and imposing, but Phen wasn't afraid. He decided that being a lying, stealing, murdering outlaw had hardened him to fear. He told himself that, right up until the giant geka lizard, with its four zard-men riders, came scurrying down the road toward him at an unnatural clip. His heart nearly stopped and he was forced to correct his assumption. He wasn't immune to fear.

If the zard riders wanted to do him harm, it would have been done. Phen was defenseless, save for a few spells. Loak's ring was on his neck chain, so he couldn't just disappear. Four well armed zard would have no trouble dispatching him. Their mount could have eaten him whole. Phen was glad when they passed without considering him. They only hissed and laughed when he and his horse ducked like terrified rabbits into the trees at the side of the road.

Later in the day, the forest grew dense. It wasn't the thick wet jungle they'd been in on the island. It was more like the Evermore, with oaks, and elms, and a few pine trees scattered among them. The trees were full of chatty birds and the occasional squirrel or rabbit darted across the shady narrow wagon road.

Phen decided that these woods would be a good place to hunt, but he wasn't in need of food. He wondered if Hyden or King Mikahl ever felt as he was feeling. Both had killed men to protect the realm. If this was what it felt like to be a hero, Phen wasn't sure he wanted to be one anymore.

As the sun set, Phen was debating on stopping for the night when he caught his first glimpse of the distant lights of Castleside. It was still long hours away, and it looked like nothing more than a cluster of fireflies frozen in place from his vantage on the crest of a hill. He decided to ride on.

It was almost dawn when he rode into the outskirts of the city, and when the sun finally lit the sky he saw the silhouette of Lakeside Castle rising up out of the forested hills like a dark hulking monster. It wasn't as big as the castle at Xwarda, or nearly as ornate. It was huge, though, with a dozen fat towers, all sporting black triangular banners with the bright yellow lightning star on them. Its crenellated towers and walls sported hundreds of armed guards moving about. The city outside its wall seemed reluctant to wake up in the ominous shadow.

One look at the great iron-banded wooden gate of the outer wall, and the dozen skeeks guarding it, told Phen that he would need Loak's ring to get inside. After he and Spike ate up the last of the food, he threw the saddlebag over his shoulder so that Spike would have a place to ride. He put on the ring and waited patiently outside the gate for a chance to sneak through. Once again, he found himself wondering why he wasn't afraid.

A message from Queen Willa arrived at the Red City of Dreen by bird. General Spyra quickly dispatched a rider to carry it through the Wilder Mountains to King Jarrek. The man didn't get it there in time.

Earlier in the day, a different rider had arrived at King Jarrek's command post on a horse that had nearly been ridden to death. That messenger said that more than two thousand Dakaneese sell-swords had overrun the men posted at

Seareach. The enemy troops crossed into Wildermont and took to the hills as if they were preparing for a battle.

"Preparing to fight who?" Jarrek asked. "If they sacked Seareach then there is no one to fight save our men here, and at Low Crossing." No one had an answer.

A few hours later, when the rider from Dreen arrived with the message from Queen Willa, Jarrek understood all too clearly. Leaving all the foot soldiers behind to watch over the freed slaves, he took the Highwander Cavalry, along with the mounted Valleyan troops, and sped south in hopes of saving the five thousand soldiers that Queen Rachel had sent through Dakahn. Ra'Gren had set a trap for them. Jarrek doubted that those men could be warned. He sent riders ahead with orders for all the men at Low Crossing to hurry south as well.

Once everything was in motion, and there was nothing left to do but ride, Jarrek thought about the strange offer he had received from the breed giant lord across the river. He didn't have the authority to grant Lord Bzorch the city of Locar. Only King Mikahl could do that, and as much as the might of the breed giants could soon be needed to defend Wildermont, Jarrek didn't think that Mikahl would agree to such a strange bargain. The breed giants had raped and killed their way across Westland for Queen Shaella. Mikahl wouldn't be able to forgive or forget the atrocities they committed. Mikahl had been at the Battle of Coldfrost. Besides that, Jarrek didn't have any idea where the High King was at the moment. Still, the ferocious man beasts would be a great ally in the inevitable war that was to come.

Even if Queen Rachel's troops were caught in the trap, the narrow passage, where the lower Wander Mountains, and the wide sluggish flow of the Leif Greyn River came together, couldn't be left to the Dakaneese. It was such an easily defendable bit of terrain that, even with his ragtag force, King Jarrek felt that he could defend Wildermont. Had he more men, Ra'Gren wouldn't have dared the surprise attack. Now that Queen Rachel had finally decided to join forces with him, he might have been able to man a proper defense. If the Seaward men were slaughtered in Seareach, though, they would be back to where they were, only without control of the bottleneck. Hopefully the men could defend themselves long enough for Jarrek and his little army of Valleyans and Blackswords to get there.

As the day's ride progressed into a moonlit dash, Jarrek wondered about the rest of Queen Willa's missive. A little surprise from Doon was coming his way. He knew that Doon was some sort of dwarven god or underground city. He understood that she was trying to convey something to him covertly, but her meaning was lost to him.

Willa was a strange woman, but her free spirit and strong demeanor had captured Jarrek's heart. Her beauty and elegance were things that crossed his mind frequently. He was sure she didn't know how he felt. Once his people were freed from Dakahn, he hoped to find the chance to tell her. There was much to do before that dream could be realized, though.

Late the next afternoon, tired and hungry, Jarrek's troop crossed the bridge at Low Crossing. They could see carrion in the dusky sky, circling to the south, so they didn't rest the horses long. Instead they pressed on with dread building in their hearts.

They found the battle in the dark. Jarrek barely had time to don the wolf skull helmet that completed his red enameled armor before a blazing torch went hurling by his head. There were other torches, mostly on the ground, and deeper into the fray an oil keg had been smashed against a tree and set aflame. Not many fighters braved the illuminated areas for fear of the enemy archers in the hills.

Jarrek rode his horse deep into the skirmish, and despite his fatigue, he fought in a precisely controlled rage. Steel rang on steel. Men cried out in agony, while other men danced around them in the wild shadows. Every few minutes, at a different part of the battle, a torch went sailing down from the hills. Mercenary arrows would then come streaking into the illuminated area. Queen Rachel's men, and now King Jarrek's, would suddenly sprout quills, while the swift sell-swords would dart in with their steel then disappear.

More soldiers, uniformed Dakaneese, came up behind the Seaward force. There was no retreat. Along an alley barely half a mile wide, between the river and an up thrust of mountain, thousands and thousands of men fought savagely through the night.

The men were tired and the horses exhausted, but they battled anyway. When dawn finally broke Jarrek was still darting his horse into the Dakaneese ranks hacking and slashing fervently. Seawardsmen and Dakaneese sell-swords lay dead or dying everywhere. The uniformed soldiers, Jarrek saw, were mounted city guard from O'Dakahn. They pushed hard, trampling the bodies under their mounts. By midday, the surviving Seawardsmen, and what was left of Jarrek's group, had been pushed back over the bridge at Low Crossing. The Dakaneese seemed content to stop there. It was obvious why. They now held the passage. The bottleneck was behind them. Maybe fifteen hundred of Queen Rachel's five thousand men had been saved, but the single most important piece of land in the realm had been lost. Defending Wildermont from a full Dakaneese invasion would be all but impossible now.

Jarrek decided that, since this was now all-out war, he would promise the breed giants Locar in the High King's name. If Mikahl didn't back him, he would give them a piece of Wildermont instead. It would take a long time to get more men from Valleya, much less Highwander or Seaward. If they didn't force the

Dakaneese back beyond the bottleneck before they fortified the position, Wildermont was lost.

Jarrek handpicked an escort, commandeered the freshest of the horses, and rode with haste back to Castlemont. He would bargain with this Lord Bzorch. If the savage breed beasts were willing to fight for Wildermont, King Jarrek wouldn't deny them the opportunity.

The only thing Queen Shaella loved more than flying on a dragon's back was Gerard. But, since she had been deprived of the glorious feelings of flight for so long she couldn't help herself. The Silver Skull of Zorellin and her hell-bound, mutant lover could wait just a little while longer. After putting on the controlling collar, she boldly mounted the young black drake, her blood electric with giddy anticipation.

"Fslandra, go fetch my staff," she ordered her zard servant. Then to her two wizards, "I was about to ink a reply to a request from King Ra'Gren," she told them. Cole, Flick's near twin, was standing beside him holding the Silver Skull. Flick was beaming over having delivered Shaella the artifact and her gift successfully. He had spent all afternoon getting Shaella's dragon harness adjusted down to the black wyrm's size.

"I think I'll go see the bastard instead," she giggled and patted the creature.

Behind the two bald-headed wizards, the three remaining red-robed priests of Kraw looked on in awe. The will of their demon god was at work before their very eyes.

The group was gathered on the long stairway in front of the castle's great arched entry. A reluctant group of uniformed zard had formed a loose ring around them because a crowd was beginning to gather. Tales of the beast had spread like a wildfire through the inns and taverns, and soon everyone inside the vast walls of Lakeside Castle knew about it. Everyone wanted to see the Queen and her new dragon.

Phen eased around the spectacle and positioned himself by the great oaken doors to the castle. Flick had given the Silver Skull to another bald-headed wizard—a thinner, taller one. Phen planned on following him when he came in, so that he could nab the skull, or at least see where it was placed. All the attention the sleek black-scaled dragon was drawing made it easy for him to move around. He figured that he didn't even have to be invisible to get into the castle. Nevertheless, he kept the ring on his finger. There was no sense in tempting fate.

The dragon's mighty roar caused him to look back. He was halfway up the steps. The dragon looked at him, and Phen knew beyond any doubt that the wyrm could see him. Luckily it was in no position to worry about him. The sound of hurried footfalls startled Phen back around just in time to avoid a young zardess. The reptilian girl, defined by the feminine cut of her strange attire, was carrying a wicked looking staff that had a melon-sized crystal orb for a headpiece. She didn't slow as she made her way through the group of people past the ring of zard soldiers to the dragon's side. With little show of fear she handed the staff up to Shaella.

With her partially scarred scalp and her long raven black hair, Phen thought that Shaella looked even more beautiful and intimidating than the rumors portrayed her.

Too bad you're gonna die soon, Phen thought as he started up into the castle to wait on the skull. He was wondering why he still wasn't feeling afraid when the dragon leapt from its haunches into flight. Zard soldiers hissed and people jeered and cheered alike. When a man heaved open the door, Phen steeled to the task, and darted into Lakeside Castle.

Chapter Thirty-Five

Shaella was exhilarated. The young black drake wasn't nearly as big or powerful as Claret, but he carried her effortlessly. His anger suited Shaella's demeanor. Before long it was clear that the dragon favored her too. They were flying east over the vast expanse of her kingdom. She was the Dragon Queen, and he was her wyrm.

Even though it wasn't necessary, Shaella leaned forward and spoke loudly over the wind. "What are you called?" she asked.

"Daragrathomlegenvrot," the wyrm replied into her mind.

"Dar-agra-thom-legen-vrot," Shaella repeated carefully. "I'll just call you Vrot."

"You are the ones with control," Vrot chuckled sarcastically. "Call me whats you will."

As they circled higher, Vrot picked up the scent of fresh death. Through the link of the controlling collar, Shaella sensed it as well. She told him to seek out the smell.

At first Shaella thought they were going to fly over the marshland that separated Dakahn from lower Westland, but Vrot followed the scent north of the swampy regions. Soon the dragon was circling the lower Wilder Mountains where they met the split in the Leif Greyn River.

Vrot flew high enough that the men below didn't notice him. Shaella cast a spell that allowed her vision to zoom in and focus on details below.

Thousands of corpses lay in scattered masses, from Low Crossing all the way to Seareach. A torn and bloodied banner lay among them displaying the rising sun of Seaward.

So Ra'Gren wasn't exaggerating, Shaella mused. Nearer to Seareach where the passable land narrowed, there was more life. Men in uniform, flying the Dakaneese trident had made an encampment. Seeing that Ra'Gren had sent his own men told her how serious he considered this matter. King Jarrek had jabbed a thorn deeply into his pride.

When they circled back around they saw that there was another encampment north of Low Crossing. Shaella could tell by the banners fluttering in the breeze that this group was a mix of Highwander men, Valleyans, and Seawardsmen. At the moment they didn't look like much, but Shaella knew that if all three of the other eastern kingdoms had come together to help King Jarrek, soon many more men would be marching to his aid. Now that she had the Silver Skull of Zorellin, she could summon Gerard into the world, and other demons as well. She thought that it might be wise to quell the enthusiasm of this eastern coalition before it grew too strong. If King Jarrek and the High King somehow managed to defeat Dakahn, then Westland would certainly be next.

She wasn't worried about King Mikahl and his sword anymore. Soon he would be in the red priests' trap. She worried about Queen Willa's Blacksword soldiers, and all those vicious, tattoo covered bastards from Seaward. She didn't have a sizable force of men to lead into a war, but she had a dragon.

She wondered if it might be wiser to let Willa and Queen Rachel send more of their fighters. That way the demons and devils she intended to release from the Nethers could have them all at once. In her mind's eye she saw Gerard's fearsome demonic visage, and knew that it would be up to him. He would tell her what to do. He would reach through her staff and fill her belly full of sticky heat, the kind that scalded her insides. He would get his way.

She started to urge Vrot northward so that she might investigate the wall that she'd heard Lord Bzorch was building around his city, but she changed her mind. She had to laugh. The stupid breed giant had hated the magical walls King Balton imprisoned them behind at Coldfrost. Now he was building his own walls around himself. Whether it was made of stone and wood, or of magic, to Shaella, a wall was a wall. If all Bzorch really wanted was to be isolated with his own people he could've just stayed in Coldfrost. Did it matter who made the walls?

She wasn't worried about the Lord of Locar, though, she was the one who had freed him and his people from the eternal prison of Coldfrost. She wouldn't let him forget that.

Gerard's image formed in her mind again and she longed for him. The red priests were preparing to call him forth, but she still needed to visit Ra'Gren. She needed to assess his battle plan and wanted to remind him of her might.

Below them, near Seareach, a small group of men were heaving body after body into the Leif Greyn River. The snappers and dactyls would be thick along the edge of the marshes, all of them fighting to get a taste of the ripening human flesh as it floated south toward the sea. By the looks of it there would be plenty to go around.

Farther south a large troop of Dakaneese foot soldiers was marching toward the passage. She had to respect Ra'Gren. The dead were far too fresh for him to have sent the reinforcements after the battle. He had done so in anticipation of victory.

The Dakaneese cities all long the marshy Leif Greyn passed under them quickly as Vrot sped toward O'Dakahn. They soared over the fishing villages of Pearsh and Owask, then Osvoin, where Shaella's mother had lived her pitiful life as a swamp witch. Pael had planted his seed in her and disappeared into the mountains north of Westland. He'd ignored Shaella until her first menstruation.

Then out of nowhere he'd arrived and given her a spell book. Gifts that caused her to have to use her mind arrived irregularly. Then came Flick and Cole, and the grand idea to train the zard and conquer Westland. Shaella had only learned recently from reading Pael's journals that her two wizards were literally under her spell. Pael had charmed them to her long ago. They had no choice but to obey and adore her. This was disturbing because she had long thought them her true friends.

Looking back, she realized that Pael had loved her. After all, he had conquered Westland for her when he made King Glendar empty it of able bodied men. The knowledge of the spell he cast over her wizards allowed her to order them around more objectively now. Pael had left a trail of information that led her directly to his journals. She'd spent most of her life thinking that he had forgotten her, that he loved Prince Glendar and had really wanted a son. Now she understood that a lot of what he did had been done for her, at least until he found the power of Shokin. She still hated her father, though. He killed Gerard.

Gerard had become more than human, and she longed for him like a desert longs for water. She growled with frustration as O'Dakahn came into view below them. Here she was fussing with King Ra'Gren when she could be bringing Gerard out of his hellish prison. The King of Dakahn had pointed out in his missive that she owed him, and maybe she did. His pirates had helped capture the barges of weapons and supplies that sustained her zard army while they prepared to take Westland. But Pael had paid him handsomely for the aid. She owed Ra'Gren the courtesy of hearing his need, but nothing more.

She was a true Dragon Queen again, and her lover was about to provide her with an army of demons. Ra'Gren needed to understand the only reason he was sitting his throne was because she allowed it. If anything, *he* owed *her* for that.

After a meal of sea-born delicacies that was followed by the slow satisfaction of a young slave girl's mouth, King Ra'Gren reconvened his court. The announcer's staff finished booming, and his mouth opened to call out, but the news of Queen Shaella's arrival burst through the door in the form of an overly excited messenger boy. The poor runner was as terrified of catching the King's trident in his chest as he was of the sleek black dragon outside.

"Welcome her in then," Ra'Gren ordered one of the men lingering near his throne.

"She says for you to come to her," the boy said before darting back out of the throne room as fast as he possibly could.

It was hard to tell whether the long low sound that escaped Ra'Gren was a sigh or a growl. After a moment of brooding, he rose. "Very well," he conceded. "Gather my personal guard."

A few moments later Ra'Gren's procession made its way out of the front doors of his lavish palace. At the bottom of the long flight of stone stairs that led into the statue-strewn bailey, a sizable young black dragon sat, looming over Queen Shaella. Its slitted yellow eyes held enough challenge in them that some of Ra'Gren's court scurried back to the higher steps. Ra'Gren might have felt fear himself, but he didn't show it. The captain of his guard did, though. His trembling was so pronounced that his armor was clattering. When Ra'Gren was five steps above Shaella, he stopped.

"I like what you've done with your hair," he said with a slight bow and a smirk on his face. "You've grown into form, I see."

Shaella didn't let his remark about her burned scalp bother her. She wasn't a vain little girl. She knew that her scars were ugly. Instead of reacting, she had Vrot stretch his long sinuous neck over her so that his acid dripping maw was inches from Ra'Gren. The King of Dakahn's face went as a white as his hair. It was obvious he was fighting not to tremble as the fetid stench of Vrot's corrosive breath blew his hair back.

A long silence ensued, while Ra'Gren gathered himself. "If your dragon is hungry, Shaella," he said as he pushed the clattering captain of his guard toward her, "this one has volunteered to be his meal. A captain who would allow a dragon to land at my doorstep without even a warning is worthless to me."

As the soldier stumbled forth, Vrot didn't wait for Shaella's Command. He clamped his mouth down over him. The sound of crunching bone and corroding metal drowned out the man's screams. The dragon then tilted his head back and chugged the body deeper into his maw. In two heartbeats the captain's kicking legs disappeared down the dragon's gullet. Somewhere higher up the steps the sound of retching and the splatter of vomit was heard.

"Enough foolishness," Shaella snapped.

"I agree," said Ra'Gren. "Tell me, Shaella, why is it that you sold me all the Westland nobility that resisted you, but you'll not have a slave in Westland?"

Shaella smiled. "Slavery breeds weakness."

"Slaves can be bred to be strong or weak," retorted Ra'Gren.

"No," she corrected him. "Slavery breeds weakness in the master. If you take away all of your slaves, Ra'Gren, you and your overlords are helpless." She laughed at his expression. "When you have sons, I hope they are wiser than you are."

His growing scowl made her want to laugh even harder, but she calmed herself. "What do you want from me?" she asked harshly.

"Who are you to..." Ra'Gren's angry roar was cut short when Vrot's head came striking down at him.

"You'll do well to remember who needs who," Shaella snarled. With a wave of her hand she stopped the dragon's attack. Ra'Gren's face was a bright shade of red now. "You wrote that Westland owed you, but you are mistaken. Who sent you all these wagon loads of Wildermont gold, and every man, woman, and child that remained in Wildermont after my father wasted it?"

"King Glendar gave me those gifts," Ra'Gren argued with impotent defiance.

"My father's puppet," said Shaella hotly. "Why do you think Pael would give you these things? Do you think he did it so that you could insult his daughter, and try to claim debts you're not owed?"

Ra'Gren took a deep breath and tried to temper his rage. "Shaella..." he started.

"Queen Shaella," she said. "If you want to see what power is, I will show you here and now. I will crumble your castle and let your slaves dance on your throne. If you want Westland's aid, and are willing to ask me for it, you might get what you need. Now tell me, Ra'Gren, what do you want from me?"

Amazingly, Ra'Gren still seemed more angry than afraid. The people around him were terrified. With a scowl of distaste showing plainly on his face, he finally spoke. "I need to know that, if Queen Rachel and Willa the Witch come marching through Valleya, you will take up arms against the east and finish your father's failed conquest." Ra'Gren was glad to have said it the way he did. He hadn't expected Queen Shaella to be this strong.

"You're impossible," she spat. "I will aid you against the east, but for my own reasons. Not for yours, or my father's."

Vrot lowered his head and she climbed up onto his neck. Once she was comfortable she looked down at the King of Dakahn. "You'd have me fight off the whole of the east just so you can take Wildermont. It would be easier for me to take both, Dakahn and Wildermont, for myself." She laughed as he realized the truth of her words. "Remember that, Ra'Gren."

As the dragon leapt into the air, Shaella was lost in the rush of her power. She'd almost forgotten how it was supposed to be. With a dragon under her, it all came back. She decided that she would reward Flick handsomely for the gift. Then she realized that the gift had truly come from Pael. After all, he was the one who had placed the charm on Flick that gave him the desire to serve her so well.

She had no doubt that Pael loved her, but she still hated him for killing Gerard.

Chapter Thirty–Six

Hyden was starting to worry about Mikahl. His friend wasn't sleeping, and on those rare occasions that he did manage to find slumber, the High King tossed and turned. He was sweating profusely, as if he were feverish, but only when he was dreaming. Every now and then he would mumble something about, Princess Rosa, or King Balton. Sometimes he would wake suddenly and look around as if he were a lost child.

Hyden knew that Mikahl had plenty to worry about, but as they drew nearer to Westland, and the dangerous task they were set on taking, he found he was concerned. Mikahl was possibly too ill to attempt sneaking into the Dragon Queen's castle. If anything, the High King's exhausted condition would be a hindrance. Hyden hoped to help his friend sort out whatever was the matter as he didn't want either of them to get caught. He approached Mikahl with these concerns one evening, after Mikahl woke from a troublesome dream.

The ship they were on was called *Shepherds' Goddess*. As the name implied, it was mainly used to haul stock. Prince Raspaar purchased it from a yard in Salazar where it had been sitting in dry dock for most of a decade. At least it held water and seemed sturdy enough in the one storm they sailed through. In its hold, forty head of prime Valleyan breeding stock whinnied and stomped about in the narrow stalls. Even on the deck with the breeze, the rich earthy aroma of digested oats was potent. Below decks the smell could only be described as ripe.

Hyden and Mikahl shared a tiny cabin. There was barely enough room for both of them to stand up at the same time. Hyden noticed Mik was awake and leapt from his upper bunk. He took a seat on the footlocker near his friend's feet. Mikahl looked terrible.

"What is it, Mik?" Hyden asked. "You have to tell me. We can't go into Westland with you half awake."

"I have to go," Mikahl said harshly. "I don't expect you to follow me. If you don't think you can trust me, or the state I'm in, then beg off."

"Trust you?" Hyden's voice was tinged with anger now. "We've been through too much for this. Tell me what the problem is or I'll call the whole thing off, at least your part of it. I have to find Phen, and I'll somehow get Rosa free if I can, but you're sick, Mik. How are you going to keep from being discovered when you call out in your sleep?"

"How could you stop me from going?" Mikahl asked. He propped himself up on an elbow and it was obvious that he was more curious now than aggravated. The effects of his dream were fading, save for the sheen of the sweat that slicked his face.

"I'm a legendary wizard, Mik," Hyden joked. He was relieved to see Mikahl grinning. "I can send you to another plane of existence. While you're there you can go on a quest to find Oarly's other boot."

"Aye," Mikahl chuckled. "The stumpy bastard told me about his boot, and the cinder pepper." Mikahl cringed at the idea of it. "Brutal."

"Aye," Hyden nodded. "Talk to me, Mik. We have to succeed here. It's not just me and you who will perish if we fail. If something happens to you, the kingdom will lose Ironspike's might."

"Bah," Mikahl huffed as he reached for his boots. He pulled a shirt from the pack by his bunk and tried to shake the lingering effects of the dream as he dressed.

Mikahl hated the dream. It sickened him to see his father's haunting, worm-ridden visage. And Rosa was bleeding and pleading for him to save her. Even now he could hear her in the recesses of his mind.

"Come on, let's get some air and I'll try to explain." Mikahl stepped out the door to make room for Hyden but called over his shoulder before he got too far, "Bring the flask Oarly slipped you. I think I'll need a sip or two."

They made their way up onto the deck. After long weeks of traveling on the *Seawander*, Hyden was spoiled to its luxuries. The *Shepherds' Goddess* was a ship of purpose, not built for comfortable travel. The peak of the bow offered the only bit of open space large enough for the two of them to speak privately.

Hyden decided it was like being on a balcony that overlooked the sea. Seeing his friend's troubled expression, he handed Mikahl Oarly's flask. Mikahl took a long pull from it and winced.

"By the gods," he hacked into a hoarse cough. "Did that fargin dwarf piss in this?" He wiped his mouth and spat. "It's got the aftertaste of a refuse pit."

"Hyden laughed despite his growing concern. "It's Wyndall's home-brew," Hyden explained. "Persimmons and some pink fruit fermented in a goat's bladder."

Mikahl blinked a few times. "It's strong enough. I nearly swallowed my tongue."

"Aye," Hyden agreed as he took a sip and made a sour face. After he managed to swallow, he spoke in a hiss, "I should've filled it with squat weed juice to pay you back for your departing gift."

"That was masterful, wasn't it?" Mikahl was serious. "I had no part in the thing with the cinder pepper though. That was all Oarly. Dugak warned me he was a great trickster."

"He is," Hyden agreed. "He made us all think he was dead on Cobalt's island. You should've seen Phen crying like a babe." He stopped himself. The thought reminded him of the matter in hand. "I have to go fetch him. I'm not sure what it is, but there is something special about him. He kind of reminds me of you."

Mikahl shook his head. "They are torturing the Princess, trying to draw me into a trap."

"How do you know?" Hyden asked.

"I'm not sure, but I keep having this dream that's not just a dream." Mikahl faced Hyden and his eyes were grave. "It's like seeing things that happened through someone else's eyes. They've violated my father's grave and mutilated the Princess. Something tells me it's a trap, but there's no way I can keep from trying to save her. It's as if I've been spelled from afar."

"Phen would know of such spells," Hyden said, chiding himself for not learning more about magecraft now that he could read. Phen had taught him a dozen cantrips. Not illusionary tricks and the like, but real magic. Nothing formidable enough to take on a sorceress like Shaella, or her bald-headed wizards, though. Hyden couldn't even find the boot he'd made vanish. He did have some of Phen's spell books in his pack. He decided he would study them. Maybe he could find something that could help?

Talon swooped down and landed on the rail between them. He kept his wings partially open to keep his balance as the ship rolled and swayed on the sea.

"He's gotten huge," Mikahl observed calmly. He remembered when Talon was barely a foot off the ground. Now the fierce looking hawkling was twice that or more. The bird's wingspan from tip to tip was as long as Ironspike.

Hyden beamed like a parent. "He's strong too. He carried a fish twice his size up out of the sea to the deck of the *Seawander* once."

Mikahl nodded and reached for the flask again. Hyden let him take it.

"I guess we need to figure out how the bitch is planning to trap you," said Hyden. "Or at least make a plan better than what we've got." Hyden was glad that Mikahl wasn't taking the matter of his sickness lightly. He could tell that it would be impossible to try and stop Mikahl from taking part in what was to come. He didn't like the situation, but then again who would? His faith in Mikahl was returning.

"Gods... Ughh!" Mikahl coughed as Wyndall's brew stole the breath from his lungs. "You don't like our plan?" he asked after he'd regained his breath. "We take to Lion Lake, swim into the underwater tunnel that Lord Gregory told us about, and follow his map through the dungeons. Then we go up into the castle and start killing skeeks and bald-headed wizards until there's no one left to kill."

"Is that really your plan?" Hyden snatched the flask back and took a longer sip this time.

"Do you have a better one?" Mikahl grinned stupidly.

Hyden forced the liquor down his throat and made as if he were a dragon breathing fire across the sea. "Not yet, Mik," he managed to answer. "But by the White Goddess, and all the gods of men, we'd better come up with one."

Invisible, Phen followed the skull to the hall the red priests had turned into a temple of Kraw. The priests didn't like the idea of the Queen's wizard standing over them while they worked, but apparently there wasn't much they could do about it. After much debate, the three priests finally convinced Cole to relocate them and the Silver Skull. Phen overheard most of the conversation and it scared him. The priest needed a larger room, preferably with a high ceiling, so that any larger demons or devils, and especially the great Kraw, would have room to move about once a gateway to the Nethers could be opened. Cole asked them how a large demon would be able to leave such a chamber without destroying the walls to get out. That caused another argument, about the shape changing capabilities of demon kind.

Finally the decision was made to move the whole mess outside where there was plenty of room. There was a large enclosed garden off of the royal chamber. The gazebo, the priests decided, would make a perfect dais. The skull was placed on a table while the priests transferred their candles, tomes, and other accessories. Cole made zard servants hang curtains from the eaves of the structure so that the curious eyes of the tower guards wouldn't intrude. A lectern, stolen from the castle's chapel, was draped in black silk and the skull was eventually placed atop it in the center of the octagonal floor of the gazebo. A long table was covered with candles, bowls and other items, such as likenesses of Kraw in wood, gold, and stone.

Phen was in the garden, watching from a distance. He shuddered when his eyes met the milky green chips of jade that stared out of the Silver Skull. It almost seemed alive, as if it were anticipating the red priests' spells. Phen overheard Cole grumbling about Shaella's extended flight with her new dragon.

The eager priests soon grew fidgety, but Cole seemed like he couldn't care less about any of it. Long after dark, Cole took the skull back into the castle. He laughed at the priests, then he threatened them when they protested. Phen followed him down stairways and through twisting halls. He was led through several rooms, and a passage that no one but the wizard seemed to know about. He had to stop his pursuit when he looked up and realized he was lost. But at least he knew where the skull would be when the priests got around to using it. Luckily Spike found him and led him back to a familiar place in the castle before disappearing again around a corner.

Phen found that he was hungry, but ignored the sensation for now. He figured he could sleep in the corner of the room the priests had been using. It didn't look like they would be leaving the gazebo. He decided that, if they came back to the hall, it was big enough for him to stay out of their way.

Feeling secure in his immediate plans, Phen decided that he needed to eat. He reached out to Spike through his *familiar* link and went to find the lyna. He ended up at a pantry that was built under a set of little used stairs.

To Phen's great surprise, several lyna were gathered there. None of them, save for Spike, seemed very friendly though, and they gave the boy plenty of space.

"Hello, Spike," Phen said as he dropped into a squat to rub his *familiar* behind the ears. Spike loved it, and as long as Phen only rubbed toward Spike's tail, he didn't get pricked. "Who are your friends?"

Spike didn't answer him with words, but conveyed that the other lyna were pets of the zard, or had been delivered there in the shipping crate they'd been born in. Phen was privy to the odd thoughts that Spike picked up from the others of his kind. When he asked Spike to help him find some food, a female lyna urged them both to follow her.

Spike conveyed that the female lyna belonged to the Queen's servant zardess. Phen remembered seeing Queen Shaella take her staff from a zard girl before she'd taken flight on the dragon. He noticed Spike's smug strut and could tell by the peculiar glances he was getting that his *familiar* knew how to cultivate the acquaintance.

"I'll bet she can't hear the Queen at night," Phen said to Spike.

"Sticka, I am," the female lyna's unexpected response found Phen's mind. "She talks to her demon lover with her magics. She'll use a silver skull soon to call him back from the dark place he is in."

Learning that another lyna could sense his thoughts disturbed him, but his nose was suddenly filled with the warm wholesome smell of cooking bread. His mouth began to water and his belly growled. He hadn't eaten since dawn, and by his best guess it was near the middle of the night.

The two lyna distracted a cook while Phen pilfered himself a healthy meal. A short while after he ate he fell asleep in the pantry under the stairs where the castle's lyna congregated.

Cole found that many perks came with the duty of running Westland in Shaella's name. One of the boons was getting to oversee the dungeon. Like his mentor, Pael, he had a great interest in crossbreeding species. They had different goals in their experimentation, though. Pael wanted to create a race of creatures he could control and use as an army. Cole, however, just wanted to create one terrible and powerful beast. Something he could control, that was capable of battling a pack of breed giants, or an entire troop of men. In the winter, Flick had captured for Cole a real giant. After the invasion of Westland, Flick lorded over the northern lands until Shaella loosed the breed giants. The giant herdsman had ranged down into Westland, chasing after a stray devil goat. Flick captured him and kept him in the cells below the keep at Northwatch. Cole had secreted the giant here to Lakeside Castle's dungeon. Shaella either didn't know about it, or she didn't care. She stayed wrapped up in her chamber most of the time, using the Spectral Staff to communicate with Gerard. She had her twisted world, and Cole had his.

She wasn't concerned with his experimenting. At least Cole didn't think she was. After all, he was following in her father's footsteps. His prisoner was forgotten for now, though. He was curious about the Skull of Zorellin. According to history, Shokin had used it to open a gateway into the Nethers. The priests were going to try and bring their god back through just such a gateway. Cole knew that the skull had capabilities other than opening portals into hell. Like his mentor, Cole had studied the spell books religiously. He learned that with the power of the skull he could summon a thing or two that he could use in his experiments, and more importantly, he could bind certain creatures to his will.

That is exactly what he hoped to do with a thing he accidentally loosed into the lower levels. It was a malformed creation—part cave bear, part breed giant. A sentient creature, it had escaped its confinement and was loose. Until he killed or contained it, the lower levels of the dungeon were useless to him. Not even he dared to go down there. He knew that it would eventually starve if he left it alone, but he wanted to try and bring it under his control before that happened. He knew he didn't have much time to use the skull. When Shaella returned, he was certain that her full attention would be invested in using it to free her lover.

Cole had already ordered his zard servants to prepare a test subject for him. The lizard-men relished the chance to nab an unsuspecting breed.

The exauhsted beast growled out and pulled at the chains that held its arms splayed wide. Blood dripped from the wounds that shackles had dug into its wrists. Its legs were in chains too, and stretched so that that the creature couldn't bend its knees.

"It'll be over soon," Cole comforted ironically, earning a hissing laugh from the zard was watching over the captive. He then sat the Silver Skull on the breed beast's chest and spoke a series of ancient words three times over. There was a slight humming sensation, but nothing else happened.

Cole, fearing that the controlling spell hadn't worked, moved the skull to a table and gave the creature an order.

"Get your hands out of those irons. Do it now."

For a moment he was disappointed, but then the zard attendant started hissing and pointing at the breed. The huge beast began yanking and jerking at the shackles, tearing the skin from its wrists until a bone finally snapped. It screamed out terribly, but didn't stop trying to get free. Cole wasn't paying anymore attention. The skull could do what he needed it to do. He had to prepare so that he could finish before Shaella returned.

Chapter Thirty–Seven

The dragon-blooded beast that had once been Gerard Skyler was angry. He'd lost the ring. His long clawed finger stretched it to its limit, and in some recent battle it must have snapped off and clanked away into the endless darkness. He couldn't even say how long it had been missing.

It wasn't a necessary thing for him. Its magic was puny compared to his, but he coveted it. Gerard's twisted power had grown exponentially. Blistering magical attacks, stout defensive shields, and tricky illusionary castings now came to his mind when he was trying to kill. The things he had consumed, Kraw, and both halves of Shokin, along with a dozen or more of the lesser devils and demons, all chanted the incantations on his behalf. They would protect their host vehemently, but while they were a boon in battle, the rest of the time his mind was filled with arguments and psychotic babbling. At the moment, the intensity of his rage had stilled them. He'd lost the ring.

He let out a raging roar of frustration, letting a long jet of flame blast from his maw. He then sent a great crackling bolt of crimson lightning streaking through the blackness. He'd searched for what could have been ages, but hadn't been able to find his prize.

There were many things in this hell that were equal to his power, and thousands upon thousands of hell-spawned creatures that feared him, but there was one dark hulking monster that was greater than him: Deezlxar, the Abbadon, the dark master of hell. The demons of Gerard's mind whispered that Deezlxar had found his ring and kept it. Gerard searched the carcasses of every kill he could remember. He scoured the endless brimstone plane interrogating the lesser things and challenging the others. Some fled, some fought and died. Those were consumed hungrily. Some of them sent him this way or that with lies manufactured to buy themselves distance from the powerful malformed creature that he was. Every path he followed led to more frustration, until there was nothing left to do, save confront Deezlxar.

Demons were born into a hierarchy. Some were just more powerful than others. Shokin's essence told him this. Devils had a hierarchy as well, but they weren't born into it. This he gathered from Kraw. He was neither demon, nor devil, yet he was both. He was human, and dragon too. He was a god in his own right, and the urge to challenge the Abbadon was growing. He would have his ring back, even if he had to devour the master of hell and order every inhabitant of this blackened place to search it out for him. He wasn't part of a hierarchy. He wasn't created to serve. He'd fed on the yolk of a fire dragon's egg and was transformed.

The power he possessed was power he took from others. He wasn't subject to the laws of the hells. He wasn't like any other entity that was trapped here.

Some of the denizens of the dark had taken to following him; they listened to his ramblings of the gateway, and they often did his bidding. These lesser demons went out in search of the ring, but only brought back tales of Deezlxar.

Gerard found himself searching for ways to go deeper into the planes of hell. He would find this Deezlxar and learn what the Abbadon was about. Thoughts of the ring, and the mighty evil that had stolen it from him, consumed Gerard. He came upon a great circular stairway that led down into a more potent blackness. Shaella's sweet voice was the only thing that stopped him from going down. She was calling to him again.

He forced the chaos in his mind away and responded to her. In his mind's eye he could see her sprawled on her great bed. He saw that she wasn't clad in seductively revealing silks this time. She was wearing a leather riding dress that was stretched open across her abdomen, hip-high leather boots, and a high collared riding cloak, that almost hid the controlling collar she wore like a choker, finished off the imposing look. She seemed as she had when he first met her at the Summer's Day Festival; strong, confident, ready to conquer anything that stood before her.

How long ago had that been? His brain couldn't reach back that far. The part of him that was still Gerard was fading. Gerard's memories had been trampled into oblivion, but nothing could remove his longing for Shaella. Her voice, and her presence in his mind, is what drove the chaos away. She was as deeply embedded into his being as the urge to breathe.

"Oh, Gerard," she said happily, almost cheerfully, to him. Neither emotion seemed to reach its way through his gloom. "My wizard, Flick, has brought me the Silver Skull. I have it." She sat up on the bed excitedly. "And a dragon, my love; he gifted me with another dragon to replace the one your brother stole from me."

"Brother?" Gerard rasped deeply. A flicker of a memory, of laughing with a black-haired boy while some giant woman told them a tale, shimmered away. A feeling of his love for Hyden almost formed, but his twisted brain came around to what else Shaella had said, and all that was forgotten. "You have Zorellin's skull?"

"Yes, my love," she cooed. "The red priests are preparing to open the way for you now, this night, at the peak of darkness." She looked around, suddenly distraught. "It's midmorning now, my love. In just hours there will be a way for you to come back to me."

He looked at his hand, at the long dark finger where the ring should be, and growled. "Not this night," he rasped. "I have one more feast to attend before I can come give you the world."

Shaella deflated at the words. Her excited eyes pooled with tears. The idea that being with her wasn't the most important thing to him was like a knife in her breast. A deep wound that sent ripples of uncertainty through her. The first tears she could ever remember crying spilled down her cheeks. "What is it that would keep you from me?" she asked in a cautiously controlled tone.

"If I were to come to you this moment, love, I could give you the earth to rule," he told her. No matter how malformed he was, with his elongated, almost snouted head, plated brows, and ropey hair, his eyes were still Gerard's. The devilish look in them pierced into her and set a fire in her belly. "If you can wait until I finish this, I will make you the queen of hell, and earth. Then we can make the heavens tremble in fear, together."

She had no designs to rule hell and earth. She wasn't that concerned with ruling Westland. Oh, the times she would have traded her kingdom just to have him with her again. His deep voice, intense eyes, and his hot slick promises, had rekindled her fire.

"How long must I wait?" she asked breathlessly. Her tears were distant memories, the doubts forgotten, like clouds blown on the wind.

"Not long," he said gruffly. "Have my priests open a portal this night. I will come to you for a time. Have your binding spells ready. I will bring you a taste of what is to come."

Phen woke to the itchy, almost painful abrasion of Sticka's nettles. Spike lay nearby, sprawled with glazed eyes and an overfull belly. Immediately, Phen began to panic. He didn't know what time of day it was, but he knew he'd slept far longer than he'd intended.

"What time is it?" he asked the lyna, realizing how foolish a question it was to ask a prickly cat.

"Something happens soon," Sticka conveyed to Phen with uncanny clarity. "The Queen's master comes."

Phen gave Spike a glare and went off to find a window so that he could assess the time of day. On the way he nabbed part of an uneaten meal from a cart. When he was finally able to follow one of the priests out into the garden, he saw that it was only afternoon. There would be time for panic later. A surge of frightened energy snaked up his spine. He decided right then he was going to try and grab the skull.

The priests were burning a great symbol inside a circle in an open space of the lawn. It was a seal, or a gateway symbol, Phen knew from his studies. He found it easy to slip across the yard and into the curtained gazebo. If the skull had been there, he could've gotten away with it, but it was nowhere to be found. Phen figured that Cole still had it. He had a mind to alter the symbol the priests were burning into the lawn, thus changing their spell. All it would take was an extra mark or two. He decided that he might make things worse by tampering. Before Master Targon died, he'd preached about the consequences of such actions. There was still time, so Phen decided to try another tactic. If Queen Shaella was readying herself for Gerard, then maybe her dragon's collar was lying about her chamber somewhere.

Phen hadn't seen the dragon since Shaella returned, but it was the talk of the castle staff. Eavesdropping as he moved invisibly through the castle searching for Shaella's apartment, Phen heard all sorts of rumors. After wasting an hour looking, and learning nothing, he went back to the pantry and coaxed Sticka into showing him where Shaella slept. Spike had digested his meal by then and was eager to come along.

Sticka led them up a circular flight of steps to the castle's second level, then down a long wide hall that was lined with statues spaced evenly along the walls. Huge tapestries and paintings of landscapes were centered between the statues. Phen noticed that the scenery was deceptively lifelike. It was like looking out of a window instead of at pigmented oils on canvas or woven threads. A great waterfall in one of them formed a cloud of misty spray that seemed to radiate off the canvas. Another was of a pasture of sheep. When Phen looked directly at it everything was still, but from the corners of his eyes he would swear that he saw the sheep gnawing at the grass. After careful inspection he saw that some of the artworks were signed. He knew immediately that the names were elven. He cast a spell to detect magic on the painting before him, and was pleased that his instinct was right. He made a mental note to look into the type of magic it would take to paint such a vision. It would have to be a potent spell to last thousands of years.

The big oak double doors at the end of the hall suddenly parted. Queen Shaella looked out with narrowed brows. Phen realized that he'd made a stupid mistake casting his spell. The look in her eyes told him that she sensed it. There was nothing he could do about it, though, because he was captivated by her beauty. She was naked, save for a towel that was wrapped around her waist. Her dark wet hair hung down over her breast on the side that wasn't scarred. Her nipples were the size of coins, and even though he was terrified, Phen couldn't peel his eyes away from them.

"Who dares to disturb..." Shaella started, but she stopped when her eyes found the two lyna pacing in the hall.

A bit of movement from the statue at one side of Shaella's door drew Phen's attention. It was still now, but he thought that the hand had reached to the hilt of its sword.

"Fslandra!" Shaella yelled over her shoulder.

From behind her, the zard girl appeared, looking as sheepish as a bulbous-eyed lizard girl could look.

"Yes, Masteress?" Fslandra hissed in some strange version of the common tongue.

"It seems your Sticka has found a suitor," Shaella's eyes scanned the hall again, looking for what it was that had alarmed her. "The two of them must have been making magic," Shaella joked without a smile. She spoke the words of a detection spell but nothing triggered a reaction. If she'd cast the spell a few seconds sooner she would have seen Phen running as fast as he could to get out of her entry hall. He was certain the statue moved, and he remembered that Shaella was more than just a queen with a dragon. She was a sorceress— Pael's daughter no less. The statues were probably magicked guardians or the like. Either way, he didn't plan on approaching her apartments that way again. His heart was still hammering in his chest so hard that he thought his ribcage might burst. The curve of her body had been so distracting that he didn't even remember if she'd been wearing the dragon collar or not. When he was far enough away from her room that he felt he could relax, he leaned against a wall and gathered himself. *I have to have patience*, he told himself. He wondered if Spike had escaped the hall. As he went back to the pantry he called out to his *familiar* to find out.

Later that night, when Phen was able to slip back into the garden again, he found he was too late to get at the skull. He couldn't just open and close doors by himself. He had to wait on someone and creep in with them. The scene he saw was worrisome at best. He didn't think that there was any way he could stop the ceremony the red priests were preparing to perform. The skull was already in its place on the lectern, and both of Shaella's bald-headed wizards were conferring over something in the gazebo. A filthy young woman was half hidden behind them. Her hands were tied together with rope. The three red-robed priests, and a few other men wearing black robes, were scurrying about lighting candles and placing different items about the garden. Then came the Dragon Queen.

"Who brought her down here?" Shaella snapped sharply from the balcony above. At first Phen thought she was falling over the rail, but the smooth way she floated down in her flowing silk gown reminded him of the power she possessed.

When her bare feet were on the ground she started toward the filthy girl. Phen realized then that it was Princess Rosa. The only parts of her that weren't covered in grime were the twin streaks of white below her eyes where her tears had been running.

In answer to the Queen's question, Flick pointed at the priests and shrugged.

"Answer me, man," Shaella ordered one of the red-robed necromancers. "Why was the Princess brought here?"

"If the High King comes to save her during our ceremony," he answered nervously, "we wouldn't be able to spring the trap. She must remain in sight until the portal has been closed. To do otherwise would risk losing her while our attention is focused here."

Phen decided that Princess Rosa was more important than the skull. As the ceremony began, he worked his way over to where Flick and Cole were standing. Phen noticed Cole looked tired and sickly. His eyes were set into deep dark sockets. Shaella's body shone through her gown as if the material wasn't even there, yet no eyes lingered on her. She began casting a spell, and implored Flick and Cole to join her.

Phen recognized the nature of the binding wards they began to recite. He almost cast a spell of his own, but was scared that he would alarm the menacing sorceress or her wizards.

"Shhh, Princess," Phen whispered from right behind Rosa.

"Who's theere?" she yelped. "Don't touch me, troll!"

Flick looked back at her and scowled. "Silence," he hissed sharply. "No one is going to harm you this night."

"Shhh," Phen whispered again after Flick went back to his casting. "You'll get me caught."

Rosa looked around wide-eyed and terrified. Phen saw that one of her hands was swollen to twice its normal size and that a finger was missing from it.

"Who is there?" she whispered to the thin air around her. Her voice was so quiet that Phen barely heard her.

The murmuring of the red priests had turned into a droll howling chant and the air around them was beginning to fill with the crackling static of powerful magic.

"Look closely in the direction of my voice on the count of three and you'll see me," Phen told her. "One... two... three," Phen pulled the ring from his finger for just an instant and shoved it back on.

"Oh!" she yelped in surprise.

Flick glanced back when he sensed magic behind him, but he didn't see anything.

"Where are they keeping you?" Phen asked. The sound of the chanting priests and the popping noise of the erratic magical light that was flashing over the seal drowned out his voice so that only Rosa could hear.

"In Pael's tower, in a room called the nest," she answered.

"Here," Phen touched her cheek and gently moved her head so that she would have some sense of where he was.

"Wheere are Kang Mikahl and Hyden Hawk? Is my motheer seending the Royal Guard?" she asked hopefully. "I remember yew, yer Hyden Hawk's apprentice, Pin."

"My name is Phen, and there's only me," he told her. "I came to get that." He pointed at the Silver Skull then realized that she couldn't see his hand. "The Silver Skull," he added, hoping his embarrassment wasn't evident in his voice.

"What's it feer?" she asked, but Phen didn't have to answer. A great grinding roar filled the night. It was accompanied by a blasting gout of flame that shot up high into the sky.

As soon as Phen saw it, he knew that it was Gerard. The thing stood with its head level with the second floor balcony and was covered in thick plated skin. Its leathery wings stretched wide and were dripping with stringy mucus. Its claws looked like daggers, as did its teeth. It had short thick hind legs and an elongated torso. Its neck was stretched and its rope-like hair dangled from a huge half-snouted head. Its skin was glossy black and at its elbows and knees wicked looking spikes had formed. Bright eyes, as big as cantaloupes, looked out from under angry brows. Other than their size, the eyes looked perfectly human. That's how Phen knew that it was Gerard. They were so much like Hyden's eyes that he shivered with disgust.

Princess Rosa fainted, collapsing into a heap beside Phen. *It's probably for the better*, he thought. He was having a hard time controlling his fear. Any time, one of the wizards, or even a priest, might sense his presence. The sound of the priests chanting, and a deep humming whistle of wind, kept him from hearing the conversation Shaella was having with her lover, but he could see by the way she was touching him, and herself, that the two of them were sharing something deeply personal.

Had there not been such a resemblance, Phen would have discounted that this thing was once his friend's brother. How this monstrosity of might had once been human he couldn't fathom. Nor could he understand why it leapt back into the gaping maw of the seal. A few moments later, a pair of panther-like hellcats peered cautiously up out of the hole. Shaella let loose a binding spell and they leapt into flight. Then came another winged demon. This one shot up out of the hole, straight into the sky. By the look Shaella gave Cole, it was clear he had failed to bind it with a spell. Shaella cursed and screamed orders at both of her wizards. They moved around for better position, leaving Phen alone with the Princess.

He hoped that she would turn invisible when he grabbed her, but she didn't. Worse, she was too heavy for him to lift, much less carry to safety.

A great commotion near the priests' gateway commanded Phen's attention. Something that radiated evil like a foggy stench crawled up out of the hole. It was huge and hairy, with long apish arms, and cherry eyes. It stood on two legs and carried a massive bone as if it were a club. The end of the bone was knotted and gnarled, and the shaft was the size of a healthy tree. When the thing stood upright, its wolfish head was above the balcony. Several smaller things crawled out at its feet and Cole spelled each of them as quickly as he could. One was a scorpion as big as a goat. There was venom dripping from its curled stinger.

With a sharp pop that left Phen's ears ringing, the hole suddenly disappeared. The three priests collapsed into heaps on the garden lawn. Flick was casting a spell that was far beyond Phen's understanding. Then the bald-headed wizard scooped up the Princess and strode away. It was all Phen could do to keep up with him as he wound and twisted and climbed through a labyrinth of hallways to Pael's tower lift. Phen couldn't go up with the two of them, but that was all right. He heard the command Flick used to make the lift rise. As soon as Flick came back down, Phen got on and, with a word, rode it up to the nest. It was several hours later, after he had somewhat healed the infection in Rosa's hand, and tended the stump of her finger, that he realized he didn't know the command to send the lift back down. Not only would he soon be discovered, he couldn't get away.

Chapter Thirty-Eight

The three-thousand Valleyan cavalry that General Spyra somehow managed to round up were a welcome sight to King Jarrek and his men. To learn that just as many infantry, both swordsmen and archers, were marching through the pass, bringing with them much needed food and supplies, was even better. Jarrek couldn't wait for the foot soldiers to arrive, though. He had to attack the Dakaneese and drive them back through the bottleneck before their reinforcements got settled in. It was the only option.

Master Wizard Sholt had arrived in a startling flicker of sparkles a few days earlier, bearing messages. The sudden presence of Queen Willa's high wizard unsettled Jarrek, but Sholt was welcome. So was the news that Queen Willa sent with him. Her missive stated that Queen Rachel was already organizing her troops to make the short march across lower Valleya to attack Ra'Gren at O'Dakahn. Her anger at having her men ambushed and slaughtered in Seareach, and the frustration of not knowing her daughter's fate, seemed to bring out the aggressiveness in her. King Jarrek hoped her attack would keep Ra'Gren's attention on the defensive and distract him from Wildermont.

The strangest news of all came with Sholt as well. A small army of dwarves was on its way to aid them and would supposedly arrive any day.

"Have they reached Dreen yet?" Jarrek asked Sholt after hearing the news.

"They're not traveling overland," said the wizard with a shrug. He glanced down at the front of his stark white robes as if looking for a stain. "They have tunnels. General Diamondeen, the commander of the force coming our way, assured me that he and his twelve hundred fellows would arrive here ready to fight by the turn of the season."

"The turn of the season," Jarrek's mind went blank. "That is... that's..." He realized he didn't know when that would be.

"Summer's Day is only three days away, Highness."

"Three days?" Jarrek couldn't believe it. "Almost a full year since this madness began. It seems like only a few months have passed, but then again, it feels like it's been decades."

"I understand," Sholt agreed. He had fought Pael's undead army from the walls of Xwarda too. His mentor, High Wizard Targon, had been snatched from the wall by the Choska demon. Sholt had walked the heaping piles of his city after Mikahl killed Pael. He'd helped restore a city that had more corpses than carrion in the streets. He'd exhausted himself of spells daily for months alongside Master Amill, trying to clear the rubble and stench from Xwarda's districts so that the survivors might start again. For a while, time had lost all meaning, for all of them.

"I assume you will attack soon," Sholt said, looking down at the maps strewn about the table.

Jarrek had moved the main body of their occupation south from Castlemont to an abandoned farming village north of Low Crossing. The stronghold there, which was really only a large rock house with a piled stone wall built around it, had become King Jarrek's command center. It was crowded, but it sufficed. Sholt could tell that the man had long since given up the luxuries of his station. The King of Wildermont used the open privy pit like the other men, and ate most of his meals from a field tin with them. It was clear that they respected him for it. Hardly any of the men behind him were from Wildermont. The zeal and fervor with which a soldier will fight to defend his homeland wasn't in them, yet King Jarrek's determination, and the way he led them, caused them to believe in his cause wholeheartedly.

"On the morrow," Jarrek answered Sholt's unasked question, at first light, a company of breed giants will lead the attack."

"Breed giants?" It was Sholt's turn to be surprised.

"I took some liberties as the situation dictated." Jarrek let an ironic smile creep across lips. "Had I known I'd be getting all of this help from Xwarda, I might have left them out of it." He looked at Sholt seriously. "It will come as a blow, albeit a small one, for Queen Shaella to find a large number of her ferocious breed giants have betrayed her."

"What does the High King think of this?" Sholt asked, showing genuine curiosity at what the answer might be. "It was reported that breed giants savaged the people of Northern Westland for some time."

"Mikahl went off into Westland some weeks ago and no one has heard from him," Jarrek frowned. "I have no men to defend with, and I can't afford to wait."

"That is grave news about the High King," commented Sholt. He wiped again at the front of his pristine robes. "Queen Willa is under the assumption that the High King is in contact with either you or General Spyra. Queen Rachel thinks he is trying to rescue Princess Rosa." Sholt shook his head sadly. "The realm needs Ironspike. If we lose Mikahl, we lose its power for all time."

"I know, but I can't afford to dwell on it, Sholt," Jarrek said. "I have a country to protect and a kingdom to rebuild. Ra'Gren still holds thousands of my people as slaves. He has already slaughtered innocents in the street. High King or no, I'll do what I have to do. I have to think of the greater good."

"No one will doubt your judgment, Highness," Sholt said with a nod of respect. "After I report back to Queen Willa, I will spend the rest of the day preparing spells for battle. I am at your service."

"Sholt," Jarrek stopped him as the wizard started out of the room. Jarrek found that he couldn't find the words for what he intended to say. He settled for, "Let Willa know that I appreciate everything she's done for Wildermont."

When dawn broke, eighty breed giants stormed across the Wilder River at the village of Low Crossing. They didn't use the bridge. Water that would be chest deep and encumbering to an armored human barely came up to a breed's waist. For the most part, the primal beasts didn't wear armor, only loose fitting trousers and vests made of layered elk hide. A few of them wore chest plates, scraps of mail, and helmets that they'd gathered from the ruins at Castlemont on the journey south. One of the hairiest of the breed wore nothing at all save his fur.

Right behind them, four hundred swordsmen stormed the bridge, while archers rained down steel tipped death to cover their crossing. In moments, the battle became heated. The surprise factor of the morning attack wasn't nearly as effective as the sight of the battle-crazed tree-swinging breed giants. The Dakaneese soldiers were terrified of them. Battle Lord Ra'Carr's men were driven back quickly at first, far enough that a thousand Valleyan cavalry braved the river to join the fray. A good half of the horsemen were mounted archers, and the amount of damage they sent streaking into the deeper ranks of the Dakaneese was substantial. As the day wore on, though, the backbone of Ra'Carr's soldiers stiffened. King Jarrek's troops were going nowhere.

Master Sholt rode cautiously over the bridge on a terrified horse. He was surrounded by half a dozen shield men whose sole job was to protect him from stray arrows and such. The Highwander wizard cast several spells. Lightning shot forth from his hands and arced over the main knot of battle into the unengaged troops beyond. Because of Sholt, Dakaneese fighters died terrible smoldering deaths by the handful. Then a great ball of flame appeared in his hands. He rolled it, and worried it, and caressed it, until it grew as big as a barrel keg and then he hurled it into the forward ranks of Dakaneese. An unlucky female breed giant got caught up in the explosion of flames that came when it impacted, but at least a score of the enemy fell into burning, writhing heaps. The breed giantess roared defiantly as she was consumed in flames. She continued to hammer away at the Dakaneese before her until she finally burned to death.

Jarrek commanded the rest of the crossing, looking as intimidating as ever in his red enameled plate armor. The ruby eyes of the wolf skull mounted on his helmet sparkled in the sun.

Day wore into night and, yard by bloody yard, King Jarrek's force pressed the Dakaneese back. Sholt used the cover of darkness to gain a better position so that his line of sight spells would have better effect.

Men died, and breed giants fell. Steel clanged on steel and bone pummeled flesh by the light of the moon. By dawn, all of Jarrek's main force was across the river and engaged. The bottleneck was in sight, and it seemed that victory was in their grasp. Then the screeching roar of some winged beast came from the skies to the west.

Flick, looking ever so much like Pael, was riding a great bat-like Choska demon. On either side of him was a terrifying looking hellcat. The horse-sized panther-looking creatures dove away and swooped down into the skirmish below. With tooth and claw, and severe lashes of their long treacherous tails, they cleared away soldiers and breed giants as if they were batting flies. Screams of terror erupted and Jarrek's men had no choice but to fall back.

Sholt caught his breath and sent a series of streaking pulses of magical energy up at the Choska. One of them found its mark, causing the beast to roar and dive away. Jarrek raised his sword high and charged one of the hellcats. "Make way!" he screamed, trying to get through the ranks of men battling for their lives. "Make way!"

He yelled and charged his horse and came in swinging vicious arcs with his blade. He had to dodge a claw, but his sword bit flesh repeatedly. The hellcat roared, and a nearby breed giant, whose chest was striped with bright red dripping slashes, brought his tree-limb club down across the hellcat's back with a crunch. Jarrek spurred his mount around and leaned down, thrusting his blade. It sank deeply into the hellcat and his men swarmed over it before it could recover.

"Do not fear them!" Jarrek screamed, holding his bloody sword high for all his men to see. "They bleed and die! They bleed and die!"

The men got the message and found some courage in the actions of the Wolf King.

The Choska, with Flick on its shoulders, came screeching down. Sholt saw its target plainly. King Jarrek's red enamel armor with the glittering wolf skull helm made him stand out in the fray. Even more so, since he was standing in his saddle, with his sword raised high. For lack of options, Sholt calmly cast a spell, and blasted Jarrek right out of his stirups with a fist of wind. The Choska's powerful claws would have closed on Jarrek from behind, but it missed.

Flick snarled and found the white-robed wizard at the northern edge of the battle. He cast a spell that caused an invisible web to fling across the Highwander mage. Then, while Sholt squirmed to get free, Flick assaulted him with swirling blasts of wizard's fire. Due to the constrictions of the web, Sholt wasn't able to cast a protective counter. He took the full brunt of the searing blast.

Flick brought the Choska around to attack again but was suddenly jarred from his seat and nearly tossed. A spear was embedded deeply in the Choska's neck. The beast arched and writhed in the air and screeched out in pain, but it could do nothing more. It was all Flick could do to settle the demon beast.

Flick twisted back to see where the missile had come from and found himself looking down at Shaella's Lord of Locar. Bzorch was surrounded by a dozen of his breed giants, each of them carrying big coils of rope. Bzorch was holding a... *What? A giant crossbow?*

Looking at the spear jutting out of the Choska's neck with a dozen feet of rope dangling from it, Flick realized that the huge breed giant was toting a dragon gun.

"Shaella will make you pay for this, Bzorch," Flick said to the wind. He urged the Choska away from the battle. He had no choice but to flee the area. The Choska was wounded and needed to land before it crashed. Each wing-beat ground the jagged spear tip into its tendons and muscles that much deeper. Shaella wouldn't be pleased with Flick for retreating, he knew. But she would take her anger out on the breed giants of Locar, not him. Flick couldn't believe they'd betrayed her after she set them free. He could only wonder what Jarrek and the Squire King promised them for their treachery.

The dragon gun didn't matter. Queen Shaella and Vrot would soon lay waste to Locar for this, Flick was certain. The zard would relish helping her—they hated the breed.

If for some reason Vrot failed her, Flick was sure that the terrible thing that used to be Gerard would annihilate the whole city. Flick, even while watching Pael, charged and raging with his raw demonic might, had never felt anything half as powerful as Gerard. Kraw, Shokin, whatever Gerard was now, was the epitome of dark power. Flick almost felt sorry for the realm.

Jarrek didn't know what hit him, but he saw the great dark shadow of the winged demon pass over as he was knocked from his saddle. He was immediately surrounded by Highwander men and Valleyans, who kept a protective ring around him. His horse lay twitching on the muddy ground, a pair of deep slashes across its back. Jarrek couldn't help but shiver at the sight. A Valleyan captain held out the reins of a horse that had lost its rider. Jarrek found his sword in the muck and climbed on it. The other hellcat was dancing on its wings just over the battle. It would dip and claw and then rise up before a spear or a sword tip could find its belly. Several arrows stuck out of its hide, but it seemed unconcerned with the minor wounds. Jarrek was having trouble breathing—the hard fall had broken his ribs, so he made his way back to the bannerman. He was glad to see that his men were still pressing, but the cost was high. Everywhere around him, men who were fighting for a kingdom not their own lay dead or dying. They hadn't died in vain, though. Once Jarrek could see the whole of the battle, he knew it. The rise of the rocky foothills was at their left, and the wide expanse of slow flowing river was at the right. They were at the mouth of the bottleneck. The day was almost won. It was all the Dakaneese could do to retreat without killing each other as they were forced backwards into the narrower field of battle.

Battle Lord Ra'Carr gave out a defiant cry and charged the lines of Jarrek's force right behind the remaining hellcat. The call he gave was, "For Ra'Gren! For your king!"

The hellcat ravaged a path for the Dakaneese to fill and much ground was lost. Jarrek's estimation had been premature, but then another battle cry rang out, a deep and savage call. Jarrek looked around to find the Lord of Locar trying desperately to get a clear line of fire for his weapon. Jarrek almost laughed at the welcome sight. Then he stood in his stirrups and tried to help the half-breed. "Clear back from it," he screamed, urging others to repeat his cry. "Clear away from the flying beast."

Whatever happened next worked for the breed giant because Bzorch fired a spear. The hellcat gave out a horrible shriek as the barbed bolt shot through its gut. It flew up into the air, but couldn't get away. Three breed giants had the other end of the rope. The hellcat looked like a huge malformed kite, swooping and twisting in the wind as it tried furiously to get itself free. But the barbs on the spear, and the rope, held it true. The three breed giants on the ground, heaved and pulled, and heaved and pulled, slowly dragging the creature down to the blades waiting below.

While this was going on, the Dakaneese pulled out of the bottleneck. Jarrek's men held their position instead of pursuing. Having lost the passage, the Dakaneese soon realized there was nothing left to fight for here. Slowly, the sounds of battle fell away. To punctuate the end of the bloody ordeal the Lord of Locar let out a deep primal yell as he bodily beat the last bit of life out of the skewered hellcat. It was a victory scream, and feeling the rush of conquest surge through them, King Jarrek, and many of the men, raised their swords and joined in the call.

Chapter Thirty-Nine

Seeing the *Shepherds' Goddess* raising sail and easing away from them made Mikahl shiver. The little rowboat he and Hyden were in was heavily loaded with supplies that they knew were ultimately useless, and the slow rolling waves were huge. Mikahl let out a nervous laugh. Beyond the ship, the bright amber sun was setting.

"What's funny?" Hyden asked, as he gathered up the oars and began to row them away from the sun.

"You and I, Hyden," Mikahl laughed again, shaking his head in disbelief. "We're either daft or just plain ignorant." He turned away from the silhouette of the departing ship and looked at Hyden. Hyden had bright rays and a bunch of long dark hair in his face and was squinting. "We're miles from land in a fargin rowboat, with the sun going down no less. What if we get switched around and row all night in the wrong direction? What if the current carries us right into Kingsport? We'd be caught and killed. What if...?"

Hyden spoke over him. "What if you quit acting like a worried old crone?" Hyden joked at his friend's obvious nervousness. "In all of our travels, Mik, you've been the brave one. You're the reckless swordsman, the one who shows no fear." Hyden looked around them, and for a fleeting moment he felt as insignificant as an insect. "You're afraid of the sea, aren't you?" he asked with a grin.

"Not while I'm on a ship," Mikahl admitted, with a scowl at Hyden's mirth. His scowl faded as Hyden's grin slowly turned into a shocked look of fear.

"Oh gods, Mik," Hyden gasped, pointing behind Mikahl toward the sunset. "It's a giant serpent!" Mikahl's eyes grew wide and he twisted around clutching the sides of the boat.

Hyden burst into laughter. "You... are... as white... as a ghost," he managed between guffaws.

"Stow it," Mikahl growled. "That wasn't funny."

"Oh yes, it was," Hyden laughed even harder. After a moment his glee subsided. He started rowing again and spoke in a somewhat serious tone. "You'd rather be out here at night, Mikahl, trust me. The sun would burn us alive, especially since you're wearing your mail." He shook his head at his friend's lack of forethought. "Can you swim in that?"

Mikahl looked at him a moment then began peeling off his belts and packs so that he could get out of his mail.

"I don't know why you even brought it." Hyden began laughing again. "We're supposed to swim through the underwater passage into the Dragon Queen's dungeon. What were you thinking?"

Mikahl couldn't help but laugh with his friend, though his laugh was tinted with sarcasm. "It's a good day's hike from where we're making land, just to get to the lake." He paused to get the shirt of armor over his head. "I brought it in case we're attacked on the way."

Talon called out from overhead, and after circling the rowboat, came swooping in to join them.

"Talon is our compass," said Hyden. "You've forgotten who you're traveling with, Mik. I'm a wizard with a *familiar* that can sense the land, even now. "

"A jester and a glorified chicken is more like it," Mikahl returned.

Talon cawed his disapproval of the remark.

"All right, Talon," Mikahl conceded. "A jester and his chicken hawk."

Talon flew to Hyden's end of the boat and settled into a coil of rope on the floorboards as if it were a nest. Hyden rowed until the moon was above the sea, then turned the oars over to Mikahl.

It would be impossible to go the wrong way, Mikahl decided. The lights of Kingsport were tiny, yet clearly visible to the northeast. A glance over his right shoulder at them, every few pulls, kept him confident of his course. Before long, the sounds of the waves breaking against the rough shoreline told them that they were close. Talon took back to the sky and flew overhead. Hyden shared Talon's vision, and the hawkling guided them safely to land.

"Should we wait until dawn?" Hyden asked.

"Aye," Mikahl replied. "Let's rest our arms, and at first light I'll get my bearings. There is still a wild thing or two in this part of Westland. They don't call Lord Gregory the Lion Lord for nothing."

"There are lions in Westland?"

"Of course there are; far worse things too." Mikahl shook his head as if to think otherwise was absurd. "Why would Westland's banner boast a prancing lion if there were no lions in Westland?"

"Westland's banner is the lightning star now," Hyden reminded. "Or haven't you been paying attention."

Mikahl growled as they pulled the little boat up through the surf onto the shore. Once it was secured safely in the underbrush they ventured a few hundred feet inland and made camp.

"They call it a lightning star," Mikahl said, "but I have to agree with Lord Gregory. It looks more like a fancy yellow snowflake."

"They have a saying about yellow snow in the mountains where I come from," Hyden said.

"Exactly," Mikahl watched with curiosity as Hyden lit a small fire with a flame he conjured to his fingertip. "You'll do loads of damage with that spell," he commented dryly.

Hyden laughed and shook his head. "Go to sleep, Mik. I'll take the first watch."

Mikahl lay back and closed his eyes, but he dared not sleep. If he did he might dream, and that was the last thing he wanted to do now that he was back in Westland.

Dawn came sooner than either of them expected. They decided to leave the excess supplies Raspaar's crew had loaded into the dinghy for them. They ended up flipping the boat upside down over the stuff and covering it with brush, but it was a hasty job and would only be camouflaged from distant passersby. Anyone who came close would be able to spot the deception. They hoped that they wouldn't need the boat to make a retreat from Westland later, but neither truly thought that a clean escape in the little tub was a likely conclusion to this incursion. This was an all or nothing gambit, and both of them were committed to it.

"Hyden strung up his elven longbow before they started, and Mikahl donned his chain mail shirt and made sure Ironspike was loose in its scabbard. Each of them shouldered a leather pack of rations and waterskins, and then started off.

Hyden found himself searching for signs of lions. He'd never seen a lion, save for a sketch of one in one of Dahg Mahn's volumes. He saw two paw prints, and plenty of geka scat, even a feeding area were some long dead carcass had been strewn about by the predators, but he didn't see a lion.

"The gekas must stay close to the lake," Hyden observed. "They're amphibs by nature."

"Then why would they leave the marshes?" Mikahl asked. "Why would they leave a naturally protected environment that suited them?"

It was a good question. The zard were amphibs too. Hyden had read about them in books that Phen showed him in Xwarda's Royal Librarium. *Why would they leave their natural habitat for the Westland plains?* He pondered the question as they continued through the day. It was an uphill hike the whole way, and they were both happy to come over a rise early in the evening and see the great shining surface of Lion Lake glittering in the shallow valley before them. It was too late to attempt the swim, and they were too far away. They skirted the shoreline toward the castle, being sure to stay in the cover of the wooded hills as they went. It wouldn't do to have one of the zard-men on the high gray walls spot them creeping around. They moved away from the water, back over the rise. There they could build a fire and not be seen. They made camp and rested after eating a solid meal of salted beef, bread, and dried fruit. Then the two of them eased up to the ridge and looked out at the looming mass of stone and steel that they would soon be inside of.

Hyden had Mikahl point out Pael's tower. It was the one closest to the southern corner of the castle. Hyden made a smug face. It wasn't nearly as impressive as Dahg Mahn's tower back in Xwarda—now his tower, he corrected the thought. He hoped that saving Phen and the Princess, and stealing back the Silver Skull would be as easy as winning through Dahg Mahn's trials had been. In his heart he knew better.

Talon swooped in, landed on a nearby tree and began preening himself. He was tired from watching over them all day.

Mikahl didn't see a great hulking castle across the glassine expanse: he saw home. A wealth of emotions flooded through him as he gazed at the place where he was born. The joy, relief, and comfort one should feel when returning home was absent, though. Anger at seeing those zard-men patrolling the walls, and the disgust that flared every time he saw the lightning star took their place. He ground his teeth. He had a mind to draw Ironspike, call forth his bright horse from its symphony, and go riding over the walls wreaking havoc. The longer he sat there, the harder it was to keep from doing just that. His thoughts must have shown plainly on his face.

"You'll have your chance, Mik," Hyden said from beside him. "They want you to come running into their traps. Don't oblige them."

"She's just right there," Mikahl argued, but with fading conviction. He knew Hyden was right. They had to be cautious and stick to the plan. One more sleepless night wouldn't kill him. "We should go long before the sun rises," he said trying to calm his anger. "We should use the cover of darkness to get up against the wall." He sighed and turned away, putting his back against a rock. "We'll have to stay in the water a while. I doubt we could find the marked stones Lord Gregory told us about in the dark, but I think it's a better plan than trying to swim in the daylight."

"Aye," Hyden agreed, remembering what the trout looked like in the lake from Talon's perspective. The tower guards would be able to see them even when they were underwater. He thought that he could probably climb straight up the wall if he had to. Getting there was the trick. He gave Mikahl a pat on the shoulder. "Just be sure you leave your chain mail here. I'm not going to spend the morrow dodging arrows while I'm diving to pull you up from the bottom."

Inside the castle, Spike followed Cole down into the upper levels of the dungeon. The wizard had put the Silver Skull in a leather sack and was toting it over his shoulder. Spike had to stay a good distance behind because the scorpion-like creature that Cole had bound was following him as well. Phen was trying desperately to see through Spike's eyes, but it was hard. Sometimes he could, and sometimes he couldn't.

Rosa's untimely questions were driving him mad. Not only did they break his concentration, they were taking away his confidence. It seemed that every time his mind was relaxed enough to see with his *familiar*, she couldn't help but ask a question.

Phen saw Cole pass a hallway that he remembered. It led to a smaller hall that went to the base of the tower where he'd gotten on Pael's lift. Yesterday, Phen learned the command to lower the device. There were a few terrifying minutes of waiting to see who or what was coming back up on the lift after it suddenly eased down out of the room. Cole had come up with a tray of food and a pitcher of water. He set the items on the floor and looked around curiously. Seeing nothing but Rosa's huddled form and the stirred up dust, he'd huffed, stepped back onto the lift, and spoke the command for it to lower.

Phen tried to make a mental map of Cole's passage from the point he recognized, but it was no use. Too many turns and archways, and then two sets of stairs. Phen saw the wizard come to a dark alcove with a great iron door centered in its far end. Cole rapped on the steel and a head-high window opened inward spilling orange torchlight in a rectangular beam. A pair of dark skittish eyes looked out. Then after a loud clank the door creaked open. Cole spoke to the man at length, allowing the hell-born scorpion, and then Spike, to ease into the area. Spike had to scurry past them all into the deeper shadows in order to keep Cole's venomous pet from seeing him.

The dungeon guard was terrified of Cole's new creature. His fear caused the wizard to cackle with delight. Soon Cole's zard assistant arrived. Phen overheard part of their conversation.

"Let us see if that thing running loose down there can survive my new friend," Cole told the zard.

"Thinkss we'll be rid of it soon," the zard said.

"I hope so. I didn't mutate that breed bastard so it could take over our lower levels," Cole snarled. "The giant Flick caught me has probably starved to death by now. It's a pity we had to leave it in chains. He might have been able to rid us of the breed freak."

"A curiouss battle, Masster Cole," the zard commented. "One I would haves liked to ssee."

Cole nodded his agreement. "Escort this hell-spawn to the lower gate, Zalvin; maybe it will rid us of our problem so that we can at least examine the pure blood's internals before it starts to rot."

"Yessss, Masster Cole," Zalvin gave a short dutiful bow. Cautiously, as if leading an angry dog, the zard urged the scorpion down a darkened stairway and disappeared.

After Cole left, the dungeon master shut the iron door behind him. The instant the door banged shut, Phen lost contact with Spike. He began to worry about his *familiar*. Phen tried and tried to reestablish his link with the lyna, but just couldn't do it. With a frustrated sigh he put his head in his hands and tried to think.

"Are yew all right, Pin?" Princess Rosa asked.

He started to correct her pronunciation of his name, but decided that it would be pointless. To her, she was saying Phen. It was her Seaward accent that caused her to pronounce it wrong. Earlier he had asked her what the people of Seaward call the little appendages that helped a fish swim. "Feens," she'd replied. After that he gave it up.

"I'm all right, m'lady." He forced a smile. "It's just that I need to get that Silver Skull away from here." He doubted that Queen Shaella even knew Cole was tampering with its magic.

"Eat and rest." Princess Rosa was barely older than him, but her smile was motherly. She offered him the bigger part of the meal that had come up. "Getting some rest will help you think."

"Aye," he agreed and reached for a piece of the hard bread on the tray. "What's this?" he mumbled. He could see the corner of a gap in the floor. He snatched up the bread and took a bite, and then held it in his mouth as he moved the tray over and began dusting the filth off of the wooden floor. In a matter of moments he revealed a rectangular trapdoor with a finger hole in one end to use as a handle. He stuck his finger in it cautiously and raised the hatch, revealing a ladder that led down into the darkness. Chewing his bread, he smiled at the Princess.

He cast an orb of light into his palm, causing Rosa to yelp, then he leaned his head into the hole. Phen was delighted at what he saw down there.

"What is it?" Rosa asked, peering down to see what had the boy grinning so broadly. "It's just a room full of old books."

"No, m'lady, it's much more than that." He grabbed one of the sausages from the tray and started down the ladder. "It's Pael's library. There's more power hidden in this room than anywhere in the world, save for maybe Xwarda."

"What will you do?"

"Hopefully, I'll be able to find a spell that will help get us and that Silver Skull away from here."

"Do be careful, Pin," Rosa said rubbing the stump where her fingers used to be. "Pael's was such an evil sort of magic."

Phen reached up and gave her good hand a squeeze. "It wasn't his magic that was evil, Princess," Phen said, hoping that it was true. "It was his heart."

Chapter Forty

Gerard could smell the evil radiating from the archway before him. His eyes saw nothing but black on black, for there was no light here. The darkness was so thick, so absolute, that a torch flame would have been swallowed whole. But his ears heard the shape and texture of the walls, and his nose smelled the sweet taint Deezlxar left in the air. The dark master of hell was close. Gerard could feel it. The battle lust began to boil in his blood. His teeth ached for demon-flesh and his heart was pounding a potent rhythm in his chest.

After craning his elongated neck to and fro to stretch his shoulder muscles, he eased through the archway into the greater blackness beyond. He was ready to face the thing that stole his ring. He was ready to face his destiny—or so he thought.

"How dare you come seeking my destruction!" A voice so deep that it shook Gerard's guts exploded all around him. "What are you, that you think you can challenge me?"

"I'm the one that terrorizes your domain, the thing that you cannot control," Gerard growled back defiantly. "I'm the thing that makes your minions tremble. Now show yourself."

A sweeping blow sent Gerard tumbling sideways. He hadn't seen it coming, or what had made the attack, but whatever it was, it was huge. He saw that he wasn't mistaken about its size when he sent an orange gout of flame up into the air above him. The illumination revealed a three-headed crab-like monstrosity that had six legs. It was already bearing down on him again. This time Gerard ducked the coming appendage and raked his claws across the creature's underside. His claws found thick leathery hide and hard bone where he'd expected to find vitals. The beast squatted down, almost pinning him to the hard flat floor, and only the slick greasy coating on Gerard's plated flesh let him slip free.

Gerard sent a churning blast of purple energy into the demon's side as he rolled away. It struck with a thump and exploded, sending wet pieces of matter everywhere. The thing howled out in pain as it danced around to face Gerard. As big as it was, the great gouge in its side was only a minor wound. It retaliated with its own magic, a triple blast of white-hot demon's fire, one coming from each of the dragon heads that loomed over Gerard. Gerard howled out a primal roar and charged right through the scorching blast. He was part dragon and therefore fire, even demon's fire, had little effect on him. He leapt at Deezlxar's chest, where the three necks branched away, using his long hand and toe claws as if he were a raccoon leaping up on the side of a tree. The monster shrieked and darted one of its other heads at him. The blackness was now punctuated with long bright burns in his vision, but Gerard somehow sensed the attack. He jumped away and latched onto the attacking head just as its jaws clamped down on itself with a bloody crunch. Then Gerard blasted out another fiery roar. One half of Shokin cackled, while the other spoke a spell. Ancient whispers sounded in his mind and a static lavender blast pulsed from his hand exploding a chunk from the head he was now clinging to.

Gerard had to dive away from the beast as it twisted around and screamed. He somersaulted through the air, churning his tail and contorting his body so as to land on his feet, but Deezlxar continued around with a bone crunching lash of one of his six appendages smacking Gerard in midair. Gerard spun and flailed, trying to land well, but it didn't happen. Mostly his head and neck caught the floor with the bulk of his body coming right down on top of him. He crunched into himself so hard that his tail bones impacted the back of his head. Bones were broken. One of them jutted up out of his arm. He could feel raw, nauseating pain where exposed nerves and marrow were touching air. With his other arm he yanked the broken one crudely back into its proper shape and let loose a horrific yell. Then he turned and called forth blast after blast of magical energy, while Kraw, and both halves of Shokin did the same inside his mind. A swarm of poisonous insects, a jagged streak of crimson lightning, then several balls of roiling purple energy came pulsing out of his fingertips and assailed the beast.

Deezlxar countered most of them with shielding spells. The poisonous bugs found his blood more toxic than they were and they soon sputtered to the ground and faded into nothing. The lavender blasts charred the Abbadon's flesh as it advanced, but none of it did enough damage to stop the coming attack.

Another streak of lightning found Deezlxar's wounded head, and sizzled the life out of its eyes, but still Deezlxar came on. The Abbadon had taken Gerard's best and it was still ready for more. Gerard knew that he had to retreat and regroup. There was no way that he could win this battle, not this day. His armor plates were crooked and several other bones were broken besides his arm. The gore that had splattered his body was starting to sizzle on his flesh.

Gerard spun and clawed deep slices across one of the Dark One's necks, then he did the only thing he could do to survive. He flashed himself away with a spell.

He appeared in the empty blackness somewhere away from Deezlxar and immediately began trying to heal himself with his magic. He wasn't done with the Abbadon yet, but he was no fool.

As much as Shaella wanted to march the huge, hairy, bone-wielding gorax into Locar to straighten out the breed, she couldn't. She'd promised Ra'Gren aid, and the gorax would go far toward keeping Queen Rachel's army from crossing into Dakahn. Shaella had to remind herself that it was Bzorch and his barbaric breed giants she was mad at. Not all of the people of Locar had betrayed her, just the breed.

She found that she couldn't be mad at Flick for retreating from the battle as he had. His Choska had been critically wounded, and Ra'Gren's men lost the fight anyway. The feel of the wind in her hair, and Vrot's young, strong muscles churning his wing strokes under her, confirmed the decision.

Cole was another matter. She was completely infuriated with Cole. Despite her orders, he'd let one of the Choska slip into the world without being bound, and had instead bound the will of an overgrown insect. Gerard hadn't loosed those demons for her to squander. She wasn't sure if Cole was going mad down in the dungeons, where he spent most of his time these days, or if he had some strange purpose that she didn't know about. Cole had always been more like her father than Flick. Maybe that's what it was. She would deal with him soon. It had to be done.

Shaella hated having to bother with Ra'Gren again, but it was necessary. She was certain he would put her in a mood. She decided that she would save dealing with the breed for last, that way the fires of her wrath would be fully stoked when she found them.

The statue-filled bailey before Ra'Gren's palace was crowded as she circled low over it. Clouds were building up in the sky and she wanted this part of her day over with so that she could fly above the coming storm on her way north to Locar.

She loved to skim the tops of the storm clouds. The kinetic energy built up in them was powerful and seemed to charge her blood.

The people below cleared away for her as she brought Vrot smoothly down. With a wide snap of his wings his hind legs touched the ground. The dragon took a lurching step before his front claws went forward and his wings pulled in. Shaella didn't bother to dismount.

"Go fetch your king," she ordered a uniformed man who was posted at the top of the steps. His expression showed his reluctance to do any such thing, but he didn't balk. He glanced at the dragon fearfully, then turned and strode into the palace entrance.

It didn't take Ra'Gren long to appear. He was followed by a dozen of his overlords, all but two of whom chose to stay high up on the stairway away from the dragon. Ra'Gren's expression was angry, yet curious, as he strode powerfully toward her. He stopped when he was on a level with Shaella's eyes. Just to be difficult she had Vrot raise her up a little higher so that Ra'Gren was forced to look up at her or back up a few steps.

"You failed me in Seareach," Ra'Gren barked. "Your creatures were of no real help."

"I didn't agree to help you take Wildermont," Shaella snapped. "I only agreed to help you defend against the Eastern Alliance. Those hellcats were supposed to be a gift to help you guard the pass, but still you lost it."

"Nevertheless, those things failed us." He looked at the messenger who'd arrived earlier with the particulars of the battle. It irritated Ra'Gren that Shaella knew what happened before him. "My man tells me that your half-breeds betrayed you and helped Jarrek win the day. If this is the sort of assistance you give, I'm not sure I want it anymore."

"You're an old fool." She hawked and spat at the ground a few steps below him. "Do you even know what sort of threat approaches?" She looked at him hard, hoping he would try to come down on her for calling him a fool in front of his court. His face was red, and cords throbbed under his clenched jaws, but his eyes kept darting down to Vrot's slobbery maw and then back to her. His voice was level and controlled when he spoke.

"Tell me of this threat."

"An army, twenty thousand strong, is marching across Valleya as we speak. They mean to storm your border and attack here at O'Dakahn. Queen Rachel didn't like the party you threw for her men in the Seareach passage." Shaella allowed herself a smug smile. It was nice having a spy in General Spyra's bed. "Are you prepared to defend your borders, and if not, are you prepared to defend the city?"

Ra'Gren's mouth opened and closed like a fish, but no words came to him.

"That's what I thought." Before he could respond she waved him to silence. "If you don't want my assistance, if my aid isn't to your liking, then I'll be on my way." She started to urge Vrot into flight but, as expected, Ra'Gren stopped her.

"Queen Shaella," he said in a way that hid his deprecation in the tone of his voice.

Shaella heard the inflection and knew it for what it was. It was a plea.

"What can we do?" he asked her when she didn't fly away. "I have men, plenty of soldiers, but it would take days to get them all to Oktin and Lokahna to defend the bridges."

Shaella waved her hand and spoke a word in the language of demons. The huge gorax appeared right in the middle of the bailey among the statues in a brilliant flash. People gasped and yelled and nearly trampled each other trying to get away. Even Vrot took a cautious step back from its sudden appearance. The wolf-headed gorax growled out loudly and waved its huge bone club about. It stood over twenty feet tall, and its black ape-like chest rippled with muscle that contrasted with its thick gray fur. As if irritated at being called upon, the demon bashed one of the marble statues into a crumble. The head and shoulder of the destroyed monument flew ten feet and bounced into the base of another statue with a heavy thumping crack.

"My new friend can keep the Seaward army from crossing at Lokahna. That will buy you some time to get troops to Oktin. I doubt Rachel's army would want to march that far north anyway, not after losing the element of surprise. Send a few thousand archers to help the gorax cover the banks of the river, and a few hundred cavalry to round up any stragglers that might win their way past him, but warn your men to stay clear. If it is in his way, and alive, the gorax will kill it if he thinks it came across the river into your kingdom."

Looking at the gargantuan demon beast Ra'Gren found that, for the first time in a very long time, he was speechless.

The *Shark's Tooth* fought its way up the channel against the mild current of the Leif Greyn's diffused flow. They had long since passed under the shadow of the Dragon Spire and were nearing the open marsh where the Leif Greyn River split. Once, the route would have been impossible to travel due to Claret's presence, but now the spiking volcanic formation was nothing but a sinister landmark amid a swampy half-submerged jungle. The normally snapper-filled waters seemed empty of life. Even the insects seemed to have better things to do than bother Lord Gregory, Lady Trella, and Oarly as they stood on deck and watched the swamp go by.

Maxrell Tyne, now Captain Tyne, with the aid of his partner Grommen, had readily agreed to take them. After all, Mikahl owed Maxrell a fortune, and he wasn't about to forget it. They'd taken on a Water Mage to help power the ship against the current, and so far he had done well, but he was tiring. The Lion Lord hated it, but the ship was flying the lightning star banner. This served to kept the few curious eyes they came across from lingering. Save for in the night. At night it seemed like there were always a dozen pairs of eyes watching them from the marshy darkness.

The hardest part of the voyage was going to be getting past Seareach, where the Leif Greyn's flow was most potent. The *Shark's Tooth* would travel at a snail's pace against the current, and for a time the ship would be in the archers' range from either side of the river. Once they were through they could hug the Wildermont shoreline and make their way slowly up to Castlemont, where King Jarrek was supposed to be trying to regroup.

As the ship moved into the dangerous run of river, Lord Gregory ushered Lady Trella below, using the dark clouds building in the sky as his excuse. He'd spotted a bug-covered, half-consumed, human body floating in the water and wanted to spare his wife the sight of it.

"There's why we're not being eaten alive by the flies, Lord Lion," Maxrell Tyne said. A look from Lord Gregory, as he gently turned Trella's eyes away, spoke daggers. Tyne cringed and shrugged his apology.

After the lady was below, Oarly pointed out a few more bodies to the crew. "Them snapping marsh monsters are bloated and sleeping," the dwarf surmised. "I think the arrow in that last body was fletched in Dakahn."

"I seen one with inked skin," Grommen called from the back of the ship, where he was scanning the marsh behind them, making sure nothing was following. "Tattooed from head to... Well, what was left of the bastard was covered with the ink."

Captain Tyne had the best view from the wheel deck. He put his hand on his brow and looked around them. "It was no small battle that put this much death in the river," he said as he reached for his brass looking glass.

"There," Oarly said, pointing. "One of Queen Willa's men, a Blacksword." He was a little drunk on Wyndall's liquid fire, as he had been for days. There was an unopened keg of the stuff lashed on the deck, and several flasks stashed in his gear.

"I hope we're not too late to be of aid to King Jarrek," Lord Gregory said after the hatch door closed behind his return.

"We'll be able to see Seareach soon," Captain Tyne said, as he peered to the north through the looking glass. "We'll be able to tell more about the situation then, assuming of course that this weather holds off."

A turn of the glass later Captain Tyne asked Lord Gregory to come up and have a look. The sky had darkened considerably, but it hadn't begun to rain yet. That it would rain, was inevitable.

When he looked, Lord Gregory couldn't help but bark out a laugh at what he saw.

"He's held the passage, man," Gregory observed loud enough for Oarly and Grommen to hear. "It cost a lot of men, but they held the passage."

"A hell of a battle had to take place there," observed Tyne. "Look at the corpses."

"Aye," Lord Gregory agreed, scanning the Wildermont shore northward. There were jams of bodies bobbing like pale white logs caught against the far shoreline. He paused and twisted the outer casing of the brass tube to focus the lenses. "What in all the hells?" He took the device from his eye and polished its lens with the hem of his shirt and looked again. "By the gods, there are breed giants roaming among Jarrek's men." Lord Gregory swung the looking glass southward and, after a moment, found what he was looking for. "The Dakaneese are still positioned near the mouth of the pass, but they don't seem to be preparing for anything."

"Licking their wounds and waiting for reinforcements," said Tyne. "That's how I see it."

"Aye," Lord Gregory agreed. He looked again at the breed giants mingling with all the human soldiers on the Wildermont side of the pass. He had bloodied his sword well against them a decade earlier, at the Battle of Coldfrost. He didn't know what to make of it.

Oarly came up the ladder, his curiosity getting the better of him. He'd been listening to the conversation and wanted to have a look for himself. "May I?" he asked.

"Please do," Lord Gregory replied. "There are some of your people among Jarrek's men as well."

"My people?" Oarly asked with narrowed brows. He took the tube from the Lion Lord. "That's impossible," he said as he put it to his eye.

"Not impossible. I saw them," Lord Gregory pointed his finger to the north. "Look for the breed giants gathered round the bonfire, you see them?"

"I see the wild looking bastards," Oarly answered.

"Now take a look just to the left of them, you'll..."

"By Doon!" Oarly did a hop-skip in place without moving the glass from his eye. "The Lion's got it right. Not just a few of them." Oarly looked at Lord Gregory, then at Captain Tyne. "You know what this means?" he asked them excitedly.

Neither Lord Gregory nor Maxrell Tyne had any idea what it meant. Tyne shrugged because Oarly was about to tell them whether they cared to know or not.

Not even the loud pattering of the fat raindrops that started to fall could dampen the dwarf's enthusiasm. The dwarves of Doon had not only returned to the surface of the land, they'd come to Wildermont to fight with the Red Wolf.

Chapter Forty–One

The rain limited visibility. Even from the great height of Locar's newest wooden structure, a monstrosity of a gate tower, it was hard to see for more than a few hundred feet in any direction. The open space in the tree trunk wall, where the actual gate would eventually be, was wide open. Through it ran the Midway Passage, a well packed road that stretched across Westland from east to west. In this weather, Sorvich was sure that no one would be traveling in or out of the city. Still, he looked on vigilantly from the tower platform, even though his fur was saturated with rain. Sorvich, had a huge swivel mounted dragon gun at his disposal, but he never once thought to look up.

Shaella urged Vrot straight to the commandeered building where the Lord of Locar normally ruled his roost. The stone structure gurgled and hissed, and slowly began to melt away after Vrot drenched it in his acidy spew. A few screams resounded through the rainy gloom as those who were out working in the weather caught sight of the sizable black dragon sitting in the middle of Locar's main thoroughfare. It didn't take long for a full alarm to be sounded. Shaella sat patiently on Vrot's back, waiting to see what sort of action would be taken. While she waited, she let Vrot satisfy his hunger on a couple of breed that came close enough for him to reach. Before long a somewhat organized group of breed giants, with a few humans thrown in the mob, cautiously approached from down the street. A few of them sported her lightning star on their leather service armor. Two of the breed carried large crossbows like the one Flick warned her of. The others carried axes or swords. Upon seeing that it was Queen Shaella sitting on the dragon's back, about two thirds of the group bowed to her.

"Where is Lord Bzorch?" she yelled through the drizzle.

One of the braver breed giants, one who was loyal to Bzorch and his cause, stepped forward. He didn't lower the dragon gun he held. "He's not here," the breed yelled back.

Shaella sighed. The breed giants were like pack animals. They all followed the alpha male. In this case they were about to start following the alpha female or pay the price for not doing so. "I can see that, fool." With a thought she had Vrot blast the breed with his corrosive breath. The spear launched out of the breed's weapon at an odd, harmless angle, and in seconds the screaming half-beast was nothing more than a gory puddle in the street.

Most of the onlookers walked quickly away then. Those who stayed lowered their weapons and stepped back cautiously.

Another breed giant came forward holding both of his hands up to show that he was unarmed and suppliant. He bowed graciously then spoke. "Your Highness,

I am Lord Bzorch's hand. My name is Cozchin. The Lord of Locar is across the river in what used to be Wildermont, trying to expand the limits of the city." He wiped the rain from his snouted face and tried to disguise his fear. With his primitive features, the expression looked more like a snarl.

"I know what Bzorch is doing," she yelled at them all. "If you people didn't know, the Dakahneese are our allies, not our enemy, yet Bzorch seems to want to help King Jarrek defend against them." She glared at those who remained. "How did they cross the river?"

"I assure you," Cozchin groveled. "I... We had no idea what he was intending to do while he was..."

"How! Did! They! Cross! The river?" Shaella screamed each word. Vrot's head shot down and stopped only inches from Cozchin's face. Hot fumes vented across the breed giant out of nostrils that the breed could have fit his fists into. Cozchin nearly choked on the rancid stench. It was all he could do to keep from running away.

"A barge," Cozchin answered quickly, trying to get the words out before he retched. "They turned a lumber barge into a ferry."

"Where?"

"At the old bridge."

"You, you, and you," Shaella pointed out three of the breed giants that hadn't bowed or bothered to lower their weapons after recognizing her. "Step forth."

After they hesitantly obeyed, Shaella motioned for Cozchin to step away. He didn't wait to comply. His footfalls made large splashes on the wet road as he jogged a dozen paces to the side.

"Bow," Shaella commanded the three before her. "I had you people destroy the bridge for a reason," she said when they did. "I am your queen. If it were not for me, and me alone, you would still be freezing to death and eating each other in Coldfrost where King Balton left you." She pumped a fist high and Vrot reared up and let out a deep rumbling growl. "How easily you forget my kindness. How easily you turn on me!"

Vrot snapped his jaws down on one of the breed that was kneeling before them and shook him violently. Before the other two could get up and move away the dragon tossed the mangled corpse from his jaws and blasted them with his acid breath. As they writhed and gurgled into bubbling puddles, Shaella continued her tirade. "This is how I repay treachery. Cozchin is your lord now. Bzorch will not survive this day. Anyone who crosses that river has crossed me, and you can see right here what fate that will bring you." She spat at one of the puddles.

As if the gods meant to punctuate her authority, a crackling streak of lightning split the sky behind her, then thunder rumbled through the air. The people looked on in terror from behind lifted curtains, and between buildings. Vrot took one long smooth stride then leapt back into flight. He didn't go far. Shaella had the menacing black dragon blast the ferry with his breath and watched until it sank out of sight. Then she had him tear down most of the tree trunk wall that had just been built around the city. It was only by some great stroke of luck that Sorvich, and the new gate tower, with its big swivel mounted dragon gun, didn't come crashing down with it.

Sixty-four of the breed giants that survived the battle at Seareach were trudging north through the rain. They were less than a quarter day's march away from the makeshift ferry that would take them home to Locar.

Only Bzorch and his personal dragon gun crew stayed behind. The breed lord was enjoying immensely the height of the pedestal the human fighters put him on. He had to admit, watching breed giants yank the hellcat out of the sky, and then him rushing in and pounding it to death, had to have been an awesome sight to behold. The arrival of the dwarves of Doon from the nooks and crannies of the Wildermont foothills had been amazing too. And now that the position at Seareach was fortified to the hilt, the mood in Low Crossing was celebratory.

Amid the drinking and storytelling and all the bonfire bravado, Jarrek was still busy making plans. He wanted Bzorch to be a part of them, so he asked the breed lord to stay around. The unexpected arrival of the Lion Lord and his party created a venomous tension. King Jarrek's captains and the dwarves worked hard to keep the old enemies at a distance. Neither Lord Gregory nor Bzorch seemed ready to forget the bloody days they spent warring out on the tundra. Little did Bzorch know that the sixty-four breed giants he'd sent back to Locar were not going to make it. Their orders had been to prepare for Shaella's retaliation, but Shaella and Vrot never gave them the chance. They showed them no mercy when they swooped down out of the sky and eradicated them.

The breed giants fought tooth and claw, as best they could, against the dragon. One of them managed to get a shot off with the dragon gun. The spear hit Vrot in the hind quarter, but the young black wyrm used his corrosive breath to eat through the attaching line before it could pull taut. Queen Shaella responded by casting a spell that blasted the breed with a ball of sticky yellow wizard's fire that clung to them and burned even as they rolled and thrashed and tried to extinguish themselves. Vrot landed among them and dispatched a handful of breed with his claws while he disfigured half a score more with gouts of his potent acidy spew.

A patrol of Jarrek's Highwander men rode out from an outpost and tried to help them, but only managed to get killed and corroded themselves. Shaella missed only one of the sixty-four traitorous man-beasts, and she chased that one south until she was sure it wasn't Bzorch. She decided to let it live so that the absconder might plant the seed of fear into everyone he told of what had happened. Her only mistake was that she assumed Bzorch was among the group of dissolving corpses her dragon had dispatched. Had she known that he wasn't, she might have flown south and unleashed some more of her fury on King Jarrek's encampment at Low Crossing. As it was, she assumed Vrot had killed the alpha breed and decided to save the destruction of Jarrek's forces for another day. She was spell weary, tired and wet. Vrot had part of a spear hanging out of his flank. It pleased her that her young dragon hadn't complained about the wound. She knew it pained him. When they returned to Lakeside Castle she would reward him with a fat geka to sate to himself on. Flick, or the priests, could remove the spear and heal the wound. No, she wouldn't trust the priests with her dragon. Flick she would trust with her life. Either way, she would make sure that Vrot was comfortable, and that his loyalty was not forgotten. It wasn't like she had anything better to do. Gerard was off fighting battles of his own in the Nethers. She had already decided that she wouldn't call out to him again, not until she knew he was ready to emerge. Just thinking about it seemed to ruin her otherwise wonderful mood. She spent most of the flight back to her castle trying to get him out of her mind.

The trap the red priests set for King Mikahl hadn't been sprung. Shaella decided to worry about that after she'd had a bath and a meal. A few well chosen words of encouragement to the necromancers might rectify the situation. It seemed to her that Princess Rosa just wasn't very good bait. Either that or the High King just didn't care about her. At least she could use Rosa to halt Queen Rachel's advance on Dakahn if she had to. The lives of Jarrek's slaves, and revenge over Ra'Gren's ambush couldn't be worth her daughter's life, could they? Shaella laughed, thinking that she just might find out very soon what Rosa was worth, and to whom. She would pay a visit to the Princess later as well. It never ceased to amaze her how weakness and fear poured out of the wretched girl when she confronted her. In the spirit of keeping the day's mood aloft, she might just cut off another finger.

Phen re-read the incantations of the spell for what seemed like the hundredth time. It wasn't the type of spell that you could cast and then release later with a word, so he wanted to be sure he had it memorized. The chance to use it might present itself anytime, and he was determined to be prepared. He'd learned a lot from Pael's texts. Mostly trivial knowledge that wouldn't help him or the Princess, but the spell he was working to memorize now would throw off the Dragon Queen's entire scheme if he could just get himself in the presence of the Silver Skull again and cast it, especially if he could cast the spell while the red priests were using the artifact.

It turned out that the Silver Skull of Zorellin was really a skull that had been dipped in molten silver by a sorcerer named Zorellin. The birth name of whose skull it actually was, was also the key to the spell Phen found. Pael, or maybe Shaella, had written the name in the margin of the spell book. Now Phen knew it.

He finished the review and almost closed the book. He shook his head and sighed. Better to go over it one more time, he told himself, and started reading again. A hurried scrabble of footfalls from overhead stopped him. It sounded like Rosa had stumbled and fallen over. Her tangled hair fell down into the rectangular hole above him and she looked at him with worried eyes.

"Someone ees coming up, Pin," she squealed. "Put the lemp eewt and hide."

"Aye," he replied. "Move away, I'm coming up just in case." With a wave of his hand he extinguished the lamp and started up. Once he was in the nest with her, he closed the hatch door and scrambled to get the ring from his necklace onto his finger.

"Hurry," Rosa whispered as the top of the lift came up into the room. Phen vanished just as Queen Shaella's menacing smile cleared the floor.

"Who are you talking to?" Shaella snapped. Her eyes darted around the room quickly. "Who's here?" It wouldn't have surprised her if King Mikahl had managed to circumvent the priests' trap. They had assured her that he was close at hand, and that it wasn't possible, but she was smart enough to keep from underestimating Ironspike. She found her heart fluttering with the fear that Mikahl might be behind her and whirled around.

"I was talking to you, Queen Shaella," Princess Rosa answered sheepishly. "I'm so very hungry." She began to cry, more from fear than anything, but the tears helped her be convincing. "You brought no food," her sobbing grew deeper.

"Stop it," Shaella snapped. "I'll have some food sent up when I'm through here." She stepped from the lift and strode to one of the tall narrow arrow slits in the wall. Once they had served as releasing and arrival perches for Pael's army of messenger birds. *What I would give to know who half of his spies were*, Shaella thought to herself. Even with all of his information, and his strength of will, he had failed, she reminded herself. His quest for power had ended on a battlefield in Xwarda when Mikahl took his head. She shook the thought away, and returned her attention to the Princess.

"It seems that your High King may be coming for you after all," Shaella smiled wickedly. "He hasn't contacted you yet has he?" She studied the teary-eyed girl and decided that she looked too helpless to have had any good news. "It's likely that he soon will. He might just fly his little fire pony up here and try to save you. He'll be surprised to find that he's expected." Shaella started to pace around the circular room, forcing Phen to have to tiptoe out of her path. The swirl of air his movement caused made Shaella stop and stare at the space he had just been occupying for a long moment. A few heartbeats later she scrunched her nose at her paranoia and resumed her leisurely pace.

Phen wished with all his heart that he still had the knife Hyden Hawk had given him. The wooden handle had been ruined in the fiery mishap on the *Slither*. He almost talked himself into casting a spell on Shaella, but he knew that she was far more powerful than he. She could probably turn the magic against him with a thought. With the dagger, though, he could have just thrust it through her heart. He'd killed before, and he was certain he could do it again. He tried to pay attention to what she was saying about King Mikahl, while wrestling with his murderous thoughts.

"Oh, he will come get you, love, and start away, and then—oop!" Shaella giggled, causing Rosa to sob even louder than she had been. Phen had to put forth great effort to keep from bashing the Dragon Queen in the face for torturing the poor Princess this way.

"You saw my Gerard the other day, didn't you?" Shaella immediately regretted letting her mind go to her lover, but she finished the thought before stepping back into the lift. "Once I'm done dismembering the High King, I think I'll feed you to Gerard. He'll be hungry after taking over the hells for me."

Shaella stepped onto the lift, her mood ruined by her own gloating thoughts of Gerard. It made her a little jealous that King Mikahl was coming for this miserable wretch. Gerard wanted power more than he wanted her, and the tiny void of doubt that left in her confidence made her angry.

"Some food will come up soon," the Dragon Queen said before speaking the command to lower the lift. "Eat it all," Shaella added as she sank into the floor. "Get fattened for the kill."

Phen hoped that Shaella wouldn't notice anything amiss in the library below as she passed through it. He waited until the lift had time to clear the floor beneath the library before he pulled off Loak's ring and went to the Princess. He put his arms around her hesitantly and let her cry into his shoulder.

"Don't worry," he told her. "We'll find a way out of this mess." *At least I hope we will,* he added to himself.

Chapter Forty-Two

Oarly was in the middle of his sixth or maybe seventh toast to the return of the dwarves of Doon. For centuries they had been underground. During that time, the few hundred dwarven families remaining on the surface dwindled in number, down to barely a score. All of them resided in the hills east of Highwander where Oarly had grown up. Why the dwarves had gone under was hard to determine. If you were to ask one of them, you were likely to receive an hour-long spiel that told you nothing. The most common response was that the sun affected their skin. This couldn't be true because anybody who looked at them would know that the only part of the dwarves' skin that ever saw the light of day was their hands and their big bulbous noses. For the most part, the rest of them was covered in hair.

The dwarves brought bad news to the surface with them. The Hammer of Doon, one of Ironspike's counterparts, had been lost in a great molten sea of lava when the King of Dwarves used it to kill an elemental. It was a sad affair, but it happened so long ago that the dwarves who'd returned to answer Queen Willa's call thought of it as just another story.

Bzorch was half asleep with his dragon gun crew near at hand. A watch had been posted among the breed in their area of Jarrek's encampment. Lord Gregory's sudden presence had eroded away most of the bridge of trust that Bzorch and the King of Wildermont had built. The hate between Westlander and breed beast was far too personal to let go of. Westland lords, just like Lord Gregory, had hunted down the breed as if they were vermin. They were mutilated and tortured, the remains left on display for months on end in the bloody snow.

Lord Gregory had about as much tolerance for the breed giants as Bzorch had for him. The breed had come out of the mountains in Northern Westland and raided, pillaged, and plundered for years, until finally they'd grown bold enough to attack a troop of Westland soldiers stationed at the Frozen Outpost. Lord Brach's sister had been there attending a wedding. Thus what had previously been only occasional violent skirmishes between the races graduated in to a hateful, bloody war.

Lord Gregory spent his time with King Jarrek discussing the situation at hand, and what the possible courses of action were. An escort to take Lady Trella through the Wildermont Mountains to the safety of Dreen was already being assembled. Lord Gregory hadn't told her he was going to stay with Jarrek to provide logistical aid. Both the Lion Lord and the Wolf King were of a mind to take full advantage of the current situation in Dakahn. Diamondeen, the dwarven general, had hinted at some possibilities that put their minds to churning. They were just waiting on a few messengers and scouts to return with current information before calling a full battle council.

It was late in the evening when the single breed giant that survived Queen Shaella's attack, came stumbling into the camp. The bloodied creature found Bzorch and told the tale. King Jarrek and the badly scarred Sholt both hobbled out to hear the news. Lord Gregory watched and listened from a distance. He wasn't welcome, nor did he want to go into Bzorch's area of the camp. He found himself wincing at the gruesome details he heard, and he even grew angry at the idea that the breed had been melted away with acidy dragon's breath. He imagined how he would feel if it were Westlanders Shaella killed that way. Oarly came to his side but said nothing, choosing to listen to the story from a distance as well. The celebratory mood of the encampment dissipated quickly, and the harsh realities of the war they were entangled in strangled the life out of the evening. After King Jarrek and Bzorch spoke in private for a while the breed began gathering their things to leave. Bzorch swore before them all that he would kill the Dragon Queen and her pet wyrm, or die trying. Then he and his troop loped away northward, intending to cross back into Locar on the ferry.

For the first night since Jarrek's soldiers had taken back the bottleneck, the encampment was quiet. At least until Lord Gregory told his wife that he wouldn't be traveling to Dreen with her. Lady Trella's anger rang through the night like a shrill bell hammered by an ornery child. Her rage was soon replaced with sobs of disappointment and worry. Eventually, though, the Lion Lord made her understand. He wasn't going into battle, he was just staying to help make plans and advise King Jarrek as the High King would expect him to do. Despite her anger and disappointment, she made love to him. His ever dutiful sense of loyalty to the good of Westland and the realm was one of the things that had attracted her to him in the first place. He promised to come to her just as soon as things were worked out and the battle plans were made.

"You'd better," she told him severely from his shoulder. "I didn't suffer that crowded ship and that smelly dwarf just to be sent away once we got to the mainland. I would have been plenty safe back at the Lost Lion with Zasha and Wyndall."

"Aye, m'lady," Lord Gregory sealed his promises with kisses. "I'll be with you again before you even get settled."

"You'd better be," she repeated, as she gave in to temptation and kissed him back. They made love again, and she managed to convince him to let her stay at Low Crossing with him for one more day. That way she could take the messages for General Spyra herself, at least that was the excuse she used to get him to agree. He didn't like the idea of her staying, but he couldn't resist her.

Two messengers arrived in the morning, one with news that made Jarrek swear and Sholt shake his head in disgust. Oarly and Lord Gregory, as well as General Diamondeen and a few others, hurried over to find out what had the normally reserved King of Wildermont cursing loudly in this pavilion.

"More Dakaneese cavalry arrived at Seareach during the night. Four, maybe five thousand men, and thrice as many are coming behind them." Jarrek looked to the other messenger, who was holding a scroll case bearing the mark of Queen Rachel of Seaward. "Ra'Gren's going to try and take back what we've just regained. He'll have the men to do it this time."

"And most likely a dragon riding wench in the sky too," added Oarly.

Jarrek looked at the seal on the scroll he pulled from the case. The impression in the wax was one he didn't recognize.

"Come on, General," Oarly suggested to the leader of the dwarves. "Let's go have a look at those tunnels you were telling me about." He and General Diamondeen excused themselves while Jarrek opened the scroll and read it to himself.

At first Lord Gregory thought the Wolf King was laughing, but then the man wiped a tear from his cheek and sniffled.

"What is it, Majesty?" Sholt asked. He gave Lord Gregory a look. "As if we needed any more bad news."

"Enough of the 'Majesty', Sholt," Jarrek replied with a strange smile on his face. The tears were flowing freely now. "It's not bad news this time. It's amazing. Sir Hyden Hawk Skyler truly is one of the greatest wizards to ever grace this realm."

"What?" Lord Gregory asked, not sure if he'd heard the Wolf King correctly. "According to the High King and Master Oarly, Hyden has yet to cast a spell that worked properly."

"Let me see," Sholt took the parchment from King Jarrek's hand, and after skipping over the formalities, began to read it aloud:

" '688 *women and children of Wildermont, formally held in Dakahn, have arrived in Seaward City. Other ships carrying similar numbers have left Dakahn and are en route as well. Already we have negotiated the purchase of several thousand of your people's freedom. As soon as the great treasure that Sir Hyden Hawk's party found is recovered, we will proceed to extricate as many of them as possible. The transportation of such a number of freed slaves has become an issue, but I assure you that we are working on that problem as well. We were concerned that the wealth Ra'Gren is amassing because of our purchases might work against your other efforts, but after his vicious actions against innocents were reported to us, we decided to free as many of your people as we can, as quickly as we can, in order to save them from a similar fate.*

Queen Rachel and Queen Willa are working to fund and provide food and shelter for them.'

"There's more, but you get the gist." Sholt shook his head at the wonder of it. "It's signed by a Lord Northall, of Salazar." He handed the curling parchment to Lord Gregory.

"Northall must have acted on Hyden's initial suggestion with coins out of his own coffer," Lord Gregory told them. "Captain Trant and Master Biggs couldn't possibly have recovered any of the pirate booty yet. We just left them on Salazar Island a week ago."

"It doesn't matter why, or how," King Jarrek said. "With ideas and words alone, that mountain boy cast a spell that has freed thousands of my people."

"He is a remarkable young man," Sholt agreed.

"I wouldn't wish the burden he carries on the Dark One himself," Lord Gregory said.

"How so?" asked Jarrek.

"He holds himself to blame for everything the Dragon Queen has done as of late. Apparently he had the chance to kill her once and didn't do it."

"We must call a war council, Your Highness... King Jarrek," Sholt corrected. His expression showed that he didn't like breaking the hopeful mood with the matters at hand. "We must be ready in case Ra'Gren or Queen Shaella try something. Far too many men are amassing to the south of the Seareach passage for us to do otherwise."

"It would be a shame for all those who've just found freedom to not have a land to return to," Lord Gregory observed. "It's bad enough that they will have to come home to ruin, even if we do keep Ra'Gren out of Wildermont."

"I tend to agree with what you were discussing yesterday evening, Lord Lion," Jarrek said with a huff of defiance and some newfound determination in his voice. "I think it's time to take the fight to the Dakaneese."

Later, in a pavilion tent, around a couple of tables that had been pushed together and covered with maps, King Jarrek gathered his war council. Sholt, Lord Gregory, Oarly and General Diamondeen, along with several captains from the Seaward, Wildermont, and Valleyan forces, all stood in the crowded canvas structure listening to the sad count of troops, and the dire news of the preparations that the Dakaneese were making. The only good news was that Queen Rachel's

Seaward army would soon cross the Kahna River into Dakahn and hopefully give King Ra'Gren something other than the passage at Seareach to worry about.

"It's not just the men you've got to worry about," said Oarly dramaticly. "It's the fargin dragons, and demons, and all them bald-headed wizards." He was more than a little drunk.

"And don't forget the Dragon Queen herself," Sholt added. "She's more powerful than any of her minions, I assure you."

"How do we defend against them?" one of the cavalry captains asked. "Our archers have little effect, and we have no real defense against the spells they cast."

"Unfortunately, my colleague Master Amill is with the Seaward army," Sholt said. The heat of the bodies all crammed into the pavilion had him sweating. The salty perspiration was finding its way into the burns on his back and legs that hadn't healed yet. He looked as uncomfortable as he felt. "I've asked Queen Willa to send some of our more accomplished apprentices, and any others who might be able to help shield the men from the arcane, but it will be days before they arrive."

"If only High King Mikahl and Hyden Hawk were here," one of the captains of the Highwander Blacksword said, "they would keep the wizards and demons busy so that we could handle our own bloody business."

A round of agreement, and some argument, followed the remark. The captain who'd spoken was hoping to learn that one or both of the heroes were on their way. They weren't.

"We have to work and plan under the assumption that they won't be able to help us," said Lord Gregory coldly. "If either of them do happen to return, it will just be a boon."

"Are we putting too much faith in Queen Rachel's army crossing the Kahna?" asked Oarly.

"We're the finest fighters that ever lived, dwarf," one of the big tattoo-covered Seaward captains said defensively.

"Calm down, man," Oarly returned with as much aggressiveness, if not more. For a moment it seemed that the dwarves and the Seawardsmen might go at it, but General Diamondeen gave Oarly a look that caused him to step away.

"What Master Oarly means, is that the Dragon Queen still has Princess Rosa. If she wants to aid Dakahn, then she can use the girl to halt Queen Rachel's advances."

"I guess we'll have to settle for defending the passage," King Jarrek conceded, his hope deflating visibly. He so badly wanted to take the fight to Dakahn, but the situation didn't seem to allow for it. He didn't have enough men. The risk was just too high.

"No! No! No!" Oarly barked as he shouldered his way up and crawled onto the map strewn table. "What you need to do is funnel all of your troops through the tunnel General Diamondeen showed me today." Oarly scowled at Lord Gregory, who was looking up at him as if he were daft. "The tunnel comes out in the Dakaneese hills north of Alliak." Oarly turned toward King Jarrek and continued. "As a matter of fact, as soon as the Dakaneese charge the passage, you should retreat. Let them have it." The dwarf was grinning from ear to ear while everyone was looking at him as if he had gone insane.

The truth be told, he was as drunk as he had been in weeks, but a grand idea had struck him.

"Have you gone mad, Master Oarly?" King Jarrek asked over the murmurs of disappointment and disapproval.

"He's just drunk," Lord Gregory said.

"No, lads," General Diamondeen called out as Oarly's brilliant plan came clear to him. "Oarly's got it right." He went on to tell them what he and Oarly saw while roaming the mine tunnels under the southern foothills during the day. Then, as he told them what the observations meant, what Oarly had so cleverly figured, both King Jarrek and Lord Gregory burst into laughter. It *was* an insane idea, but it was the best plan that either of the two formally educated military battle strategists had ever heard.

"I suppose I owe you an apology, Master Dwarf," Lord Gregory said to Oarly after the laughter died away.

"No, Lord Lion," Oarly spoke more of his drunken wisdom. "You owe your wife a trip to Dreen. The plans are made, so now you can go with her on the morrow."

Everyone in the pavilion, and the entire encampment, had heard Lady Trella the night before, and each and every one of them murmured their agreement.

Strangely enough, Oarly's plan of attack was so solid that Lord Gregory actually felt he could leave the situation behind and enjoy the trip through the mountains with his wife.

Chapter Forty-Three

Swimming in the darkness, out to the base of Lakeside Castle's wall was terrifying. Both Hyden and Mikahl felt extremely vulnerable as they swam, mostly underwater, beneath a windy gray sky where the moon was bright enough to backlight the clouds. Talon circled above them as they went, but there wasn't much the hawkling could do to help. Every time they came up for air they expected arrows to come flying down, or shouts to ring out. Luckily no one noticed them.

The long night of clinging to the wall, and paddling in place, was tiresome. Thankfully they found the oddly chiseled keystone before the sun was fully risen. A dozen feet below the marker, under the surface of the water, was the promised tunnel. They emerged into a dark sizable chamber. The faint glow of daylight refracting through the water was detectable, but it wasn't enough for them to see by. Mikahl started to draw Ironspike, but Hyden stopped him.

"Watch this," Hyden said proudly. He cast his plum-sized orb of light into existence, just as Phen had taught him. It appeared, hovering just above his palm, and emitted a warm yellow glow similar in radiance to an oil lantern. "The sword's power will draw attention, Mik," Hyden told him, as he willed the orb to hover up to a place just above his head. "Don't use Ironspike unless you absolutely have to."

"So you *can* cast a spell?" Mikahl shook his head at the wonder of it.

They took in the big stone-walled chamber they were in. The dark, slick-looking block walls were covered with a thick moldy moss. A few rusty torch sconces hung precariously from the sides of an open archway big enough to drive a wagon through. The water they were standing in was very deceptive. From the archway it appeared that the whole floor was just a shin deep pool of water. The hole they had swum up through was undetectable. An unsuspecting person walking across the span would fall right into it. Hyden didn't figure many people were roaming the lower levels of Lakeside Castle's dungeon, though.

"Why is the archway so big?" Mikahl asked.

"What did you Westlanders keep down here?" Hyden shrugged.

"This stuff is centuries old, Hyden," Mikahl said. "I never knew if King Balton used the deeper dungeons for anything or not. I doubt it. The upper levels held a murderer or two, awaiting the headsman, when I was growing up, and at least one breed giant in the early days of the breed war, but I've never been down here."

"Since it's your castle, you get to lead," Hyden indicated the big archway. "Keep your sword ready, but don't draw it unless you have to," he reminded. "As soon as I get a dry string on this bow I'll have an arrow ready to loose."

"I doubt there's anything down here," Mikahl said hopefully.

At the archway, the floor stepped up into a long hallway that paralleled the outer wall of the castle. On the left, spaced about every twenty paces, were alarmingly large rusty iron doors. None of them appeared to be locked, and most of them were open. One was hanging askew. The bottom portion of the iron had been bent into a fold, and the upper hinge pins had been pulled out of the block wall. When they passed that one, Hyden stopped and looked into the cell.

"By the gods, Mik," he said. "Whatever they kept down here was huge."

"Aye," Mikahl agreed.

The hall eventually came to a junction. They could either keep going forward or turn left and go deeper under the castle. "Which way do you think?" Mikahl asked.

"Think about what's above us, Mik," Hyden suggested. "Now that I'm not shivering and waterlogged, maybe I can concentrate. I'm going to have Talon check the tower to see if that's where they're keeping Rosa."

Pael's tower wasn't hard for the hawkling to find. When Hyden found Talon's vision, the bird was already perched on its sharp peak, preening himself in the morning sun. With Hyden's urging, Talon circled the structure cautiously then landed on the sill of one of the upper arrow slits. The room was empty, save for several bird cages that lined the walls, and a pile of dirty clothes on the floor.

The hawkling started to fly away, but the pile of clothes stirred. Through Talon's eyes, Hyden saw that under a tangled mop of filthy hair was Princess Rosa. She was sleeping, if restlessly, but at least she was alive. Without waking her, Talon leapt back into flight.

Hyden let go of his extended vision. He'd thought about making his and the High King's presence known to her. Surely she would remember Talon, but he decided that getting her excited and full of hope, when they were still a long way away from being in a position to help her, would serve no purpose.

"She's there, just like you said," Hyden said.

Mikahl was several yards down the left hand branch of the hallway, looking around in the dim reaches of Hyden's magical light. As he returned to the junction, the satisfied grin on his face told Hyden that Mikahl had heard him.

"If we're at about the same level as the surface of the lake, then we are at least five stories below the main floor of the castle." Mikahl looked from one tunnel to the other. "I guess this way." He started them deeper into the structure.

"I'm following you," Hyden said as he made an arrow mark in the mold on the wall. It pointed back the way they came from.

They roamed the dungeon for several hours. Hyden lost track of how many marks he made. They'd come up three separate staircases so far, and the cells on the level they were currently on were not nearly as large as those below, but they were still big.

"We were just here," Mikahl said with a frustrated huff. Hyden's mark was on one of the other walls pointing off to the hallway across from them.

"We go left," Hyden said.

"Are you sure?"

"Just..." Hyden stopped his voice short then whispered, "Did you hear that?"

"No."

"Shhhh," Hyden hissed. "Listen."

They both strained their ears into the darkness. Apparently some of the keen senses Hyden shared with his *familiar* were beginning to stay with him when they were apart. Mikahl couldn't hear anything, but Hyden was sure he could hear a long low groaning. After he heard it again, he started off toward the sound, leaving Mikahl no choice but to follow.

Hey took a few turns that Hyden didn't bother to mark, and found another stairway leading up. The sound was coming from somewhere on the floor above.

"I don't hear anything," Mikahl whispered.

"It sounds like somebody in pain," Hyden replied softly.

"After you," said Mikahl, making a show of the fact that Ironspike was at the ready.

Hyden checked the tension on his bow string. His arrow was nocked as they started up.

"Why are you sneaking?" asked Mikahl.

Hyden looked back with narrowed brows.

"Your light is already shining into the hallway up there. Let's get up before something traps us in the stairway."

Hyden had to laugh at himself this time. He hurried his pace and, once he was standing in the wide cell-lined passage above, the source of the sound became apparent. He walked straight to a locked cell door. A look in the head-high window hit him like a fist in the gut. Before Mikahl had even caught up to him, Hyden had the bolt thrown and was starting into the cell. Behind him, Mikahl was protesting, but it was too late.

Lying chained in the corner of the putrid smelling cell was a body, nothing but skin and bones really. It was obviously that of a giant. The poor starved figure was easily thirteen feet from head to toe. He was so near to death that Hyden thought it might be inhumane to try and save him.

The giant moaned again, "Booohhhrrrg."

Hyden knelt beside the emaciated form and took its huge head into his lap. He poured a few drops of water onto its swollen cracked lips. "I think he's calling for Borg."

Mikahl found himself raging. He could imagine King Aldar's fury if he were to see this. He could imagine Borg's fury. He rummaged through his wet shoulder pack and found a satchel of meat that was only semi-damp. "Here." He handed it to Hyden.

"Booorrghh."

"Borg's not here," Hyden said. "Eat this." He put a small piece of the soft jerky in the giant's mouth then dribbled some more water.

After the giant finally swallowed he spoke in a raspy whisper. "Tell Borg they..." the giant started quivering. "They killed Dalla." He shuddered and gasped in a breath, but then fell still.

"By the goddess, don't die," Hyden pleaded with tear-filled eyes, but he knew it was too late.

"He's better off now," Mikahl said, putting a hand on Hyden's shoulder. Had he thought the touch of his blade wouldn't just kill him, he might have used Ironspike's magic on the giant. "Did he say to tell Borg that they killed Dalla?"

"Aye, and I will, but..." Hyden raised a hand to still Mikahl and cocked his ear to the side, listening again. He started to say that he heard something, but just then a big dark figure came up out of the hall behind Mikahl. Hyden tried to warn his friend, but wasn't nearly quick enough. A huge clawed paw smashed the High King across the cell into the wall with a thumping clatter.

Hyden slid out from under the dead giant. He'd sat his bow down and it was half a dozen paces across the floor. As he started for it, he realized that he wouldn't get to it before the grotesque beast got to him, but it was too late. He was committed to the action. He pulled an arrow from his quiver as he strode, and just as his hand closed on the grip of the weapon, the beast kicked out at him, causing his legs to come over his head. Just before he crashed into the floor he saw something else skitter into the cell. It wasn't nearly as big as the beast that was attacking him, but it looked pretty dangerous. It was some sort of scorpion-like thing with a long dripping stinger curled up over its segmented body. He couldn't tell any more about it because, when he impacted the wall, blackness engulfed him.

Mikahl blinked his eyes open, but still saw nothing. Instinctually, he reached to his shoulder and pulled out Ironspike. As its symphonic rush of power filled him, he rose to his feet and surveyed the room by the light of its blade.

A malformed breed beast was bearing down on Hyden, who was lying limp across the cell. Only the sudden brilliance of Ironspike's glow stopped the creature from tearing into his friend. Mikahl stepped forward and, with a mighty heaving arc, slashed at the thing before it could turn on him. The blade sliced cleanly across its back, but not deep enough to do serious damage.

The creature roared and turned so quickly that Mikahl was caught off guard. A savage claw ripped out at his chest. As he saw the sharp digits coming at him, he called forth Ironspike's magical armor. It spared him the brunt of the damage, but he was still gouged across the ribs. As he thrust his sword at the creature's guts, he felt more than saw, another presence in the cell. He dodged the scorpion's venomous stinger just in the nick of time, but in doing so he was forced to pull a blow that would have killed the other beast. By the time he caught his balance, the sword's glow was surging purple with his growing anger.

As soon as Mikahl had his feet, he charged the great hairy monstrosity with a savage attack. His first chopping blow took the beast in the upper arm and left a bone-deep gash from shoulder to elbow. His next spinning slice ripped across its middle, but not deeply enough to stop it. After that, he had to run as fast as he could across the cell to try and help Hyden. The scorpion was scurrying toward his helpless friend with thick, honey-like venom dripping from its tail spike. In all the commotion, he forgot about the huge corpse sprawled across the floor. His foot caught on one of the giant's legs and he ended up stumbling right into the scorpion's angry stinger.

It just missed his flesh.

As he went twisting by, he stabbed at the thing. The tip of his now white-hot blade hit the stone floor hard after going straight through the hell-spawned creature. It skittered across the floor into the corner, leaving a trail of thick yellow slime. He doubted it was dead, but at least it was away from Hyden.

Mikahl booted Hyden's body as gently as he could. "Hyden!" He yelled, eyeing the huge blood-drenched thing that was coming at him again. "Get up, Hyden!"

Mikahl spun away from his friend and thrust with his sword. He managed to stick the raging monster with its tip. It roared and slapped the blade aside and charged at him with savage purpose this time. As he drew back Ironspike's blade, he saw Hyden jerk up into consciousness. Mikahl started to twist and spin and cleaved the thing before him across the middle, but a sour note in the chorus of his mind caused him to glance toward the corner where the scorpion had gone. Dripping a slick yellow substance from its body, it scrabbled at him with deceptive speed. Mikahl leapt out of its way, but barely. The scorpion stinger dug deeply into the freakish breed beast's leg. The monster swatted the bug away and screamed out a horrible roar. Clutching at the wound, seemingly forgetting its attack on Mikahl, the hairy beast went to a knee. Mikahl looked on in shocked horror as the beast's leg swelled with a visible quickness right before his eyes. He didn't hesitate to take advantage of the monster's ill fate, though. He took one step, then another, and swung down at the creature's neck. Ironspike sliced through cords, bone, and gristle with almost no resistance. The monster's roar of pain ceased abruptly, leaving the cell empty of sound, save for the symphony of the blade's magic in Mikahl's head, and the splattering of blood on the floor as it spurted from the stump of the malformed breed beast's neck.

*

Hyden felt as if he'd been thrown down a flight of stone stairs.

"Are you all right?" Mikahl asked him as he stepped over the huge corpses lying in the middle of the cell.

"Aye," Hyden grunted. His voice sounded unsure. "I took a whack on the head." He reached back and found the knot forming on the side of his skull.

Mikahl reached the tip of Ironspike down and touched Hyden on the shoulder. He called forth its healing powers and sent them sparkling through his friend's body. Hyden shuddered and looked up.

"Whahh!" he said. "That feels fargin strange, Mik."

"But better, huh?" Mikahl grinned.

"Aye."

Mikahl reached down and helped him to his feet.

"Thank you," Hyden said sincerely. He walked over to where his bow lay and reached down to pick it up. It was too late when he saw the scorpion skitter out of the shadows at him. By the time he understood what he was seeing, the thing's stinger was pulling out of his stomach just below his breast bone. The pain he felt explode inside him was so intense that he couldn't even scream when he stumbled over backwards into Mikahl.

Chapter Forty-Four

"Lord Antone," Ra'Gren growled from his throne, trying to keep his anger in check. "As of this moment Battle Lord Ra'Carr is relieved of duty. He cannot demand more men."

"Who's to lead the forces against Jarrek then?" the now stupefied messenger asked.

The King of Dakahn cocked his head thoughtfully before answering. "It seems that we took the bottleneck in the first place, after Captain Da'Markell arrived with my cavalry." Ra'Gren was speaking aloud, but mostly to himself. Then sharply he commanded the attention of the court's scribe with a bump of his trident's butt on the floor. "Write up a command! Declare Captain Da'Markell as my new Battle Lord. Lord Ra'Carr is to travel to Oktin immediately, where he will take command of the forces that are arriving there. He is to use those men to defend the Valleyan border from Oktin north. There are no bridges across the Kahna north of Oktin, and the river is far too deep to be waded, so he might just be able to manage the task."

The scribe chuckled dutifully, as did a few of the other court attendees.

"Also," Ra'Gren added, "have Lord Cryden accompany him. "The slave trainer did well harassing the Seaward troops as they marched through Archa, and Alliak. Rank him as lieutenant and make sure he knows to report all of Lord Ra'Carr's actions to me."

A representative of Overlord Paleon of Oktin had been listening from the front pew. He stood and bowed his head and waited for the King's attention. Ra'Gren stared at him for a few long moments then harrumphed and gave the nod for the man to speak.

"Majesty, I am one of Lord Paleon's underlords. He sent me to request troops to replace those that the Seaward army killed when they passed through, but I see that your wisdom is far ahead of our requests. How many men can I tell my lord that he should expect and what…?" He made a pained expression of confusion. "What pray should I tell my lord of Ra'Carr's ascension to the command of his men in relation to my lord's current position."

Ra'Gren sighed. He was of a mind to empty the coffers into the hold of a ship and sail to Harthgar, leaving these boot-licking cowards behind. Either that, or put on his armor and lead his army into Wildermont himself. These fools wouldn't dare ask half the questions they did, not if he was hefting his trident on his shoulder.

"Tell Lord Paleon that, until a time when the military concerns of my kingdom are settled, Lord Ra'Carr is assuming the position of overlord of Oktin.

Assure Paleon though, that he will assume the seat that Pa'Peryn's death left vacant once this skirmish with Valleya and Seaward has reached a conclusion."

"My thanks, Majesty," the advisor groveled with a deep bow. "May I enquire the number of men you're sending?" he asked hesitantly.

"You may not," Ra'Gren dismissed him with a wave. Out of curiosity, the King asked a man sitting at the scribe's table a question. "How many men did we leave here in O'Dakahn?"

The man began rummaging through scrolls, most of which tried to curl back up as quickly as he unrolled them. After a moment he scratched his head. "Some forty-five-hundred cavalry, approximately eight thousand swordsmen, and twenty-five-hundred archers are left, Majesty."

"It seems to me that, with Ra'Carr and Cryden guarding the Northern Valleyan border, the Dragon Queen's demon beast guarding the Lokahna Bridge, and Battle Lord Da'Markell pressing Wildermont, we need not worry about being attacked here." Ra'Gren spoke matter of factly, but he was fishing for suggestions, or faults in his line of thinking from those gathered at court. The only fault of thinking, though, was the fact that he actually thought someone might speak up and point out an error in his judgment. He'd gigged more men with his trident in the last few months than he had in a decade. No one dared to voice an opinion.

"Even if Shaella's demon fails, she has Princess Rosa," Ra'Gren continued assessing the situation aloud.

Lord Antone listened intently. He had been sent here to get more men for the upcoming invasion of Wildermont, and he liked where his king was headed.

"If we leave twenty-five hundred cavalry, half the swords, and fifteen hundred archers to guard O'Dakahn, that leaves what, ten thousand men to send to Seareach? Do you think that will be enough to take Wildermont?"

The question wasn't asked to anyone in particular, and Lord Antone didn't want to correct his King's arithmetic, especially since the error was favorable to his cause. "Ten thousand more men would serve our new Battle Lord perfectly," Antone said encouragingly. "In fact, with the reinforcements you've already sent, the taking of Wildermont under Da'Markell's leadership should go quite smoothly."

Ra'Gren smiled at Antone as if the young lord had just helped him defeat some great enemy. "Is there anything else we need for the invasion?"

"Should we expect any help from the Dragon Queen, or her wizards?" Lord Antone couldn't help but ask.

"Do you think they're needed with all of those men?"

"No, Majesty," Antone said. "I just wanted our new Battle Lord to know what sort of aid to expect. Of course, their presence couldn't hurt our efforts."

"Once Wildermont is ours, your work here won't be forgotten, Lord Antone. Is there anything else at hand? I'd like to be finished with the day's buisness before anyone comes bursting through the door."

The court officers and the regular attendees had a good chuckle at that. After the mirth subsided, the announcer answered the King's question.

"All that's left is another request from Lord Northall for the purchase of two thousand more head."

"If the crown can claim half of the transaction, approve it. But slip in one of our better handlers among the slaves. That's six thousand head of mostly Wildermont folk he's purchased already. I'd like to know what he's doing with all of them. Do you know how he is shipping so many out of Dakahn so quickly?"

"Majesty, the rumor is that Salazar has purchased a large amount of Harthgarian ore and is using the slaves as smiths to work it," the announcer answered.

"Nevertheless, I want one of our men in the next herd. Once those orders are written, have someone find me." He stood and stretched, and strode out of the throne room, pausing only to give the announcer the order to dismiss court.

"What in the devil is it?" the tattoo-covered commander of the Seaward muster asked Master Wizard Amill. They were standing on the Valleyan side of the bridge at Lokahna, looking at the huge gorax beast standing guard vigilantly across the span.

"Exactly that," the Highwander wizard answered. "A devil or a demon of some sort, as best as I can tell."

"Should we try to cross?" Commander Escott asked.

"Those are Queen Rachel's orders, though I don't envy you the task," answered the wizard.

"It's a fargin big bastard," the commander said. "But if it bleeds, we can kill it." He gave Master Amill a look. "It does bleed, doesn't it?"

"Who knows?" Master Amill responded with a shrug. "Most demon kind are formed supernaturally. Their earthly bodies are just shells that can die. The essence of the demon moves on. With devils, who knows?"

"I guess we are about to find out." The commander wheeled his horse away from the wizard and rode back to where his nervous troops stood. "Long archers come forth!" the commander yelled. "First pike, form up six abreast at the bridge. Captain Galen, I want your swords to follow them across on my command. Archers, get lined up along our side of the river. I want that thing killed. Send your arrows at the beast until our men get across and engage it. Then give them cover where you can. I see a few hundred Dakaneese cavalry camped at the city's edge over there. Make sure they don't get to our pike men."

As the men formed up to make the crossing, Master Amill rode over to the commander. "I'll blast it with a kinetic ray to start things off," he said. "It will most likely stun the thing long enough for your men to swarm over it and finish it off." He glanced back at the several thousand troops formed up behind the ones making ready. "I think that, if it falls, you should get as many men across as you can. We can see those cavalry camped over there, but if Ra'Gren has any sense, there are a few thousand more soldiers hidden in the city as well."

Commander Escott nodded his agreement. "Let me know when you're ready to send your kinsmatic wave, or whatever you called it. I'll order the attack on your mark." The commander spurred his horse back into the ranks of soldiers, calling out orders for them to follow across in an orderly fashion.

The Seaward commander was an intimidating looking man, with his huge muscles and bird of prey body tattoo. The point of the ink-worked beak started at the bridge of his nose and ran back over his bald head giving his brow an extremely angry looking 'V' shaped set. Nearly all of the Seaward soldiers were heavily muscled, covered in tattoos, and in prime fighting condition. Commander Escott was bigger than most of them.

The Seaward soldiers wore sleeveless chain mail hauberks that belled into knee length skirts below their wide leather belts. High plated boots and similar gauntlets finished the uniforms. Some of them wore helmets. Some chose to let the wicked ink that covered them from head to toe work as intimidation. Dragon skulls, fierce demon eyes, and huge toothy shark maws could be seen among the ranks.

Master Amill didn't envy the commander for having to send his men to face the gargantuan demon beast, but deep down he had more sympathy for the huge monster. These men looked like they would savage it to pieces if they had the chance. When he was ready to cast his spell, and in a favorable position for his work, Master Amill gave the commander a nod. After making a few last minute adjustments and calling out orders, the commander returned the nod and raised his long serrated sword up into the sky.

Master Amill made the finishing gesture and spoke the word that released his spell. As the crackling static roar of it shot forth from his outstretched arm, Commander Escott dropped his sword, sending several hundred arrows hissing up from the thumping bowstrings along the riverbank. They seemed to be chasing the hot purple swath of magical energy that shone plainly in the brightness of the day.

The ray of magical force hit the gorax full in its slick black chest, but it only staggered back two steps and growled. The heavy clawed hand that wasn't clutching the huge knotted bone club shot out, pointing directly back at Master Amill. Powerful magic flowed from the demon in a searing streak. The blast exploded a divot of earth out of the Valleyan shore before the Highwander wizard. Master Amill and a few dozen Seaward archers went tumbling through the air. One was shredded to bloody pieces. Another man impacted a tree like a limp sack of grain. Master Amill hit the ground hard, but rolled to his feet. Blood and angry disbelief poured from his face equally. The demon seemed indifferent, even as arrows came raining down about its head and shoulders. The missiles all seemed to tangle in the beast's thick silvery pelt before they could actually pierce its flesh.

The bone club came crashing down into the first wave of pike men who crossed the bridge. Several were smashed flat and others were severely maimed. Then the monster took a full swing with its weapon, batting several more of them across the ground. A small group managed to get by the huge monster, maybe a hundred men, but the demon was making short work of anything that came within range of its deadly weapon. The middle of the pike men's group halted midway across the bridge, stalling the flow of men to a complete stop. None of them wanted to face the creature.

"Retreat! Come back," Commander Escott yelled. He watched in horror as the group of Dakaneese cavalry came riding up and started harrying the knot of his men who had managed to get across. On foot, the Seawardsmen had no chance against the swift horses and expertly wielded spears of the Dakaneese.

The screams of a drowning Seawardsman, fighting with all his might to keep afloat in the river with his armor on, added to the horrible chaos of the debacle. Less than half an hour after the crossing had started, the bridge was empty. The Seaward army was two hundred and seventy-four men lighter than it had been before. Other than a few arrows that had found the demon's hide, the Dakaneese force hadn't taken any injury. Whether to discourage further attempts at crossing into Dakahn, or just out of sheer meanness, the Dakaneese cavalry made a show of herding the last few of the Seawardsmen they had corralled toward the demon. Tired and utterly defenseless against the forces around them, the stranded men were either crushed by the pounding club, or run through by the cavalrymen's spears. It was a sickening sight to behold, and both Master Amill and Commander Escott swore to avenge the brutal show of butchery.

Their oaths wouldn't be easy to keep though. To kill the heartless Dakaneese cavalrymen they had to find a way to get across the river. And at the moment, that seemed like that might be impossible.

Chapter Forty-Five

Hyden's abdomen swelled to the size of a small melon, but only for short time. The dragon's tear medallion he wore around his neck was like a fountain, sending warm sparkles of healing magic showering over his body. Mikahl was adding to the effect by using the melodies of Ironspike's song as well. The damage the poison was doing to Hyden's body was being continually healed, but the poison itself was still inside him. Its potency didn't seem to be diluting. Its deadly effects were still trying to shut down his vitals. Over and over he felt the horrible explosions of pain the venom caused in his gut. It was unbearable. Hyden found himself on the verge of wishing that death would take him so that he didn't have to stand the pain.

Mikahl was at a loss. He was scared out of his wits. Every time he touched Ironspike to his friend, he prayed to the gods that the sword wouldn't take Hyden's life. Mikahl could see plainly that Hyden was in a bad way. His friend's normally tanned skin was a sickly greenish color and his clothes were soaked with perspiration. Hyden was trembling as if he were freezing cold, and Mikahl had no idea what to do about it. He found himself having to fight back tears as Hyden's nearly unconscious body began to shudder and shake violently.

"All the gods be damned!" Mikahl yelled at the dingy stone ceiling. "If this man dies, then you're no gods at all!"

Hyden's hand found Mikahl's. "Go," he rasped. "Save Princess Rosa."

"I'll not leave you to die alone," Mikahl said with tears flowing freely down his face. He couldn't help but hiccup as a sob overtook him.

The magic of the teardrop soothed Hyden, if only slightly. "You have to go," he said, a little more forcefully. "They'll know you're here now. Get Rosa and go."

"Not without you."

"I'll not be leaving." Hyden stopped to cough. The pain was debilitating. It was a long time before he found his voice again. "Not leaving with you." His hand fell away from Mikahl's and his eyes rolled back into his head. Through tears and curses Mikahl used Ironspike's magic on Hyden again. After a few moments Hyden's eyes fluttered open. "You're still here?"

"I'm not leaving without you," Mikahl promised.

"You have to." Hyden's greenish face split into a weird grin. His hand went to the medallion at his neck. "I have a trick left up my sleeve, Mik. Trust me. You have to go."

"What are you going to do?" Mikahl asked.

"If you'll go away, I can call the dragon, Claret. She'll come and heal me properly." Hyden had no idea if Claret could heal him, or if she could even answer his call. He didn't doubt she would come if she knew he needed her, but he didn't think she could help him while he was down in the dungeon. She could be on the other side of the world. He just knew that he had to do something to get Mikahl on his way. He would rather die miserable and alone, with the hope that Phen and Princess Rosa might escape the Dragon Queen. He definitely didn't want to go thinking that their only hope was down here waiting to get caught because of him.

"What do I do?" Mikahl asked himself more than Hyden.

"You go. You get Rosa and get her safe." Hyden squeezed Mikahl's hand. He was starting to tremble again. "Once she's safe you come back and try to get Phen." He coughed again and the pain made him drain of all color.

"Aye," Mikahl agreed. He leaned down and hugged Hyden tightly. "Are you sure you want me to go?" he asked through his anguish.

"Aye, Mik, before you get caught." Hyden managed to get his trembling arm around Mikahl and hugged him back weakly. "Hurry, before Claret comes."

"Aye," Mikahl agreed, making his voice sound as confident and hopeful as he could. "Sir Hyden Hawk, I love you like a brother."

Hyden released him. "Aye. Go, Mik. Hurry."

Mikahl rose and wiped away his tears, then turned and nearly ran out of the death-filled cell. As soon as Mikahl was gone, Hyden sought out Talon's vision. He found his *familiar's* sight. After it combined with his own into a spectral view of the land below the soaring bird, he began calling out, not to Claret, but to the goddess of his people. He was about to die, and he wanted her company as he went. He needed Talon to make the journey to her. He knew that he was far too weak to make it alone.

Mikahl stopped and leaned against the wall outside the cell. He was certain that Hyden was dying. He understood his friend, and he knew that Hyden wanted him to finish what they'd started. To do otherwise would make Hyden's death pointless. After he steadied himself, and got the tears to stop flowing from his eyes, he decided to dispense with the subterfuge and started back through the dungeon the way they had come.

He walked for a while in a daze. His mind couldn't stay focused. It kept drawing him back to his friend and the horrible death that he was probably facing at this very moment. He found himself at the cross passages where Hyden had first heard the dying giant. It was the third time he had been there since he'd left Hyden. At least that's where he thought he was. It looked exactly the same, yet felt different. He forced the dire thoughts of Hyden's situation from his mind and tried to concentrate. After a few minutes he realized what it was. He hadn't gone back down any stairs yet. This crossway was probably exactly over the other one, just on a higher floor. He started for the stairwell, which he thought he might know the location of. As he turned a corner, he heard a distant conversation taking place. He nearly tripped over a small creature, a cat, or maybe a big bug. It fled into the shadows before he could see exactly what it was. It didn't matter, though. The conversation suddenly stopped. It took him only a moment to figure out why. The deep blue light of Ironspike's blade had found those who were speaking.

A scuffling sound came from ahead of him. He squinted into the gloomy edges of Ironspike's light trying to see what it was. Just as he took a step in that direction, a zard-man leapt from the darkness at him. Its toothy pink mouth was open wide. In its big black-orbed eyes, Mikahl could see his own distorted reflection growing larger. He didn't panic, nor was he startled. Almost casually, he sidestepped the creature and let its own momentum carry it across Ironspike's blade. The zard was dead before it hit the floor.

Mikahl strained his ears over Ironspike's roaring chorus to listen for the other one, but he heard nothing. He took a few quiet steps back toward the intersection of tunnels he'd just left and chanced a glance down one of them. He saw nothing but darkness. He held his sword up to extend the range of its light and still saw nothing.

Suddenly, he heard a crackling roar from behind him. His own shadow leapt forward down the hall as a sun-bright flash exploded at his rear. The blow hit him in the back and sent him sprawling. The massive jolt jarred him to the bone. He could barely see now, and would have surely been cooked by the magical lightning had Ironspike's protective wards not absorbed most of the blast's power. He rolled and called forth shields from Ironspike's symphony. A translucent shell formed around him, but not before he was blasted again, this time by some bright red kinetic beam. After the shield stopped its burning power from reaching him, he looked down to see a big smoking hole in his shirt. The smell of burnt chest hair and flesh filled his protective globe. When he looked back up he saw the demon-wizard Pael looking back at him, and the rage that filled him turned the bluish glow of Ironspike's blade white.

As Mikahl gained his feet, another red blast exploded before him, but this time his shield diffused it. The bald-headed wizard at the end of the dungeon's hall wasn't Pael, he realized, but the bastard sure looked like him. The wizard was a bit worried too, now that Mikahl was shielded and on his feet. The black-robed mage started to charge down a side passage, but wasn't quick enough. The swath of magical energy that shot forth from the end of Ironspike's blade evaporated everything in its path. Stone, steel, and flesh flashed into nothing more than dust, leaving Cole half there. His shoulder, part of his ribcage, and a portion of his hip had been vaporized. Shocked, and still trying to flee, the wizard took half a step before folding in on himself and smacking wetly into the dungeon floor. He screamed as he realized his condition. Cole couldn't cast a spell even if he could have mustered the concentration it took to do so. He only had one arm now, and his guts were draining onto the cold stone. He let out a bone-chilling wail that echoed down the corridors, but Mikahl didn't hear it. His blast had burned through the dungeon wall, and several more walls, including the outer wall of the castle. Ironspike's symphony was raging in his mind and he was moving toward the sunlight. Purposefully, he strode to the first hole and started to duck through it.

"Please," Cole begged.

Mikahl spat, and left him to die in misery. He followed the big holes he vaporized until he found himself looking out over Lion Lake. He was maybe forty feet above its surface. He took a few steps back, and then he charged and jumped into the open air. As he fell toward the surface of the lake he called forth the bright horse from Ironspike's symphony. In a brilliant flash of golden flames, the winged stallion came into being between his legs. Its wide powerful wings caught air, and some ten feet over the shimmering water they swooped round and started to rise.

It was late in the day and still the bright horse stood out like a lantern in the evening. Mikahl didn't care anymore. He flew straight for Pael's tower.

When he was hovering outside of the upper chamber where Princess Rosa was being held, he used Ironspike to blast a hole into the wall, big enough for a person to crawl through. Once the pieces crumbled away, Mikahl was shocked to see that it wasn't just Princess Rosa staring out at him—Phen was standing beside her. The boy was fumbling crazily at his neck for something, but stopped when he saw that it was him.

Rosa was crying, but smiling, and trying to get her fingers through her tangled hair. It was clear that she was foolishly worried about how she looked. Her embarrassment seemed to fade when Mikahl smiled brightly at her.

"Phenilous," Mikahl called sharply. "Are you a prisoner too? Did they take the ring Oarly told me of?"

"I still have the ring, but you are in peril. It's a trap. They've used Rosa as bait."

"I'll worry about that." He shook Ironspike in his hand, as if its presence could foil any trap that existed. "Hyden is down in the dungeon. Do you know how to get down there? He needs help badly."

"Aye," Phen nodded, thinking about the creatures he knew to be down there too, including his *familiar*. "I can find the way." He helped Rosa out onto the bright horse. He could feel the urgency of Hyden's situation radiating off of Mikahl, and as soon as Rosa was on the fiery magical creature he yanked the ring from his necklace.

Rosa hugged herself so tightly to Mikahl that he could barely breathe. "Hurry away before they come," she said to Mikahl. Then she turned back to the gaping hole in the tower. "Thank you, Pin..." She was going to say more, but the space was empty and she didn't know if he was still there or not.

Mikahl heeled the bright horse away from the tower. After the magical stallion put it a few dozen powerful wing strokes behind them, Mikahl began to think that the trap had failed. Already he and the Princess were hundreds of feet away.

"Oh, King Mikahl," Rosa sobbed between his shoulder blades. "I'm so glad to see you."

"I couldn't resist the chance to save the most beautiful girl in the realm," Mikahl replied, oddly thinking of Lord Gregory's smoothness with his wife. It was the last thought he had before a wave of thick blackness came over him. It was like he had flown into a glob of honey. Princess Rosa, the bright horse, and even Ironspike faded from his world. There was nothing but himself, the blackness, and the sensation of falling.

At first he waited for the bone-crushing impact, but eventually he realized that he wasn't falling at all. He was lying in a garden. He couldn't move, not even his eyeballs. The woman looking down at him seemed blurry. The pink teardrop scar on her cheek, and the bald patch on one side of her head were alarmingly familiar, though. She smiled a wicked, sinister grin. He'd never seen Shaella up close before, and he had to admit that she was beautiful in her own dark sort of way. He tried to speak, tried to lash out at her, but he could do nothing. He felt as if he had been turned to stone.

Chapter Forty-Six

Shaella woke to Fslandra's gentle touch. Sunlight was streaming through the half open shutters. The golden rays that cut across the open space of her bedchamber were alive with sparkling motes. By the angle of the beams she could tell it was midday.

"What is it?" Shaella snapped rather harshly. The young zardess recoiled with a hiss. Not conversing, or even communicating with Gerard for the last few tortuous days had taken its toll on Shaella.

"The priests are calling for you, Mastress," the zard girl hissed. "They have caught something in their trap."

Shaella sat up quickly. "The priests have caught the High King?" she asked to make sure she had heard correctly.

"Yesss," Fslandra hissed. "The priests are calling for you."

"This is wonderful news, Fslandra." Shaella stood and strode to the wash basin. "Get me my armor," she commanded as she began to cleanse her naked body with a soft cloth.

A few, short moments later, she was looking like the imposingly powerful Dragon Queen that she was. Under a studded leather girdle, blackened Harthgarian mail shimmered like scales, as she made her way down to the gazebo where the red priests had erected their temple.

To Shaella's delight, Ironspike was lying unsheathed on the altar to her lover. The High King was lying on the wooden floor beside Princess Rosa.

"How long will they stay like that?" Shaella asked.

"Indefinitely Your Highness," one of the priests said.

"Unless we lift the stasis," added another.

"No, don't do that," Shaella told them. She leaned down and looked into Mikahl's eyes. She gave him a big gloating smile. "Does he see me?" she asked as she stood back up.

"Were not sure," one of them answered. "He's still able to blink, so it's likely."

"Would you like us to kill them now?" the third priest asked. He was hovering over Princess Rosa. The girl's raggedy clothes were torn and one of her breasts was exposed. Shaella gave him a disapproving look that caused him to back away from her.

"The Princess is to remain unmolested," Shaella barked. The look on her face made clear that she was serious. "I may have need of her in Dakahn."

She dismissed the priest by smiling broadly past him at the person who was approaching across the lawn. It was Flick. He was grinning and nodding as if he were impressed with the sight before him. "He really isn't much is he?" the wizard said as he came to stand over Mikahl.

"Not without that," she pointed at the sword lying on the altar. "I was just debating over what I should do with him."

"Take your time," Flick suggested. "Ra'Gren has need of us once more. It seems he is about to try a run into Wildermont through the Seareach Passage again. His men will be decimated if you or I don't lend our assistance. I would have gone already myself, but I thought that you might enjoy a chance to unleash Vrot on Jarrek's troops."

"It seems that you've become a mind reader as well as a great wizard," she told him. "I think a ride on my dragon is exactly what I need. You're coming on the Choska?"

"Of course, Mastress," Flick said with a flourishing bow. "With both of us there to harry Jarrek's archers, the Dakaneese troops should be able to retake the passage with ease."

"Ra'Gren's fools will find a way to muck it up," Shaella said, showing her distaste for the King of Dakahn with her expression. "They are so dependent on their slaves that they've grown lazy and weak. It makes me almost ashamed to be half Dakaneese."

"What are we to do with the High King?" one of the red priests ventured.

"Leave them where they lay, both of them. I will post a potent guard around the altar before I go. Make a prayer to my lover telling him what you've done here, but do not disturb him otherwise."

Commander Escott gave Master Wizard Amill a dubious look. "Do you really think it will work?"

"That demon can't be in two places at once," said Amill. "I think that, with what Queen Willa and General Spyra are doing to aid King Jarrek, it will all work out in the end." He turned to the tattoo covered commander. "At least as long as it still looks like all our troops are stalled over here when the sun comes up."

"Making five thousand men looked like ten thousand isn't so hard at a distance," said Escott. "It's making them look like twenty thousand men that's the trick."

"My spells will hold as long as your men don't go scattering about."

"After the last debacle I think that they'll do anything you say, Master Wizard. You saved a few thousand of them from getting roasted."

The night after the first crossing attempt failed, they'd tried again. They stormed the bridge in a great snaking line of soldiers, six abreast. Once across, they went in three separate directions, forcing the demon beasts to go to extreme measures trying to stop them all. It seemed to be working until the monstrous thing began using its magic. Demon fire, in hot emerald gouts, clung to flesh and earth alike. Only a powerful wall of force that Master Amill cast into existence between the demon and the retreating troops saved them.

Hopefully, sending fifteen thousand men north to the bridge at Oktin under the cover of night would allow them to get past the demon so that they could attack O'Dakahn as planned. The new tactic would work if Commander Escott's men, and Master Amill's spells, could convince the demon that the Seaward force was still across the river from them waiting.

"We'll learn in the morning if they suspect anything," Master Amill finally said.

"The light of day will surely tell the tale," Commander Escott had to agree.

Gerard saw them—pairs of eyes in the blackness. There were thousands of them, and they were everywhere. Some were brighter than others, some bigger, or farther away, but all of them were looking at him. They backed away as he passed, giving him ample room. Some of them did this out of respect, but most of them backed away out of fear.

From all over the hells, the demons and devils, as well as other things, had come to witness the impending battle. They gazed in awe at the only creature that ever grew bold enough to try Deezlxar a second time.

Gerard was tense. By all rights Deezlxar could set these things on him. So many attackers at once would be impossible to overcome. The Master of Hell was vain, though; the Abbadon chose not to destroy Gerard that way. He would make an example of the thing that had challenged him. Deezlxar knew that if a creature like Gerard could come maul him and get away with it, soon, other power hungry entities would try him. Such was the way of things in the Nethers.

Deezlxar wasn't ready to hand his domain over to the likes of Kraw or Shokin just yet. He was ready to destroy Gerard, though, and he planned on doing it in fantastic fashion.

The shape of the archway that led into Deezlxar's chamber could be seen by the deep crimson glow of all those eyes. As Gerard strode cockily up to the arch, a hissing murmur echoed through those gathered around. The buzz of anticipation was intense. The time was at hand.

Gerard learned a lesson last time. Deezlxar wouldn't just fold under his dominant will like the other malignant creatures of this place had. Gerard's quickness and savagery weren't going to be enough. He had to be not only faster, but smarter. It was with that thought that he darted into Deezlxar's chamber.

As expected, the Dark One was ready too. There were no threatening words spoken this time. The snapping teeth of one of the Abbadon's heads, and a powerful sweep of his long spidery limbs and the battle began. After dodging the severe fangs that clacked closed just in front of him, Gerard would have been batted away by the club like appendage coming at him, but he expected such an attack this time. He flashed away in a flurry of rose and lavender sparkles, reappearing behind the Dark One. Then, with a vicious series of hacking slices, he tore into the great devil's tail stalk. He couldn't get all the way through the heavy member before the creature spun, but he did manage to sever the bony central core where the tail's nerves and tendons were.

Deezlxar whipped around, but without his tail to stabilize his momentum, he spun too far. Gerard, like before, leapt and charged up one of the Dark One's two remaining necks. He saw that the Abbadon had chewed his headless trunk down to a grisly nub. Before the thing could respond, Gerard leapt from its neck to its bulbous spider-crab body. Gerard figured that if its weak spot wasn't on the underside, then it most likely was on the top. He landed with his dagger-like toes puncturing fleshy hide for traction, and then he tore into the thing like a badger digging a hole in the earth to escape a hungry wolf.

Skin, blood, and thick slimy matter flew out from behind him. He ripped, and thrashed, and dug a hole the size of a water well into the Dark One's back.

The chorused roar of both of Deezlxar's remaining heads was earsplitting. By hacking its tail, Gerard had thrown its whole equilibrium off kilter. There was little Deezlxar could do, and he had to do something quickly. His heads couldn't reach back and over to snap at Gerard.

Gerard was digging deeper into the Abbadon's body one moment, the next, he felt an icy wave pass through him. It was so bitterly frigid that his fiery dragon's blood had to fight to move through his veins. Stiff and rigid he teetered and rolled from Deezlxar's back. In a crash that nearly shattered him to pieces, he hit the flat featureless floor of the chamber. The only thing that saved him was the fiery nature of his body's core. Had it not worked to thaw him from the solid block of ice that he had momentarily become, he would have shattered into a thousand pieces.

While he was still sluggish and groggy, and trying to regain himself, one of Deezlxar's dragon-like heads came down on him. Huge jaws snapped shut over his body. He nearly choked on the hot fetid breath. Teeth bore down on his middle, digging sharply into his armored skin. He found that his head and shoulders were inside one of the mouths. He could feel the immense pressure of the Dark One's jaws smashing at his middle, but the teeth couldn't penetrate his plated body. It was no comfort, because he knew the other head would soon snap closed on his legs and tear him in two. The protective nature of his hide wouldn't be able to save him from that. He felt his lower half being shaken violently and fought down his panic. He tried to tune out the pain and focus on his magic.

Blast after blast of crackling purple energy shot forth from his clawed hands. The first and second of them seemed to do little, but the rest of the blasts caused his world to still. After that, he felt air from outside the mouth flowing past him. A jarring crash told him what he wanted to know. The jaws slackened on his body and he crawled forward into the head through the thick soupy the mixture of blood and tissue left by his spells. He came out of the gaping hole his blasts had caused in the, now limp, dragon's head. He was met with a heavy blow that sent him spinning head over tail through the air. Before he landed, another blow rocked him, causing the blackness to fill with explosions of white light. Just before he smashed into the floor, he snapped himself away in a crackling pop of lavender sparkles. He brought himself back into the chamber high overhead, and with the sudden extension of his torn leathery wings, he righted his fall.

He landed on Deezlxar's back and instantly started tearing another hole into the Dark One's flesh. This time he stopped after penetrating into the mucky yellowish goo. Before the Abbadon could throw him, he cast a spell, and dove away to avoid the blast of the energy he'd loosed inside the beast. The shower of gel-like matter that exploded up out of the hole splashed across him like mud. A moment later he leapt back onto Deezlxar and skittered to its back and blasted again.

The agony the second concussion sent through the Lord of Hell kept Deezlxar from being able to use his magic. He could do little more than buck and twirl. For a long while, Gerard continued assaulting the Abbadon by blasting and leaping away as fast as he could manage. Long after the Dark One's form had stilled, Gerard was still clawing and blasting. He didn't stop until he was exhausted. By then the Abbadon was a mushy ruin.

The last thing Gerard did before he let out his brutal victory roar was to call out to Kraw's priests and tell them he was ready to come into the world. Then, after the echoes of his savage roar subsided, he told all the terrified skulking creatures of hell to be ready. Soon they would be able to celebrate his victory with a feast of man flesh.

Chapter Forty-Seven

As if caught between a fantastic dream, and some horrible nightmare, Hyden spiraled in and out of consciousness. One moment he was with Talon flying over lush green tree tops. The next, he was convulsing in the dungeon cell next to a starved giant's corpse. Somewhere, not too far away, he could feel the vibrations of kinetic explosions. A fleeting thought of his friend Mikahl came and went. Hope and fear, in a vivid flash. He couldn't remember where Talon was going, but he could tell that the hawkling was moving with great speed and purpose. There was no circling or lingering on this flight.

Pain in his abdomen gripped him again, stealing his breath. Then the relieving magic of the dragon's tear medallion surged through him. His mind went back to Talon's and he watched the world pass below. At least until the hot pile of coals in his guts began to flare, pulling him back into the helpless pain-filled reality of the dungeon cell he was lying in. The tear pulsed again and he was flying over a river. Over and again the pain consumed him, and the magic of the dragon's tear eased it away, but eventually his thoughts found a daze of semi-reality where both sensations collided into confusion.

Talon flew round and round the cell, and Hyden fell from the sky into a swirling cloud. *Wait*, his subconscious screamed, *I'm still in the cell. Talon is in the air.* The hawkling screeched out in protest as Hyden started to slip away. Like a hot needle, Talon forced his vision into Hyden's spinning brain. A sea of green swaying leaves leapt up, and when it seemed the emerald mass was about to slam into them, they went right through. Branches, streams of mote-filled sunlight, and then the sound of other birds filled Hyden's head. The dizzying flight carried him through the undergrowth to a place where a gurgling stream had pooled. Talon landed on a large moss covered boulder at the edge of the water and screeched out again. A thundering cloud of smaller birds, and a few of the smaller four-legged creatures, exploded away from the fierce sound. Gliding from his perch down to the stream's edge, Talon began splashing the cool liquid over him. Hyden felt the chill of it. It helped him focus. Using all of the strength of will he could muster, he stared deeply into the rippling pool. Just then, a white, pillowy cloud passed overhead. Its reflection made the surface of the water appear milky-white, chased with silver. A particular swirling of ripples spun and wavered, and slowly, as if she were the sky herself, the White Goddess formed into being. Her arms opened wide in welcome, but the beautiful smile Hyden expected to see wasn't on her face. Her look of sadness as she took him in filled him with dread.

"I think that I've failed you, m'lady," Hyden said. "I'm at the door of death and our enemies are ushering me in."

"You must go into the darkness, Hyden Hawk," she said gently. "Only there can you find the light."

"Aye," Hyden responded. He had no idea what she meant. "I need not go anywhere. The darkness is coming to me."

"You must suffer the pain Hyden," she commanded. "You are not dead yet. Pull yourself to your feet and seek the darkness. Only there will you find the light. The light can save you, but you must hurry."

"I don't understand," he rasped as her image started to fade.

"Find the light in the darkness, and the balance will be restored, Hyden." She was fading from view. "Get up Hyden," she urged, but then she was gone.

"Get up, Hyden Hawk," he heard the echo in his mind as the image of the forest faded to gray. Then Talon leapt into flight, jarring him back to reality.

"Fight it, Hyden," a familiar voice said from close to him. "Get up. You have to get up, Hyden."

An odd scratching sensation raked across his cheek and his eyes fluttered open. The pain in his guts was overwhelming, but not so much that it kept him from trying to scrabble backwards away from the toothy thing that was crawling around his face.

"Ahhhhghhh!" he yelled as he managed to scoot barely a pace backwards. The creature before him hissed and hunched into a prickle.

"Thank the gods," said Phen from beside him. "I thought you were gone. You have to get up and walk."

Hyden tried, but couldn't speak. The pain of moving was akin to being roasted alive from the inside out. Phen grabbed him under one arm and pulled him up into a sitting position. Hyden's complexion went from pale green to ghostly white. Phen poured cool water over his head and let it run down his face. Then he helped him sip.

"We have to get out of here, Hyden," Phen said. He didn't do a very good job of hiding his fear, but he tried. "Mikahl took Princess Rosa from the tower, and the Dragon Queen's priest caught them in a spell." Phen shook his head, trying to clear the worry from it so that he could think. "I tried to warn them, but he didn't listen."

"Never does," Hyden mumbled.

"I can't carry you out of here," Phen said. "You have to get up and walk."

Hyden took a few long breaths, then the dragon's tear pulsed a soothing blast of energy into him. It didn't do much to quell his pain, but it gave him the strength he needed to climb to his feet.

"I have to find the darkness," Hyden murmured.

Phen put his arm around his friend's waist and helped him take a step, then another. "A moment ago you said you needed to find the light."

"The light …" Hyden whispered. " …is in the darkness."

"Whatever you say," Phen agreed with him. "We're going to get you out into the daylight, if we can manage to get there without getting caught."

"Aye," Hyden put more effort into helping Phen help him. "Into the light."

Phen found that he was fighting tears of sorrow as he helped Hyden along. His friend was dying, and he knew it. Even so, he would get Hyden to daylight. He wouldn't let him die down here in the dungeon. If Master Sholt or Master Amill were at hand, Phen thought that maybe a healing spell of higher magic might help, but he doubted it. The thing that had pumped Hyden's gut full of venom looked terribly wicked, even lying dead on the dungeon floor. The malformed breed giant's leg was swollen to the size of a cask. Phen held little hope for Hyden. He fought his tears and concentrated on helping him take each step. It was all he could think to do.

Shaella was enjoying the swift rush of early summer air as it whipped through her long dark hair. Flick was a hundred feet away, perched atop the bat-like Choska demon's neck. It was slightly larger than Vrot in body size, but not nearly as long. It didn't have a sinuous tail or neck. Still, it was a fierce creature, with razor sharp claws, a wide mastiff-like head, and a mouth full of nasty teeth.

As always, clutched in Shaella's hand was the staff with the Spectral Orb mounted at its head. As the thick blue winding line of the Leif Greyn River came into view in the distance, she saw a glimmering red light swirling around inside the crystal. She brought it closer and let Vrot guide them while she studied it.

The distorted image of one of the red-robed priests stared out at her with a perplexed, yet excited look on his face.

"What is it?" she snapped, bringing the man's attention to bear like a whip crack. "This had better be good."

"Queen Shaella," the priest bowed.

"Out with it," she snapped.

Flick heard her and urged the Choska closer to the black dragon.

"Kraw has commanded us," the priest said excitedly. "We are preparing to bring him out of the Nethers."

"Wait for me," she said, feeling an electric tingle run through her belly. "I'm turning back now. Do not open the seal until I'm there."

"Yes," the priest said in a tone that made her think he might not obey.

"Flick!" she called out. "Go on! Aid the Dakaneese in my stead, then see what else Ra'Gren requires, at your discretion of course."

Flick felt a sinking feeling inside as he nodded that he understood her orders. It was Gerard, he knew. He could tell it by the gleaming of her eyes. With only the grim satisfaction that she was happy to motivate him, he agreed. Then he winged the Choska away before his expression could betray his emotion. Flick found that he felt a little more for his queen than he should. He knew that she didn't return the affection. She was in love with Gerard, but nonetheless, Flick loved Shaella.

Shaella wheeled Vrot sharply around and gave her dragon a loving pat on his sleek scaled back. "Fly, my dragon," she ordered. "Fly as swiftly as you can." The idea that Gerard was coming to her now filled her with an ecstatic hope. She was literally trembling with excitement. It was all she could do to stay seated as Vrot churned his way through the air with his powerful wings.

In a moment of clarity Hyden called out to Claret. Not for himself—he was done. He thought he understood now what the White Goddess meant about the light. Even if he succeeded, though, he didn't see a way to get back from where he had to go. It was Phen who needed a way out of this place. Not just out of the castle, but out of Westland completely. As Hyden leaned heavily into the corner of a hallway just above the dungeon level of the vast castle, he struggled to get his medallion's chain over his head. When Phen returned from scouting the hall, Hyden hung it over Phen's neck then sagged into the floor.

Phen didn't question the deed. It would have choked him up too badly to do so. As he struggled to get Hyden back to his feet, he suddenly had an idea of his own.

"Here," Phen said, taking Loak's ring and pressing it into Hyden's hand. "Put this on."

Hyden's moment of clarity was gone now. He looked at the boy, then at the ring. It took his scrambled brain a moment to make sense of it, but he finally understood. He let Phen slide the ring onto his finger and saw that, even to his own eyes, he disappeared.

Phen got his arm under Hyden's and pulled him back to his feet. He knew that he looked quite insane moving through the castle hugging an invisible person, but he figured that he could prop Hyden in a corner if he had to. He struggled to get them walking again. Once he did, he felt for his connection with Spike. The lyna was up ahead of them, scouting for danger. All of the guards and servants were either hiding or trying to find a view of what the red priests were doing in the garden. Something was happening out there now, Phen guessed, for the hallways were completely empty.

Without the magic of the teardrop to fill him with relief, Hyden knew that he couldn't go much farther. "Go on, Phen," he whispered. "Tell me where Mikahl is, and go."

"I'll not let go of you, Hyden Hawk," Phen argued stubbornly. "You'll fall into a heap without me."

"Then get me to Mikahl," rasped Hyden. "After that you have to get away from here."

"Not until I destroy the Silver Skull," Phen said. "I know how to render it useless Hyden, but it will only work while it is being used."

Hyden found some strange relief in that. In the foggy mess of his brain he tried to untwist the thoughts that were tangled there. After few moments he stopped them in the middle of an empty passage.

"Aye, Phen," Hyden whispered. "Wait until the seal is open, and then destroy the skull. But I have to be there."

"You need to..."

"No!" Hyden cut the boy a off as harshly as he could manage. "I'm going to die, Phen. Do not argue with me." He used all the strength he had left in him to grip the boy by the shoulders and shake him. "Promise me, Phen. Promise me you'll get me to the seal, and then destroy the skull while it's open."

Phen couldn't hold back his tears any longer. He didn't quite understand Hyden's motives, but he understood the finality of them.

"Aye," he whispered. "I'll try my damnedest, Hyden. I will."

Chapter Forty-Eight

The same day Lord Gregory and Lady Trella arrived in the Red City of Dreen, so did Queen Willa. The two parties, however, arrived in quite different manners. The Lion Lord and his wife came into the city on horseback, after spending many days of hard riding over the well-worn passage through the Wildermont Mountains. Queen Willa used a witchy device that was hidden in the depths of her castle, called the Wardstone Waygate. Used properly, the Wardstone Waygate could take its user, and a handful of others, most anywhere they could imagine. It was a one way teleportation though. No matter where you went, you had to use conventional means, or other magical ones, to return to Xwarda. Only a handful of people knew that it existed, and as far as anyone knew, the gateway was the only one of its kind.

Queen Willa had her hair pulled back into a fat single braid, and was dressed for battle. A knee length shirt of fine silvery chain mail was fastened around her middle by a plated leather girdle. Over her shoulders was a custom formed breastplate that maintained her feminine form. High, shin-plated, boots, a helmet of gold worked steel, and a long narrow sword completed her garb. She brought with her a small escort, four of her fiercest Blacksword warriors as a personal guard, and King Granitheart, the ruler of the dwarves. Several days earlier she had dispatched from Xwarda ten thousand of her Blacksword soldiers, and half again as many mounted pike men. King Granitheart sent the remainder of his force with them, some three thousand battle eager dwarves. The entire force was currently marching west and Willa figured they would be almost to Kastia by now. A pair of her Master Wizard's apprentices, young men who barely qualified as acolytes, were with the troops. The idea was for Master Sholt, Master Amill, the apprentices, and herself to be able to communicate by way of spells and other magical means so that the separate groups of soldiers could work together.

Willa came because she was a capable, battle-tested sorceress in her own right. She had every intention of taking the place of an apprentice once things started to get bloody. Her excuse was that the youngsters had no experience. In truth, she just wanted to be there.

After dinner she called a war council. General Spyra gave his full cooperation; after all, he was Willa's man.

Of course, Lord Gregory was invited, and the King of the Dwarves as well. Master Sholt had conveyed to her the Lion Lord's unofficial rank and role as the High King's adviser and friend. Lord Lion's opinion wasn't to be taken lightly. Attending, by way of being close to Master Wizard Sholt, were King Jarrek and General Diamondeen. Commander Escott was with Master Wizard Amill as well.

It seemed that Queen Willa was going to take control of the situation until the meeting actually began. When it did, she made it clear that King Jarrek was the one in charge.

There was no way to get troops where they were most needed, not fast enough to do any good. Ra'Gren was about to attack at Seareach. Jarrek asked that the others concentrate on getting forces into Dakahn along the Valleyan border at Oktin and Lokahna. Diverting Ra'Gren's attention from Seareach was a priority. The demon beast guarding the bridge at Lokahna had to be eliminated first, explained Master Amill. He conveyed commander Escott's thoughts about attacking the hulking creature from the Dakaneese side of the river and told them that the bulk of his troops should be at Oktin very soon. Master Sholt told them Master Oarly and General Diamondeen's plan, though he let Lord Gregory fill in the details.

The mood of the evening was somber. The fact that neither High King Mikahl, nor Sir Hyden Hawk Skyler had been heard from for weeks left little room to hope for their survival, much less their aid. To make matters worse, it turned out that they had underestimated the timing of Ra'Gren's aggression. In the middle of the battle council, the Dakaneese forces charged the Seareach Passage with a full out attack. King Jarrek and Master Sholt assured the others that they had things under control for the time being. They would follow the plan they laid out, but they had to leave the others and attend to the matters at hand.

When Master Sholt ended his spells of communication the others were left feeling helpless.

"If your men are at Kastia now," Lord Gregory said to Queen Willa and the King of the Dwarves, in an attempt to generate some positive action, as well as some hope, "then they should be diverted immediately toward Oktin. If they are allowed to march all the way here, then they will lose maybe two days."

Queen Willa nodded that it would be done, and then went about casting a *sending* to the apprentices to convey the orders.

Lord Gregory had to laugh at himself. Queen Willa was a far cry from the twisted conniving witch queen that rumors had portrayed her to be. He couldn't imagine the beautiful headstrong woman eating people, or feeding them to her armies. He could, however, imagine her trying to turn a drunken lecherous lord into a hog—something else she had supposedly done.

"If Commander Escott and Master Amill are still at Lokahna, then the troops they sent to Oktin will have no serious brass to direct them," General Spyra said hopefully. He was suggesting that he get the appointment, and was blatantly eager about it.

"That's a good point," said Lord Gregory.

All eyes fell on Queen Willa to make a decision, but she was busy speaking softly to an apprentice mage who was nearly a hundred miles away.

Lady Mandary, General Spyra's wife, was outside the service entrance that led to the council room where the meeting was taking place. Her ear was pressed to the wooden door. A moment before, her eye had been glued to the key hole, surveying the group. She was giddy with a devilish excitement. Queen Shaella would love to hear of all the scheming troop movements. She would especially want to hear the little bits that Lady Mandary learned about the trap Jarrek and the dwarves were setting at Seareach.

"What, pray tell, are you about?" a loud female voice startled Lady Mandary nearly out of her false skin.

A heartbeat later she flushed with anger. She was the Lady of this castle and her husband was the current ruler of the kingdom of Valleya. She didn't have to answer to anybody.

"Mind your business," she snapped as she turned to see who was speaking to her. She expected to find a servant, or one of the maids. Instead she found regal Lady Trella glaring at her.

"That is exactly what I would say to you," Trella said before moving on.

Trella was hungry, had been since they arrived, so much so, that she left the General's prying wife and continued on her journey to find something to eat before the kitchens closed for the night. As soon as she was gone, Lady Mandary's ear was pressed back against the door.

"...of course, General," Queen Willa was saying. "But you are doing such a fine job here. I will go. I have King Granitheart and twenty thousand men to protect me."

Lady Mandary cursed under her breath. She'd missed something important. Why wasn't her husband being sent to war, she wondered? He was a general after all.

During the interruption of her spying, she hadn't seen the dwarven king move about the room. It was all she could do to keep from getting cracked in the face as he hurried out the door in search of a chamber pot. She squealed and put on her best face for him, feigning that she had just been passing by, that he had startled her. He was in no condition to question her. The gallons of wine he'd drunk during the meeting were about to flow out of him on their own. Frustrated that she'd missed an integral part of the planning, she decided that she had enough information to warrant a *sending* to Queen Shaella. As fast as she could, she hurried to her quarters, pricked herself, and squeezed a drop of blood into a finger bowl.

Shaella was just getting back to Lakeside Castle when the orb at the head of her staff filled with the persistent image of her marsh-witch spy. She was in no mood for a gossipy chat. Her lover wanted to be let into the world. Gerard wanted to be with her, and she longed for him. Nevertheless, her curiosity wouldn't let her ignore the calling.

Her spy told her that King Jarrek had a surprise planned for Ra'Gren's troops in Seareach. She was in no position to do anything to stop it. Vrot was already coming down to land her in the bailey yard that had been set aside for the dragon's comings and goings. All she wanted to do was hurry to the red priests' temple garden and welcome Gerard from the Nethers. She ordered Vrot to fly like an arrow to Dakahn and to do as Flick bade him. The dragon could warn her wizard of Jarrek's trap, but she figured that it would be too late by the time he got there. She could cast a *sending* to Ra'Gren herself, but that would take too much time. All she could think about was her lover. With a frustrated huff she decided that she wouldn't leave loyal Flick unwarned.

As she watched Vrot leap back into the air and wing away eastward, she used her staff to call out to her friend so that he would be aware of everything she had been told. After that, her only concern was the coming of Gerard.

"Are you ready?" King Jarrek asked General Diamondeen.

"We'll know in a moment," the dwarf pointed to another of his kind who was approaching.

Jarrek greeted Oarly with a smile and a slap on the back. "Are we ready, Master Oarly?"

"As ever we will be," Oarly nodded. "The relay is set. Just give one of those torch bearing dwarves on the hill the signal when it is time."

"It'll take some patience to draw them in," Jarrek said.

"I hope it takes till dawn," said the dwarven general. "I want to see the looks on their faces."

"What of the tunnel? Is it cleared?" Jarrek asked.

"Since supper call," Diamondeen answered proudly. "We've been sending a few through since then, but most of my dwarves are already at the far end."

"Good," said Jarrek giving the two dwarves a nod of appreciation. "I don't know how to thank you."

"When the battle is over you can get us drunk," said Oarly with a grin.

"Why wait until the battle is over?" General Diamondeen asked seriously. "Everyone knows a dwarf fights better when he's drinking."

"If you can find it, you can drink it," Jarrek laughed. "I have to get to the front." With that he strode off to find a horse.

As everyone expected, the Dakaneese came hard. The Seaward forces under Jarrek's command held them for a long time, but finally, around midnight, the call to retreat rang out. After that it was all about fighting on the run. The Dakaneese swarmed into the passage and pushed with mighty force. By dawn they controlled the position completely. The Choska demon came tearing through the ranks and the bald-headed wizard riding its back was strangely trying to keep King Jarrek and his troops from retreating. In between attacks, the wizard reined the Choska around, flying low over the Dakaneese and calling out to them. Soon they too began trying to retreat out of the passage too.

King Jarrek saw what was happening and cursed in disbelief. Somehow the wizard knew about the trap. Still, several thousand Dakaneese infantry were in the passage. Jarrek knew that it was now or never.

"Retreat! Full retreat!" he called out to his men. He turned his horse and charged back toward Low Crossing. As he went, he commanded the attention of the torch bearing dwarves on the ridge. "Let it go!" he ordered as loudly as he could scream.

The dwarf waved a flaming brand in a certain motion. Another dwarf up the way repeated it, and so on, until Oarly's group, who were positioned underground, saw the signal and went to work.

For a long time, nothing happened, but then a great rumbling shook the earth. The Dakaneese hadn't been expecting the sudden lurching of the ground beneath them. In the seconds of their initial fear and confusion, King Jarrek's men broke from all engagement and charged away from the battle with breakneck fury.

From overhead, Flick tried to stop the retreat. He knew he couldn't save the Dakaneese troops, but he figured he might cause quite a few of the enemy to get caught up in the trap.

The earth shook again, and this time the passage collapsed right out from under the Dakaneese fighters. Huge chunks of rock and earth fell away beneath their feet. Cracks shot across the earth that grew and shifted until it seemed the whole world was caving in. A loud roar filled the morning. Horses and men screamed and scrabbled but to no avail. As the ground beneath them was crumbling and falling, water from the mighty river was rushing in to fill the void. Armored men sank away and horses thrashed in the flow. King Jarrek and his Seaward soldiers had to fight through rows of thorny vines and treacherous thickets that hadn't been there before. Flick also hindered their way by sending great exploding blasts into the earth in front of them, causing the horses to rear up or balk. A wall of fire erupted, cutting about half of the retreating force off before they could get away.

Those that kept themselves and their horses calm were able to leap through the flaming obstacle, but many were lost as their animals turned and ran into the expanding hole that was forming where the passage had just been. Jarrek went back, his horse leaping through the wall of flames as if it wasn't there. He took the time to urge many of the men past the burning barrier, but soon he could wait no longer.

The caving pit had collapsed into the Leif Greyn River's deepest channel and a wall of water and churning muck was rushing in with alarming force. Jarrek charged his horse straight back through the flames and up to higher ground as swiftly as he could. To his surprise, Bzorch and his dragon gun crew were there. They said they hadn't been able to cross back into Westland because their ferry was destroyed. Streaking spears, followed by uncoiling lengths of rope filled the air and the Choska was forced to carry Flick away from the area.

Jarrek surveyed the scene. He took his time, letting his men catch their breath as he did. The bottleneck passage, and most of Seareach, was gone, as was most of the land that stretched from there up toward Low Crossing. It was all under water now. A great lake now blocked the southern border of Wildermont from Dakahn. The only way between the two countries now was over the Wildermont Mountains, and they were far too steep and craggy to allow any sort of sizable force to pass.

The first part of the plan had mostly worked. They could have drowned twice as many of the Dakaneese soldiers, had Shaella's wizard not caught on to the plan. Considering this, Jarrek decided that the mage had to have been informed. There was no other way their movements could have given away what was going to happen.

Either way, it was time to start the second phase of the dwarves' brilliant idea. King Jarrek was glad to see Bzorch and their big heavy weapons. When his forces came out of the earth on the other side of the secret mountain tunnel he was sure the dragon-guns would prove to be useful. If they moved swiftly enough, the breed might be able to catch up with the dwarves and the Highwander men who were already trying to come up behind what was left of Ra'Gren's force. It would be a rout if they could pin them against the new body of water.

Jarrek glanced to the west. Already the *Shark's Tooth* and a few other vessels were moving into the new lake from the river. As much as Jarrek didn't like sell-swords, he'd grown fond of Maxrell Tyne and Grommen. The ships under Tyne's

Command were to spend the day transporting archers into the mountains, where the dwarves had cleared positions overlooking the confused Dakaneese.

Jarrek nodded to himself that he was ready, and went to round up and count the survivors of his Seaward front. Once they were regrouped they'd have a long ride underground and a few more battles to fight. As much as he hated to, he broke up the reprieve and ordered them to move. He found the troops eager to comply. None of them forgot how the Dakaneese had trapped and killed their kinsmen. In moments, they were following the breed giants into the dwarven tunnel.

It was time to take the battle to Dakahn.

Chapter Forty-Nine

"I can't help you get around out there without getting caught," Phen said. "You're invisible, I'm not."

Hyden sucked in a deep breath and let go of the boy. Standing on his own, he had to reach down deep to muster the strength to stay upright, while doing his best to block out the pain. "Where's Mikahl?" he asked through gritted teeth.

Phen peeked out the door and Spike shot between his legs into the grassy garden area. The lyna found a thick shrub and hid beneath it. From there, Phen watched through his *familiar's* eyes. The sun would be setting soon, and the bailey was already bathed in shadow. The garden was bustling with people, though. The red-robed priests were lighting torches and candles, and making preparations. Queen Shaella was standing amongst four white clad men—no, they were statues. The statues from outside her bedchamber, Phen realized. She was speaking to them with closed eyes and making subtle hand gestures. She was in the middle of some sort of spell, he guessed.

Beyond her in the gazebo, he could see one of the red-robed priests lifting the Silver Skull from its podium. He recognized part of Rosa's dress on the floor nearby.

"In their temple," said Phen. "I can see Princess Rosa lying there. Surely they're together."

Hyden peeked around the edge of the door and used Phen's shoulder to hold himself steady. "Where will the seal open?" he asked. His vision was blurry at best. He could barely make out the structure on the lawn.

"Can you see where they burned the symbols in the grass?" Phen asked.

The marks were nearer to the door, and Hyden could see the shape. He recognized the ancient symbol that was burned inside the circle. He had eradicated a more permanent version of it in the Dragon's Spire, so that Mikahl could kill Pael. "Here," he grunted, pulling Loak's ring from his finger. "Put it on. Go see if you can help Mikahl and the Princess."

Phen took the ring and watched as Hyden leaned heavily on the wall. He looked like he had sweated all the liquid from his body, as if his eyes were sinking away. Outside, the priests were beginning to chant. Phen gave Hyden a quick hug then wiped the tears from his eyes. He wanted to speak, to say goodbye or something, anything, but no words would come.

Hyden forced a smile. "Put it on, Phen," he said weakly. "Be sure and destroy the skull after."

"After what?" Phen asked, as he faded from sight.

"You'll know when it's time." A tremor shook Hyden. "When she... she comes for you, tell her what hap... happened to me. Now go. Ta... take care of Talon."

Hyden didn't wait for Phen to respond. He shoved Phen's invisible body gently out the door and quietly latched it closed behind him.

*

Phen had no idea what 'she' Hyden was talking about. Hyden was obviously feeling the effects of the poison and not thinking clearly. Hyden was about to die. Phen knew he would never be able to laugh or joke with him again. Phen was so overcome with grief that he had to fight to keep from sobbing out loud. He couldn't...

A deep whooshing sound blasted from somewhere under the seal. It was so deep and powerful that it startled Phen out of his grief. The rush of fear-driven anxiety hurried his pace across the garden. Just as they had before, the red priests had moved the skull from its place atop the podium to a small altar built at one end of the symbol they'd burned into the lawn. The skull sat so that its wicked jade eyes looked over the place where the world would soon fade away into blackness.

Phen noticed that Shaella's statues had taken up new positions. He hadn't seen them move. Two of them now stood guard on each side of the short set of wooden steps that led up into the makeshift temple. He had no choice but to go between them. He glanced at Shaella as he passed her. She was fidgety, yet focused. Her eyes were glued to the place where Gerard had appeared before. Just as Phen started into the gazebo the whooshing sound came again, only this time it took on a deep thumping that pulsed in time with the diminished harmony the priests were chanting. He knew he had to hurry. He could feel the static drawing in.

He didn't want to have to tangle with the marble guardians. He had no idea how formidable they were, but he was sure that they were plenty capable of stopping a terrified boy from getting by if they had to.

Remembering that Spike was about, he called to his *familiar*. The lyna shot toward him across the yard like a startled rabbit. It bounded up into the gazebo without a thought. Phen watched the statues carefully, but saw nothing, not even the slightest of flinches. Through Spike's eyes, he looked about the inside of the structure and saw that the walls were nothing more than heavy curtains. If he had to, he could get out through the seams where they overlapped. Mikahl and Rosa were lying as still as the statues that were guarding them. A shining glint on the altar caught the lyna's eye. It was the tip of a blade. Phen hoped that it was Ironspike. Hyden had told him once that all of King Mikahl's powers were held in the blade. If Mikahl ever lost it, or dropped it, he would be vulnerable. Hyden explained that this was why the High King trained so rigorously and regularly with it.

Phen heard Shaella gasp and glanced back toward the seal.

It was opening. He had to hurry.

He took a deep breath and charged between the statues. He didn't look back. If he had, he would have been frozen with fear. Both marble guardians were starting in right behind him.

Phen saw that it *was* Ironspike on the altar. He snatched it and started over to where Mikahl lay beside the Princess. The weight of the sword caused him to drop it when its blade slid off of the altar. It hung in the satiny tablecloth that was draped over the table. Phen grabbed that and pulled a candelabra and a statue onto the floor with a clatter. The first marble guard that came in charged at Phen as if it could see him, but it got tangled in the tablecloth and fell face first. Its reaching hand fell just short of Phen's ankle. The second one stumbled over the first, buying Phen just enough time to boot the sword against Mikahl and wrap the High King's hand around the hilt.

Phen wasn't sure what he hoped would happen, but he'd expected more than nothing. His heart sank. It would apparently take more than just the sword to pull Mikahl out of the spell he was under. Phen looked back, and one of the guardians was on him. He wasn't sure what happened next, but he knew that Ironspike's blade flickered blue for a moment. He dove over the wooden rail of the gazebo into the drapery that hung there. His weight tore the heavy cloth from its hangers and he fell the few feet to the ground on the back side of the building.

Thinking that the stone-formed guard was right on his heels, Phen rolled to his feet quickly. He ran to a place a few dozen feet behind Queen Shaella. There he began silently reciting the words to the spell he would use to destroy the skull.

It was getting darker, but the hole in the world was far blacker then any Westland night had ever been. Already the seal was opened wide, and over the physical roar of power it caused, Phen could hear something coming up from within.

Mikahl felt the rush of Ironspike's magic. It didn't come on like a symphonic tidal wave this time. The sound came slower, the trickle of whistled melody, an echo of a reverberation that was eventually joined by another strand of audible power, and then another. Slowly it worked its way around and through the spell that was cast on him. The thick muck he felt trapped in gave way to a more viscous resistance. Then gradually he was able to move and stretch his limbs.

The first thing he did was raise the blade up into the strange white-painted man that was charging over him. Even when he'd been spelled, he could see. Knowing that Phen had the ring that made him invisible, he assumed that it was

Phen who'd moved his sword across the floor and put it in his hand. The man over him wasn't a man at all, he found, when his blade sent a showering of stone chips across his face. The sword cleaved through a stone leg, though, leaving the heavy granite limb to crash into his body. The rest of the animated statue crumbled into gravel as it fell.

Mikahl shoved the leg away and sat up. Another of the stone men was untangling itself from an overturned table and cloth. Mikahl wasted no time. He sat up and lunged with his sword so that its tip punctured the marble man's chest. He saw his stupidity as the man cracked apart and began to crumble over them. He had to roll and crawl over the limp form of Princess Rosa to keep the heavy chunks of stone from bashing into her delicate body. Luckily, the back of his head and shoulders took the brunt of the damage.

A few heartbeats later, Mikahl started down the wooden steps of the gazebo only to see the thing that was once Gerard Skyler standing over a black hole in the lawn. Mikahl saw the back of Shaella's half-scorched head reflecting the flickering torch flames, just as two more of the marble guardians came closing in on him from either side. The eyes of the beast in the hole locked onto his. He felt a chill tear through him when the striking resemblance to Hyden registered in his brain. Shaella whirled on him as well, with the makings of a spell already on her lips.

It was all Mikahl could do to call Ironspike's magical shield forth from its symphony as he spun with his blade extended to slice a complete circle around him. Both of the marble guardians shattered at the sword's touch. Then a hot crimson blast shot forth from Shaella's hands hitting his crackling blue shield in an explosion of prismatic light. But the concussion of raw power that Gerard sent hurling at him was far more potent. Mikahl went flinging backwards through the gazebo and right out the other side of the structure. He came to a tumbling halt on the lawn on the other side, so entangled in drapery that he had to fight just to extend his legs.

"Gerard," a weak voice called out from behind the thing standing in the seal. It was Hyden. "What have you done to yourself?" he asked. The tears flowing from his eyes were bloody. Inside the thick plated body of the thing before him, he could plainly see his little brother, and the idea of it ripped at his heart like a jagged claw.

"Hyden?" the thing said in a voice so big and deep that it shook the walls of the castle.

"What have you become?" Hyden asked, as he fought to stay on his feet.

The recognition in Gerard's eyes was fleeting. The voices and thoughts of too many powerful entities were swirling around his brain. The minute part of him that was still human could find no purchase to grasp hold of.

"I am the Warlord now," Gerard boomed. He stepped forward, moving his gaze from Hyden to the depths of the black hole beside him. "I am the Master of Hell and Earth," he called down into the Nethers. "Come, my pets, relish the freedom you have been denied."

A huge black thing with a buzzard's head and wide leathery wings crawled out of the darkness and leapt into flight. Behind it, a trio of hellcats shot straight up into the air. They were followed by another winged creature that might have been part insect.

"No!" Hyden yelled as he charged across the few feet that separated them.

Shaella sent a spiraling strand of yellow force streaking out at him. It wrapped around Hyden and squeezed him tightly in place. If she'd let the force go, he would have fallen into a heap. He didn't have the strength to struggle. Instead, he said a prayer to the White Goddess to help him find the chance, and the strength, he needed to do what she had told him must be done.

Phen had the last word of his casting on the tip of his tongue, but held it in his mouth. He could see what Hyden intended to do now. He whirled and looked back to see King Mikahl kicking and crawling out of the tangle he was in. Relief flowed over him. He hadn't been sure if the vicious blow had killed the High King or not. His attention was pulled back to the scene before him as the buzz of a few dozen sheep-sized insects came skittering out of the hole like swarming ants. Fear swam through his veins as two of them started toward him. They looked like giant roaches, or water beetles, with sharp pincers extending from the sides of their clacking beak-like mouths.

Phen could cast a spell against them, but he would lose the one he needed to destroy the Silver Skull. As one of them darted forward to attack, indecision froze him. Out of nowhere, Spike leapt onto the creature's swiveling head and started clawing and tearing at its red glowing eyes. As the thing behind it started forward, another lyna came leaping out of the shadows, then another, and another. Before long, the two demon bugs were in a frenzied battle with a half dozen of the small quilled felines.

"Hyden Hawk," Mikahl yelled from just behind Phen.

"Let him be," Phen warned. "Kill the Dragon Queen. Hyden knows what he's about."

Phen couldn't believe that he'd just ordered the High King like he was a kitchen maid. Then again, he couldn't believe he was standing before a gateway to the Nethers, surrounded by all sorts of terrible creatures. He had forgotten completely that he was invisible. It seemed that all of the demon-kind could see him plainly, and things weren't looking good.

Mikahl slashed his way through the battling insects, swinging Ironspike around to force them back. The lyna of took full advantage of their fear of the sword's power and soon had the bugs fleeing over the walls of the bailey garden or up onto the balcony of Shaella's bedchamber.

Gerard roared and sent a sizzling purple blast at Mikahl as he came up behind Shaella. Mikahl sent a white hot raging streak to meet the demon magic. The two channels of power collided in a blinding explosion and hung there. Mikahl's magic wasn't as strong as the Lord of the Hells', and the surging purple ray moved back toward him swiftly. Using all his will and rage Mikahl fought against it, but it was no use. Already the tip of his sword was turning from its bright white radiance to a dull amber. The Abbadon was draining the power out of it. Mikahl fell to his knees, trying to avoid the tainted magic. He glanced at Hyden, who was still trapped in Shaella's eldritch rope. He didn't know what to do. Nearly the whole length of Ironspike's blade was coated with viscous amber goo. A deathly icy feeling was creeping into the hilt now, and he could feel it reaching into his hand, and up his arm.

Suddenly, Talon's ear shattering shriek split the night. It was so loud and fierce that even Gerard looked up into the sky.

Like a streaking shadow, the hawkling swooped. Raking claws shot across Shaella's face. She had no choice but to let go of the hold she had on Hyden as she clutched, screaming, at her ruined eyes.

Hyden felt the magical force let go of him and gave a roar of his own. He stumbled, then charged, leaping onto the thing that had once been his brother. His presence caused the creature to give up its attack on Mikahl. Hyden took a step up. Using Gerard's thigh, he leapt onto his neck. Reaching around his brother, he rammed his hand into one of Gerard's eye sockets with all he had left in him. As he did, Mikahl charged up behind Shaella with three running paces, and with a massive swing of Ironspike's blade, sent her head tumbling through the air.

Gerard saw the blow with one eye. He saw the blood fountain up out of the stump of Shaella's neck and pour down her cleavage. He saw her body crumple to its knees and then pitch forward. He even saw the shocked expression on her face as her head hit the lawn. What he didn't see was the blast from Mikahl's sword that hit him full in the chest and sent him staggering over backwards into the hole that he'd come out of.

"Jump away, Hyden!" Mikahl screamed to his friend. The beast was falling back into its hell and Mikahl didn't understand why Hyden was still holding on.

Phen understood, and he cast his spell, calling out the name of the man whose skull the wizard Zorellin had once dipped in molten silver. The three priests screamed in fear and pain as the form of the Silver Skull suddenly began to shrivel and melt away.

Mikahl watched in terror as his friend clung viciously to the back of the raging demon god. For an instant, it looked like the powerful beast was going to catch air with its wings. A clawed hand found the edge of the hole and held on, and again it looked like the thing might pull itself back out of the seal, but first one lyna, then another came streaking across the lawn. The prickly-furred cats attacked Gerard's gripping claw until it let go.

"No, Spike!" Phen screamed as his *familiar* went over the edge with Hyden. Just as they fell away, the great whooshing sound of the seal faded, and the hole in the earth cinched closed.

A screaming red-robed priest came charging at Phen, but one of the big hell-born things that escaped the Nethers snatched him up before he got halfway across the bailey. Apparently, King Mikahl, Phen, and Talon all had the same thought at the same time, because all three of them went racing toward the shambled gazebo where Princess Rosa was starting to wake from the spell she'd been under.

Chapter Fifty

"Look," Commander Escott pointed with a face full of confusion.

"By the gods!" Master Amill muttered. "Is it leaving?"

"Let us hope so," Escott answered in dismay. "If it is, we can walk right into Lokahna."

"It might be a trick."

Just after the sun set, the great bone-club wielding demon turned and started walking north. For days it had vigilantly guarded the bridge. Now it was trudging away.

"I would think that since all of Queen Willa's troops, the dwarves, and three fourths of our men are converging on Oktin, it's heading there," said Master Amill.

"I agree," commander Escott nodded as he moved away. A moment later he was barking orders across the encampment.

Master Amill made a *sending* to Queen Willa to warn her of the approaching gargantuan beast.

Escott was smart, Amill decided. The man was ready to take Lokahna with the troops he had. They hadn't seen any foot soldiers across the river, only a small detachment of Dakaneese archers and cavalry. He really didn't think he would be needed, other than to tend the wounded. Still, he concentrated his preparations on both attacking spells and those of healing. He could tell that the Dakaneese were as surprised by the beast's departure as he was. He couldn't imagine the coming battle to be anything less than a rout, but he wanted to be prepared for anything.

Phen was closest to the gazebo, and he got there first. A small blaze had started off to one side of the octagonal construction where the altar candles ignited some of the drapes. One of the red priests pulled Rosa up to her knees by her hair. A gleaming blade was at her throat. He didn't see Phen, but he saw Mikahl barreling up the wooden steps at him. Phen had to leap to the side to avoid Mikahl and his white-hot blade. Just as the priest started barking threats and pushing the edge of his steel into Rosa's throat, Talon came round in a banking streak. The hawkling's claws caught his hair and hood. Talon's beak came down hard into the man's eye. A thin ribbon of red appeared at the Princess's throat but to Mikahl's surprise the priest suddenly fell away. An invisible blow had caved in the back of his head. He crumpled forward, leaving Talon fluttering. Mikahl had to dive to catch the limp Princess before she came bashing down face first into a jagged piece of broken marble statue.

"Was that you, Phen?" Mikahl asked, once he had Rosa's head cradled in his lap.

"Aye," Phen said. He pulled Loak's ring from his finger and became visible again. "Can you break the spell on her?" he asked. In the time he'd spent comforting the Princess he had grown fond of her.

"I think Ironspike can pull her out of it." Mikahl looked at the boy and noticed the streaks that tears had made on his dirty face. "What's Hyden about?"

"He's dying," Phen said, taking in a deep sucking breath to keep himself from breaking down into sobs in front of the High King. Talon fluttered down and landed on Phen's shoulder. "He said he had to go into the darkness to find the light."

"That thing that stung him was a real bastard," said Mikahl. He didn't try to hide his tears either. The brightness of his blade slowly faded from its white glare to a warm radiant blue. The smoke from the gazebo was starting to smell like cooking meat as the fire found the priest's body.

"I don't think I can carry you and her both on the bright horse," Mikahl said as he and Phen pulled Rosa out of the burning structure.

"Get her to safety," Phen said, as he took in the moonlit garden. "Those things are gone now, I think. I destroyed the skull. I can hide, and work my way to safety. Besides, I think that Shaella's dragon collar is out there in the grass somewhere. We wouldn't want that to end up in the wrong hands."

"Aye," Mikahl gave the boy a nod of respect and a pat on the shoulder. He gently laid the flat of Ironspike's blade against Rosa's leg. The cobalt glow flared carmine for an instant, and a few seconds later the Princess was mumbling something and her eyes were fluttering open. When she saw Mikahl, she looked around fearfully, until her eyes fell on Phen. Then they grew wide and filled with confusion.

"Oh, Pin, I had a dream," she whispered shakily.

"It was no dream," Mikahl said, causing her to jerk her head toward him. When she saw him, a beautiful smile crept across her grimy face. He gave her his hand and helped her up.

"I'll get her to Dreen, where she'll be safe," the High King said. "Then I'll come back for you."

"Aye," Phen nodded. He held up Loak's ring. "You may not see me, but I'll be looking for you." He hoped to find the dragon's collar and be able to leave right behind Mikahl. Even through all of his grief, the prospect of a riding a dragon put fire in his blood.

Phen had to squint when the bright horse flared to life. Mikahl led Rosa to the fiery magical pegasus and helped her climb on. Talon cooed his awe into Phen's ear as Mikahl joined her and the bright horse carried them away.

Phen tried in vain not to think about Hyden. He started searching the garden grounds for the dragon collar, but it was hard to see through the river of tears.

*

At an altitude higher than the breed giants could shoot their dragon guns, and using a spell that allowed him to see quite clearly what was below him, Flick surveyed the strange movements of Jarrek's troops. Vrot was flying dutifully beside the Choska Flick was riding. Even the dragon was amazed at what they were seeing below. The Wolf King's army had all but disappeared from the face of the earth. It took them a while, but the cunning black dragon finally figured out that they had gone into a tunnel or a cave. Once that notion was established, Flick deduced that the dwarves he'd seen had been instrumental in sinking Seareach. The squat men were fabled diggers and rocksmiths who'd once had a great kingdom in the realm. How Jarrek persuaded them to return and fight for him, Flick couldn't guess. The wizard realized that they were probably going to come up out of the ground in Dakahn somewhere. An attack was the only reason he could think that they would travel in such a manner. He had Vrot and the Choska making long sweeps as they worked their way south, hoping to find a sign of where they were going to emerge.

A short while after the sun went down, the dragon came near to him and spoke. Flick didn't have the collar on, but he understood enough of the old language to make out some words.

"The Queen has coupled with the darkness," he mistranslated. He figured that Vrot meant Gerard had come forth. The dragon's actual words were, "The Queen has found her death."

A short while later, when the dragon peeled away and sped off to the west, Flick assumed that Shaella had called him back to her. He put it out of his mind. She'd ordered him to aid Ra'Gren at his discretion. If he could find the place where Jarrek and his dwarves we're going to come out of their tunnel, then he could try and block it, or cave it in. If he couldn't find it, he would be forced to fly to O'Dakahn and consort with Ra'Gren. That was something he didn't want to do. He could barely stand to think about the Dakaneese King.

Flick searched until the sun began to lighten the sky in the east. If they were coming out near Seareach, in the foothills along the border, then they were waiting for something, he decided. He half hoped to see Shaella flying to his aid from the west, but he knew that she wouldn't leave Gerard so soon after his return. He wondered why she'd called Vrot to her. Discouraged, and feeling more than a little jealous, he willed the Choska southward toward O'Dakahn. He decided that ousting the repulsive king of slaves and sell-swords out of his bed before dawn might make him feel better.

Phen found the collar Shaella had been wearing, but a few heartbeats too late. The surviving red priest was huddled in a dark corner, trying to fasten it around his neck. It was so bloody that the clasps kept slipping between his fingers. Talon tried to attack the man, but was batted away brutally. Phen didn't know what to do, so he cast the first spell that came to mind. A sudden burst of thorny vines shot up from the earth and entangled the priest. The priest was mystified, searching the garden yard for his unseen attacker. A ball of fire flared forth and burned the prickly foliage away. He looked around frantically, but all his eyes could find was Talon, who was nursing a dislocated wing and hobbling toward the base of one of the stone walls that surrounded the garden yard. The priest gave up fumbling with the collar for a moment and began casting another spell.

Phen was overcome with panic. The spell was obviously directed at Talon. He racked his brain for something that might help them. Distraction was the best he could come up with.

"Don't you dare do it!" Phen warned ominously. He darted a few feet away from where he had spoken, just in case the old man had sharp ears.

"Who goes there?" the priest yelled. He began trying to get the collar back on his neck. At least he seemed to have forgotten about Talon.

"I'm nothing but a wisp," Phen said as he cast his little orb of light into being. It appeared in his hand then floated slowly up and came to rest above his head. The priest's eyes locked onto the glowing ball and his brows narrowed. Phen used the same spell that Hyden had used to make Oarly's boot vanish. He strode forth, touched the collar, and made it disappear, before quickly backing away. The collar reappeared in a little space of Phen's making. Unlike Hyden, he would be able to retrieve it later.

The priest's face seemed to draw in toward a point at the bridge of his nose. His snarling growl was so deep and angry that it startled Phen. An icy grasp reached into Phen and clasped his heart. He knew then that he was in trouble. This was far more than just an old devil-worshiping priest. Already the dragon collar was back in the man's hand.

Out of the corner of his eye, Phen caught sight of Talon struggling to get his wing back into a normal position. Inside his chest the grip seemed to be strangling the beat of his heart. Its coldness took his breath away.

The priest murmured some words then grinned as he saw plainly what his magical grip had taken hold of. He took his time then, and carefully got the collar buckled around his neck. The whole time the anticipation of getting to kill the boy who had ruined the Silver Skull was growing inside him.

Phen tried to struggle free, but couldn't. He could see the hatred forming in the priest's eyes. He wasn't invisible to the man anymore and he knew it. He should have known better than to have underestimated the old mage. The red priests had managed to summon Hyden's brother with the Silver Skull, and they'd trapped the High King and taken Ironspike. Who was he to tangle was such a force?

He glanced around, searching for anything that might help them. Talon seemed to have snapped his wing back into position, but wasn't able to take flight. The poor hawkling was trembling and in obvious pain. Phen thought it was possible that the priest had a similar grip on Talon's heart. He felt his pulse fading. His heart was being crushed and it seemed as if his guts were freezing solid.

"I should tear you into little bitty pieces for what you've done, boy," the priest growled. He put his hate filled eyes inches from Phen's. His breath was hot and smelled of onions and fermented fruit. "I would relish the sounds you'd make as you came apart." Spittle sprayed from his mouth as he spoke. "Kraw would enjoy the taste of you, I think."

The icy grip inside Phen let loose then, and he gasped for breath. A brutal backhand took him across the face, knocking him to the ground. "A quick death would be too good for you," the priest snapped.

Talon hop-flapped across the lawn, and ended up on top of Phen's chest. The hawkling cawed at the evil necromancer.

"I'll think I'll save you for later." The priest murmured a few words and made a quick gesture with his hand. The world stopped then. A bitter chill, far more potent than the grasp, consumed Phen. Then everything slipped into blackness.

Had Flick flown just a little farther east when he was searching for Jarrek and the dwarves he would have found them massing in the town of Alliak. They had quickly taken it over and we're now preparing to march west to try and trap the remaining Dakaneese forces against the new lake.

If Flick had been farther north, he might have seen the bright white shining magical Pegasus that carried the High King and Princess Rosa over the Wilder Mountains toward Dreen, but he saw neither. All he saw was the huge filthy cesspool of O'Dakahn growing larger and larger on the southern horizon as he raced to get there before Ra'Gren could crawl out of bed.

High King Mikahl and Princess Rosa landed inside the fenced protective walls of Dreen's modest castle yard just after sunrise. After escorting her to General Spyra and placing her into his care, Mikahl found Lord Gregory and told him what happened in Westland. It was hard to be happy with the news of Sir Hyden Hawk's fate, but the prospect of retaking Westland from the zard excited the Lion Lord. Lord Gregory outlined King Jarrek's current plans, and Mikahl promised to come to their aid just as soon as he went and retrieved Phen from Lakeside Castle.

It was with much elation and a sense of new found hope that Lord Gregory dispatched a rider to catch up with Queen Willa and King Granitheart, who were on their way to Oktin. After that, he had Lady Trella see to the needs of Princess Rosa and wrote a proper letter to Queen Rachel telling her that her daughter was now safe and out of the Dragon Queen's hands. Then, as soon the messenger bird was away, he found the map room and began making preliminary plans to take Westland back from the skeeks.

Chapter Fifty-One

In the light of early morning, Flick strode up the long run of stairs that led to the entrance of Ra'Gren's palace. A pair of guards hurried behind him protesting his passage, but they were too afraid of the bald-headed wizard to try and stop him. He had, after all, flown into the grounds on the back of a giant, ember-eyed bat. Flick ignored them. He gained the top of the long flight of stairs where another pair of guards stood. They dutifully crossed their pikes in front of him to block the ancient wooden doors. With a dismissive wave of his hands, Flick caused the panels to fly open. The wide-eyed guards were so unsettled by the blunt display of magic that they pulled their pikes up and let him through.

"I will be waiting in the throne room," Flick said. "Bring me your king, and be quick about it." Flick was grinning inside. The haughty bastard would be flaming mad. Ra'Gren was easily riled, and Flick loved to push the limits of the man's tolerance. He just couldn't respect a man, a king no less, who did nothing for himself. To be rousted out of his bed full of slave whores would have him on the edge of bursting.

As Flick entered the throne room, he looked around and caused the unlit torches ensconced along the walls to flare to life. He almost took a seat in Ra'Gren's fur covered throne, but decided against it.

A long hour later, King Ra'Gren, dressed in nothing but a filmy robe of coral green silk, came into the throne room. He was carrying his iron trident on his shoulder as if to throw it. His white hair and beard were disheveled, and his face was a bright purplish color. The half dozen guards around him had their weapons drawn and looked a little more formidable than the ones Flick had met outside.

"What is the meaning of this?" Ra'Gren snapped. His level of alarm dropped only slightly when he saw who was waiting for him in his throne room.

"King Jarrek has closed off of the Wildermont passage and over a third of your men are floating home in the river." Flick found that he was enjoying himself more than he expected. Ra'Gren's eyes were as big as eggs and the worm on his forehead looked like it might crawl away. "What's more," Flick continued. "...the Red Wolf has a legion of dwarves aiding him now. They are tunneling into Dakahn as we speak."

"Dwarves? Underwater?" Ra'Gren looked at the trident in his hand then back at Flick as if he were judging the distance between them. "Are you mad? Tunnels?"

Flick couldn't help but laugh. Ra'Gren roared out at the blatant show of disrespect, but somehow managed to keep a hold of his weapon. The sound of his frustration caused the men around him to step back and cringe. "You're telling me that the Red Wolf is attacking my kingdom now?"

"If he's smart, he will try to pin your troops against the giant lake that now sits where Seareach once was," Flick said casually. "If he manages to pull it off, your men will have no escape."

"This is preposterous," Ra'Gren snapped. "Where is Shaella?"

"Queen Shaella. She is attending to her hell-born pets. She sent me to help you. At my own discretion, of course," Flick added with a grin. "It seems your plans always go awry. I'm not one to dabble in failure."

Ra'Gren started to bark out an angry response, but a sudden whooshing sound accompanied by a bright yellow swirling light filled the space between him and the wizard. Reflexively, Flick called forth several protective wards for himself and a powerful kinetic blast that he could unleash with a word.

Ra'Gren moved back from the strange apparition as well. Two of his six guards stepped up bravely between their king and the spiraling cloud.

The magical energy took the smoky form of a plump young lady, whose dire expression was as intense as it was grave. She never fully came into form, but through the cloudy shape the blonde sheen of her curly ringlets and the icy blue of her eyes could be made out quite clearly.

"King Ra'Gren," she said with a slight bow and a nervous glance at something that those in the throne room couldn't see. Her back was to Flick, but he knew exactly who she was. He had seen her reflection in Queen Shaella's scrying bowl on occasion.

"What is it, witch?" Flick asked sharply. The idea that Shaella's spy was giving information to Ra'Gren as well as his Queen angered him to no end. She whirled around and peered through the light of her spell as if he were hard to see. Flick could tell by the terrified look on her face that his anger was misplaced.

"Cole? Flick? Which one are you? I can't see well enough to tell you apart," she sobbed. "He's killed her. Tell me it's not true. Tell me our queen is not dead."

"What is this?" Ra'Gren growled through his unease.

Flick held up a hand to still the angry king. He could tell that something was terribly wrong. "Who said she was killed?" Flick asked.

"The High King and his Princess," Lady Mandary cried. "He said he beheaded Queen Shaella after killing you, and some priests. The bastard brought Princess Rosa to Dreen then went off after someone named Fin."

Flick was staggered by the news and immediately began reaching out to Shaella for confirmation.

"Are you sure?" Ra'Gren asked.

Lady Mandary turned back to the King of Dakahn. "I saw the High King and the Princess with my own eyes," she sniffled and gulped in a breath. "There's a great army coming through Oktin; Seawardsmen, dwarves, and the Blacksword of

Highwander, led by Queen Willa herself." She looked away and her eyes grew wide. Her voice became a hurried whisper. "They're coming for you."

Another voice, that of an angry woman, was heard in the background, and then Lady Mandary's apparition was gone. The cloud of yellow smoke slowly dissipated.

Ra'Gren started to say that it wasn't just his plans that sometimes went sour, but the look of pure hatred and anger on the bald-headed wizard's face stopped his voice in his throat. Instead of saying anything, he walked to his throne and sat down. He wasn't sure what Flick was capable of, but he knew he needed to turn the wizard's anger to his advantage. With Shaella dead, and his force at Seareach trapped, he would need every ally he could muster.

Lady Trella was in the middle of fetching more hot water from the kitchen pot for Princess Rosa's bath when she heard the General's wife speaking crazily. She stopped to listen, thinking that Lady Mandary might have hurt herself and possibly needed aid. As she went to open the door and ask if everything was all right, she heard the woman's words. "... and some priests. The bastard brought Princess Rosa here to Dreen..." It was all Trella needed to hear. The woman's disrespect of the High King, and the tone of her words, only confirmed what Lady Trella had suspected since catching the woman spying on the war council. She burst into the room, just in time to see General Spyra's wife warning King Ra'Gren.

Before Lady Mandary could move to defend herself, Lady Trella punched her hard across the jaw. The woman crumpled to the floor. Trella wasted no time. She swept the scrying bowl off of the vanity into the floor. Then she tore a strip from the bed sheet and bound Lady Mandary's hands behind her back and hurried off to find her husband.

She found him with General Spyra, both speaking hopefully over a map of Westland that was held open on the table by an empty bottle of wine and a trio of goblets. She was glad the bottle had been empty for a few days. She didn't want to tell the General about his wife's treachery at all, but since she had no choice, she would rather him hear the news sober.

"Sirs," she said politely, interrupting their conversation. She didn't give them the chance to ask what was wrong. "I've caught Lady Mandary," she said. "I caught her in a treacherous act, and I've subdued her."

General Spyra looked up and blinked in confusion. "What? Lady Mandary?" He looked to Lord Gregory for some sort of explanation, but the Lion Lord looked just as confused by his wife's accusation.

Lady Trella explained in great detail what she'd heard and seen, both times that she'd caught the General's wife acting suspicious. General Spyra looked stricken.

Half an hour later, Lady Trella was dismissed to tend Princess Rosa. Lady Mandary stood unbound before her husband and Lord Gregory. She swore that lady Trella was a jealous liar. The conniving marsh witch had her husband convinced that she was innocent and was urging him to challenge the Lion Lord to a duel to prove her honor. Lord Gregory declined the challenge, explaining to Lady Mandary that the High King would be back soon, and with the power of Ironspike, he would be able to see the truth of the matter.

Speaking to General Spyra, Lord Gregory said, "If your wife is still willing to deny Lady Trella's claim before the King of the Realm, and the might of his blade, then I will place myself at your mercy, but I promise you, friend, my wife is no liar, and King Mikahl will know the truth."

Lord Gregory felt for the General. The man was as honorable as they come, and so in love with the woman that he couldn't see past his heart. Lord Gregory's statement hit home with Lady Mandary, though. Already she was starting to make excuses to leave Dreen.

"I thought you were my husband," she spat at General Spyra while glaring daggers at the Lion Lord. "If you've not enough rocks in your britches to defend my honor, then you'll take me home to Xwarda now."

General Spyra took his time and weighed Lord Gregory's statement in his heart. Already he knew that, even if his wife was proven to be innocent of Lady Trella's accusations, the woman would never love him or respect him as she had before. A man who didn't fight for his wife's honor wasn't worthy of her love.

He almost did it. Even after the Westland lord had declined the challenge. He almost drew his blade. Common sense kept him from it. All along he had known that it was too good to be true. Lady Mandary loved him a little too much, a little too perfectly, always catering to his pride while gently prying information from him.

Fighting a tear, and the dead weight of a lifetime of hope pulling at his heart, he cursed out loud and called for the guards to come. *What a fool I've been,* he told himself.

Thinking that her husband was going to have Lord Gregory put in chains, Lady Mandary said, "It's about time you came to your senses. These greedy Westland nobles just want your seat."

"I suppose you're right, my love," General Spyra said to her as a pair of Valleyan guardsmen stepped into the room. "It is about time that I came to my senses." Then to the guards he said, "Take her to the upper cells and treat her well. She may be a traitor, but she is still a lady."

"You coward," she yelled at him as the guards grabbed her arms. "You're a fool, a buffoon. Wraaagh!" She spun and twisted free of the men holding her. She was far stronger than either of them thought possible. Her golden ringlets began to grow thick and grey and her chubby cheeks deflated to pale spotted leather-like skin. Her wide proud shoulders drooped, and her breasts sagged to her belly. In a matter of seconds she transformed from the plump young Lady Mandary into the old wrinkled Dakaneese swamp witch that she really was. Her long nails raked one of the guards across the eyes. He brought both of his hands to his face while the other guard was fighting through his shock to draw his sword. She sent a sizzling blast of static into his chest that sent him staggering backwards. The smell of burnt flesh quickly filled the room.

The marsh witch whirled on the open-mouthed General and began barking out the words of a spell. He was entranced by her sudden transformation, sickened that he had loved such a thing. He had kissed that rotten toothless mouth and run his fingers through that matted gray mop of hair. She smelled of decaying fish and looked as if she were older than the Maker. It caused him to heave. Suddenly leaning over, he was vomiting on the floor.

The fiery red streaks of magic that shot forth from her fingertips passed right through where his head would have been had he not gotten ill. She was cackling loudly now, and in the process of bringing her razor sharp claws down across the General's back when Lord Gregory made his move. Drawing his sword, he took two steps then made a chopping swing that left him way over extended. He felt his sword tip bite into flesh, and heard the witch's howling scream, but his breath was forced out of his lungs as he hit the hard stone floor squarely with his chest. The world filled with exploding white stars for a moment. When he opened his eyes, he looked up and saw the anguished General's tear-streaked face as he pulled his sword out of the witch's gut. The shining blade was covered in thick black blood. When the Lion Lord rolled over to push himself up, he saw the clenched hand and forearm that his sword had severed from her body. As he stood, he looked at the General. He saw an embarrassed, heartbroken man who was about to crumble. "I'm sorry, sir," was all he could manage to say, but he said it as sincerely as he could. Then to the bloody-faced guard that was huddling over his fallen comrade, "Go. Find a healer for him, if it's not too late."

"I'm a fool," said General Spyra after the guard was gone. He was trying desperately to hang onto at least a scrap of his dignity. "If you'll excuse me," he managed to say before turning. After a few paces he stopped and drew in a deep breath. "Can you have your wife recount exactly what the traitor told our enemy," he asked Lord Gregory without looking back.

"Aye," Lord Gregory answered. "Why?"

"If we know what they think we are about, we can change our plans and regain the element of surprise," the ever dutiful General said before walking away.

"Aye," Lord Gregory replied with an unseen nod of respect. He wanted to say something that might ease the heartache the General was feeling, but he could think of no words that would help. "I'll go to her immediately."

"Lord Gregory," General Spyra turned this time. His wet swollen face showed the depths of emotion he was feeling. He started to say more, but the look he saw on the Lion Lord's face suggested that words were not necessary. They exchanged curt nods of understanding, and then Lord Gregory went to find his wife.

General Spyra scrunched up his face and roared through clenched teeth. After glancing at the young Valleyan guard, who was possibly dying on the floor, he kicked the marsh witch's corpse in the face with sickening force. He let his sword fall from his grasp and clatter to the floor, then hurried away to find a private place where he could let loose his anguish without shaming himself further.

Chapter Fifty-Two

Hyden felt himself being lashed and pummeled, but the blows were nothing compared to the pain in his abdomen. He was falling, and the blackness around him was absolute. He couldn't tell which way was up, which way was down, or if he was conscious or not. Even after he became oriented to the cold stone floor under him, he was confused. For what might have been moments, but could have been days, all sensation, save for pain, stopped for him. His agonized state was eventually disturbed by an insistent scuffing sensation along his arm. When he swatted at it, it responded with an irritated meow. Hyden's eyes blinked open to see that he was still in darkness. He reached out with his mind and felt the warm prickly lyna that was trying to wake him.

Hyden couldn't see the creature, but he remembered it from when it had woken him on the dungeon floor.

He felt chilled, and his skin turned to goose flesh. Strangely, he noticed that his gut didn't feel as if it were on fire anymore. Further investigation reminded him that his muscles and tendons, and maybe even his blood, were saturated with venom. His hair felt like icy needles prickling into his scalp, and he began to shudder. He was weak. His body felt as if it were melting into mush from the inside out. He knew he should have been hungry. He hadn't eaten in days, the thought of food made him retch and he went into a coughing fit that lasted far too long. By the time he had his breath again, he found he could make out subtle shades in the blackness. He sat with his knees drawn up into his arms for a long time, trying to gather his thoughts. The lyna wiggled up against him, content to preen and purr. Eventually, Hyden cast the little ball of light into his palm. Its dull glow barely illuminated his face, and he soon began to feel like some sort of bait, so he extinguished it. He closed his eyes and sought out Talon but couldn't find his *familiar*. He tried to find the hawkling's vision with his eyes open, and though Talon didn't connect with him, he found that his eyes focused into a crisp sort of clarity, even in the darkness. He found that he could see the edges of himself and the shape of the lyna lying beside him. It wasn't much, but it was something.

"We found the darkness, Spike," he rasped to the creature. "Now it's time to find the light. We have to hurry, though, the stuff inside me is going to melt me into a puddle."

The fact that his voice didn't reverberate reflected the vast emptiness he was in. As he stood, the lyna hunched and stretched. Hyden wanted to do the same, but was afraid he wouldn't snap back into shape if he did. He slowly turned, peering into the emptiness, searching for a sign, or a glimmer of anything that might indicate which way he should go. As he looked, he wondered where his brother had gone and why he hadn't killed him. He only vaguely remembered falling out of the garden yard and battling. He forced the thoughts out of his mind because he loved his brother fiercely. Thinking about him made him sad. He couldn't afford to wallow in emotion. He could actually feel his body breaking down.

Spike saved him from having to choose a direction. The lyna raised his tail up high and, with a quick glance back, started off as if he knew exactly where he was going. Hyden shrugged and staggered after him. The direction was as good as any. The place, Hyden decided, was the definition of featureless.

They walked for a very long time. Hyden had to stop once due to another fit of coughing that had him spitting out coppery tasting chunks of phlegm. Then he leaned over and vomited out most of the liquid that was left in his body. After that he fell to a knee and vomited some more. His head spun so bad that, for a time, he forgot where he was. He recovered, though, and continued staggering after the lyna. Once, he heard something growling low, and far too near. He saw several pairs of ember eyes watching him from a distance, but he we was too ill to be afraid of them.

Suddenly, it seemed that the lyna was hovering over the smooth floor. Hyden looked on curiously until the sharp edges of a stairway defined themselves in his eyes. Spike was leading him upward. He hadn't seen any sort of light down here so he gnashed his teeth together to bear the stress and started up after the lyna. The stairway circled ever upward and seemed to have no end. Hyden, drenched in his own fluids, and shivering with fever, climbed up them for what might have been forever.

Mikahl was somewhere over Westland riding on the back of his magical Pegasus when he spotted a big dark shape winging its way toward him. He was glad to see that Phen had found the dragon collar and was riding in the right direction. He reined the bright horse into a hover, and then let a wide crimson swath of magical energy burst up into the air as a beacon for the boy to see. The dragon banked and came toward him for a short time. Then suddenly it dove and sped away to the south. It was all Mikahl could do to keep up, much less gain on the sleek flying wyrm, but somehow the bright horse managed it. Mikahl saw that it wasn't Phen on the dragon's back. It was one of the red-robed priests he had seen gloating over him when he was incapacitated, and another rider. They were the ones who had set the trap for him and Princess Rosa. He decided that he didn't want to miss the chance to eliminate such a formidable enemy. He urged the bright horse into a position above and slightly behind the powerful looking wyrm and then let loose a ripping streak of jagged yellow lightning at them. The crackling blast missed the riders, but tore a sizable hole in one of the dragon's wings.

The wyrm roared out in pain and wheeled itself in a new direction. The priest sent a spiraling blue blast of energy back up at Mikahl, but Ironspike's shields absorbed the attack. The bright horse might have been slightly faster than Vrot, but it wasn't nearly as agile in the air. The young black dragon used his long sinuous body to turn and spin and sent a spewing blast of its sizzling acid breath over Mikahl. Once again the High King's sword absorbed the attack, but the vapor of the corrosive stuff made his eyes fill with tears and took his breath away. By the time he could see again, the wyrm had carried the priest far to the south. Mikahl's eyes were streaming and blurring. He knew that, even if he caught back up with it, the dragon could outmaneuver him. He could barely fight the pain in his lungs. He cursed as he was forced to circle his fiery steed down to the earth.

The bright horse was a magical extension of himself. It was manifested through Ironspike, but it wasn't a real winged creature that could see, or act on its own accord. It couldn't guide Mikahl if he couldn't see. He didn't have a choice, he told himself. Phen could remain invisible and hide awhile longer.

Mikahl was glad when he saw that he was coming down over the marshlands south of Westland. There was plenty of water there. All he could think about by the time he had his feet on not-so-solid ground was washing his stinging orbs. It was with great relief that he knelt along the spongy shoreline and finally splashed water onto his face. Luckily for him he still had Ironspike in his hand, because an explosion of water and teeth came lunging up at him and took him by suprise.

The winding stairway finally ended and another smooth expanse of blackness spread out in all directions. Another coughing session racked Hyden to the core, until he felt like he'd spat up half of his insides. He had to spend some time lying on the cold floor.

Soon the lyna was moving purposefully away again. Hyden struggled to follow and found confidence that at least Spike was going where he wanted to.

Hyden just wanted to lie down and die. All the moving and sweating was doing nothing for his body except spreading the venom deeper and deeper into him. He was glad that Mikahl, Phen and the Princess were all right. He'd seen Mikahl cleave Shaella's head, and he'd felt the rage surge through the thing that used to be Gerard after it happened. How he'd survived the monster's wrath was beyond him. As best as he could figure, he had been so out of it that Gerard probably thought he was dead. Or maybe, a tiny bit of him hoped, some inner part of Gerard had fought through to protect him. He'd seen his brother's eyes when they first recognized him. The thing had even spoken his name. A shiver ran through Hyden and he started to cough again. He fell to his knees, leaned forward, and hacked for a very long while.

For a time, he thought that this was it. He couldn't breathe, he couldn't focus. It was over. Thick drool ran from his mouth. It tasted strongly of blood and was full of tiny granules of his dissolving body. After a while, where all he could do was gasp for air with deep rasping heaves, he leaned his head back and said a prayer to the White Goddess.

It was a short prayer, and not very polite. Why she would send him so far into hell just to die in a puddle of his own fluids was beyond him. He longed to be with Talon just one more time, to fly through the heavens and feel the air rushing past him, or maybe to climb to the heights of the nesting cliff, where Gerard had found the hawkling for him, so long ago. He coughed again and nearly heaved when he had to spit small bits of rotten flesh from his mouth. Tilting his head back to draw breath, something registered in his brain.

"Light."

Hyden cocked his head. Had he heard that? Or was he just losing his mind as well as his innards? He looked around. The lyna was a few feet away walking in a curious circle. Hyden wiped his sweat drenched face with his shirt sleeve and tried to stand.

"Light."

He heard it that time, but knew that he hadn't heard with his ears. He looked at Spike. The lyna stopped and returned his gaze. He could barely see the little cat-like creature, but he knew it was what had spoken to him.

"Light, follow," Spike said and started off again.

Hyden stumbled after the creature. He finally caught his pace so that he was walking more than falling. After a short exhausting jaunt, the lyna stopped.

"Light," it said simply.

Hyden looked ahead of them. There it was, like a single star shining in the sky—a speck of light. It was impossible to judge how far away it was. A thousand yards maybe? A league? Who could say? Hyden didn't care. He had to get to it before he collapsed into a fit. He knew he couldn't survive another one.

The light grew as he approached. Was it a doorway? A lantern? He couldn't tell. After a few hundred more steps his heart sank. It hadn't grown at all. It was still just as far away. To make things worse, he began to hear a scraping, grunting sound coming from behind him. Deep heavy breathing accompanied the noise. He wasn't the only thing attracted to the light. He hurried his pace as best he could without falling down. He was sweating so profusely that he was leaving a trail of wet footprints. A glance back revealed a huge spidery shape with several legs. It was dragging something laboriously as it came, but it was coming nonetheless.

"Hurry, light," said Spike.

"I'm falling apart," Hyden replied out loud, thinking that the lyna didn't understand, or care. Spike's response surprised him.

"The light can save you."

"Aye," Hyden grunted, remembering the White Goddess saying something similar to him. In a rush of determination he focused his gaze on the illumination and pushed his pace. What the glowing speck in the distance was, he had no idea, but he told himself he would get there before the thing behind him caught up, or he would die trying.

The long grueling hours of practice that Mikahl pushed himself through every morning paid off in one quick instant. He was on his knees at the edge of the water in grass that was as tall as his shoulders. The waterline was completely hidden, for the grass grew out of the water, as well as on the muddy bank. Mikahl was splashing handfuls of cool liquid up into his burning eyes. He didn't see the wide swath of grass parting as an ancient snapper slithered toward him. His splashing masked any noise it might have made, except the exploding roar as it shot its huge bulk up out of the water at him.

Mikahl's lightning quick reflexes and brute strength allowed him to use the snout of the huge beast as it came down at him. He pushed himself just out of the snapping jaws and rolled away through the muck as fast as he could. For once he was glad not to have his chain mail on. If he had been wearing it, the marsh monster's teeth would have surely caught in it.

He could barely see as the low-bodied gator ran at him across drier ground. Its mouth was a gaping pink smear against a darker background. It was huge. He could tell that it was big enough to bite him in half if it got a hold of him. He jabbed Ironspike at the thing and the sharp blade dug into the roof of the creature's mouth. It stopped its charge then and backed away hissing. Mikahl could barely see it, but he took advantage of the snapper's hesitance and charged. He waved Ironspike around menacingly until the big creature turned and slithered back into the water in search of an easier meal.

It took a long while for Mikahl's thundering heart to slow down. It took even longer before he felt that he could see well enough to chance the bright horse again. By the time he made it back to Lakeside Castle to look for Phen, the sun had long since sunk beyond the ocean. It came as no surprise to find that Phen was nowhere to be seen.

Chapter Fifty-Three

Through the night, Mikahl waited for Phen to show himself. He sat on the balcony of Queen Shaella's bedchamber looking out over the destroyed garden area where he'd left the boy. He called his name every so often, but there was no reply. He even walked the corpse strewn yard using Ironspike's light to search the bodies. He didn't find Phen, but he learned that Shaella's head and body were no longer there. He was woken from a nap he'd fallen into when someone started banging on the door to Shaella's chamber. He used all the shields and guards he could find in Ironspike's symphony and then threw open the door ready to fight. What he found was a trembling young zard girl.

At that moment Mikahl realized something: Westland was still full of zard. He couldn't just vent his rage and start killing skeeks, though. He looked over the zardess and saw a trio of others at the end of the long, wide entry hall. Two skeeks were guarding a human woman. The woman took a step back and her hand lifted to cover her mouth. Mikahl vaguely recognized her as Lady Able of Eastwatch.

"It's true, then?" she asked through tears of joy. Almost immediately, her shoulders squared and she shoved her way past the two startled lizard-men who were guarding her. Her walk was dignified and she held her head proudly as she strutted toward Mikahl. When she neared the door she spoke to the young zard girl. Her voice, though tender, had a cold edge to it. "Tell your kind to leave the castle at once, Fslandra," she said. "Your Dragon Queen is dead," she looked at Mikahl for confirmation of the fact. He nodded. "The zard have no place here anymore. Tell them, Fslandra. Go."

Mikahl was dumbfounded. He wasn't ready for this. "M'lady," he said to Lady Able. "Leave them be for now. Come, I will take you to a place that is safe." A thought occurred to him. "Are there any others who need to be escorted to safety?"

She looked at him as if he were mad. "The people of Westland don't need to be escorted anywhere, they need their king." She looked him in the eyes and her expression deflated. "You're not here to take back our kingdom?"

"Soon, m'lady," he said, feeling awkward and foolish for not expecting to be needed in such a way by these people. "There's only myself and this." He indicated Ironspike's softly glowing blade. "I cannot defend the entire kingdom alone."

She nodded understanding. "I'll fetch the girls then."

Girls? Mikahl wondered what he was getting into.

A glance back down the hall revealed that the two zard guards and the young zardess had fled.

Mikahl hoped that Phen was all right. He'd given the boy plenty of opportunity to rejoin him. The idea that maybe the priest or the dragon had done the boy harm crossed Mikahl's mind, but if that were the case, there wasn't anything he could do about it. He had faith that Phen was capable of taking care of himself. King Jarrek and the eastern army needed him. He needed sleep, and time to think too. He didn't really have time to be carrying women to safety on his magical stead. At least that's what he was telling himself when three young girls ranging from two years to maybe seven came scurrying into the chamber. Each one of them was a bit smaller and more afraid than the last. They looked terrified just to be in Mikahl's presence, and suddenly, getting these teary-eyed angels to safety was the only thing Mikahl could think about. To his surprise another face, one he recognized, and the huge bosom that went with it, came into the room with Lady Able. A pair of nervous servant men carrying large kitchen knives followed protectively.

Missy, the kitchen girl whose breasts were so large that they were often spoken of around campfires all over the realm, gave him a dirty-faced smile, and then went to herding the young girls into a tight group.

Not long after, Mikahl, with two tiny bodies in front of him, and the third slip of a girl clinging to his back as if her life depended on it, rode the bright horse off of the balcony and began winging their way eastward. Mikahl had promised Lady Able and Missy that he would return when he could. He explained that there was an army waiting on him in Dakahn and that he would have to stop there for a time. The two men understood and one of them went down to the kitchens to get more supplies in case they had to hole up in the chamber for a few days. Mikahl waited until he returned and was glad to see that a few more castle folk had joined the group.

During all of this, Phen lay down in the bailey yard, half under a shrub at the corner of the garden with Talon nested on his chest. The High King had passed them by half a dozen times through the night but hadn't seen them because they were invisible. Even if they'd been conscious, neither Phen nor the hawkling could have moved. Before flying away on the back of the black dragon, the last red-robed priest had turned both of them to stone.

Escott, commanding the fifteen thousand troops sent to Oktin, had taken the city the day before Queen Willa and King Granitheart arrived. Now a force that was over thirty thousand strong was turning south to march toward O'Dakahn. The first night they made camp was the only night they met any resistance. The huge gorax demon came stomping through the encampment in the predawn hours and killed nearly a thousand men with its brutal club and potent spells. But the great black-chested beast was only passing through.

Nothing the humans did managed to do so much as irritate the hell-born creature. Even Queen Willa's witchy spells did little other than rankle it as it pounded a bloody path through the ranks. But it didn't stay and fight, it continued north as if it had an agenda, as if the time spent killing thousands of men had made it fall behind schedule.

In Lokahna, Master Amill and Commander Escott watched as Queen Willa and her formidable army came marching in from the north. Once the two forces combined, they numbered over thirty-five thousand men and dwarves. Now that they held the two main crossing points, getting more troops from Seaward was only a matter of making the orders.

They didn't know it in Lokahna yet, but already the Queen of Seaward was mustering up another sizable force to join them. After learning that her daughter was safe in Dreen and that Rosa had been tortured and maimed, Queen Rachel vowed to give the High King her fealty and to help him eradicate any who held even the slightest bit of loyalty to the lightning star.

Queen Willa let King Granitheart and Commander Escott take command of the huge force and left Master Amill in charge of communicating with King Jarrek and Master Sholt, who were now marching their men and dwarves south to meet them. She decided to return to Dreen. General Spyra's situation was affecting his judgment, and Lord Gregory had no designs to rule over Valleya in his stead.

King Granitheart and Commander Escott agreed that a direct march on O'Dakahn was best. Their forces were far too large to try to sneak around. They figured that they could easily push Ra'Gren's might behind O'Dakahn's walls and force a siege.

They underestimated the enemy, though. Neither of them counted on Flick and the Choska demon, or the young black dragon. If they had, they might have been able to save half of the great army they commanded from the horrible death that awaited them.

Hyden was only a dozen paces away from the source of the light he had been staggering toward. The very instant he realized it was the ring his brother had found on the hawkling nesting cliffs so long ago, he also realized it was on something's long claw-tipped finger. What the long dark insectoid creature was, he couldn't say, but he felt sorry for it when it started to attack him as if it were the one springing the trap.

Behind the creature, in the dim light of the ring, Hyden saw Gerrard coming down claws first. The mantis-like demon wearing the ring crumbled and screamed beneath the self-proclaimed Warlord of Hell. Hyden had to dive out of the way to keep from falling right into the fray. He was mortified at the savage power that Gerard unleashed on the creature. It took the same amount of time for him to stumble to the floor as it did for Gerard to tear the thing into slimy shreds.

The light of the ring faded as the life of its wearer leaked away. The victor began feeding on the greenish gore of the creature, which helped Hyden disassociate the little brother he had loved so much from the monster before him. This wasn't Gerard. It might have eyes that looked like Gerard's. It might even have fleeting thoughts that stemmed from some piece of Gerard's memory that survived deep down, but it was not Gerard. It was some malformed demon beast that was content to be feeding on the ruined body of another hell-born creature.

Hyden managed to crawl to the edge of the bloody mess and locate the ring on the dead beast's finger. He reached for it and grabbed hold of the elbow that was still attached to the lower part of the limb. As he pulled it toward him, Gerrard saw the dying twinkle of the ring and roared. His huge head loomed down and peered at it.

Looking up at Gerard's soft-eyed gaze, Hyden saw recognition flare in those eerie orbs again. Hyden yanked the limb to him and began fumbling with the ring, trying to get it off the limp bloody finger.

"No!" Gerard thundered. "Mine!"

Hyden almost let go of the limb and fled. The beast's voice, though deep and as powerful as shattering stone, still sounded somewhat like Gerard. The pleading look on its face cut through Hyden's resistance straight into his heart. Still, he managed to get the ring from the dead thing's finger, and when he did, its glow vanished completely. Darkness enveloped them again.

Hyden rolled over half a dozen times, trying to put distance between him and Gerard. The dizziness that followed caused him to fumble the ring from his hand. Terrified and confused, he felt out in the direction he heard it tinkling on the floor. He couldn't see it. The world was spinning and he was starting to cough up his mushy guts again. He could feel Gerard coming up behind him. He could almost feel his brother's savage claws tearing him to pieces. The heat and moisture of the evil creature's breath grazed his neck. Desperately, he felt for the ring, but his hands found only flat cold stone. Defensively, he rolled to his back and looked up. The slick glistening shape of Gerard was there. And in the darkness those eyes looked nothing like his brother's. Deep inside them, reddish orange flames flickered and glinted prismatic hate. The Warlord, the Abbadon, the new Master of the Hells took a long step toward him out of the bloody gore of its kill and huffed out a low growl.

"Minnnne," the word sounded so inhuman and evil that Hyden felt his heart stop. Whatever this thing was, it was about to destroy him. He hoped it would be over quick. He had suffered terribly and he didn't want to die thinking of how he had failed the White Goddess. All he could do was throw an arm protectively over his face as the thing that was once the brother he loved, lurched down at him to feed.

King Jarrek's troops managed to trap about half of the Dakaneese forces against the new lake at Seareach. The other half fought tooth and nail to help win their fellows free of the Seawardsmen, Valleyans, and the savage dwarves. It wasn't meant to be, though. King Jarrek and his troops closed the gap and killed the Dakaneese they had trapped, to a man. They would have pursued the thousands of Dakaneese that escaped the trap, but the Choska attacked and stopped them from it.

The demon bat had no rider this time and it was able to attack them with a speed and agility that it hadn't been able to employ before. It was ferocious as it swooped in at impossible speeds and yanked men out of the ranks.

The bald-headed wizard was riding on the back of the black dragon's shoulders now. They came out of nowhere and rained acidy spew and wizard's fire over Jarrek's men to great effect. Master Sholt managed to cast a protective ward over a couple of buildings that still stood, but only a few hundred men could get under the protection. The dwarves, at least some of them, found refuge in the foothills. The breed giants fled as well. In a matter of a few moments the angry wizard and his dragon managed to maim or kill most of Jarrek's men and nearly half of General Diamondeen's dwarves.

Against all the odds, King Jarrek had managed to defeat the Dakaneese force that had caused him so much trouble, but now he was left huddled under a roof like a rabbit in a fox den. It was only a matter of time, Master Sholt warned, before his wards wore off. Then the dragon and the Choska would be able to pick them off as the structures they were hiding under were eaten away by the dragon's saliva.

Chapter Fifty-Four

After dropping the three Westland girls in Dreen and hearing about Lady Mandary and the General, Mikahl and Lord Gregory made to review the known situation in Dakahn. Before they were able to get started, a Valleyan mage named Cresso, who had been communicating with both Highwander wizards for Lord Gregory and the General, came hurrying into the map room.

"It's King Jarrek," he said. "They are trapped, southeast of Seareach by the black dragon and a winged demon." The brown robed young man didn't even stop to draw a breath as he went on. "Master Wizard Sholt said there isn't much time. There aren't enough of them left to mount a defense. If the Dakaneese troops that slipped out around them regroup they are... They are done... Uh..." he realized that he was speaking to the High King and his jaw fell open and hung there.

"Where are the dwarves?" Lord Gregory asked. "And the breed?"

"The breed?" Mikahl asked sharply.

Lord Gregory put up a hand to still Mikahl's question. He nodded for Cresso to answer him.

"Some of the dwarves may have managed to get into the foothills," Cresso repeated what he had been told. "Nothing was said of the breed giants."

Mikahl's sharp look told Lord Gregory that he needed to explain.

"A handful of the breed giants deserted the Dragon Queen and joined King Jarrek's cause. I have to admit they have saved a lot of men and managed to put some serious thorns in Shaella's side." Lord Gregory didn't tell Mikahl what King Jarrek had promised them in return for their service. Now wasn't the time for that.

"I'm going," said Mikahl, shaking his head in disbelief as he started out onto the balcony.

"By the gods, Mik," the Lion Lord started after him. "We're so close to being able to take O'Dakahn, and Westland too. Be careful."

"Aye," Mikahl said over his shoulder without slowing. "I will, but Jarrek fought beside me in Xwarda. I'll not leave him stuck out." With that he drew Ironspike and called forth the bright horse.

Hyden waited for the death blow to come. He heard it whooshing deeply through the air at him, but before Gerard's dagger claws could tear into his flesh, the blackness of the Nethers exploded with lavender light. The kinetic blast of energy was so intense that it made Hyden's hair stand on end. It was so bright, that it burned his eyes through his closed lids.

He had to squint under his arm to see what was happening. A ray of magical energy had seared into Gerard from above. As it died away, Hyden saw a spider-like body with what appeared to be two dragon's heads connected to it. One of the heads hung limply, but the other was baring its teeth to attack. The creature was coming down hard and fast at Gerard. Hyden glanced back at where he thought the ring might be. As the afterglow of the magical attack faded, he saw the finger-long shadow it threw, but it was about twenty feet away.

Above him, a great roar, followed by an earsplitting scream, filled the darkness. The sound of tooth on bone, and wet, tearing flesh came next. A cerulean pulse flared between two large freakishly entangled bodies and the grunting of the battling creatures filled the darkness that followed.

Hyden crawled on his hands and knees toward the ring. Another lavender blast, this one shorter and more concussive, guided him to it. Once his hand closed around it, he somehow managed to get to his feet and started sprinting away from the horrific mêlée behind him. A glance back, at the same moment Gerard blasted forth a long streak of fire from his maw, revealed a ragged looking stump on the spidery beast, where a third head must have once been. The main bulbous bulk of its body had several wet glistening holes torn into it and Gerard was on its back now, making another. With short ripping claw strokes and searing gouts of fiery dragon's breath, Gerrard attacked relentlessly. Just before Hyden turned away he saw a deep emerald beam shoot from the spidery demon's eyes. It shot directly into Gerard's chest. The rays cut right through Gerrard and he screamed out in agony as he went tumbling to the smooth stone floor.

The scream sounded so much like his little brother that Hyden's heart clenched in his chest. He ran until a sudden breathlessness caused him to fall hard to the ground. Another racking fit of vomiting followed. He couldn't swallow. He couldn't get any air. When he coughed up a chunk of something the size of a quail's egg, which tasted of infection, he realized that this fit wasn't going to subside. The blackness around him began filling with tiny white star bursts and a loud roaring of rushing blood filled his ears. He fumbled with the ring again and found that it had been stretched to a size far too large for any of his fingers. He coughed again and nearly inhaled his tongue when air shot into his lungs.

He shoved two fingers through the hole in the ring and thought for a minute that he had dropped it because nothing happened. Then, the world exploded into bright blinding whiteness. If something other than death was happening, he couldn't fathom it because the stark absolution of the brightness that he found himself in left him as blind as it did thoughtless. Strangely, after a few moments of utter nothingness, everything began to make clear and perfect sense.

Everything.

Gerard felt the emerald rays burn through his thick chest plates and sear him to the core. He felt the strange magical energy rapidly heating his guts, and then he felt it burst out of his back as it passed completely through him. He had to let go. The pain was excruciating. After his tormented scream died out, he rolled under Deezlxar and blasted out a white hot stream of dragon's fire straight up into its underside. It might be bony underneath, but as Gerard just learned, even bones cook. Gerard sucked in air quickly and let out another blast. Deezlxar seemed not to notice at first, but then the heat worked its way up into the bottom of its body.

Like a crab skittering across sand, Deezlxar went left, then right, almost dancing on its many segmented legs. It spun around and leapt off of its foe, and then sent another searing emerald blast into the dragon-blooded demon-god that was Gerard. Gerard cast a spell of his own and this time an angry yellow bolt of lightning hit Deezlxar right in the base of its remaining neck. Deezlxar's emerald rays burned into Gerard too, and both of them roared out in agony.

Somehow, the true Lord of Hell managed to get Gerard in his teeth again. It didn't bite down as it had before. Instead, Deezlxar shook its dragon head violently about until the sound of splintering bone and tearing flesh could be heard. Then it let go, leaving Gerard spinning through the air, to come crashing down into a tumbled heap on the floor.

At once, Deezlxar pounced on the would-be-usurper. But Gerard wasn't done. An explosive change, born from hatred, and anger, and the raw demonic power that both Kraw and Shokin afforded, came over him. He wasn't going to die here in this endless blackened place, he told himself. He was going to eat the man who had killed his Shaella bite by bite, and he couldn't do that if Deezlxar killed him. His dragon blood boiled, and his demonic essence swelled and morphed him. His devilish armor projected and exploded into a plethora of long sharp spear like projections. What Deezlxar landed on flared crimson and exploded into an orange and white bone-crunching blast. There was no escaping the power of it. The Master of Hell felt the projections shooting up through its under armor into its brain cavity and searing its life away. All the Dark One could do was use its bulk, and its last dying bit of magic, to try and destroy the thing that had just killed it. It let out a defiant death roar then turned itself to stone as it came down hard on top of Gerrard.

Gerard was pinned under the bone-crushing weight as it pressed on him. After the breath was driven from his lungs and the settled weight stopped snapping his twisted bones, all he could do was lay there and gasp. But then, as with all the other hell-born creatures he had killed and consumed, Deezlxar's demonic essence, rushed in and filled him to the point of bursting. A darkness unimaginable reached up and enveloped him, and he was gone.

Flick could see the fading yellow aura of the weakening protective magic below him. It wouldn't be long, he knew. Already Vrot's acid was eating through the shell in places. Soon King Jarrek and his remaining men would have to come out and face him. If the shield somehow managed to hold, the few thousand Dakaneese soldiers who were circling back from the southwest would root them out and end them that way. Flick wanted so badly to kill King Jarrek himself, though. The Red Wolf King would be a poor substitute for the vengeance he wanted to unleash on the High King for killing Shaella, but for now Jarrek would have to do.

Flick was racked with emotion over the death of his friend and queen. She had been far more than either to him. Sure, Gerard had come along and stolen her heart away. How she had kept such strong feelings for the stupid mountain clan boy after he got caught up in Pael's madness, Flick never understood. All he knew was that her happiness meant everything to him, and if that thing Gerard had become made her happy, then so be it. But now she was dead, killed in cold blood by the mighty High King. If what the red priest said was true, she hadn't even had a weapon in her hand.

Flick was fairly certain that the man hadn't lied to him. His spells would have detected the dishonesty. Besides, the priest had dutifully brought him the dragon's collar and helped him perform the healing on Vrot's wing. Flick sensed that the priest was hiding something, but if it had been important then Flick's mentally intrusive magic would have picked up on it. Now was not the time to worry about the last priest of Kraw, though. Flick was about to slake his thirst by killing King Jarrek, and he intended to save his revenge for the High King.

Vrot cut a hard arc through the air and blasted forth another gout of wet sticky acid. It came raining down over the feeble shell that was protecting the building below. Flick snaked out with his mind and contacted the Choska demon. It was circling to the north, waiting for the dwarves to show themselves.

"Kill any and all of them that you can," he ordered the winged demon. "No mercy whatsoever."

The Choska didn't comprehend mercy. It thrived on fear, and it lusted to kill and devour human flesh. It would follow Flick's commands explicitly.

Flick wheeled Vrot around and darted to the southeast awhile. He spied the Dakaneese force marching double time toward him. Whatever Battle Lord that Ra'Gren had put in charge of them was pushing them to their limits. This would have pleased Ra'Gren, but Flick wanted them to take their time. If they arrived before the Red Wolf's wizard's shield failed, then they would get the pleasure of stomping over the King of Wildermont themselves. Flick wouldn't get to do the deed. He looked at the last tendrils of sunlight reaching out of the sea to the west and estimated that, at their rate of travel, it would take them at least until the middle of the night to reach Jarrek's force. He doubted that the spell shield would last that long, but he had learned long ago not to underestimate a determined Highwander wizard.

He sighed as he brought Vrot back around. Either way, Jarrek would be dead. As they flew back to the battlefield a thought occurred to him. After he, his dragon, and his Choska demon stopped the eastern forces from invading Dakahn, and after he took his revenge for the cold-blooded murder of his friend and queen, who would run Westland? The zard were still there, but would they follow him?

"King Flick," he said out loud. It didn't have the ring he would have liked, but the sound of it didn't taste bad on his tongue. "The Dragon King," he decided, sounded much, much better.

The Choska saw movement below and darted down toward it. A pair of dwarves were creeping out of the rocks and peering upward, looking for winged danger. General Diamondeen spotted the Choska a moment too late. The demon had tucked its wings back and was coming down in a streaking dive. The dwarven general had to leap head first into the rocks, but the Choska was the one who received the surprise. Just as its razor sharp claws would have torn into the General, a spear came launching out of the boulder-strewn hillside nearby. It missed horribly, and a few jeers at the shooter's lack of accuracy came from the dwarves hiding in the surrounding hills. The missile shot past the Choska and buried itself in the ground a few hundred feet away. The rope attached to the spear fell like a dead snake across the earth.

The Choska shot back up out of range and sent warnings to its master. Had it known that three dwarves had wrestled one of the dragon guns against a rock and managed to fire it, it would have been far less wary, but the demon had to assume that at least one breed giant was hunkered below.

Just to remind them of its might, the Choska sent a cherry red blast streaking into the rocks where the limp rope ended. Two of the dwarves crouched there were killed instantly; the third was hurled through the air in the opposite direction, his flaming hair and trousers lighting the arc of his trajectory in the darkness.

A couple of heavy stones and an axe went hurling up out of the rocky hillside, but none of them came close to the winged beast. The Choska marked the location of one of the hurled objects and sent a blast that way. Another dwarf met his end, but two others managed to scurry to different hiding places undetected.

Mikahl flew too far south. Fearing that time was running out for his friend, he sped back to the north scanning for any sign of them on the ground. He had to pay attention to the skies as well. On his way he came across the fast marching Dakaneese troops that were coming to finish off King Jarrek's force. In a sharp, steep diving swoop he shot across the ranks and let loose a series of massive lighting blasts. The crackling streaks split the force nearly in two, leaving hundreds of soldiers dead or writhing on scorched strips of earth. Mikahl let loose a few more blasts of lightning, and enough of Ironspike's magical fire to burn down a city. When the Dakaneese lost their structure, he blasted them some more. Most of them survived, but they were no longer on the march.

Mikahl left them and found Jarrek's position by the fading yellow glow of Master Sholt's shield. The sun was gone now, but the evening sky had just a touch of rose left to it. As Mikahl swooped in to land, a soldier braved the open and waved him away, pointing up toward a sinuous shape in the distance.

Mikahl didn't have a plan. He could think of nothing other to do than engage the dragon. He could tell by the pale egg-shaped head of its rider that it wasn't the red-robed priest that had flown away from him over the marshes earlier. He could also see that the damage Ironspike's blast had done to one of the wyrm's wings had been healed somehow.

Men were shouting at him from below as he started toward the young black wyrm, but he couldn't understand them. Flick sent a streaking fiery blast at him, and Mikahl was forced to twist himself out of its way. He answered with a crackling lightning bolt. The dragon veered around it with only the slightest tweak of its wings.

Mikahl thought he could see Flick laughing as the two of them came close to crashing in the sky. At the last moment both of them dove away. Mikahl managed to thrust Ironspike's blade out into the dragon's hide, but the wound was only superficial. Flick, however, cast an invisible wall into being in the air right in front of Mikahl. When the High King hit it, the sudden blunt impact caused Ironspike to twist from his grasp.

When his sword left his hand, the bright horse disappeared, as did all of Mikahl's magical defenses. He fought crazily while tumbling from the sky to grab the sword that was tumbling with him. With catlike agility he twisted and finally managed to wrap his hand at around Ironspike's leather wrapped hilt. The sword filled his lungs with breath and he called forth the bright horse only a few dozen feet above the ground.

As he righted himself into a hover, he found he was looking down the sights of a massive crossbow. He was so close that he could see the striations a sharpening stone had left on the barbed tip of its spear-sized bolt. Beyond that, a mud-covered breed giant seemed to light up with angry recognition at the same moment Mikahl did. The breed giant he had watched his father publicly disgrace before sealing them all away at Coldfrost sneered hatred as he fired the spear from his weapon. Mikahl had no chance at all to get out of its way.

Chapter Fifty-Five

"Something bad must be happening," said Cresso with absolutely no emotion whatsoever. He tried to convey the messages he sent and received in a smooth soft monotone so as not to confuse the emotion he was feeling with that of the sender. The effect made him seem to be cold and uncaring of the events taking place around him—at least Lord Gregory thought so. "Master Sholt is not responding," Cresso explained.

"Could he be...?" *Dead?* Lord Gregory didn't want to say it out loud. He was so worried about the High King that he went to the mage to try and learn what was going on.

"No," Cresso answered matter of factly. The certainty in his expression relieved the Lion Lord. "My spell message is reaching him, he just isn't responding." Cresso wrapped a finger and thumb around his long narrow beard and slid his hand down slowly. "He is most likely preoccupied." The last was said with a little concern showing in the mage's voice. Lord Gregory noted the fact that it was the young man's own thoughts, not a conveyance from another that he was voicing at the moment. It made him feel more comfortable.

"If you would, Cresso, keep trying until he responds," Lord Gregory said. "I will be at the map table or in the throne room."

In most instances, a trip from a wizard's tower top chamber was a strenuous journey that involved traversing countless stairways and passages. In the palace at Dreen, it was only a matter of descending three flights of stairs and then following a short hall that led to the keep's main entryway. For a man as greedy as King Broderick, Lord Gregory mused as he trotted down, there wasn't much opulence about. Nothing in the palace was over luxurious.

Lord Gregory's thoughts were cut short by a hurried set of footsteps clanging up the stairs toward him. The frightened face of one of General Spyra's men looked up at the Lion Lord. The man gulped and wiped the sweat from his brow. He was dressed in full armor and had to be sweltering in the summer heat. He started to speak twice, but heaved for breath both times.

Finally he said, "To the balcony, m'lord." He pointed up at the door to Cresso's room. "You'd best see it, rather than hear me describe it."

Lord Gregory knew true fear when he saw it, and this man was afraid. He turned, racing up the steps and started to knock on the young wizard's door. It opened before his knuckles ever touched wood. "Lord Gregory," Cresso was almost bowled over when the Lion Lord rushed in.

"M'lord," Cresso urged Lord Gregory over to the western facing balcony.

Once they were outside, the mage pointed southwest. The Red City, as it was called, was low built. No structure was over two stories tall save for the palace. Still, with the huge cattle pens and stable yards everywhere it was a large, widely spread metropolis. Less than a mile away a huge hairy head and shoulders rose above the rooftops. The massive beast was howling from its wolfish snout in what might have been rage, but just as easily could have been glee. The great club it carried was bashing in roofs and most likely crushing people and stock animals too.

"It's the beast that tore through Queen Willa's ranks south of Oktin," Cresso explained.

"The General was... is readying to ride out to meet it," the armored soldier huffed from the doorway. "He's surely off by now."

"He must be stopped," Lord Gregory said. Spyra was in no condition to rage off into battle with a monster. He was far too emotionally distraught. A glance back at the loud destructive beast made Lord Gregory think that the General might have lost his mind.

"Cresso, can you get out there and warn the people to stay clear of it? Tell them to let it pass. I think that it will just move through." He looked at the now fidgeting mage for reassurance, but found none.

"I can't get out there any faster than anyone else," Cresso looked sharply at the armored guard. He didn't want to go out there. He was terrified, but he took in a deep breath and gathered his confidence. "...but I suppose I can do it far more effectively." He shouldered past the soldier and disappeared down the stairs.

"You," Lord Gregory said in a commanding tone. "By the order of the High King, the General is to be headed off before he manages to get himself, or his men killed. Use whatever means necessary outside of killing him. Order a troop of pike men to be ready if the thing turns toward the castle. And tell the stable man to ready my horse, just in case."

When the young man was gone, the Lion Lord watched the creature from the balcony as it worked its way north through the Red City at a steady pace. It was a great relief to see that it held its course. If it kept going as it was, he decided, it would eventually end up in the Giant Mountains. The terrifying looking thing was quite a bit bigger than Borg and his kin, but the giants numbered in the thousands and would surely put a stop to its intrusion into their kingdom. Lord Gregory decided that a warning was the least he could do for the gargantuan men who had so kindly guided Mikahl to his destiny. He made a long study of the creature's passage to make sure that it was well past turning on the castle, then went to the desk in Cresso's room, found a parchment and a quill, and began scribbling out a message to King Aldar, the ruler of the giant folk.

The spear Bzorch launched from his dragon gun sliced painfully across Mikahl's face, right through his cheek and ear. The roar that erupted just behind his head, though, told him that the breed giant had hit his intended target. Mikahl twisted around to see the huge Choska seemingly halted in midair by the shaft jutting out of its upper chest. Its sharp terrible claws were closed on the air where he had just been. He had to lean and twist to keep the bright horse from sliding into the ground just beyond the big breed giant. Then he had to duck under the swiftly uncoiling rope that another of them held. As if a great muddy boulder were coming to life, another huge breed giant rose up from the ground in front of him and aimed a similar weapon. Then Mikahl was past them.

His whole left side was covered in blood. It was no small wound on his face, but as soon as he thought about it, the symphonic power of his sword sent cool, tingling magic through him into the cut. He brought the bright horse around and sent a crackling bolt of lightning at the gigged Choska. The impact of his blast folded the flying beast in half and sent it flailing backwards. The unsuspecting breed giant that was holding the rope was yanked from his feet and pulled across the rocky ground for twenty feet before he finally let go. Mikahl heard Bzorch bellow out a laugh at the terrible folly.

Mikahl turned back just in time to dodge a searing crimson blast of Flick's magic. It missed him, but Mikahl didn't get clear of Vrot's corrosive breath. As he flew right through the misty edges of the blast, Mikahl felt his skin start to sizzle. He hadn't had his shields up and already he was choking and gasping for breath. His skin burned and bubbled. The horrible death scream of one of the unlucky breed giants behind him filled his ears and then abruptly ended in a gurgling gasp. Mikahl couldn't see, nor could he stop the acidy muck from eating into his flesh. Instinctually, he landed the bright horse then began streaming through the melodies of his sword's powerful song. He was searching for anything that might help him. He looked at his affected left arm and saw that most of his skin was already dripping away like melting wax. In a few places he could see muscle, tendon, and bone. Finally, in a panicked daze, he did the only thing he could think to do. He fell to his knees and called forth all of Ironspike's power at once.

The tip of Pavreal's sword shot skyward as if Mikahl had thrust it up. It was all Mikahl could do to hold on to the hilt with both hands as a deep thrumming rush exploded up from the earth, through his body, and out of the blade. A swirling pillar of smoke shot into the night. Some hundreds of feet above him the cloud flattened out and spread across the sky, turning dark and angry like a roiling storm. First one lightning strike split the distant darkness, then another. Then, as if the bottom of the heavens had burst, a cold soothing rain came pouring down over them all.

Vrot had to flee out from under the clouds to avoid the wicked bolts of lightning that were streaking down all around him. Flick didn't like it, but he let the dragon's instincts carry them to safety. He'd managed to give the High King great pain, and fill him with fear. He doubted any amount of healing, magical, or otherwise, would be able to repair the damage Vrot's breath had done. For now, that would have to satisfy his lust for vengeance. In his departing rage he decided to do something drastic, something that the High King and his pitiful followers would never expect. He urged Vrot westward toward Settsted Stronghold where droves of zardmen, long beaked dactyls, and big toothy gekas were doing little more than awaiting orders. There was no way the swampland creatures there could know of Shaella's death yet. Flick had the dragon, and he knew they would follow whatever orders he gave them.

He remembered that Pael's failure was due to power-lust and greed, and that Shaella's demise was brought about by love. Flick felt none of those emotions. Hate, anger, and the need for vengeance would guide him on his attempt to take over the realm. He didn't think it would be that hard—nearly every able bodied soldier left on the continent was about to converge on O'Dakahn, and he had a dragon.

By dawn of the next day, Lady Able had assembled a sizable force of castle staff. They, along with a few townsfolk who fled the riotous conditions of Castle View City, and the mayhem outside the walls, were slowly taking over the castle. Floor by floor, room by room, they moved about gathering weapons and chasing zard away as they went. Before long, all of the upper floors were rid of the scaly invaders. Armed groups of porters, stable men, and cooks ranged out and brought back supplies, just in case they had to bar the doors. With each excursion, the group gained a new member or two. Lady Able, a far different and more humble woman than the haughty noble she had once been, helped secure and fortify their area of the castle.

Only once was the group challenged. A half dozen fully armored zard, looking to see proof of their queen's death, stormed through the big double doors of a formal dining hall that allowed access to Shaella's apartment. They were set upon by men and women alike, wielding weapons ranging from kitchen knives and ornamental spears, to serving trays and garden tools. It didn't take long for the rest of the zard to figure out that they were unwelcome. For every zard that fled, two loyal Westlanders joined with the group. A few men with military training began organizing, with Lady Able's permission of course, and soon a structured sense of control was established. By the second night, Lakeside Castle was completely retaken from the zard.

Lady Able made certain that the Westland patriots knew they still had a son of Balton Collum for a king. She also made sure that they knew he had Ironspike on his side.

She had no doubt that Mikahl would make a great king. Seeing the way those little girls melted his resistance revealed the true nature of his heart to her. She silently vowed that, when he returned to his castle, he would find some semblance of order here.

The last of the red-robed priests, Solidar was his name, didn't look like himself as he sat nervously beside the wagon driver who was carrying him and his cargo through the crowded shipping district of O'Dakahn. He'd shaved his black beard so badly that his chubby pale face looked as if a cat had attacked him. His long hair was hacked short, and he wore a plain woolen tunic and rough spun britches instead of his silky red robes. The robes were in the crate that was riding in the bed of the wagon with him. Also in the crate was his most precious cargo: two, no, three items that his god would reward him for salvaging. He could only hope that the spells he'd cast over them would last throughout the sea journey from O'Dakahn to the Isle of Borina.

Solidar was sure that he was being followed by one of Ra'Gren's men, or maybe one of Flick's. His eyes darted to and fro, and he often glanced behind him, not only at the road and the sea of people that closed in behind the passage of the cart, but at the cargo as well.

The sharp crackling sound of magical static caused him to yank his head around. He was relieved to see that it was only a whip lashing into an unruly slave. He wrinkled his nose at the scene. Forty or fifty people, all chained one leg to the next, were being herded in a long line toward a grimy warehouse. Each time one of the slaves missed a step, or fell behind, the driver lashed the whip across them, leaving a dripping crimson streak. It was none of Solidar's concern, he decided. The ship that would carry him and his cargo back to the isle, and theTemple of Kraw, was the only thing that worried him now. That and those bastards that were following.

Reflexively he looked back over his shoulder again, first at the people, then at his precious crate. He mentally went through the series of preserving spells he'd cast on its contents. He wanted to be certain that he had been thorough. It wouldn't do if Shaella's body, or head, started to rot while he was at sea.

The third item in the crate was Shaella's staff. With the spectral orb mounted on its head, he would be able to reach his god directly. Kraw would tell him what to do, and he would prosper.

Chapter Fifty-Six

After a night of heavy lightning and pouring rain, King Jarrek, General Diamondeen, and High King Mikahl, with the help of Master Oarly and Master Sholt, trudged through the gore and rounded up the survivors of the black dragon's terrible acid bath. Some six hundred men and four hundred dwarves survived. Those too wounded to continue were carried back to the cavern where others tended their injuries under heavy guard.

The four surviving breed giants kept their distance from the High King and his sword, but the fifth's eyes never left Mikahl. Bzorch had saved the man's life, but had nearly taken his face off to do it. He wasn't sure if he had lost, or gained footing with the deed. He could see that only an angry red scar remained where his huge bolt had sliced the High King's flesh, but that was only one of the terrible wounds that the seemingly indestructible young man had taken. The power of Pavreal's blade was staggering. It regenerated new flesh over the High King's open wounds, and the wounds of several others. It didn't seem to have replaced some of the stuff that had been eaten away inside, but the corroded pocks closed over and ceased to bleed. To Bzorch, seeing this was miraculous. He had never seen magic used for good. For the first time, he saw King Balton's infamous blade in a different light. He decided that he would try to speak to King Jarrek privately soon, so that he could find out where he stood. Until then, he and his kind kept their distance.

Mikahl informed King Jarrek of the Dakaneese soldiers he'd harried to the southeast of their position. Jarrek decided that his numbers had dwindled just a little too far to face them. He handpicked a hundred men and had the dwarven general do the same. He then ordered the rest of the men to retreat to Low Crossing through the dwarves' tunnel. He told them to set traps as they went, and seal the passage for good once everyone was safely back in Wildermont. He and the men he had chosen were going to try and speed south along the river, avoiding the other force altogether. If they made it clear, his intention was for them to converge with the larger force of Willa's Blacksword, and King Granitheart's dwarves. From there they would methodically put O'Dakahn under siege.

King Mikahl, still burning and itching from the deep destructive wounds he had taken, approved of the plan. Though Ironspike had somewhat healed his flesh, his left forearm and hand were ruined. He could barely grip a cup, and the length of limb from elbow to wrist looked more like a stick than anything human. Other than that, his shoulders had several deep pocks corroded into them, and they were itching terribly. He could scratch the ones on the left side, but reaching the ones on his right hurt his left arm so badly that he had to suffer the irritation.

He was well enough to give Jarrek and the dwarves protection from the back of the bright horse, though. When he was sure that they were clear, he was going to carry Master Sholt to Lakeside Castle so that he could aid the Westlanders and establish communication with Lord Gregory.

Just before they started south, Master Sholt informed them that Queen Rachel had organized a flotilla of Seaward ships. They were already en route to take up positions along the Dakaneese coast to prevent Ra'Gren from receiving supplies and fortifications that way. It would take some time to get them into position, but already five thousand more soldiers had left Ultura and were marching toward Lokahna.

With Master Sholt riding nervously on the bright horse behind him, Mikahl conversed with Lord Gregory. The Lion Lord didn't tell Mikahl of General Spyra's mad charge, or the demon's destructive passage through Dreen. He rightly figured that just having knowledge of those events would distract Mikahl from what he was about. Mikahl asked the Lion Lord to explain the breed giants' involvement in all of this, but Lord Gregory quite bluntly told him to ask King Jarrek.

Mikahl contemplated the fact that Bzorch had saved his life, but still it was hard not to hate the breed. When he was King Balton's squire they had come out of the northern mountains and regularly attacked Westlander innocents. He had been at Coldfrost, and though he was never allowed to raise his blade against them, he saw many a man meet a gruesome end there. He remembered clearly watching Bzorch from across the icy flow through the glassine shield King Balton had created. He remembered wondering what so many huge beasts would eat on the small glacial island prison.

He knew now.

They had eaten each other.

He had never really understood the happenings at Coldfrost. His friend King Aldar, the ruler of the true giants did, though, and since he had a message to deliver to his friend Borg, he decided that when this was through he might pay them a visit. Thoughts of the starved giant he and Hyden had found in the dungeon, and the venomous wound Hyden Hawk had taken there, saddened him. Mikahl's heart grew hollow for a time.

His mood lightened when he flew low enough over Jarrek's group to see the dwarves flailing in the saddles of the horses they were riding. Their stumpy legs weren't long enough to actually straddle the big Valleyan destriers. If the horses hadn't been so well trained it would have been a fiasco. Even with the big steeds compensating to balance the squat little men on their backs, a few of the dwarves hit the ground tumbling. Luckily none of them were seriously injured, and even with the occasional delay of waiting on a dwarf to dust himself off and remount, the small group managed to get beyond the reach of the Dakaneese troop that was marching to Seareach.

Mikahl was thankful that they were safe. He was fighting exhaustion. If he fell asleep, he was certain that the ground would be the last thing that ever passed through his mind. He couldn't remember when he last slept. Not since he was trapped and put under the red priests spell could he remember even resting.

Before he and Master Sholt peeled off for Westland, Oarly rode up under them and waved them down.

"I know you're the High King and all," the dwarf said, choosing his words carefully. "Young Phen is my friend, as was Sir Hyden Hawk Skyler. I know that Hyden's soul will rest easier if Phen is located." Oarly picked at the knee of his pants for a minute, letting his emotions cool. "The lad is a hero in my book."

"I looked and looked for him, Master Oarly," Mikahl told him. "I swear I'll put Master Sholt, and any other I can, to the task of finding him."

"Aye," Oarly conceded, seeing the sadness and fatigue on the High King's newly scarred face. "If I could get there, I'd search the fool boy out myself," he added before urging his horse away.

"On my honor, I'll do my best to find him," Master Sholt called after him.

"Tell King Jarrek that I'll be back as soon as I can," Mikahl yelled as the bright horse lifted them away.

Mikahl took them north to check on the progress of the men and dwarves that had been sent back through the tunnels at Alliak. On the way, they passed over the body-strewn field around the buildings where Flick had trapped King Jarrek's force. Some of the Dakaneese were arriving and milling about the carnage aimlessly. Another group of them were huddled around the big Choska's carcass. Mikahl's lightning bolt had pretty much cooked its insides and then the dwarves had swarmed over it and finished it off.

A small group of Dakaneese looked to be following the trail of the men bound for the tunnels. Mikahl, with Master Sholt gripping him more tightly than the tiny girl had, dived on them. He sent them scattering with a pair of hot crackling lightning bolts. Master Sholt relaxed a little bit and sent a few fiery blasts of his own down among them. After a second pass, the pursuit stalled and the remaining men began skulking back to their commanders.

Apparently Jarrek's men, and the dwarves, had already gone into the tunnels. Mikahl didn't see any of them out around the opening. He took this as a good sign and wheeled away to the west.

The sun was setting into the ocean when they came down out of the clouds over Lakeside Castle. Mikahl noticed that an attempt to clean the garden yard had been made. As he landed his magical pegasus on the balcony of the Royal Apartments, the half dozen people milling around the bedchamber screamed in startled fear. When they saw who the rider was they quickly recovered, but stayed away nonetheless. Master Sholt found a divan and collapsed into it. He leapt back up with a yelp when his arse hit something solid and invisible that was already lying there. He was too sore and worn from the long ride to worry about what it was, and he quickly found another place to rest.

Lady Able straightened the hem of her apron and smiled broadly at Mikahl. She ushered him to the side of the great bed and called for food and refreshments to be brought. Mikahl managed to introduce Master Sholt, and then listened as Lady Able proudly told him the reasonably stable state of things at Lakeside Castle. Mikahl only heard about half of it, and when she was done, he conveyed that the Highwander master wizard he had brought with him was at her service. After that he lay back in the soft feather bed and fell into a deep, much needed slumber.

Lady Able eyed Master Sholt suspiciously. She wasn't sure what to think of Willa the Witch Queen's master wizard. He and the High King both had burn scars about their neck and shoulders, and holes worn all through their dingy clothes. She wondered if she should find Master Sholt some frogs to eat to be hospitable. He looked to be as worn and weary as the High King was. Already he was snoring softly where he sat. Rest is what these men needed, she decided, and she left them to go find some clean garments for them to wear when they woke.

Flick sat at King Ra'Gren's table. He had been busy flying along the western bank of the Leif Green River from one Settsted outpost to the next, rousting the zard and the marsh beasts, and giving them orders. He had returned to Ra'Gren's palace to enlighten the man of his new plans.

The two of them were alone, but the table held enough food for twenty. Huge game birds, both fried and baked, several types of fish, and edible crustaceans, along with a good sized honey-glazed piglet were among the many different dishes laid out before Ra'Gren and his sole guest.

The King of Dakahn could afford such opulence a thousand times over, Flick knew. After Pael had leveled Castlemont he'd ordered King Glendar to load the gold and jewels they pulled from the wreckage onto wagons and haul them to O'Dakahn with the survivors of King Jarrek's kingdom. The wagon train of slaves and wealth had been given to Ra'Gren, not only as payment for arming and armoring the zard troops Shaella had used to take Westland, but also to purchase several ships that had eventually sailed, carrying King Glendar and his personal battalions. A strange illness had come over the King's ship and it was reported that the captains of the other vessels set it afire and sank it so that the affliction died with it.

Flick wasn't interested in Pael or Glendar, though, he was curious as to what happened to the men from those other two ships. He knew something about them that no one else knew. As he had done with his entire army, Pael had poisoned those men and spelled them to rise again after death. Flick had an idea how to use those few hundred undead, if he could find them.

After hearing how Flick planned to save O'Dakahn from the mass of eastern soldiers that were marching across Dakahn unhindered, Ra'Gren happily sent out orders to seek out and capture the men that Flick was interested in. Ra'Gren knew who captained those ships. Other men on the docks would know who the crews were as well. Some of them would be easily found, and information about the others could be gained from them. It was a small price to pay to have the new, self-proclaimed Dragon King of Westland, and his army of skeeks, crush King Jarrek and Queen Willa's forces against his walls when they arrived to put him under siege.

Chapter Fifty-Seven

Mikahl woke to a grave faced Master Sholt. The High King had slept for two whole days. Sholt stubbornly wouldn't tell him what had him looking so somber until after Mikahl bathed, put on fresh clothes, and ate a healthy meal. Only then did the Xwardian wizard explain what he'd found.

"Turned to stone," Sholt said. "A fine white marble like substance anyway? He had an elven ring of invisibility on when he was transformed, or petrified, however you want to classify it. It won't come off without breaking the finger off with it. Without a spell, or a handful of flour, you can't even see him." Sholt rubbed his eyes with a thumb and a forefinger then sighed heavily. He was exhausted. Casting the spell required to see Phen while examining him, had drained him.

Mikahl put down his goblet. His eyes were filled with sadness. "That's terrible," he mumbled. "It won't be easy breaking the news to Master Oarly." He looked at the ceiling. "Isn't there a way to break the spell?"

"Before I answer, Your Highness, there's more." Master Sholt stood and walked to the large window of the small private dining room. "It seems that Talon, Sir Hyden Hawk's *familiar*, was guarding over Phen when it happened. The bird is in the same condition as the boy."

"Talon," Mikahl growled and stood abruptly up from the table. His sadness slowly morphed into an angry simmer. "Can't you do anything? Can Master Amill? What will it take?"

Sholt held up a hand, trying to politely stall the High King's emotion. "I don't know yet," he said honestly. "There may be ways to undo what's been done, but I must study the situation. I don't want to exaggerate the sliver of hope I hold. When I say *sliver*, I mean parchment thin, Your Highness."

"Aye," Mikahl sighed. Over the last few years he had lost more friends than he could count on his hands. With Hyden gone, and Phen and Talon possibly dead as well, he didn't think that he could feel any more sorrow than he already did. "You have my leave to do anything and everything necessary to revive them, Master Wizard. Spare nothing," Mikahl said sternly. It was all he could do.

"Rest assured, I will do all I can," Sholt promised.

A long hour later, after a trip to the guard barracks where he'd often trained in his youth, Mikahl was wearing a heavy hauberk over his clean shirt, and flying east on the bright horse. He was going to join Oarly, and King Jarrek. He had no idea how far south they had gotten while he slept, so he flew over the marshes, hoping to find them close to O'Dakahn. As he passed over some of the deepest swamp he'd ever seen, he noticed a flurry of activity below. A large group of creatures was moving through the overgrown terrain with a purpose. He circled lower and made a few passes. He scared up a small flock of the big long-beaked dactyls, but saw nothing like what he thought he'd seen. A few large gekas and a pair of zard-men rooting around in an area that was infested with snappers was all. They were probably hunting. As he winged the magical pegasus back on a southerly course, he wondered why he'd thought he'd seen so many things moving. Tired eyes he told himself.

When the marshlands were behind him, and he was over Dakahn, he flew south, pushing the bright horse's pace to its limits. He experimentally took some sharp turns and other evasive maneuvers. He'd seen how agile the dragon was in flight and wanted to mimic that grace. If he met Flick again in the air, he wanted to know what his own capabilities were. After only a few attempts to move as the dragon had, he knew that there was no way to out fly the wyrm. With its long tail to balance it, it could spin and stop, or twist in midair, right out of a streaking dive. With its elongated neck it could fly in one direction and attack with its acidy breath in another.

The one thing Mikahl knew for certain was that he did not want to be anywhere below the dragon. He knew he would have to be more than lucky to win a battle with a creature like that. He hoped it didn't come down to an aerial confrontation, but he was pretty sure that it would. How else could he keep the wyrm off of the troops? Maybe one of the breed giants would get lucky and pull the nasty black bastard out of the sky.

Breed giants! Mikahl shook his head in angry wonder. The breed acted controlled, almost civil, while he and Jarrek were speaking. They weren't the savage animalistic beasts he remembered from Coldfrost. Mikahl wondered what sort of an arrangement Jarrek had made with them. The way Lord Gregory passed the subject on to the old Red Wolf made Mikahl wonder. He trusted Lord Gregory and King Jarrek explicitly, though, so he decided to let that concern wait until another day.

Mikahl wondered what King Aldar would say about the situation. He knew that the true full-blooded giants hated the breed. He found that he didn't relish his role as High King of the realm. There was far too much to worry about, too many responsibilities and decisions to weigh. His old horse, Windfoot, a good long bow, and a camp in the Reyhall Forest, or the Northwood, sounded far better. No battles, no dragons or demons, no slaves or skeeks, just a good old fashioned hunt for a boar or a stag. He could almost smell the pine needles and feel the soft earth under his boots.

His reverie was broken by the sight of not only Jarrek's small group and the tattered Red Wolf banner they still carried, but another far larger force flying the rising sun of Seaward, the Blacksword of Highwander, as well as the red and yellow checkered Valleyan shield. From his vantage point in the sky he could see the dark smear to the south that was O'Dakahn. It was a huge metropolis, larger than Xwarda, Southport, and Dreen combined. The size of the encampments of soldiers below paled in comparison, and suddenly Mikahl didn't feel so confident with their plan. Pael had failed to take Xwarda with an army that was twice as big, with soldiers that couldn't die. He decided that, as soon as he landed, all the commanders and wizards, all of the kings, and queens as well, needed to be gathered. If he had no choice other than to be the High King of the realm, then at least he was going to try and be a good one.

Mikahl was glad to learn that the group of soldiers he'd been looking at was only two thirds of the force they were about to bring to bear on O'Dakahn. Other troops were still marching wide around the city to take up a position at O'Dakahn's southern gate, nearer to the busy port.

According to the maps of the city that were laid out in Commander Escott's war pavilion, the wall around O'Dakahn had only three gates set in it. One opened onto the docks and warehouses of Port Dakahn. King Graniteheart and Master Amill were already leading a large division of men and dwarves that way. The northwestern gate opened onto the road that ran up the east bank of the Leif Greyn River to Seareach and into Wildermont. It was the biggest of the three portals, and King Jarrek quickly asserted that he and General Diamondeen would be leading the force that took up position there. Everyone agreed.

Commander Escott was assigned the northeastern gate that opened onto the road that ran to the crossing bridges of Lokahna and Oktin. One of the Highwander apprentices was to go with him, and the other with King Jarrek to replace Master Sholt, leaving Mikahl free to defend against the dragon, or anything else that might come at them from the sky. Each of the northern groups had a breed giant with a rope hauler. There were only two of the bulky crossbows left. Bzorch chose to go with King Jarrek to the northwestern gate. It was the gate nearest King Ra'Gren's palace, which sat inside another set of walls. If the wizard was aiding Ra'Gren, Bzorch assured them, the dragon would most likely be defending that area.

Later that evening, before the main force split, they were all lingering around one of the bigger fires near the command pavilion. Many of the captains and sergeants were crowded around, seeking favor from their commanders, and trying to set their eyes on the High King. Mikahl's battle with the demon-wizard Pael was the stuff of legends.

Suddenly, Bzorch stood up and drew everyone's attention to himself with a loud primal roar. He let it be known to all that he had sworn to kill the dragon that had destroyed his kin. He warned soldiers and commanders alike, and even the wizards and kings, to give him much room if the dragon showed itself. Then, to everyone's surprise, he and the three other breed all took a knee before High King Mikahl and bowed. Mikahl looked quickly at King Jarrek for answers. Jarrek cringed and backed out of the firelight as Bzorch began to speak.

"We might only be four, King," the alpha breed beast said slowly and with deep conviction, "but we are willing to die to earn the right to control the crossing. Coldfrost is a painful memory that we will never forget it, but it is a memory nonetheless."

Mikahl wasn't sure what crossing Bzorch was talking about. Locar? Surely not Oktin, or Lokahna. He looked for King Jarrek again, but didn't see him anywhere. He didn't want to disrespect the breed giants' show of fealty, and he absolutely didn't want to dishonor the wild looking half-blood that had saved him from the Choska's claws. Mikahl wasn't sure how to react, so he gave them a deep nod of respect and did his best imitation of King Balton.

"I pray you get the chance to slay the dragon, mighty Bzorch. It has killed far too many. As for Coldfrost, I had no part in the battle there, other than as squire to my father and king. King Balton's reign over Westland has ended. Mine is about to begin. None of us who were there can forget, but we *can* stand together and start anew."

"One king, one kingdom!" someone yelled from beyond the fire's light.

"One king, one kingdom," another repeated loudly. Others took up the chant as well, including King Jarrek, and many of the dwarves.

It was in that spirit of unified purpose that the forces marched away the next morning toward their positions outside the city gates of O'Dakahn.

The few Dakaneese people who hadn't sought safety inside the city's walls were escorted away from the massive dwellings and shops that had been built against the protective barrier. It took most of a day to get them clear. Hundreds of stubborn families were displaced and sent north out of harm's way. The besieged Dakaneese inside the walls didn't waste any time taking action. During that first night they doused the structures with oil and set them to burning. They had no intention of letting the Eastern armies use them to build on, or the wood to build siege engines.

Lord Gregory's planning counted on them doing this. They weren't planning on building siege engines, other than for the sake of show. They would sit there, outside the city, and wait for the rest of the reinforcements Queen Willa and Queen Rachel had dispatched to arrive, while the dwarves dug a huge collapsible cavity under a single section of the imposing wall. The charred and smoldering structures outside the barrier gave the dwarves excellent cover when they crept in close and started to dig.

According to Oarly, the wall's size and weight would bring it down. All that was needed was a large well placed gap under the foundation, and a little push. Oarly took his sappers away from the gate in search of a favorable area to collapse. Other crews of dwarven diggers were spaced around the barrier, each trying to bore a passage under the wall that might allow a small human force to gain entry. If they got through, the sheer number of people that lived in O'Dakahn would make it easy to blend in. If a small group of men could manage to get one of the gates open from the inside, then the eastern armies could just swarm in and go to work. Still, Oarly and many of the other dwarves agreed, collapsing an area of wall to make their own gate would be much more effective.

*

A day's march due west from O'Dakahn, on the bank of the Leif Greyn River, sits the marshland village called Nahka. For several days, the zard and their gekas used the powerful current of the Leif Greyn's main channel to carry them from the marshes. Larger dactyls carried roped bundles of weapons and supplies, while flying in small unnoticeable flocks. The snappers that resided in the marshes didn't bother with the zard, and only one geka met its end during the crossing. By the time O'Dakahn was ringed with the fires of the structures burning outside the city's wall, fifteen thousand zard-men had gathered along the river.

Flick, on the back of his dragon, flew high overhead during the night. He had rallied the zard with the telling of how sneaky King Mikahl murdered Queen Shaella in cold blood. The zard loved and respected the Dragon Queen. She had armed them and trained them and led them out of the swampy muck that the Westlanders had spent centuries driving them into.

Flick reminded them of all she had done, and incited their desire for vengeance. It wasn't that hard to get them riled and moving, not with Vrot sitting proudly beneath him. Now he was studying the forces that had besieged Ra'Gren's massive cesspool. Flick wanted them to attack outside the northwestern gate first. He had seen the ragged Red Wolf banner of King Jarrek fluttering among those soldiers earlier. His instincts told him to move on the southern gate first, though. The zard were extraordinarily silent swimmers and the forces that were gathering there wouldn't be expecting an attack from the bay. The zard could slither through the water carrying weapons and creep up on the men before they established position.

Confident that he was making the right choice, Flick turned Vrot northward. The Dakaneese pirate ship that the sell-swords had taken over was speeding south to warn Jarrek and the High King of the zard movement. His zard had been watching the ship for days from the lake that now stood over Seareach. It baffled Flick how a king without a kingdom, with no coin chests, could buy up Ra'Gren's well paid sell-swords. Maybe the High King had promised them land and titles in his make believe realm. Flick couldn't imagine any real Dakaneese mercenary not demanding payment, at least partial payment, up front. It didn't matter, Flick decided. The traitorous bastards were about to be snapper food. He brought Vrot down out of the sky in a streaking dive then leveled the dragon a few dozen feet over the river's surface. Ahead, the boat could be seen riding the current swiftly southward.

Maxrell Tyne opened his mouth and screamed out a warning as he took a leaping stride and dove from his ship. Grommen looked up into a searing splash of corrosive breath. For long moments after the top half of his body was eaten away, his legs and lower torso stood frozen in place. The other men were either directly covered, or splattered and sprayed with the acidy liquid. The *Shark's Tooth* was eaten through and sinking before the dragon's tail had swept past it.

The pieces of the crewmen that weren't eroded to a pasty liquid were quickly gulped down by hungry snappers. And those that were whole swam desperately, trying to get out of the water as quickly as they could.

As Flick brought Vrot around in a hard banking arc, his blood was alive with glee. A few snappers were now floating dead. The acid residue from the human flesh had eaten through their innards and killed them almost as quickly as it had killed the men. Flick shivered at the sight. His body was full of anticipation and the lust for vengeance. He couldn't wait to destroy the High King and the eastern armies so that he could claim his place as the new king of the realm.

The Dragon King.

Chapter Fifty-Eight

Master Amill was having a rough time of it. Between conferring with Master Sholt on Phen's condition, and helping the dwarves clear out civilians from the ships and warehouses at Port O'Dakahn, he was exhausted. He was more than pleased to find his tent had been erected and that a meal of stew and biscuits was waiting inside with his things. The stew was cold, but he wolfed it down anyway. He didn't bother to unpack his small satchel of books and personal necessities. This night, if it was actually still night, lasted far too long and he had only one thing left on his mind. Sleep.

With the practiced ease of a man who'd been afield for several weeks, he snapped the straps on his bedroll and kicked it. It rolled open invitingly. A heartbeat later he was stretched out and trying to clear his mind so that sleep would take him.

The situation with Phen was too disturbing to think about, so he forced it out of his brain completely. He wished that Queen Rachel's flotilla would hurry and arrive. Keeping the harbor clear would be far easier once they had support from the sea. The extra soldiers those ships carried would come in handy as well. He figured that the other two gate areas were easier to clear. Merchants, traders, and travelers had to be more cooperative than the hardened crews, pirates, and salty dogs they came across here. It was done, though. The harbor area was clear of all but the men and dwarves under King Granitheart. And now Master Amill was finally slipping into slumber.

The zard came silently and swiftly, from under the docks, from the rocky jetties that extended out into the bay, from the lightly forested shore. Small groups creeping on clawed feet snuck through the shadows or slithered through the alleyways of the shipping district. Several of the human sentries had to be killed to keep alarms from being sounded, but otherwise the first part of the zard assault went unnoticed.

When the zard were littered about the sleepy encampment, Vrot came roaring out of the sky and bathed long swaths of tents and pavilions in acid. Flick sent fireballs streaking down that erupted in half a dozen places.

When the waking soldiers, who weren't corroding away, went to defend themselves they were overrun by heavy-footed gekas, and the swift silent attacks of the zard, and dactyls. The men and dwarves on watch duty were the first to be melted or scorched into oblivion by the aerial assault. Swift flying flocks of swamp birds swarmed down and shredded anything they could with their long sharp beaks. The dwarves fought bravely, with both hammer and axe, but even with their fierce determination they were no match for Vrot, the wizard, or the overwhelming number of slithery zard. Flick showered them all with bright fiery concussions and Vrot spewed entire lanes clear with his horrible spray, at least until his venom glands ran dry.

Master Amill woke from a twisted battlefield dream to find a huge patch of his tent hissing away. A glance outside the flaps sent a chill of terror through the master wizard. Over half of the company was destroyed, either fizzling into a gory soup, or smoldering in flames. He contained his panic long enough to cast a *sending* to Master Sholt. As it was cast, he realized that Master Sholt was no longer with King Jarrek. He was in Westland now, but it was too late, the spell link was already forming. Master Amill heard a great groaning creek and turned to see the massive city gates opening. A stream of Dakaneese soldiers came pouring out, and in moments the chaotic encampment was overrun.

Master Sholt woke to an insistent itching sensation in his mind. It felt like someone was scratching the inside of his skull. He sat up and glanced hopefully at the deep indentation that Phen's heavy body was making in the soft feather bed. Realizing that it was a *sending* that had woken him, he rose out of the divan he was sleeping on and strode across the royal bedchamber to the balcony. He threw the doors open and let the breeze stream in. Once he had shaken the cobwebs from his head, he reached out and grabbed a hold of the magical voice that was calling to him. The faint light of the night sky was blacked out momentarily, but Master Amill's panic stricken *sending* drew his focus. As he listened, he stepped to the balcony rail and looked up curiously. Seeing nothing other than stars, he turned and looked back at the bed.

The words of his friend and peer suddenly sank in and filled him with worry. "By the gods, the zard *and* the dragon?" he replied. "Get yourself and King Granitheart out of there. He is royalty, man... Amill? Amill?"

The *sending* ended abruptly, leaving Master Sholt trembling with concern. He knew that he had to warn the others. It was possible that the zard were planning on attacking all three of the siege forces. He closed his eyes and began speaking the words of another *sending*, but a sudden looming presence behind him stopped him cold.

The starlight had been eclipsed again, only this time whatever had blocked it out hadn't passed over. It was still there. Master Sholt began to shake as furnace hot breath that smelled of rot and brimstone blew across him. He was sure that one of the many demons that had climbed up out of the hells was behind him. He felt his hair curling and could smell the harsh acrid scent of it burning. A voice that could have been a crumbling mountain growled behind him.

"Where is Hydens Hawkss?" it asked.

Master Sholt took two steps toward the room and turned with the balcony doors in his hands. He was ready to throw them closed and run. What he saw staggered him to stillness.

Cavernous nostrils, bigger than wagon wheels, with tendrils of smoke rolling up out of them were pressed against the balcony rail. Half a dozen feet behind them were luminous yellow eyes that were slitted vertically by pupils as long as a man is tall. They blinked with lids that rose from the bottom upward then narrowed fiercely.

"Where is Hydens Hawkss?" the monstrous thing asked again.

When Sholt heard the voice this time he realized what was speaking to him, but the knowledge caused him to faint into a heap on the floor.

The massive red dragon pushed its snout through the balcony entry, shattering glass and splintering wood as if it weren't even there. Then it reared back and brought its head down, using its chin to batter the balcony from the wall.

The door across the room came flying open. Lady Able, and a pair of nervous looking men bearing swords and torches charged in. The lady crumbled when she saw the giant slitted eye pressed up to the gaping hole in the wall. One of the men turned and fled screaming. The other filled his britches before falling to his knees and putting his face to the floor as if he were praying.

When Master Sholt opened his eyes, it was about midday, and the invisible marble statue that was Phen, was gone. The balcony opening had been destroyed and it looked as if something far too large for the room had been forced into it. The floor was busted downward in the middle and the ceiling was bowed up into a mangled arch. The big bed where the petrified boy had lain was smoldering and hanging out of the room over the garden yard. Only after Master Sholt gathered himself, and cast a *sending* to his apprentices and Cresson, did he begin to investigate what had happened at Lakeside Castle. He was so worried about Phen that he didn't let his grief over Master Amill's cruel fate distract him.

The only one who offered Sholt any relevant information was the man who had shit himself. He said that the huge dragon had stuck its head into the chamber, hooked the bed with its tooth, and dragged it out to where it is now.

"After that, the dragon growled so loud that I buried my head again." The man was obviously still shaken by what he had seen. Master Sholt was shaken too. He had no idea what to make of the occurrence, but he knew that the dragon had asked for Hyden Hawk by name. That meant that the dragon was most likely Claret.

Only a short few miles of lightly forested flats separated the harbor from O'Dakahn's northeastern gate. Commander Escott wasn't surprised when the zard came out of the trees like a swarm of scaly insects. When dawn broke, and Master Amill couldn't be reached by either of his apprentices, the other two forces had gone on full alert. The High King had flown over the massacre in the first light of the day. The gate was closed again, only there was no one alive outside it to keep the Dakaneese in. The gore the dragon's acid left behind was horrific.

Commander Escott's archers rained arrows on the advancing zard, but after each volley they retreated a hundred paces then turned and fired again. The idea was to get far enough away from the gate that the Dakaneese troops inside couldn't come pouring out like they had in the south. If they came out and had to stretch their number to reach the retreat, then High King Mikahl could fly in and cut them off. The dwarves who weren't digging hated this idea. They were angry and raging over the loss of their king. They wanted to attack, not back away.

It didn't work out the way anyone wanted it to. The gates never opened, and the zard came in widely spread groups on the backs of gekas and on foot. Huge flocks of deadly swamp dactyls filled the sky to cover their advance. Mikahl and his bright horse were surrounded by pecking, clawing clouds of them. They couldn't attack him due to the magical shields Ironspike provided, but they effectively kept him from being able to aid the men below.

Flick and King Ra'Gren couldn't have planned it better. With King Mikahl and his fiery steed being harried by the dactyls, and the southern force little more than a gruesome stain along the harbor now, it left the majority of Ra'Gren's Dakaneese soldiers free to spill out of the northwestern gate and attack King Jarrek. When the gates opened, Flick and Vrot came streaking over the wall and in moments cleared the way for the soldiers to pour out and attack. Ra'Gren felt so confident in the plan that he pulled on his armor and rode out with his men. He looked like some shining steel clad sea god with his flowing white hair and beard and polished armor. He rode a white destrier and held his trident high. In his other hand he carried a small glaive-like weapon that had hatchet blades on its sides and a longer blade that protruded like a spear. It was light and effective in his hands. King Ra'Gren might have been lazy and spoiled, but he was far from soft. He had killed more people in his throne room than half the soldiers on the field combined. Once the battle lust filled him he became a force unto himself, stabbing and hewing Jarrek's soldiers at will.

Vrot was relentless. After he exhausted his spew again, he carried Flick low and clawed men from their mounts, or whipped through the ranks with his powerful tail. Flick blasted flesh, dirt, and bone into rubble with his wicked pulses of kinetic energy. His wizard's fire lingered on the flesh of man and steed alike. Without the High King to contend with, the amount of destruction they were allowed to wreak was substantial.

King Jarrek fought with berserker-like intensity until he was forced to stop and gather his wits. He couldn't believe that they had discounted Shaella's wizard and his ability to rally the skeeks, much less get them to O'Dakahn so quickly. In hindsight, he realized that the threat should have been obvious. The marshland that separated Westland from Dakahn was their natural habitat, and unlike a human enemy that would be bogged down in such terrain, the zard and their gekas were suited to it and traversed it easily.

It wasn't the zard that Jarrek was fending off now, though. The long rested Dakaneese soldiers from inside O'Dakahn's wall were having their way with his travel-weary men. He wasn't sure, but it appeared that his force might have been outnumbered by as many as five to one. He had no idea how many more men Ra'Gren had inside.

He had to do something drastic, and quickly. The dragon was too much for them. He didn't know what was keeping Mikahl from a coming to their aid, but he guessed that the situation probably wasn't much better where the High King was fighting.

An idea struck him, and he found the ring of soldiers guarding his apprentice mage and gave the terrified young wizard a series of orders. A few moments later he rode past Bzorch, and was nearly thrown from his saddle as the big breed giant walked right into his path. Bzorch didn't take his eyes off of his target. He was just waiting for the dragon to get in range. His huge hairy coil-man followed closely, being sure not to let the rope tangle.

King Jarrek got himself situated and moved around them. He passed along his orders to the commanders of the battling troops and slowly the entire battle began migrating eastward away from the open gates. The way Jarrek had the men and dwarves spreading out put the Dakaneese into an advancing formation. It forced the two opposing groups to take up sides of a battle line instead of fighting in random knots and clusters. It also made it easier for Flick and the dragon to attack them, which is exactly what Jarrek wanted.

Ra'Gren roared with delight when he saw King Jarrek pulling his men back. The big white-haired seadog's armor was covered in gore. His once white destrier was a dozen different shades of red and prancing anxiously for more. He could only gape though, when a streaking spear launched up out of the fray ahead of him, causing King Jarrek's force to let out a hearty cheer. Ra'Gren twisted and looked up to see Flick scrabbling for purchase on the dragon's back as it twisted and writhed in the sky. A spear had punctured the dragon's shoulder where its left wing met its neck and body. The barbed spearhead had come out the top of the dragon's back. Ra'Gren saw the long rope attached to the spear pull taut, but a sharp pain along his calf, where a stray sword stroke bit him, reminded him that he was in the middle of a battle. Immediately, he began working away from the front. His will to be in the heat of things was fading now that Flick and his dragon were in no position to protect him.

A great roar filled the air. Vrot, with no spew left in him to blast through the rope, gave out a screeching call of frustration and pain. Then the rope yanked tight against the spear that had torn through him. He sucked in a deep whooshing breath and, with fangs gritted, pounded his wings, trying to carry himself clear.

From the ground, the half dozen men and the wide-eyed breed giant who was handling the rope came lifting up off of the ground. Some of the men stumbled and fell away, letting go of the line. The breed had tied the other end of the rope around his waist. He took a long leaping step, and when the others let go he was pulled high into the air. Vrot fought through his pain and lifted the huge half-breed up into the sky. A moment later, Flick gathered his wits, and with a clever spell, turned the spear into water. Bzorch roared out in frustration as the last coil handler went tumbling out of the sky with the rope trailing behind him. He crashed into the Dakaneese lines and luckily died from the impact before they could swarm over him.

The black dragon peeled away on surging wings and carried his protesting rider out over the vast expanse of marshland. In only moments, they were nowhere to be seen.

It looked to everyone that the dragon was fleeing due to the spear. The battle started to turn then. Jarrek's men actually started to force the Dakaneese back toward the gates.

Chapter Fifty-Nine

The Dakaneese retreat didn't last long. Within the turn of a glass Vrot was back, his glands somewhat replenished after drinking in the marsh. While the dragon rained more acidy breath over the battle, Flick killed men and dwarves by the dozen with his powerful destructive spells. The battle raged on, Jarrek's men steadily retreating eastward. King Jarrek was heartened when he finally set his eyes on Commander Escott's force. It was clear that they were retreating too. It didn't look like they had taken nearly as many casualties as Jarrek's group had.

The zard, without any form of real military leadership, had kept advancing into Escott's archers' volleys. The number of skeeks pressing them had been reduced significantly. Every now and then a big geka, carrying four or five of the braver zard, would burst through the lines of Escott's ranks and wreak havoc, but it was the thick swarming clouds of dactyls that were giving them the most problems.

When commander Escott saw Jarrek's thinning numbers easing back toward his, he cringed. The remainder of their force was nowhere near the city's gates anymore. This section of O'Dakahn's wall was relatively deserted. He knew that it wouldn't last, though. If they got backed up against the wall they would be surrounded. Hot oil and arrows would eventually come raining down from above with the dragon spume and that would be the end of it.

Escott hoped that Jarrek had a trick up his sleeve, but he had no idea what it would be. Soon enough he would be able to ask the gore-splattered Wolf King himself. It wouldn't be long until both of them were backing into each other.

Mikahl finally managed to get out of the cloud of dactyls that was harrying him. At first he thought it was his maneuvering, and Ironspike's magic, that won him free, but then he saw the sleek black dragon coming in sharply and realized that the dactyls had fled from it. They had no desire to be splashed by the wyrm's wicked slaver.

Mikahl made an evasive move to get clear of the speeding creature, then checked himself to make sure that he was shielded as well as he could be. After that, he sent a fireball streaking at the dragon. He had no choice but to peel away from his current position. Vrot altered his course and flew around the fireball as if he were water flowing around a boulder. A gout of spew went splattering across the archers at the front of Commander Escott's side of the battle. Mikahl had to look away as their bodies began dissolving. In a surge of disgusted rage Mikahl sent a trio of fireballs at the dragon in a triangular pattern. Vrot came around the first one and took the second hard in the hind quarter. The third nearly took Flick off of the dragon's back. The bald wizard held on for his life as Vrot twisted and shivered the pain from his scales. Vrot let out a roar. Flick had just righted himself when the agile black wyrm was forced to pull up into a stall to avoid one of Bzorch's whizing spears.

The breed giant cursed savagely and slung his big crossbow over his shoulder. He couldn't believe the dragon was able to stop in midair like that. Quickly, he began coiling up his line. It was the only one he had left. It wasn't easy carrying his own rope, but he was managing it. He had two spears and one line left, and a focus of will that is only attainable by a predator on the hunt.

There was a Dakaneese arrow sticking up out of the breed giant's back and a ragged cut across his waist, but he didn't seem to notice them. His intensity was frightening, even to the men of his own company. For a long while, several Highwander men had fought around Bzorch to keep him protected while he reloaded, but when Vrot swooped low the breed shouldered his way right out of his own protection and stalked into the enemy's ranks. With his club like fist and terrifying growl, he cleared his own path through the mayhem. Occasionally an arrow would streak into an enemy who was trying to make a move on the big creature, but it didn't matter—the hulking half-blood seemed to be, for the most part, battle blessed.

King Jarrek sighted commander Escott and began working his destrier that way. A Dakaneese soldier carrying a long sword made a darting charge at his mount, but the well trained horse saw the man coming. It bucked sideways and then nearly pitched Jarrek over its head as it back-kicked and caved in the breastplate of the attacker. No sooner than the horse's hooves found the ground again, Jarrek spurred the animal forward to avoid a big screaming dactyl that had been skewered by one of the archers. It crashed into the space where he and his horse had just been, taking out several men.

Jarrek chanced a skyward glance and caught his breath. Mikahl had engaged the dragon. Jarrek hadn't expected the sky to be filled with swamp birds. The archers were doing the best they could, he saw, as another of dactyl came half flapping, half spinning down into a cluster of soldiers.

Jarrek took in the city wall to the south. Archers were gathering along its top. They were sending long arcing volleys of arrows out into the fray. He glanced to the north and saw that hundreds of skeeks, all riding their quick, ferocious geka lizards, had closed off the only way left to avoid being pinned against the barrier. Jarrek realized his mistake. One of the first rules of battle was to never underestimate your enemy. Now, here they were being pushed back against O'Dakahn's wall by Ra'Gren's soldiers, Shaella's skeeks, and her wizard's dragon. The reinforcements Queen Rachel and Queen Willa had dispatched were still days away. Not only had King Jarrek failed his enslaved people, many of whom were still in chains beyond the huge city wall, he had led all these men who had come to fight for his cause to their deaths. The intensity of his regret almost outweighed the anger he felt at himself for being such a fool.

Overhead the dragon roared and Jarrek mimicked the sound from some place deep within himself. Angry beyond reason, he charged his mount into the heat of the battle.

"Follow me!" he ordered a group of mounted Seawardsmen. "We've got to get through or we are done!"

He decided that he would either carve a way out of the press or die trying. The men, seeing his intent, disengaged from their current battles and followed him, each knowing that the endeavor was next to impossible.

Commander Escott saw the realization of the situation come over King Jarrek's face. The Red Wolf had miscalculated, and now he was attempting the impossible. Escott spoke a prayer to the sun gods of his people and then ordered a dozen of his cavalry to follow the Red Wolf. A moment after they rode into King Jarrek's wake, the commander sent half a score of men after them. If the old Red Wolf was willing to sacrifice himself to carve them a way out of the trap they had fallen into, he was going to try and make sure that the sacrifice wasn't made in vain.

He began ordering men to wedge after Jarrek and push away from the wall. Better to be surrounded by an enemy on a level field then be pinned beneath the fifty foot wall that was topped with soldiers. He knew that the reinforcements could never get there in time. It was now a do or die situation. Any thoughts of besieging O'Dakahn were a fleeting memory. This had become a fight for their lives.

Mikahl managed to keep Vrot and Flick away from the men on the ground, but he could tell by looking at the battle below that things weren't going well. He saw Bzorch stomping around anxiously with his dragon gun at the ready and tried to lead the dragon into its sights, but the black wyrm, or maybe its rider, were wise to his ploy.

Suddenly the dragon inexplicably bolted northward. Mikahl rose into the sky and came around over the wall. He managed to clear the archers from a good length of its top with a series of fiery blasts. After that he swooped toward the ranks of gekas that had closed off the northern portion of the battlefield. He blasted them hard with savage lighting, alternated with streaking swaths of wizard's fire.

As he passed over the gekas and pulled up into the air, he was overcome with shocked despair, for at least five thousand soldiers were storming in from the north, the Dakaneese trident banner streaming from the flagman's pike. He cast a wall of fire across their path that startled their horses, but Flick, who was now gliding on Vrot's back, just above the charge, countered it quickly. Before the horses could even break their formation to avoid the flames, the inferno was extinguished.

Mikahl arced around and started back toward the main battle. He had to warn the others. These new Dakaneese would be on them in moments and would devastate them. As he sped back to find King Jarrek, he noticed that the dactyls had all but vanished from the sky. Only moments ago, thousands of them had been darting down and attacking the soldiers, but now they were nowhere to be seen.

A roar shocked him into the realization that Flick and his black dragon were right on the bright horse's heels. Mikahl took a jolting blow that dispersed out around the edges of the glassine globe that shielded him, but it still knocked him sideways. He was in trouble, and he knew it. There was no way that he could out fly the wyrm that was nipping at his back. He saw Bzorch out of the corner of his eye and faked pulling away from the breed's direction, but then dove straight for the big savage looking half-blood. He tried to keep his body between Bzorch and the dragon as best he could so that it couldn't see what he was intending. At the last moment he pulled up and away.

Bzorch didn't hesitate to fire his spear. The projectile tore through Vrot's hind leg at the meaty part of his calf muscle. Bzorch dove out of the way of an acidy blast and somehow got caught up in his uncoiling line.

Mikahl banked around as sharply as the bright horse would allow. He came round just in time to see the rope that led from Bzorch to Vrot pull tight. The black dragon didn't stop, but the sudden jolt of Bzorch's weight threw Flick tumbling forward from its back. Mikahl didn't hesitate either. He forced the bright horse into a dive toward the tumbling wizard.

King Jarrek seemed to have done the impossible. He and several of the mounted fighters had battled a lane clean through the zard force to the north. In a flash, hundreds of Valleyans and Blacksword soldiers, and quite a few dwarves, filtered into the gap and fought to hold it, so that their fellows could escape the closing press of the enemy. The passage wasn't open long, though. The worst possible thing that could happen did. The Dakaneese cavalry, riding in from the north, came crashing into the battle before Jarrek or his men could even catch their breath. The corridor Jarrek had fought so bravely to open gave those riders a clear path right into the heart of the battle. Within seconds, the Dakaneese began hacking and hewing away the lives of King Jarrek and Commander Escott's men. King Jarrek tried to blink away his tears when he saw what was happening, and then he was bashed from his horse by a passing Dakaneese fighter's mace. His red enameled wolf skull helmet went spinning through the air. He crashed into the growing pile of corpses on the bloody ground. Then he was trampled into the muck.

Flick cleared his mind and calmly cast a levitation spell. He couldn't fly, but he didn't have to come crashing down to the ground either. As he righted himself and came to a hover in the air, a roar so loud that it shook the city walls filled the sky. Flick ignored it and raised his arms to blast Mikahl as he came swooping in. Mikahl had hoped to catch Flick before he recovered, but he was too late. He half expected to smash into another invisible wall, but he still leveled Ironspike at the bald-headed wizard and called forth a streak of lightning.

Strangely, Flick's arms fell to his sides and his eyes grew huge. He was looking at something behind Mikahl. Mikahl didn't care what it was. He let loose his white-hot blast right into the wizard's chest. The jagged bolt of energy hit Flick with its full intensity. The shocked wizard went spinning head over heels across the sky and into the battle below. A pillar a smoke rose up from the charred husk that hit the ground and exploded into chunks of cherry embers.

Even though he caused it, Mikahl didn't see Flick's end. A gust of wind so violent that it sent him and his bright horse tumbling out of control hit him from above.

Bzorch knew he was in trouble, so he rolled under a wandering horse then looped the line over the animal's saddle horn. When Vrot hit the end of the slack this time, there was an unimaginable yank. The horse was spun shoulder under hooves and nearly torn in half, and Bzorch was snapped up into the air with breakneck force. He only came up a dozen feet, though, before darkness swept across the battlefield and a sound that might have been angry thunder blasted across the sky. He never got to see what it was because he hit the earth again in an ungainly heap.

Commander Escott heard the gigantic roar. The battle around him slowed as soldiers from both sides stopped fighting to look and see what could have made such a noise. Escott's discipline kept him from turning, and he put his sword in at least three Dakaneese soldiers, and a skeek, in the pause. Then the sun was eclipsed by something monstrous and he couldn't help but look.

His body began to tremble as his eyes swelled to take in the dragon. Not the black-scaled wyrm that had just tossed its rider, but an enormous red beast that was easily two hundred paces from head to tail. It leaned its head down casually to where the black dragon was fighting to lift the weight of the breed giant dangling limply from the line. The red launched its head out and, with a snap that sounded like a thunderclap, half of the black dragon came tumbling down out of the sky into the enemy ranks.

The sound of sudden movement brought Escott's eyes back to the battlefield. The zard were fleeing. They had lived in Claret's shadow for hundreds of years while she was bound to guard the Seal in the Dragon's Tooth Spire. They had helped Shaella and Gerard steal her eggs and trick her into a collar. Claret's wrath, and the fact that gekas were one of her favorite foods, sent the zard fleeing mindlessly from her presence. Gekas reared up and bolted out from under their riders. They trampled over the zard-men that were on foot as if they weren't even there.

Escott looked back up at the huge dragon. Sitting on its long neck, like a pixie on a warhorse, was a strange looking figure clad in stark white attire. The person pointed toward the city and then down. The dragon twisted in midair and lay a gout of flame across the Dakaneese ranks that was so huge that it literally charred hundreds of men and their mounts. With a casual adjustment of its huge leathery wings, the red dragon repeated the act again and again, making it clear that it was only going to roast the Dakaneese and the zard. After that, those of Ra'Gren's soldiers that didn't run for their lives, fell to their knees and begged to be spared.

After scattering the enemy, the dragon flew to the top of the city wall and perched there. Its huge clawed feet tore loose gigantic pieces of the structure where it gripped for purchase. It calmly listened to the white clad figure sitting on its back. Then, as if it were merely toppling over an anthill, it tore a two hundred foot section of the wall to the ground. Claret leaned forward then and started clawing her way through the city. Behind her slithering belly she left a rough path that was nearly twenty paces wide and relatively free of obstruction.

Escott had to laugh. The big red wyrm was making them a road that led directly to Ra'Gren's palace.

Mikahl somehow kept himself on the bright horse as its magical wings fought to catch air. When they were righted, he watched Claret turn the tide of the battle and was overcome with relief.

As the dragon began demolishing O'Dakahn, a white bird came fluttering down out of the sky clumsily. The High King recognized it, sort of. The bird had no color left to it at all.

"Talon?" He asked, though he knew it was. The irritated hawkling let out a long caw of sorrow then landed on Mikahl's shoulder.

"Aye," was all Mikahl said in response.

Just then, a few hundred feet to the west, a group of dwarves emerged from the rubble at the base of the wall. One of them was waving his arms excitedly. Mikahl winged the bright horse over to him. The dwarf was covered in grey brown dust, but Mikahl recognized him as Master Oarly.

"High King Mikahl." Oarly jumped up and down calling out breathlessly. "High King Mikahl, we've breached the wall. The dwarves of Doon have cleared you a tunnel."

Even though the hawkling latched onto his shoulder had him thinking of Hyden, and the field was littered with the corpses of thousands of honorable men, Mikahl couldn't help but burst out laughing.

"What?" Oarly asked indignantly with his hands on his hips.

"Just as when Queen Willa blew the Horn of Doon," Mikahl chuckled and indicated the avenue that Claret had created for them. "You dwarves arrived a bit too late."

Chapter Sixty

Four weeks later

King Jarrek, leaning heavily on a crutch, stood next to the white marble colored form of Phen, and the wavering dwarf, Master Oarly. The three of them had stood similarly in support of each other a few days earlier during the long sad funeral held for all of the heroes who hadn't survived. Brady Culvert, Master Amill, and a few thousand others had been honored that day, and the trio had drunk a toast to nearly every one of them.

Today wasn't a sad sort of occasion, though. It was a celebration. High King Mikahl and Princess Rosa were being married.

Lord Gregory was standing formally beside the High King, both dressed proudly in the green and gold of Westland. Princess Rosa looked splendid in her sapphire and flame colored gown. Three little girls stood grinning in the shadow of Lady Trella on the Princess's side of the platform.

An amphitheater had been erected by the dwarves just for the occasion. The wedding was taking place in the city of Oktin, just west of the Kahna River. Mikahl had chosen the location because it was equidistant from Lakeside in Westland and Xwarda in Highwander. A new era was about to begin, an era of hope, peace, and rebuilding. People had traveled from all across the realm to be a part it.

A new palace was already being designed. Oktin is where it would be built. By right of lineage, Princess Rosa was the true heir to Valleya, as well as Seaward. King Broderick, who was still enjoying the permanent hospitality of Queen Willa's castle, had no heir, and wouldn't be seeding one from the dungeon. Queen Rachel was his cousin by blood, and her daughter, Princess Rosa, would eventually assume the rule of both kingdoms. Dakahn was in limbo, but all of the overlords and lords who had sworn fealty to High King Mikahl and released their slaves were being unmolested and following the High King by choice. King Jarrek had already bent the knee for Wildermont, as had Queen Willa for Highwander. Thus the entire realm of men, save for the islands, had sworn allegiance to High King Mikahl and his bride.

On the great stage the dwarves had erected, Mikahl and Rosa were speaking their vows. Whoops of joy and happiness from thousands of women, and a few of the gathered men, swept across the crowd.

King Jarrek gave Queen Willa a leering smile, letting his half drunken eyes linger on her cleavage a little too long. She flushed and waved him away with the back of her hand, a pleased grin on her face. Her blue-skinned pixie advisor,

Starkle, glared at Jarrek from her shoulder. In the past weeks she and King Jarrek had been seeing a lot of each other.

"'Tis a shame Hyden Hawk's not here for this," Oarly whispered to Phen.

"Aye," Phen agreed. "We're still trying to figure it out."

"You think the dragon was right? That he isn't dead?" King Jarrek asked, after he peeled his eyes away from Willa.

Not far away, the High King was sealing his vows with a tender kiss.

"Aye," Phen answered excitedly. "Before she left, Claret told me my lyna is alive too. We just don't know where they are."

"Why did he go into the Nethers?" Jarrek asked as cheers erupted through the crowd and people started moving about them.

"He had to." Phen was forced to raise his voice over the growing sound of the celebration. The ceremony was over. The High King and Rosa were wed.

Phen and King Jarrek followed Oarly to a wine cask at the end of a long table that was laid out with all sorts of delicacies. Phen tried to ignore the looks the people gave him, the curious stares, wide eyes, and wrinkled noses. "Imagine how the battle would have ended if Gerar... the Dark Lord, had managed to escape the Nethers. If he had, legions of devils, and other things, might have been loosed. Not even Claret could defeat such an army."

"Quit staring at him," Oarly barked at a group of folk trying to get at the wine. "Haven't you ever seen a marble boy before?"

The people hurried quickly away from the disgruntled dwarf.

Phen punched Oarly in the arm. "Quit calling me a marble boy."

"By Doon, lad, that's a rock hard fist you got there." Oarly rubbed at his shoulder. Phen growled in response.

"Claret said that there is a restorative pool high up in the Giant Mountains that might make my pigments come back," Phen told them. "As soon as things get settled I'm going there."

"You're lucky your mind is still your own, Phen," Master Sholt said, as he joined the group. "A few more days, and even the dragon's powerful magic wouldn't have been able to turn you back from stone."

"Looking like you're still made of marble can't be all that bad," Oarly said.

"Aye," Phen nodded. "Has anyone seen Talon? I haven't seen the blasted bird for two or three days."

No one had.

"How's the new Locar Bridge coming?" Master Sholt asked King Jarrek, but Oarly answered.

"It would be going up a lot faster if that fargin breed giant would stand back and let my kin folk work," Oarly growled then took a long swig from his cup.

"Bzorch is very concerned with his new responsibility," King Jarrek said. "If he can keep his primal instincts in check, he'll make a great bridge master. His people have just about run the skeeks out of Westland for the High King, and I think Mik is starting to feel at ease with them."

"Bah," Oarly barked, and filled his cup from the cask again. "Fargin luggers."

"So how is it going to work now?" Phen asked. "If Mikahl is the king of the whole realm, and all the kingdoms are to be dissolved into one, where does that leave you, and Queen Willa, and Queen Rachel? What will happen to your lands?"

"We're still working that out," Jarrek answer truthfully. "But I think the kingdoms will remain as they are; the rulers as well, save for Dakahn. We will all just have to consult with King Mikahl before doing anything drastic."

Just then, Lord Northall from the Isle of Salazar came up to the group. He tried, but couldn't manage, to keep from staring at Phen's stark appearance.

Phen huffed in frustration and embarrassment. Oarly laughed at him.

"You're looking better," Master Sholt told the island lord. "Better food, and sunlight, no doubt."

"No doubt," Northall grinned. He had spent nearly two weeks in Ra'Gren's dungeon. The last five days he hadn't been fed at all because the dungeon guards had fled with most of the other palace staff. They hadn't wanted to be eaten by the dragon, or caught by King Jarrek or the High King's soldiers.

"How is Castlemont coming along?" Lord Northall asked.

"The dwarves, under General Diamondeen, appear to be making short work of cleaning up and rebuilding the city," Jarrek said, showing the reverence he felt for the dwarves' efforts. "You'll be glad to hear that two more mines are up and producing ore. We owe you a lot. What you did was kind and generous."

"It was more Hyden Hawk's doing than anyone's," Lord Northall admitted. "I'm not sure I understand his current situation, but I've never met a more selfless wizard."

"You'll be attending the feast later?"

"I will," Northall answered proudly. "It's no small honor to be invited to feast at the table of men such as yourselves."

Suddenly, a collective gasp sounded from the crowd.

"Who let the breed giant get drunk?" King Jarrek asked as he hobbled off on his crutch to try and avert disaster.

"We'd better go help him," Phen said to the others, but Master Sholt and Master Oarly were already starting after the Red Wolf King, leaving Phen to have to hurry to catch up.

*

Two sets of crimson eyes cautiously approached the huge petrified form of Deezlxar. The imposing shape still filled the beings with a chill of the power that the one-time ruler of hell once exuded. They weren't exactly sure why they had come to this place. A force that was greater than their own will had lured them here. They had no idea why they couldn't resist, but they couldn't.

Before long, a flock of wyverns came flapping noisily down into the blackness. The skitter and scuffle of many things, both great and small, filled the empty void around the bulky stone form. Deezlxar's remaining dragon head loomed up high over them all. Each and every one of the demons and devils being drawn to the scene expected it to come roaring to life at any moment. Heavier wings snapped and thumped into the air as hellcats, Choska demons, and other malformed monstrosities joined the gathering mass of hell-born entities. Soon, the great expanse was filled with thousands upon thousands of dark terrifying creatures. They milled about curiously, fearfully fighting their instincts to maul one another and claim territory. None of them knew why they were gathered there.

Just when things were getting restless and some of the creatures were growing brave enough to peck and growl at the things around them, a great cracking sound filled the Nethers. Slowly, like a great tree being felled, the last neck and head of Deezlxar started on an arc downward. Most of the things cleared out from under it as it came crashing over to the floor, but a few hadn't been paying attention, or weren't fast enough. They were crushed under dusty scree and shattering stone.

All eyes were transfixed by the shattered head of their longtime master. Murmurs of curiosity and disbelief started working through the gathering, but soon something else commanded their attention.

A vibration, deep and powerful, started to hum around them. The sound seemed to be coming from Deezlxar's fat, spider-like body. The sensation grew in volume and intensity. The demons and devils closest to the stone corpse backed away fearfully. Some were lucky enough to have gotten away, others were not.

The deep thrumming vibration began working through the floor. This was something that had never happened before, for the brimstone planes of hell were immobile. The body of Deezlxar began to rattle heavily. First one crack, then another split across its mass. Then, in an explosive wave, the stone form exploded, sending jagged chunks and sharp pieces flying outward into the masses. Some of the beasts were shredded by shrapnel, and others were crushed by huge pieces of falling debris, but none of them fled. They could not. The grip the *new* Lord of Hell had on them was absolute.

As he lay pinned under the huge mass of stone, the power of Deezlxar found its way into the thing that had once been Gerard. Slowly, his strength returned, only now he understood everything. The malformed dragon-blooded monster rose up out of the rubble in a rage, and spread his great wings. Then Gerard let out a roaring blast of hellfire so terrifying that even the most evil of demons felt their skin crawl with fear.

"I am the Warlord! I am the Master of Hell *and* Earth," the new Abbadon challenged them blatantly. "Kneel before me now, or meet your end!"

The small council hall in Oktin seemed more appropriate for a family feast than a gathering of the realm's kings, queens, and heroes. There were no great chandeliers overhead, no golden dinnerware or jeweled flagons. There was no polished hardwood table, and there were no thrones, or even cushioned chairs. A pair of old table boards had been pushed together, and seated on the hard benches that went with them was nearly all of the realm's royalty. On one side sat King Jarrek, Queen Willa, Queen Rachel, the Lion Lord, his wife, and General Spyra. On the other side sat General Diamondeen, Commander Escott, and Master Sholt with Oarly, Phen and Captain Trant. At the head of the table sat High King Mikahl and his new queen, side by side on a divan. At the opposite end of the board sat the huge form of Lord Bzorch, the sole breed giant attending the feast.

Toast after toast was made, to the hope of the future, to the dream of peace and prosperity. Master Biggs stepped in, even though he wasn't of such rank, but no one minded him joining them for a while. Greasy fingers, boisterous laughter, and general joy was the theme of the evening. Even the normally perfect and ladylike etiquette of Queen Rachel and Lady Trella was breached.

The Queen of Seaward had a gravy stain on her bosom the size of an apple, and Lady Trella laughed so hard that she snorted wine out of her nose when Master Oarly recounted the tale of Sir Hyden Hawk, the squat weed, and the cinder pepper.

After that, Mikahl told the tale of Lord Gregory, and his encounter with squat weed after being poisoned by Pael's imp.

Before long, it seemed as if a bunch of barbarians and bar wenches had decided to play dress up in a tavern. Uproarious tales were told, and more than a little frolicking took place amongst the lovers. Even General Spyra's mood seemed to be on the upside of things. But then a young soldier came bursting into the room, all breathless and brimming with news. The room fell silent as everybody took him in.

"My lords, and ladies," he said mostly to the High King. "There is something out here I think you should see." The young man looked worried and confused, but not afraid. "The message said that it should be presented to the High King personally."

Mikahl, feeling more than a little concerned now, stood and gave his wife a kiss on the forehead before making his way around the table to see what the boy was talking about. The others, at least the ones who were sober enough to follow, were right behind him.

When Mikahl stepped out into the evening breeze a shock of emotion came over him like nothing he had ever felt before. "Windfoot!" he yelled as he started toward the horse that his father had given him.

Lord Gregory smiled knowingly. Lady Trella and the rest of the guests who had come outside looked at each other with perplexed expressions. It was obvious that the High King was glad to see the horse, but none of them could figure out why there was a short stubby boot strapped to the saddle.

Phen saw it, and was filled with immediate relief. "Look Oarly," he pointed. "That's the boot of yours that Hyden vanished."

"Aye, lad, it is," the dwarf said with wide-eyed wonder as he looked drunkenly at the boot, then back at Phen. "Does this mean...?"

"Wait, wait," Mikahl said over them all, as he peered into the boot. "There's something in there."

Suddenly the quill-covered head of a small cat-like creature popped up out of the boot and looked around. Phen's mouth fell open.

"Spike," he yelled as he ran to greet his *familiar*. "It's true, Oarly. It's true," he answered the dwarf's unfinished question.

Oarly, Phen, and the High King were overcome with more relief than they thought was imaginable. The others caught on to the contagious emotion, even though they weren't sure what the new reason to celebrate was. It didn't matter, though. For the time being, hope was plentiful and all was well.

Those things alone are most always worth celebrating.

The End of Book Two

The Wizard and the Warlord - The Wardstone Trilogy-Book III brings the elves, dwarves, giants, and the dragons into the story again, as our heroes, led by High King Mikahl and the great wizard Hyden Hawk, are forced to fight for the fate of the Kingdoms. This time, they do so against the horrid creature Gerard Skyler has become, and the powerful legions of demon-beasts that he has come to command.

About the Author

There are few writers in the genre of fantasy that can equal the creative mind of M.R. Mathias – now acknowledged as a master in this genre of dragons and dwarves, and magic, and spells, and all aspects of fantasy. — Top 100, Hall of Fame, Vine Voice, Book Reviewer, Grady Harp

M. R. Mathias is the multiple award winning author of the huge, #1 Bestselling, epic, The Wardstone Trilogy, as well as the #1 Bestselling Dragoneer Saga, the #1 Bestselling The Legend of Vanx Malic fantasy adventure series, and the #1 Bestselling Crimzon & Clover Short Short Series.

You can find M. R. Mathias at DragonCon every year. Just look for the #Wardstone Dragon Car. Book signings, and booth appearances will be listed in advance, on the blog.

Use these series hashtags on twitter to find maps, cover art, sales, giveaways, book reviews, upcoming releases, and contest information:

#Wardstone – #DragoneerSaga – #VanxMalic – #MRMathias

Other titles by M. R. Mathias

The Dragoneer Saga
The First Dragoneer – Free
The Royal Dragoneers – Nominated, Locus Poll 2011
Cold Hearted Son of a Witch
The Confliction
The Emerald Rider
Rise of the Dragon King
Blood and Royalty – Winner, 2015 Readers Favorite Award,
and 2015 Kindle Book Award Semifinalist

The Legend of Vanx Malic
Book One – Through the Wildwood
Book Two – Dragon Isle
Foxwise (a short story) - Free
Book Three – Saint Elm's Deep
Book Four – That Frigid Fargin' Witch
Book Five – Trigon Daze
Book Six – Paragon Dracus
Book Seven – The Far Side of Creation
Book Eight – The Long Journey Home
Collection -To Kill a Witch – Books I-IV w/bonus content
Collection –The Legend Grows Stronger – Books V-VIII
Books IX-XII coming soon!

And don't miss the huge International Bestselling epic:
The Wardstone Trilogy
Book One - The Sword and the Dragon
Book Two - Kings, Queens, Heroes, & Fools
Book Three - The Wizard & the Warlord

Short Stories:
Crimzon & Clover I - Orphaned Dragon, Lucky Girl
Crimzon & Clover II - The Tricky Wizard
Crimzon & Clover III - The Grog
Crimzon & Clover IV - The Wrath of Crimzon
Crimzon & Clover V - Killer of Giants

Crimzon & Clover Collection One (stories 1-5)

Crimzon & Clover VI – One Bad Bitch
Crimzon &Clover VII – The Fortune's Fortune
Master Zarvin's Action and Adventure Series #1 Dingo the Dragon Slayer
Master Zarvin's Action and Adventure Series #2 Oonzil the oathbreaker
Master Zarvin's Action and Adventure Series #3 The Greatest Quest

Crimzon and Clover I-X